The Last Messiah

A thriller from our future

by V.S. Marlowe

Sinbad Books

New York, London and Dubai
2012

First Popular Edition

Sinbad Books
C/o Derek Aragon Inc.
DerekAragonInc@gmail.com

Previous books by the Author

withheld at his request

Note to readers

The book you are about to read came as a result of what seemed to be a chance encounter some months ago in the lobby of a hotel I often frequent in the Emirate of Dubai. It faces the body of water known as the Arabian Gulf to the Gulf Arabs, and the Persian Gulf to Iranians.

The encounter came on the heels of all the headlines you and I have seen for the last year ... revolution in the Arab world, threats of war between Iran and Israel, clashes between zealots of different faiths, economic chaos in Europe, fear in America.

I was relaxing one evening after a long day of travel from Saudi Arabia in the heat of early summer, when temperatures can push 125 degrees Fahrenheit.

I was tired and not in the mood for conversation. But suddenly I found a bespectacled and unshaven man sitting next to me.

Although he looked faintly familiar, I did not know him. He never gave me his name ... although I I took him to be of Middle Eastern heritage. Yet he spoke in perfect London British inflection, as though he had grown up there.

But he certainly knew who I was. I gradually concluded that he had been following me for some time.

"You must help me", he muttered. "The world is in

grave danger."

Although I took him to be disturbed, I was too tired to get up and move. And while he was odd, he was not physically intimidating.

And so I began to listen, only half-heartedly in the beginning, but with increasing attention, as his strange tale wore on.

I'm amazed to say that we sat for an entire night in that lobby, and then in the hotel restaurant, and then the lounge, and finally out on the still-sweltering promenade in front of the hotel.

We sat together until the first rays of dawn began to show in the eastern sky.

In a low voice, he narrated to me the outline and key events of the story that follows. He concluded his narration by handing me a thick typed manuscript, which after minor editing on my part became this book. Because he never gave me his name, I could not properly credit him then or now.

I continually pressed him to prove any of the things he was asserting. He responded that many of the events were historical fact, if not widely known.

But I pressed harder. I pressed him on characters and events that seemed to be pure fabrication.

His response was that not everything in the book had happened yet. But it would.

I was incredulous. How could he know what would happen in the future? Did he claim to be a seer or a psychic?

He simply smiled and said, Wait and see. It will all come true.

Because I had no way of verifying most of what he said, I present this story as a work of fiction.

As I read and reread this book while in the process of editing it, a thousand possibilities ran through my mind.

Was this book a ruse to pull me into a plot or scandal of some kind?

Was this an elaborate piece of disinformation crafted by any number of entities with a hidden agenda -- like the CIA, the MI6, the Mossad, or a political faction in Iran, Turkey or the Arab world?

Worst of all ... could this story be true?

Whatever the answer, I decided that the narrative was so compelling that the world had to hear it.

I never again heard from this stranger I met in Dubai. It was as though, like the Prophet Jonah, he had been swallowed by the whale. I often wondered what became of him ... whether he still accosted strangers in hotel lobbies. Or whether the demons pursuing him – either in his mind or in the real world -- took him down.

He remains a huge question mark. But he certainly gave me one of the more interesting evenings of my life.

I kept waiting to hear from him again... an unexpected late-night phone call, a letter, an email. I kept my email spam filters off, in the event an unfamiliar address might reach out to me, being him.

But I never heard from him again.

Then, just a few days before my publisher released this book, I received the following message in my mobile voicemail from an unidentified caller. I normally switch off my mobile when I'm sleeping to avoid being awakened by calls from opposite time zones overseas.

Because of the distortion in the sound, I assumed the call to be international. For a few seconds I thought the message might be from the stranger in Dubai. But when I heard it, I knew otherwise.

In the background was a terrible screaming, as though someone was being tortured and then killed. As I listened, my heart began to pound, for the screaming voice I heard, though stressed by fear and torment, indeed sounded like the long-lost stranger.

My doubts were quickly removed. Another voice intervened, speaking in classical Persian, which I can barely understand. After checking with a linguist friend, here is my rough English translation of what the Persian voice said:

"Listen to the sound of the cowardly informer

As he dies.

As will all who stand in our way.

Vermin of the earth

be warned,

Your end time

is here.

Your world is now subject

To our command.

We now control your leaders,

your economies,

your media.

The disorder you see

The wars, the rebellions

The economic crises

 are all of our making.

part of our plan

800 years old

 now coming to completion

We are the Elect.

You can never find us

We are hidden, invisible

Everything is now ours

 we have achieved

the ultimate prize

No one

can contest our power

no one can escape.

We have harnessed

The ultimate power

 of the universe

America, Russia, China

would kill to have this power

But it is ours

worshipped since time immemorial.

In ancient days it was called

The very light of God

Now it answers

to us alone

As will you.

There is no escape

The world is ours

The world united

In thrall to the very light of God

All hail our founder

The millennial one

All powerful, immortal, all knowing"

The phone message ended with silence, and the presumed death of the man I had met several months ago, and who gave me the book you now hold.

I will leave it to you my readers to decide whether the stranger's story which became my story is fiction or fantasy – or insanity. Likewise, I will let you decide whether this final voicemail warning is real and one to be heeded -- or the ravings of another lunatic.

Because I do not yet know the answers to these questions, I have decided to publish this book in my name, yet acknowledging the unnamed man who gave it to me.. I hope you will forgive me for being unable to verify much of this story – much less the authenticity and motivation of the man who gave it to me. But surely you will agree that the story should be told. I leave it to you to decide if it is true. Sincerely

V.S. Marlowe
July 2012

GLOSSARY OF KEY TERMS

Bedouin: desert nomads of the Arab world, residing primarily in the Arabian peninsula

Bey: an honorific salutation in Turkish; once an Ottoman governor

Bouzouki: a Greek lute

Cam i Jamshid: ruby cup of Jamshid, mythological early Persian ruler

Chagatai: a Turkic language of Central Asia

Dari: one of the official languages of Afghanistan

Dasht: certain desert regions in Iran

Dashti: reputed 13th century dissident Persian Sufi mystic and cult founder of the Dashtiya

Dervish: a Muslim mystic, including the Whirling (Mevleviye) Dervishes in Turkey

Farsi: the Iranian name for the modern Persian language

Hadith: a collection of secondary statements attributed to the Prophet Mohammad, but not given the same weight as the words of the Qu'ran.

Haoma: an ancient Persian hallucinogenic drink, used by the Zoroastrian priests and magi

Iyi aksamlar: Turkish for "good evening"

Kaaba: holiest shrine of Islam, located in Mecca, believed by Muslims to have been first built by the Hebrew patriarch Abraham and his son Ishmael

Khorasan: a region in northeast Iran

Kilim: traditional carpets woven from the Balkans to Pakistan

Mahdi: in certain Shiite belief, a quasi-immortal imam who will return to restore justice to the world

Magi: Persian-Zoroastrian priests and holy men

Mevlana: honorific title of Rumi, founder and head of the Mevlevi (Whirling) Dervishes

Masnavi: a Central Asian and Middle Eastern poetic form using rhyming couplets

Ney: a flute of ancient Middle Eastern origin

Osmanli: Turkish name for the Ottoman dynasty

Purdah: a Persian equivalent word for hijab, or the practice of veiling women

Raki: a Turkish liquor derived from grapes and comparable to Greek ouzo

Jelaleddin Rumi: 13th century Afghan-Turkish mystic and poet, founder of the Whirling Dervishes

Sana'a : capital of Yemen

SAVAK: Iranian Shah Reza Pahlevi's secret police, disbanded in the 1979 Revolution

Sems of Tabriz: 13th century Persian dervish, mentor and muse of Sufi poet Rumi

Shia: the minority branch of Islam holding that the successors to the Prophet (the Caliphs) should be male relatives of the Prophet, descended through his nephew and son-in-law Ali

Suleymanname: 16th century illustrated Turkish court history of the reign of Ottoman Sultan Suleiman the Magnificent, written in classical Persian

Sunni: the majority branch of Islam who believe the successors to the Prophet should be chosen by the faithful or their representatives

Taenia: part of the spine of a bound book

Tugra: an Ottoman imperial seal

Urdu: the main language of Pakistan, having ties to Hindi and Persian

Wahabi: the Saudi-based branch of Sunni Islam following strict interpretations of the Qur'an and other doctrine

Zoroaster: Persian religious leader and monotheist of the 2nd millennium BCE, founder of the Zoroastrians, known in his own language as Zarathustra

Book 1

Part 1

And if you be accurate in your measure
Wrapped in truth you will find the treasure
The heart of the world, in my poetry hid;
The sultan's ruby chalice, the cam-i Jamshid.
Then gaze deep into the poetry of God's 99 names,
To find the secret of the very-light,
of the stars' endless flames.

-- The Secret of Suleiman

Prologue

Raine Torkelson lived for the longest time, considering what was being done to him on that gray Istanbul morning.

He saw it all as though at a near distance, floating just above. He saw himself being gagged and trussed up like dead game on his own dining room table, laying on his side, arms and legs lashed behind his back to pull him into a human bow. But more importantly, he felt himself being stabbed to death; he saw his own blood pouring from dozens of wounds onto the table and where not congealed, still slowly dripping onto the dining room floor. He saw himself being stabbed so many times that his very edges and definition had washed out.

He felt the stabs not as sharp pains, but as dull blows, like someone pummeling him through a soft glove.

He saw himself being butchered, but he felt no pain.

Serene and ever alone, he saw his own eyes open and staring, jaw slack and slightly dropped from the

line of the upper mandible, giving him in death the most singular expression of dread and despair, a melancholy and emptiness that perhaps better summed up what Raine Torkelson was when one stripped away the armor of journalism he had created for himself -- the half-life he'd lived, always alone, never fully connecting with anything but his own aloneness and his work.

As the fog and darkness of death began to close in on him, still he realized that some kind of ceremony was being carried out. Indeed, he saw his own body placed dead center of the table, and its side leaves extended, making the table almost formal length, as if for a large dinner. Seven candles were burning, an open book of matches still on the table.

Around the body, twelve glasses had been poured, in vulgar gilt-trimmed goblets from Torkelson's own china cabinet.

There was an inscription beside his body. While the script was literary Persian, the language wasn't. The last thing Torkelson did in this world was to sound it out in his head, trying to understand.

It was classical Arabic, and its message was incongruous.

God the Abaser,

God the Humiliator, God the Judge ...

And so, with those final words and thoughts in his mind, utterly abased and humiliated, alone and without hope, his grim and desperate life finally at an end, Raine Torkelson went forward to be judged, for the very last time.

* * *

Chapter 1

As he looked back on those twenty-four hours leading up to the murder, Burt Horner would always remember them in particular detail ... not so much for what they held, but for how they culminated. While the murder itself was a small event in the scope of this city Istanbul, in the scope of his own life it was a turning point, one which changed all that came after.

Like the lunch with Torkelson that autumn Monday that started it all, the last time Horner saw Torkelson alive. It was the monthly gathering of the American Chamber of Commerce of Istanbul, known to everyone as AmCham.

Horner was headed towards 50, but still lean and rugged enough to get the periodic come-on from a strange woman. A phone or hotel room number scribbled on a napkin and slid to him, or prolonged laughter at his joke that hadn't been that funny.

In his younger days, the constant flirtations and invitations had been an irritation. Now he welcomed them as proof he was still alive.

Horner looked more like a sunburned safari guide in Africa, or a Wyoming rancher like his father and grandfather, than one of the best art historians in the Middle East. He looked more like he belonged with the Special Forces than with Sotheby's of London and New York. But he had always used the incongruity of his looks to his advantage. Even in this Asian place so far from home, people turned to him first. They deferred to him. They gave him breaks and advantages, endowed him with a wisdom that he may or may not have had.

Most of the other businessmen in the Huxley dining room were in shock about Europe's final rejection of Turkey's application to join the European Community, caused and compounded by the world economic crash, ghastly oil prices, aimless wars and political disintegration. After 30 years of rising expectations, the Istanbul stock market was in free fall. Fortunes, dreams were being lost. The future looked dark and uncertain.

Horner had come to this event in the hopes of getting the most modest of business leads. He couldn't be bothered about Europe. He just needed something, anything, to pay the bills.

And then Raine Torkelson had offhandedly asked him the most earthshaking of questions -- at least for a man like Burt Horner.

"You heard anything," Torkelson had asked quietly, "about an Iranian group violating the border and pillaging some new ruins out east, that the Turks are keeping secret? Hittite or Assyrian, up in the mountains near Ararat?"

Horner had a hard time getting his breath.

"I'm told," Torkelson continued, "these ruins were just found within the last three, four months, and the Turkish Army is all over them. Won't let anybody in, won't acknowledge anything. Won't even let the Ministry of Culture touch it. National security censor is squeezing the papers, they can't print. You heard this?"

"Who's your source?" Horner had asked as calmly as possible, already aware he'd had too much to drink.

Torkelson took his glasses off and cleaned them. When Horner had first met him 20 years ago he seemed truly one of those people marked from birth to play peripheral, subordinate roles. Back then Torkelson had been hesitant, unsure, deferent in his manner. And the squinting of the eyes, which might only have been caused by bad glasses. And his voice, which always seemed constricted by phlegm or a frog in the throat or tightened blood vessels, never resounding with any force or conviction. Horner had actually felt sorry for him years ago.

And yet now, Torkelson had come into his own. Like a little weasel of inside information burrowing here and there, he had acquired a derivative strength, that of the classic reporter, smug in his possession of the story and not about to share. Horner never had dreamed he'd be trying to badger someone like Torkelson for sustenance; years ago it had been the reverse. But Torkelson wasn't merely ignoring the conversational bait; he was stonewalling.

Silence resumed.

He got no answer.

Horner and Torkelson were seated by a vast window that overlooked the Bosporus, the water-filled canyon separating Europe from Asia and part of Istanbul from itself. They were together in a booth in the dining room of the Huxley International Hotel. Around them swirled the clatter of dishes being cleared, snatches of conversation, and the drone of workaday communion.

The world beyond the glass swam in pollution that Horner had never seen, smoke from burning garbage in dumps and soft coal combusted in wheezing furnaces, all trapped in a fall atmospheric inversion. The effect could have been uniformly apocalyptic; but it was softened somehow by the silhouettes of mosque and minaret, the boats on the water, the whirl of distant traffic spiraling up and down hillside and canyon.

"Funny folks, those Iranians," Horner ventured. "They believe in lost treasures."

"Apparently," said Torkelson. "But you'd think they'd have other things on their mind, after the Israeli attack on their nuclear sites. World War III is about to start, and they're screwing around with ruins and treasures? It doesn't make any sense."

"It makes sense to somebody in Iran." Horner said. "It started before the Revolution. Even under the Shah, the Iranians were on to something. They were searching very hard in their country ... even in Afghanistan."

Torkelson was listening.

"It was beyond big, Raine. The resources they devoted. Special SAVAK units tearing apart the mosques and tombs of two countries."

"Wasn't it just simple pillaging?"

"This wasn't pillaging. They were leaving jeweled relics and manuscripts in the dirt. They were after something much bigger."

"So what are they looking for now, in Turkish ruins?" asked Torkelson. "And which Iranians? SAVAK is long gone. Dissidents? Ayatollahs? Somebody else? The Israelis stage a preemptive attack on Iran, they miss their targets and kill about 10,000 innocent people. The whole fucking world is falling apart, and somebody from Iran is sneaking around ruins across the border?"

"Curious," continued Horner, unable to answer but

wanting to draw Torkelson out, because this sounded like Horner's big one, the one that had gotten away so many years ago and which now, in his hour of desperation and bankruptcy, just maybe had come back to life.

"The Shah," mused Horner, "wanted something so badly, he turned those crazy countries upside down looking. Hell, some say that's what incited the whole Revolution to begin with. What could it have been? What could have driven him so? A relic? Hoard? A secret?"

Christ, thought Horner as he listened to his own desperate voice through the tympanum of drink; this was his holy grail. One crappy rumor from more than three decades ago. Men like them had these stupid stories, they rattled them on, their apocrypha of commercial lore.

"And now they're looking again," added Horner, almost in a whisper. "It seems somebody new has taken up the project. Not so loudly, not so much manpower. But they're on the same trail."

Torkelson was silent as a sphinx.

"Since when," Horner continued, "do you write about ruins and relics? I thought you were on the political beat."

"I am."

"And you think this pillaging is political? Maria told me you were onto a big story about Ali Nuraddin. But I had no idea it dealt with ruins."

"I'm onto a good story," Torkelson finally admitted, sipping his beer. "The site-pillaging is only a strand. What the hell it means I don't know."

"In Iran, all comes together," said Horner. "What's your story?"

Torkelson exhaled nasally, a slight screwing of the features to let Horner know he was being pushed too hard. Some seconds passed.

"I keep forgetting not to tell your girlfriend anything. For a good reporter, she flaps her lips a lot."

"We communicate well," Horner said. "She trusts me, values my judgment. So what's your story?"

"It's politically big," the reporter finally said. "The Peaceful One. Nuraddin."

"Big plans, the Saudi boy has?"

"I think he wants to overthrow all the governments in the Middle East," Torkelson said. "Even Turkey."

"Pretty ambitious for a folk singer. Is Al Qaeda behind him?"

Torkelson smiled sincerely, for the first time all day.

"You forget Nuraddin's a Saudi Shiite, not a Sunni like Al Qaeda and Osama. And he sure doesn't talk like them. Or the Wahabis either. So he has a lot of powerful enemies on all sides. I don't know how he's lived this long. "

"Maybe they're all too afraid of him. And his

supporters."

Torkelson didn't say anything to that.

"Or they're all so distracted by the mess the Israelis made with their preemptive strike," said Horner. "Hell, every government over here could get overthrown."

"I agree," said Torkelson. "Now all this plays to the Iranians. Their brotherly Shiites are already controlling the new Iraq. And now all the post-Arab spring governments and monarchies are in trouble too. Brilliant. But the Iranians didn't make this happen. They're just the beneficiaries."

"So you think Nuraddin might take over a country?" Horner asked. "Like Saudi Arabia?"

"Not if his secret gets out."

"He has a secret?"

"Very big secret," Torkelson said. "Very bad."

"Sounds scandalous."

"In some quarters."

Torkelson looked at his watch, his unsubtle signal that he was finished revealing, that Horner hadn't delivered and so he was ready to go.

"I hate to be a pest, Raine, but this all comes together. You tell me how you heard this thing about the ruins and I'll help you figure it out."

"You aren't helping me now," said Torkelson. "All you tell me is a bunch of ancient bullshit about the Shah and you want to know who my source is."

Horner felt a wave of anger rising, but he checked himself.

"Pardon me if I sound a bit desperate," Horner finally said. "I told you what Sotheby's did to me, didn't I?"

"You said they were thinking about dumping you."

"They thought about it, and they did," said Horner.

"So sue them."

"What's to sue?" said Horner. "It was all verbal and a handshake. We worked that way for seventeen years."

"Then shed a tear. Move on. Let it go. Write it off. Next chapter."

How glib, Horner thought, his fury growing, his heart rate rising. How dare this little weasel of information tell him to move on. Move on to what? Paid by whom?

*   *   *

From there Horner had pressed Torkelson even harder for the source of the story about the pillaged ruins.

"Please give me a name I can go to about the ruins," Horner said.

"Don't be stupid," said Torkelson. His sources were sacred, more sacred than friendship, it seemed.

"People don't pillage ruins unless they're looking for treasure," Horner continued. "Iran wouldn't risk starting a border war with Turkey unless there was something very precious on Turkish soil. I was onto this 30 years ago. It got away from me. All I need is the slightest lead. A name. A source. A scrap."

"I don't disclose sources," said Torkelson.

"Help me," Horner said, ashamed to have to beg.

Torkelson looked at his watch.

"Listen," insisted Horner. "Do I have to draw you a picture of pathos? I haven't had any income in over a year now. I'm in real danger of having to start selling my clothes down there in the bazaar. I can hold off my landlord for maybe another month. I have a son in college. I am desperate. Help."

"If I hear about something in your line of work," mouthed Torkelson, "I'll try and help." His volume was not enough to make it above the background noise. He was scowling.

"Hell."

"I'm sorry," muttered Torkelson, rising to leave.

"You're sorry?" echoed Horner, spraying saliva. "Shit."

The loud expletive caused additional curiosity at adjoining booths. Torkelson was up, withdrawing.

Torkelson had begun to walk away, but Horner

abruptly followed him and grabbed him by the arm, inadvertently spinning him around.

"Break your rule this once," said Horner, right in Torkelson's face. The smaller man was mortified.

"Please let go of me."

"Help a fellow American," said Horner. "I helped you get started here and make good freelance money off Sotheby's 15 years ago. Return the favor."

The silence in the room was now deafening; even the clatter of dishes had ceased, as the waiters stood by, ready to break up the scuffle if need be. Horner was aware of it too now, some remnant of embarrassment rising through the veil of alcohol.

"Please let go," said Torkelson.

Horner saw the faces of the American and Turkish burghers around him; how he hated these puffy faces, these moneymakers who added nothing to their world. He hated them, because he hated himself in that moment. Because he was one of them. Or had been. Now he couldn't even make money.

"I've got to go," repeated Torkelson.

And so Horner let him go, since their conversation was at an end by that point. After a lull, the surrounding conversations resumed, the AmCham diners rose and walked around Horner to the buffet and carried their heaping plates back to their tables, waiters swept by Horner en route from kitchen to table, cars swirled up ramps and down hillsides, ships moved from the Black Sea to the Mediterranean.

Horner eventually made his way back to the booth, where he sat alone for an interval. He didn't move until early afternoon, when after the requisite exit farewells and collegial backslapping, the other AmCham members departed.

As he left, he learned that for the first time in his life, Raine Torkelson had already paid for Horner's lunch.

*　　*　　*

The lunch had been Horner's brief respite from the gloom of impending bankruptcy. And so, forced to face reality, he walked from the shelter of the Huxley grounds onto the once-grand avenue of Cumhurriyet Caddesi, now into its full afternoon roar of buses and motorcycles, all engines exuberantly free of pollution controls, mufflers or speed limits. The very windows shuddered in their frames, and the once-ornate facades of Victorian days darkened ever so slightly more with fallen soot and dust.

He picked up a copy of *Milliyet* and a pulpier daily from a grimed vendor with no legs, a victim of some terrorist bombing of many years ago; he skimmed the headlines about *EUROPE'S BETRAYAL!* as he paid and walked on towards Taksim Square.

Both papers chronicled the slow unraveling of the old order in Saudi Arabia, concessions the ruling family were making to the radicals. Now even open demonstrations called for their overthrow.

That, and the riots in Egypt, opposing their military's alliance with the Americans and Israelis.

And the Peaceful One's tumultuous reception in Pakistan, his face half-hidden by Bedouin burnoose so it was a blend of rock star and messianic chic.

For a time Horner sat on a bench in a park just off the square, while a loud anti-European demonstration had moved out into the square and an agitator with a bullhorn was urging Turks to return to their roots, to throw off western ways. The one positive note in this drumbeat of bad news and his awful lunch with Torkelson was the rumor of the renewed Persian treasure hunt and ruins being pillaged. He ran the idea over and over through his mind, exciting him for the first time in months. But the path to it was as sealed as it had ever been. He could never penetrate Turkish military censors without Torkelson's help. He almost wished he'd never heard about it.

That memory further darkened his mood, until he knew where he would have to go.

Horner went to a small mosque nearby.

In the years he had lived here, these places had come to be refuges for him. He had approached the issue from an academic starting point, as an appraiser of Ottoman and Islamic art and other antiquities, which required him to spend many hours in mosques and palaces absorbing the assorted designs that decorated countless ornate interiors. Glazed whirling geometry, ceramic winding vines, constellations of white fired stars in blue cosmos danced silently above and around him for years, until at some point, they'd started to become more than decoration. They seemed to be conveying something beyond.

And so had begun his gradual entry into Islam, this

Wyoming boy born on a now-foreclosed ranch, a place as far from Istanbul as was seemingly possible. He'd suppressed his curiosity for some time, wondering how he would even go about sating it. For he wasn't given to emotional religiosity; ecstasy, rapture and mind-blotting fervor weren't in his nature. No, his approach was stealthy and restrained, with an escape route always at the ready. He would attend noon prayer at mosques selected at random, intermittently, taking a position far back in the shadows, watching the ritual, the standing, the bowing, the kneeling prostrate, hearing the chants of the *imams*, the low response of the worshippers. Sometimes he got a stare or two, but figured the congregants would dismiss him as a tourist or foreign curiosity seeker, and think nothing more. Which in a sense was true. He <u>was</u> a tourist, in that he was exploring, and he was certainly curious. Other times he would simply listen to the call of the *muezzin* when it came, usually by loudspeaker. He would take some time to stand in a park or outside the mosque, following the rise and the fall of the call to prayer.

He dared not mention any of this to his other American or non-Muslim friends, for they wouldn't have understood. In fact, he didn't speak of it to anyone, until a mustachioed Turkish man in a business suit had approached him one day after Friday noon prayer in a Muslim reading room some years ago, apparently having seen him slip in on more than one occasion.

"Are you searching for something?" this man, who he would eventually know as Atilha, asked.

Horner didn't reply.

"Come join our group," this man had said, giving Horner a card, with an address, and the meeting time of Tuesdays at 7:00 pm, in Beyoglu district. Out of courtesy and embarrassment, Horner accepted the card with no intention of attending the meeting. Until a singularly gray and unsatisfying Tuesday months later. Although his business was going well at that time, and his personal life was in order, it all seemed a shallow charade, without significance or weight.

And so he found himself searching for the card, taking a cab to the address at the appointed time, scouting the site for a few minutes before entering, to ascertain any obvious signs of risk. In fact, the gathering, clearly visible from outside, was taking place openly in a storefront, a bookstore he had passed before although never visited. The sign said the shop was closed, but he could see a half-dozen people grouped inside.

Atilha was one of them. Horner reproached himself for not having told someone of his intentions or at least his whereabouts that evening. What could this be?

Nonetheless he went inside. In so doing, he took the first step into a wholly new kind of awareness, but driven by an impulse that had always been with him, an impulse to find and unlock the puzzles of life.

The group was a Sufi meditation and discussion group. Why had it taken him so long to find them?

And through that small group, he'd also met two women, one Turkish, one American, both of whom would become his lovers, but entirely different in the sort of love they offered.

*   *   *

Chapter 2

Ali Nuraddin, the Peaceful One, stood for a moment in the doorway of his chartered jet, savoring the cheers of 100,000 screaming Pakistanis at Lahore Airport. He had once been the most popular folk singer in this part of the world, and then had become a Muslim evangelist, and now some saw him as a saint, others as a revolutionary and demagogue.

As he had vowed, now he was going to meet his followers, city by city, country by country.

The Pakistani government had hesitated for the longest time, concerned about letting him in. But finally they had assented, because their hesitation had stirred so much political unrest and opposition that they feared they might be overthrown if they kept him out.

He walked down the stairway into the shrieking mob, with the lower half of his face covered by his trademark Bedouin burnoose. He spoke to the horde in Urdu, one of the six languages he had mastered on his own, without benefit of formal education, so he could speak the majority of his 400 million fans in their own tongues.

He delivered his standard message – asking his followers to help him defeat greed, rescue the poor and build a new social consensus based on love and compassion, not anger and judgement. As he said these things, he saw how young his crowd was, as everywhere under 40 years old; but what could you expect of a man who had begun as a folk singer on MTV?

In return, the audience saw only Nuraddin's eyes and his slender robed form as he spoke and read poetry, filling the airfield's loudspeakers with words ranging from whispers to a scream.

This was his first trip outside the Persian Gulf in two years. He told his Pakistani followers that it would be his first stop on a pilgrimage that would take him to all the Gulf countries, Central Asia, Egypt, Sudan, Jerusalem -- and at some point, God willing, to the holy city of Mecca.

As he said this, he and his followers knew what a gamble he was taking. There was no assurance that any of those places would allow him to enter. But as he told them, and as he felt in his own heart, he was not afraid. As long as he had breath in his body, he would press ahead for peace and social justice and spiritual rebirth.

And when he said this, his audience let up a universal shriek of approval. They knew the danger, and yet they wanted him to take the risk on their behalf.

And afterwards he was mobbed, he was adored, people fell down before him and asked to be blessed, asked him to perform miracles; though he was embarrassed by these displays, he could not stop them. The adoration went on so long that it was several hours before the airfield could be cleared of his fans, and his jet could depart.

*   *   *

Chapter 3

The memory of the lunch with Torkelson stayed with Horner on the final bus ride home; he arrived at sunset, painfully sober, expecting to find Maria, the American reporter whom he'd met in his Sufi study group and who had become his mate. But she wasn't home; and to further disorient him, the phone had rung within a minute of his arrival and it was the other woman from the group, the Turkish one, from whom he had not heard in at least two years, calling to invite him to dinner in Bebek district.

"Nilufer," he said, with hesitation, wary of encouraging the renewal of a relationship that had been ... difficult.

"Darling, darling, this is strictly business."

"Business."

"I hear you're having a bad patch."

My, the wagging tongues of AmCham had been busy. As always, she knew when he was at his weakest, and that was when she would strike.

Against his better instincts, he agreed to meet her.

They met in a bar on a wharf at Bebek by the Bosporus, a place that in warm weather is the most Mediterranean spot in Istanbul, with striped awnings and canvas chairs and white tables and water lapping just below the railing, fishing boats and yachts and motor launches all riding at anchor and lights beamed from the other side of the Bosporus pulled into gyrating chimeras on the water's surface. Though officially fall, it was warm enough tonight to sit outside. The thick haze of day now wrapped the tumbling cityscape and hillsides into a dreamlike sky, and colored the huge harvest moon a warm yellow, and it floated just above the hills of Kucuksu.

Nilufer wasn't considered beautiful -- being more voluptuous than the ideal of the day, with red hair unnaturally intense in its tint and brilliance, even when pulled back in a bun as it was tonight. Her features were lost in makeup too excessive and slightly off, plus she wore a pair of odd glasses more suited to a librarian. Yet her overall presence was one of unspeakable fertility, a femininity even in her late 40s literally bursting out of her clothes. Her hips, buttocks and bust were all enormous, and yet she had an almost tiny waist. Nilufer's skin exuded a pearly rosiness, her lips nearly blinded him with their brilliant reds, and the combination was too much for him tonight, as it had always been. Horner found himself averting his eyes, just to avoid conjuring up memories long buried of evenings years ago, of her ripeness unveiled, her openness demanding his closure ...

The old feeling was coming up in his throat and he had to fight it down.

And even when he wasn't looking at her, he was lost in her smell, a combination of a perfume he could never identify and had never detected on any other person in the world, plus another almost indecipherable subscent, a luscious reek that came over him and filled his nostrils and drew his consciousness ever downward, away from the mind, into the flesh.

God, he had to keep this in check.

To complete the picture, she was also one of the most intelligent -- or at least most intellectually stimulating -- women he'd ever known. And that had sealed the trap of her attraction for him.

"You look hungry," she said, reading him in more ways than one. "Shall we order now?"

He agreed.

"Dreadful news from Saudi and Egypt, by the way," she said. "Do you think the king will fall?"

"Who knows?" he said.

"What did your fool American president think he was going to accomplish, by letting Israel bomb Iran?" snapped

Nilufer. "He's going to provoke Iran to war. And the damned Europeans. Turkey would have been the strongest economy in Europe. Now what? I lost half my savings in the stock market today."

"I wish I had savings to lose. How've you been? Weathering the exit from politics?"

"Splendid, as always. And you, my dear?"

Since their breakup nearly ten years ago Nilufer, a onetime linguist and professor of classical Turkish literature, had been forced by financial needs to go into the advertising business. And to everyone's surprise, she'd proven a genius at it, her success, especially on behalf of the Salvation Party that won an election in part due to her efforts, leading finally to an appointment in the President's office. This he had learned of from afar, by reading the papers, and when that party had lost its power, he'd assumed she'd been out of a job.

"Dearest," she said. "Politics was an experience I wouldn't trade for anything."

The waiter brought over a smorgasbord of Turkish vegetable hors d'oeuvres, of stuffed squash, red caviar in mayonnaise, flaky pastry and white beans vinaigrette that would keep them occupied for some time.

"So what are you doing now?" he asked.

"Funny you should mention that," she said. "I have a

proposition to make."

He didn't respond.

"I want you to come work for me."

"Pardon?"

"I want you to come work for me."

He was totally flabbergasted.

"I'm pretty busy as it is," he said, thinking the conversation and meeting would come to a rapid end now.

"That's not what Raine Torkelson says."

"Raine Torkelson? He's talked to you about me?"

She smiled, lifting a skewer of shrimp to her mouth.

"We talk from time to time."

Horner was having a hard time hearing now, flustered by this information.

"What do you talk to Torkelson about?" he finally said. "Are you helping him on his Nuraddin story?"

She paused just a second too long, making him think she knew something she wasn't saying.

"What Nuraddin story?" she asked.

"Some deep dark secret that could destroy Nuraddin, the Peaceful One."

"Actually Torkelson called me about a ... Swiss client ... of mine," she said. "He wanted some background."

"Who's your client?"

"How cheeky," she said, flustered enough to make him

think he was close to the truth. "I don't name names."

"What was Torkelson asking?"

"Heavens," she said. "Some slander about my Swiss friend fronting for the Iranians."

"Is it true?"

"I don't know and I don't care. I only know that my client is charming, sophisticated, and he pays me very well."

"But why would Torkelson come to you?" Horner asked.

"He knows I have friends in high places, here and elsewhere. When I was in government we ... helped each other."

"I thought I had the same relationship with him. Today I asked the first favor I've asked him in my life. He treated me like shit."

"He can be an awfully hard <u>trader</u> in secrets," said Nilufer. "You didn't have anything of value for him, and so he stiffed you. You can't call in chits after ten years with people like him. Journalists have such short memories, Burt. Yesterday is old news, in the trash can. You were dreadfully hard on him, making that ridiculous scene at the Huxley. Have you started drinking again?"

Horner ignored the final question, and downed a boiled shrimp.

"So what's your big project?" he asked.

"In due time. I want your vow of silence, before I say more."

"Why the secrecy?"

"It's proprietary information, darling. I've worked on this one for some time. It concerns art."

"How do you connect? Are you an artist again, too?"

"I'm still a linguist," she said, "and it also connects to linguistics."

"Buying? Selling?"

"My, such a snoop. Let me think. Shall we say ... research?"

"Research," he repeated. "Linguistic, artistic research. Totally legal. No buying or selling. But is it ethical?"

She laughed.

"You're enough of a cultural relativist not to ask such a silly question. That you'll have to decide for yourself."

He was as broke now nearing age fifty as he was when he'd been twenty. Only now he was on the down curve, whereas before he'd been on the way up. The way down faded into ever deeper gloom, ever dimmer despair.

"I'll hold my tongue about your project," he said.

"I knew you would," she said. "Let's go somewhere quieter." And they went out into the night and onto the cobblestone street, for the quick ride up to her apartment which overlooked Bebek and had a commanding view of the city and the harbor, the waterways of defeated Byzantium, the fallen towers of forgotten city-states, the dusty palaces of unnamed pashas that had now become museums and orphanages for street waifs.

*   *   *

Chapter 4

As he flew back to Yemen in his jet, Ali Nuraddin was given the latest news by his retainers.

Though he was filled with belief in the rightness of what he was doing, he knew that the world was moving to a thousand different rhythms, and many of them were sinister.

He knew that these especially dark times were driving him to his mission sooner than he had planned.

He read that after the failed Israeli strike on Iran's nuclear facilities, the United States was contemplating preemptive invasions of several oil producing countries... and Iran.

The Americans would do this dangerous thing to "secure major oilfields and stabilize the world economy."

Though many would head this news and react with anger, Ali Nuraddin found himself filled with sadness, at how far the world had fallen in his own short lifetime.

It touched into the melancholy that had shaped him, and

which even now he struggled to overcome.

Then, as he looked out of the blue ocean below him, he realized how urgent his mission had become.

Powerful forces were conspiring to take the world farther into danger and disorder.

He would have to move very quickly, to complete his mission before it was too late.

He no longer had years to undertake what he knew was right in his heart.

He had only months, or perhaps weeks. He had only weeks to accomplish what hadn't been done in 1,000 years.

*   *   *

Chapter 5

Back at her apartment, Nilufer teased Horner with the prospects, without revealing her offer. This was her style; dismissing directness and honesty as bourgeois, game-playing was for Nilufer Oz the highest art.

But within an hour, he'd extracted the essence of her proposal. And the essence was a search, on behalf of an anonymous client with deep pockets, for an alleged missing chapter-folio from the illustrated biography of Suleiman the Magnificent, the Ottoman Turks' greatest ruler. The biography was known as the *Suleymanname*.

The search was based on a recently-discovered 400-year-old mystic poem -- or *masnavi* known as *the Secret of Suleiman* -- that had come from a recently-reopened Islamic library in Uzbekistan. Nilufer, educated as a linguist but earning her living as an publicist for the opposition Salvation Party, had been compelled by financial hard times to take on the project of translating the poem from Chagatai, a Turkic tongue. The author of the poem was reputed to be Yunus, private interpreter for Suleiman the Magnificent in the years 1560-1580.

A couplet rumored to be buried somewhere in the manuscript had whetted the client's appetite:

And if you be accurate in your measure
Wrapped in my verse you will find the treasure ...

Major questions remained in Horner's mind, however. For one, the existence of such a missing chapter-folio was highly doubtful. Nothing Horner had ever seen confirmed it.

Yet the client seemed to be willing to pay unlimited amounts simply for information leading to the missing chapter-folio of the *Suleymanname.* But Horner could see no reason for the manuscript to be worth so much, even if it did exist.

Nilufer would say only the missing folio was so valuable because it led to "much greater things."

What things, Horner had asked. Lost treasures, secrets, what?

Nilufer had only winked in affirmation to any and all possibilities. She was ready for him to start work right then and there, and even invited him to stay the night.

He declined the sleepover offer, but said he would

consider the larger proposal.

"We'll meet tomorrow, then, to get started."

He sighed.

"Noon?" she said. "Coffee?"

"I don't know."

"I'm so excited. A winning team."

As he drove home, the two things that kept running through his mind, more than the "project," more than the money, were these:

First, there was no person he less wanted to work with right now than Nilufer Oz.

And yet he was also tantalized by a tiny detail on the faxed manuscript copy Nilufer had shown him to convince him to take part in her search. For the fax had not come from country code 41, a code he knew well from his art dealings to be Switzerland. No, the country code was 98, the country code for Iran. And based on that and Torkelson's strange leads, it undoubtedly led back to the same client Raine Torkelson had been asking her about, who was also somehow tied in the reporter's mind to the pillaging of ancient ruins and the Saudi Peaceful One's deep secret.

Had Raine Torkelson done Horner a favor after all, by connecting him with Nilufer's project -- which might lead back to the Iranian archaeological pillagings, and the fabled treasure hunt?

Horner was so preoccupied with the conflicting prospects of doom and revelation that when he got into the taxi for the trip back to his apartment in Tesvikiye, he paid only scant notice to the deep desolation of the streets, the bearded streetcorner orators in skullcaps urging the poor to overthrow the government of Satan, the news on the cab's radio of skirmishes and battles in the rimlands taking more lives for causes barely understood. A giant harvest moon overlooked the Bosporus and the Prince Islands and the pine-fringed Sea of Marmara; an old street woman stood wrapped in shawls at the entrance to his apartment building, the embodiment of an uneasy night.

*   *   *

Chapter 6

When Horner made it upstairs, the mists of evening were already heavy on the Bosporus, and he could see only ships' lights -- diffuse, soft, ethereal -- like jewels embedded in the fogs wrapped around them.

Below him spread the quieting pulse of his street, Nuzhetiye Caddesi, widening down towards the water and at the water's edge stood the sooted ivory bulk of Dolmabahce Palace. It was there in the 19th century the last sultans had tried to put a progressive European face on their decaying dynasty with this grandiose structure to replace Topkapi, which displayed too much of its roots in the days of conquest and harem.

Across the water at Uskudar he could see the silhouettes of the many mosques concentrated there -- the Mihrimah, Yeni Valide and Semsi Pasha, surrounded by the minarets of assorted lesser shrines.

His lover Maria was waiting for him, slumped in a chair, watching television. She was shuttling between a bad and dolorous Italian movie dubbed into Turkish and CNN coverage of the worsening unrest in Riyadh and Cairo. On top of that, the Iraqi prime minister had just been shot at by one of his own bodyguards; his whereabouts and physical condition were unknown.

"Working late?" she said, into the television. He couldn't see her, or she him.

"Yes, actually," he replied.

"On what?"

"Trying to bring in a little income."

"Before I forget," she said. "Your driver Genghiz called. I think he wants to come back to work."

"I'd love to have him," Horner said. "I just don't have anything to pay with."

They were speaking of his former driver, Genghiz, who had been laid off months before for shortage of cash. Horner was talking to the top of Maria's head, her only part other than splayed feet that showed above the back of the chair. He could see she had on her splotched jeans and sneakers; she'd been at her pottery studio.

"He's a good man," she said. "Very loyal to you." The emphasis, of course, was on loyal.

"I know," he said. They hadn't even seen each other's faces yet, but volumes had been spoken.

"Starting something new?" he asked, in jovial tone.

"What?" Now she'd turned to look at him. She wore

her shirt with the tails out; her cheeks even had a smudge or two of clay. Her auburn hair was wrapped in a braided coil around the top of her head. What always amazed him was how a woman could remain so beautiful and vibrant when she spent most of her days in smoke filled newsrooms and chasing bits of information from bombastic Turkish politicians. Her green eyes and creamy cheeks glowed, looking like she'd just come from a swim in the chill Bosporus or a hike in the highlands.

This woman could have been a model or actress, professions she would have laughed at. He was lucky to have found her.

"Are you starting some new pottery?" he repeated.

"Just junk so far. Who were you talking business with?"

"But at least you're making the effort."

"Who were you talking with?"

"You don't want to know."

"Undoubtedly a woman."

"How was the newsroom today?"

"Wretched. On top of all this other stuff, Europe's rejection of Turkey was the crowning blow. Now nobody knows what will happen. Who were you with today, Burt?"

"Hell, it was Nilufer Oz."

"Oh my god," she said.

"Maria," he said, moving towards her.

"Don't," she said, putting her arm out to keep him away.

Maria shifted in mid-word to a commentator in Atlanta pointing to wall-map of the city of Riyadh, showing crowd locations, tank and police deployments. A U.S. aircraft carrier was changing course from the Indian Ocean; assorted ambassadors were shown climbing out of automobiles and going through doorways in Washington. And Ali Nuraddin was shaking hands with the Pakistani airport masses, his masked face a shadowed cavern into threat or deliverance ... the dream-messiah.

Her fit of jealously that night was a total surprise. Though it threw him off balance, in an odd way it also encouraged him about this relationship, which for the last year or more had grown so "mature" it seemed like it had no emotional component at all.

Actually, his love for her was as strong and powerful as it had always been. Perhaps even stronger. It was Maria who had changed. She was too often distant, preoccupied, cool. At certain dark times, he thought the worst. He feared maybe she didn't love him anymore. Or that she had someone else, though that would have been so far out of character. The few times he brought it up, she would brush him off, saying it was her own problem, that it had nothing to do with him.

And so he had accepted her explanation. But he couldn't deny that on top of all his business worries, to think that his relationship was in trouble added an uncertainty and an uneasiness that he couldn't shake off. God, how much he loved her and needed her. The idea of losing that love was his worst nightmare, even worse than losing his own life.

"Maria, it was just a business conversation." With that she went into a paroxysm of hollow laughter.

"I know how close you were to her," she said.

"Maria, it wasn't love. Nilufer is no threat to you in any way."

"I can smell her on you," she uttered.

"She gives off strong smell," he said. "She wears powerful cologne. Maria, believe me. I don't even like the woman. I haven't spoken to her in two, maybe three years. I haven't been with her for almost ten. Shows how desperate I am for cash. She called today, wanted to talk about a deal. I haven't been this broke in 20 years. I may have to work with her."

A period of hostile silence followed, while the television was a window into mobs in the night, fires in the vast pilgrims' campground outside Mecca, a horde trying to liberate the Kaaba and water cannons being sprayed. In Egypt, martial law had been declared. In Pakistan, 100,000 faithful bade farewell to Ali Nuraddin as his rented jumbo flew back to Yemen, where he had made his home since being expelled from his native Saudi Arabia. His next stop, if a visa could be obtained, would be Afghanistan.

Horner was stroking her arm and now her hair.

"Nilufer is poison," she said.

"I know all her tricks," he said. "As soon as something else turns up, I'll be done with her."

"Forgive my distrust," she said, not yet sounding certain she'd done anything to be forgiven for. "It was a bizarre day."

Horner wondered if her distance of the last year hadn't been worsened by the pressure of her job. She'd risen from the lowliest stringer-correspondent to WPI bureau chief in only 15 years in Istanbul and could now compete with the best.

But in recent months, the source of her moods was never certain, and when they had these rough times, he had to play a detective role figuring out what they really meant.

What made it so hard was that in the early years she'd been there for him. Thinking about those times, how much more fun-loving and adventurous and romantic she'd been, his heart would suddenly ache and it would almost bring him to tears, to see now how much she had changed. Back in those days it was he who had been more reticent. Not because he hadn't loved her. It was from his exhaustion. He'd been on the road at least two weeks a month, covering the whole Middle East. His work had been much more demanding then; he'd had so much to do. Now, it was as though they'd reversed roles. She was being worked to death and he couldn't find any work at all. If he couldn't make a living, he certainly still wanted to love and be loved. It was more important than ever.

But when her new wall grew more impenetrable, his imagination ran to some hidden wound far beyond what she had let him know,... something beyond the trauma she'd suffered in her aborted life in Iran, brought to an end by the Revolution.

*   *   *

Chapter 7

Maria had come from the blandest of suburban Chicago backgrounds. After finishing college, and working for one depressing summer as a secretary in Chicago, Maria had taken an English-teaching job in Iran, based on nothing more than her adolescent excitement on the few occasions her father had brought home one of his company's foreign managers for dinner. And it was in Iran she'd been reborn; the dryness of her life to that point had been lifted in this most unlikely of places -- in the trappings of oriental wealth and political unease, in the reinvented myths of Persia, in the simmering fervor of a religion still fresh with the fire of belief.

"Horner, I need an old-fashioned simple, tight news story," she said, breaking his thoughts. "Reporting on fundamentalists on the rise in Turkey, Ali Nuraddin flying around, the Americans planning new invasions and the Middle East falling apart, is just too big, sinister and depressing. I don't like what it's doing to me."

"Actually," he said. "I heard some talk today from your rival Torkelson. You might check it out."

At this point he passed on the tip he'd heard from the reporter: the Iranian pillaging of the mysterious ruins south of Ararat, and the Turks censoring the story.

"Interesting," she said. "Not a sparrow falls without Torkelson knowing. Where did he hear that one?"

Horner had no idea.

She was nodding, thinking to herself.

"Ararat could be a good story," she finally said.

"But how could it relate to Torkelson's big one?" Horner asked. "The deep dark secret of Ali Nuraddin?"

She shook her head.

They didn't talk for a good while; the television filled the void for them. The reconciliation would come, he could feel it; he wanted to kiss her and speed it along, but he knew it was a bit too soon. She would come to him when she was ready.

"So," he said. "You never answered. What got you back to your potting wheel today?"

She seemed moved by his concern, but didn't say anything for a moment. She was back at the refrigerator, pulling out a beer.

"This wasn't a normal day," she said. "I suppose I was looking for distraction."

"This revolutionary stuff is bringing back memories of Iran for you, isn't it?" he asked, pointing to the television.

"Yes," she acknowledged, half nodding. "Maybe. But didn't you notice the calendar?"

He paused a moment; how could he forget? It crept up on him every year, and always came out the wrong way.

"His birthday, isn't it?" he said.

She nodded, looking into the plate.

"How old would he be? I mean --"

She was waving away his correction.

"I know what you meant. Assuming he's still alive ..."

"He's probably still alive. You got letters for years, pictures, too. A whole gallery of them in the bedroom."

She didn't answer. He'd put his arm around her; he knew she was overcome, because she was wiping her eyes, and her nose had become congested.

"That's why I act this way sometimes," she said, breaking the silence as if she'd been reading his thoughts. "They tore my heart out once; I don't know if it's grown back yet."

The evening was full and rich; the lights on the water, soundless traffic on the bridges, stars twinkling over Asia.

And now he did make his move, turning to embrace her, but she still wasn't ready, even if he was. So they sat there, his arm around her watching CNN reporting the crisis.

Beyond the television, the lights of the city and harbor sank further into mist, Horner waiting for her to catch up to him, in her own time.

*   *   *

Chapter 8

When Nuraddin arrived back at his camp in Yemen, there was more news, a mix of the bad and the good.

The good news was that Afghanistan had said he could enter, he could come there within the next two months.

But this permission was bittersweet, since had Ali Nuraddin forced the issue, the Afghanistan government probably couldn't have prevented him from coming, even from making his home there.

But the most devastating news was the decision of his own homeland, the Kingdom of Saudi Arabia, to prevent his reentry after five years of exile. They said that "public peace in the Kingdom does not lend itself to visits by masked traitors, whether they think themselves sincere in their proclamations of faith, or are only cynical provocateurs."

This made him as sad as the news about America invading the Kingdom and Iran, because it meant he had so many obstacles to overcome, in such a short time.

For a moment he cried, to think that he might not be

allowed to see his beloved Mecca, that he would be an exile forever while millions made the journey every year.

But then he shook himself out of grief, and made a vow to God that he could not fail in his mission, lest humankind also remain forever in exile, from the truth of God.

He could not fail.

* * *

Chapter 9

And now it was the fateful morning, the morning of the day someone would die an awful death, a death both tragic and evil, only Horner didn't know that yet. He only knew that when he should have been at the top of his game, he was suddenly unemployed, he was broke, he was alone, he was at the end of his rope.

It was abysmally gray outside, the dead of February in Istanbul, which although depressing to the eye, promised that the filthy air of the last several days would be cleansed by rain. A strong north wind had come up out of Eastern Europe, and the rain was beating on the windowpanes. Unaccustomed to being home this late on a weekday, Horner listened with some despair as the building gradually quieted, as the pipes stopped singing, and the doors closed and locked for the last time. The stairwells echoed with final footsteps and voices as those with gainful employment or school departed for the day.

And then his phone rang; it was his journalist friend Raine Torkelson, of all people. The wretched lunch was still too painful to think about. Horner expected never to hear from the reporter again.

Yet now, only a day later, Torkelson was calling, sounding oddly unsettled, disoriented as Horner first considered, then refused, to voice an apology for the insults of the day before.

"I can't be long," Torkelson interrupted. "Where's Maria?"

Torkelson and Maria, bound only by the shared language of journalism and intrigue, nonetheless excluded art appraiser Horner and even made him jealous.

"At the bureau, as always," said Horner. "Call her there."

"I did. She's out, covering the demonstrators at Parliament."

Horner was headed towards anger again. Torkelson didn't want to talk to Horner, he wanted Maria.

"Raine, I'm busy," said Horner. "Wait for her to get back to the bureau."

"There isn't time. Burt, this is life and death. Tell her I need to talk to her about Nuraddin."

Ali Nuraddin, the Saudi folk singer turned new Islamic messiah. The one man alive who could draw Shiites and

Sunnis together, not just politicians in a conference room, but the masses, the disenfranchised, real people ... the faithful and the fallen.

"She could care less about Nuraddin," Horner said, although it was none of his business. But anger had taken over. "She doesn't want to talk to you about Nuraddin."

"Fuck off," said Torkelson. "Then I need you to get over to my apartment right now."

"What?"

"I said get over here. I've got something I want you to get to Maria."

"Get it to her yourself," Horner said. "I'm not your damned errand boy."

Horner could hear a commotion in the background on Torkelson's end. It sounded as though his front door was being rammed open.

"What the..." Horner heard Torkelson say in English, then there was some shouting in Turkish, and the phone clunked loudly as if the receiver had been dropped and was bouncing against a table leg.

Now a man, probably Raine Torkelson, screamed pitifully until he was muffled, and then there was an interval of furniture banging, bodies in motion, things falling to the floor. Grunts and odd words could be heard until the line went dead.

Frozen, Horner listened for an instant, then hung up to call the police. But the one number he had for the local precinct was busy. In desperation, Horner found his pistol and some ammunition, then ran downstairs to find a cop and hail a cab on the street.

No police were to be found. But a minute later he and the cab were off, spewing gray wastewater on either side. As they raced along, Horner checked his wallet to see if he had enough to pay for this ride.

It would be close.

*   *   *

Chapter 10

Istanbul traffic was always horrendous, worsened today by a rain-soaked parade of workers demanding some kind of retaliation against the Europeans for excluding Turkey from the European Union. But the cabbie wasn't above driving on the sidewalk. Bakirkoy was a nondescript lower middleclass suburb of concrete apartment blocks and warehouses, not far from Ataturk Airport. Horner had been there once, maybe five years ago; he was astonished now to see how the old leftist graffiti had been replaced on virtually every wall by Islamist slogans, then defaced by anti-religious obscenities.

God, how this country was changing all around him.

Another ten minutes were lost in trying to find Torkelson's building and a local police office; street signs had been knocked down or stolen, address numbers hadn't been placed on buildings. The best he and his driver could find was a pair of off-duty Turkish Army troops, who refused to get into civilian troubles. Finally Horner recognized the building;

he asked the driver to wait downstairs for him while he went up.

The moment was looming closer now; Horner didn't know this in a conscious way, but he felt it, at a subliminal level. He went about things in a deliberate manner. First he buzzed Torkelson's flat, to no response. He buzzed again, and this time, the speaker came on, but a voice barked in accented Turkish, "Very sick; go away." There was a great deal of noise in the background.

What sort of accent was that? he thought. Did Torkelson have roommates now? Another tenant opened the door from inside in order to leave, letting him enter. And now Horner could hear a scuffle in the stairwell above.

Horner took the tiny residential elevator. The elevator was about the size of a phone booth, with more religious posters plastered to the walls, and once sealed inside Horner cursed himself; too many times had he been caught in these things by malfunction or power outage.

But the elevator didn't fail.

The fourth floor landing was tiny, dank, with four flats opening off of it. With the sole light bulb burned out, the space had become a crypt. The only illumination came in narrow strips seeping from beneath the closed doors. The disturbance he'd heard seemed to be heading down the stairs below him now, perhaps a group of boys running to the lobby. As Horner groped for a lighter to identify Torkelson's place, a door burst open and a silhouette of a man ran into him face-first, the two of them colliding skulls and teeth in an awful crash; they came together so hard they literally exchanged breath, Horner inhaling an odd, bitter smell. Horner fell back into the elevator, while the other tumbled head-first down the stairs; Horner heard the man's head actually thudding on the concrete stairs as he slid down to the intermediate landing.

Stunned, Horner went towards the moaning man; his lighter threw only a flickering sepulchral glow, and Horner could barely make out a darker-skinned young man with a black scarf pulled over his mouth and nose. It had slipped mostly off. Backing away, Horner's own foot slipped, and he nearly lost his balance again. He found a heavy black string of Muslim prayer beads, presumably dropped by the man. Picking them up, he realized the beads were oversized, almost absurdly so.

Beads in hand, Horner approached the man, checking to see if he was still breathing. His eyes were wide open in a ghastly staring way, which at first made Horner think he was dead. The overall impact of the eyes was so startling that they would stay with Horner for days, on top of the shock of what he was about to discover ...

But then the man moaned.

Horner thought to feel for his pistol.

Suddenly the man revived; though obviously disoriented he took an instinctive punch at Horner, then went stumbling and falling down the stairs.

More concerned about Torkelson than about apprehending this man, Horner let him go.

Coming back up to the landing, Horner found another item dropped in the collision -- a small embroidered cloth illustration, a mini-tapestry of the type used as a resting place for a *Qur'an*, undoubtedly from the provinces, a mix of gilt and green, which he could not make out well in the gloom. He regarded it for a few seconds before gingerly picking it up. It was warm to the touch, from the grasp of the man who had dropped it.

An Arabic message was embroidered below the illustration, but in the dark he couldn't make it out either.

The door from which the man had emerged was half open, admitting a wide rectangle of abysmal outdoor light from the windows beyond.

It was Raine Torkelson's door.

"Raine," Horner called, for some unknown reason of etiquette pressing the door buzzer and hearing it blare just a foot away. The television was playing a slight undercurrent of ceremonial dervish music, lilting and melancholic with its falling Arabic rhythms, the kind of music you might hear in bazaars and parks in smaller towns, songs that spoke to the thousands who'd migrated from the countryside to Istanbul or Ankara in the last decade. While Horner found this music intriguing, it wasn't the kind Raine Torkelson listened to.

"Raine," he called again, to no response. He pushed the door further open, stuck his head inside.

The far wall of the apartment was gray light -- a bank of curtainless windows opening onto dismal day. The "on" light of a DVD player shone red at him, a tiny mournful star below the television, which showed the whirling dervish ceremony in full play, dervish dancers spinning in their white fezes.

But the next impression was polychromatic, many colors spread out upon the floor. He was looking at hundreds of glossy magazine covers, files and documents scattered on the carpet, back issues of *Newstime*, and English, Turkish, Arabic and Farsi publications from all over Torkelson's beat -- the faces of fallen leaders, the lurid photos of disaster and triumph strewn like fallen leaves in the forest, on floor, coffee table, sofa and stool.

"Lord," said Horner, dumbstruck. "Raine, what's this?"

Raine couldn't answer him. As Horner slowly turned towards the small alcove that had on his last visit served as Torkelson's dining room, he realized that Raine Torkelson was most certainly dead.

Raine's body was gagged and trussed up like dead game on his dining room table, laying on his side, arms and legs lashed behind his back to pull him into a human bow.

He had been butchered.

As in a trance, Horner went over and touched a cheek, a hint warmer than room temperature, suggesting Torkelson had died not long after the phone call that had brought Horner here. Horner winced to think the murder had been underway even as he was driving over in a cab, searching desperately for a policeman. How long had Torkelson lived after the interrupted phone conversation? Had Horner gotten here just ten minutes too late?

But for some very bad traffic, Raine Torkelson might be alive right now.

Then, both of them might now be dead, too.

But Horner hadn't yet seen the full tableaux. For as he stood there, strangely moved, he realized that some kind of ceremony had been carried out. Indeed, Torkelson's body was placed dead center of the table, and its side leaves had been extended, making the table almost formal length, as if for a large dinner. Seven candles were burning, an open book of matches still on the table.

Around the body, twelve glasses had been poured, in vulgar gilt-trimmed goblets; Horner could smell the same bitter odor he'd noticed on the killer's breath. Horner had probably drunk out of these very glasses on that last visit here, for a very awkward and mirthless New Year's Eve party Torkelson had thrown.

Looking down at the embroidered illustration he'd found on the stairwell, his eyes were first drawn to the Persian inscription in Arabic script below the illustration.

God the Abaser,
God the Humiliator,
God the Judge..

He also saw the Arabic number "99" richly embroidered to the side of the text. And now his gaze moved to the embroidered illustration itself, which he had first ignored because its colors were so muted by time and grime that it seemed an unexceptional religious scene, of generic martyrdom, perhaps the revered Shiite Imam Hussein. But now he could make out a cluster of hooded men in caftans arrayed around a fallen white-bearded dervish in a white turban. This was no *Qur'an*ic or mainstream religious story that Horner recalled .

The men in caftans were stabbing the old dervish to death, and embroidered blood poured from his wounds. Their arms were raised, their blades were red with blood, and they seemed transported into ecstasy by this death.

Horner stood frozen at the execution scene, with Torkelson's blood still dripping in the background, but with less frequency. Torkelson had wanted to pass something along to Maria. Was it here, in this mess? How would Horner ever find it? Or was that what the killers had come for? And had they found it -- the secret about Ali Nuraddin?

In shock and dumbfounded, Horner could think of nothing but to call Maria ... or Nilufer, who after years of silence had popped up yesterday dangling tales of lost manuscripts and big payoffs. Ideas were beginning to catch up with the scenery, and they weren't good. The answer lay somewhere in the sequence of yesterday's events. Only Horner didn't yet understand it, he just sensed a terrible confluence, spawning a deep paranoia that sent a chill through him, raising the hackles on the back of his neck.

A vile shiver rolled through him as he wondered if there were some deeper connection, something that had just killed one man and might kill others.

In desperation, he dialed Nilufer's number.

"Helloo" she answered.

"I am standing in Torkelson's apartment," he was able to say.

"Bertram?" she said. "You were due here at noon. I can't wait all day."

"Hush," he said. "Raine Torkelson is dead. Nilufer, he was butchered on his dining room table, with his files strewn all over the house. I'm calling the police..."

She uttered a low tremulous cry, a kind of ululation, and directed it out into the room where she was, not the phone, so it was indirect and distorted.

"The stupid fool," Nilufer finally said.

"Who got him?"

She gave the brittle wail again.

"Get out of there," she said. "Horner, get out. The idiot must have gotten in too deep with his snooping. This isn't ours. Get out."

"I'm going to call the police. Torkelson called me an hour ago, said he wanted to get something to Maria about Ali Nuraddin. Now he's murdered."

"You American jackass. You don't want to get into a Turkish murder investigation or plots around Ali Nuraddin. At least get out before you call them, call from a pay phone, untraceable. For God's sake, you were never there."

"It was some kind of a ritual killing. He's laid out on the table, there are twelve glasses, a Persian inscription on a *Qur'an*-cloth in old script. 'God the Abaser, God the Humiliator, God the Judge.' A dervish ceremony was playing on the video. One of them dropped a giant rosary when we crashed in the hall."

"I know that verse ... Horner, clean your prints off and leave."

"Hell, maybe the neighbors saw me come in. I'm here, I can't erase it. And you are too. He's probably got your name scribbled down. Maybe you should be over here with your rubber gloves."

"I didn't know he was in danger," said Nilufer. "But he should have known. Digging around about Nuraddin. It's heavy stuff."

"Heavy is an understatement. Wish I had a camera, though. This verse, those candles. I feel like I've witnessed a religious event..."

Nilufer was making her mourning sound again.

"I've got to go," he said. "I've got to ring the police."

"No," she repeated.

"Nilufer. Justice must be done."

"Come over here before you call," she croaked.

"Why should I?"

"The manuscript. Don't get yourself mixed up in Raine's mess, Burt. Because of Nuraddin, Turkish intelligence will be all over it. Your life won't be the same. Besides, I'm getting good stuff for the manuscript search. You should see it, as soon as you can get over here. References to the missing chapter-folio have already started to crop up, in what I'm translating."

He stood there a moment, watching the light of autumn storm leak through unwashed windows, the landscape of a miserable Asiatic suburb. A man was dead, surrounded by communion wine; words on a wall blessed a soul into the next world.

"You should see this manuscript first," she said, mournfully, the world now heavy with loss. *You should see this, he thought, before you do anything else.* And so softly, without speaking, as new rains fell from a sunless sky, as a man lay in state in a forgotten and forlorn apartment, another man made certain no evidence of his presence was left before he too departed, silently, closing the door behind him.

*   *   *

Book 2

Ardor and ecstasy lend pattern to the world;
Poetry without ardor and ecstasy is merely a
mourning song.

-- Jelaleddin Rumi

A caliph's crime
rests in episode lost,
in story repressed,
in memory quashed.
To find what was hidden,
by imperial shame,
read these verses about God's 99 names ...

--The Secret of Suleiman

Chapter 11

Three days can remove the details of a murder-scene from a bystander's immediate consciousness; but they don't serve to erase the feeling that lingers. For a reverential sadness prevails, even as the event recedes into the past.

Nilufer Oz and Burt Horner were talking on the parapet of the Galata Tower, used by the Genoese in the 11th century to survey their portion of Constantinople. Nilufer was standing with her back to the railing, Horner overlooking the city and the water beyond. The day had turned clear and blustery, and the city was dazzling in its brilliance. Every shadow, every rattling leaf and bare limb, every chink in stone and alleyway was edged in brutal relief. Whitecaps had sprung up out on the water, and the water was blue in all directions: Bosporus, Black Sea, Sea of Marmara. The pace of the city had quickened from the polluted torpor of earlier that week. People were scurrying about, as if preparing for winter.

"Burt," Nilufer said, trying to dissuade the grim feeling from the heart of her listener, "you're letting this wretched coincidence confuse you."

"No coincidence," he said. "An illustration of hooded men stabbing a dervish -- plus the number '99' at Torkelson's death scene, and the same thing in your 400-year-old manuscript. The cabal in your manuscript is directly linked to Torkelson's death."

"Burt, these sorts of symbols could be cliches that pop up everywhere, like crosses and smiley faces --"

"Don't bullshit me," he said. "Your translation project is deadly. How did Torkelson know you were working on a search for the *Suleymanname* anyway?"

"We were talking about other things. He asked how I was supporting myself these days and I told him a bit about the search."

"And remind me why he came to you in the first place," Horner asked.

"Like I told you the other night. He had questions about my Swiss friend."

"The same Swiss friend with a Tehran area code who's interested in the *Suleymanname*?"

She looked flustered and didn't reply. He took it to mean he had scored.

"You've got to be working for the dark side," he said. "The fact that your client has mullah links doesn't bother you?"

She snorted with derision.

"I don't care if he has ties to Vlad the Impaler," she said, "and you shouldn't either. He is a gentleman. He is wealthy. He pays in advance. I'm not in a position to turn away paying business right now."

Nor am I, he thought to himself.

"And please," she said, "Let's get over this obsession with Iran. Yes, their President is an awful little man, saying he wants to exterminate Israel. But no Iranians I know believe that could ever happen. They are the most pro-American people in the Middle East ... at least until your President let Israel bomb them. There are thousands of Jews in Tehran, living freely. Europeans, Asians, even Latin Americans do business in Tehran every day. It's just a matter of time before the Iranian people send these dreadful religious demagogues into exile. The Iranian Revolution is totally burned out. It's only rhetoric now, like Chinese Communism. No one believes that theocratic rubbish anymore."

"But," retorted Horner, "don't you care that your search is tied --through these dervish stabbings -- to the Nuraddin story ... to his deadly secret?"

"I think it's coincidental," she said.

"You're either lying to me or lying to yourself," he said.

The iron grating of the parapet was shuddering slightly with the footsteps of the other tourists moving around the circumference of the tower. Below them, medieval alleys wound beneath eaves and balconies. And one of the now-inescapable religious street demonstrations had come even here, and a street imam with a bullhorn was bellowing at tourists on a large bus to take their foreign ways outside Turkey.

"If I'm going to risk my life and work for murky clients linked to a murder," he said, "I'll have to examine this suddenly-discovered manuscript from Uzbekistan."

She seemed a bit discomfited.

"My client just wouldn't allow it. That's our agreement. I sense ... although I don't know ... that there is some considerable money involved here."

"Very dubious," Horner said.

"The manuscript isn't dubious, precious. I saw the original in ... Switzerland. As for any connection to the murder, circumstantial at best -- through poor pathetic Raine. Mystic poems don't murder people nowadays; murderers do. Fanatics, mafiosi, the like. Maybe Nuraddin's secret was too terrible for a mere mortal to know --"

With that, her eyes swelled up like anemones under threat, and she pursed her magnificent lips. Nilufer was dressed in a dark new pair of jeans that outlined her huge hips magnificently; he doubted there was any other woman of this weight and size who could look so good in jeans. She was wearing a plaid jacket, and unlike the first night she'd let down her red hair, so it was flying in the breeze.

She also wore high-heeled gold sandals, and her toenails, fingernails and lips were all painted with a color he could only call purple. Intellectually he knew it was lurid and vulgar ... but his attraction to her wasn't rational. It was pure demented obsession, he thought, trying not to look at her. At least being outdoors was keeping her perfume at bay.

"If I were you," he eventually said, "I'd think about going to the police. Speaking of ... they called me around breakfast-time. They want to come by my apartment this afternoon."

She was snapping her purse shut.

"How strange. What are you going to say?"

"The truth," he said.

"That you had a spat with him in front of 100 of the leading citizens of Istanbul the day before he was murdered ... that you were on the phone to him when he was being killed ... that you were in Torkelson's apartment while his body was still warm, even before the police got there ... that sort of thing?"

"Touché," he said. "I was thinking more like anonymously giving them the embroidered dervish cloth, and the DVD that was playing when I got there --"

"What was it?"

"The whirling dervish ceremony, as far as I can tell."
She pursed her lips.

"Darling, my sinister interpretation was meant to be a warning. As someone who has lived here a long time, you should know the Turkish truth is as twisted as those alleyways down below us."

"What would you have me do?" he asked.

"I would be discreet. I'd have an attorney."

"Discreet. As in, forgetting I was in his apartment. And forgetting he had a few conversations with you, too, before he was killed ..."

"You need an attorney," she said, "to help you understand our law."

"Atilha Atalay is my attorney."

"Darling," she said, "I respect his fine Sufi mind, but he's not a criminal lawyer. He does wills and prenuptial agreements and lawsuits for politicians whose hairpieces blow off."

"You know better than that. He was the best young physicist Turkey had 30 years ago, then had to drop his doctorate and come back and save the family law practice. And he's a friend."

Her lips were pursed, eyebrows raised in parental admonition. In this instant, it was hard for him to imagine they'd ever been close.

"If I'm going to risk getting killed for your manuscript, I'll have to be very well paid," he said.

"Burt, I'm prepared to pay you 75,000 euros in cash when you sign on. Your expertise means that much to us. There's nobody else in the Middle East we'd pay that well."

The traffic noise of the city was coming up to them as a collective sigh, with only the horns breaking the coverlet of distance -- klaxons, oogahs, sirens. But directly below them and with more clarity, the police were trying to drive the Islamic demonstrators back from the entrance to the tower. There was much shouting and taunting back and forth.

He almost asked her how the Iranian pillaging at Ararat might relate to her own well-funded search for the missing chapter of the *Suleymanname* -- but then he did not. Because in his questions, he was giving away too much about his train of thought.

And his train of thought was that a journalist's story about a Muslim messiah named Nuraddin had gotten the journalist killed. And the same journalist had also been asking why Iranians had ransacked an ancient site in Turkey. And that same dead journalist had paid Horner a favor by putting him onto an antiquities search paid for by a mysterious "Swiss" client -- with Iranian ties.

And the big one that had gotten away from Horner three decades ago -- a royal treasure hunt by the fallen

Shahanshah of all the Persias -- was almost certainly underway again.

I am, he thought, like Ahab, finding reports of the Great White Whale in tavern whispers and scraps of paper in the portside gutter.

"Maybe I've been out of work for too long," he said, laughing to relieve the tension.

"I should say so," she said, raising her enormous eyebrows again. "All the more reason to get started on our search. What better way to get this off our minds? It's no-lose. Even if you find nothing, you get paid. And if we find the missing chapter of Suleiman's court biography, sky's the limit."

He didn't say anything.

Nilufer's personal attraction hadn't diminished; today she was at the peak of her powers. Her movements set off all sorts of fleshly ripples and surges beneath the veil of fabric, and he simply couldn't stop staring as she posed with the panorama of the old city behind her.

Horner found himself comparing her to Maria, Nilufer's very antithesis on the feminine spectrum. He genuinely liked Maria, as well as loving her and even wishing they'd been able to have a child together; he didn't like Nilufer at all, found her appearance monstrous, her personality theatrical and utterly false, not to mention her skewed values and her loathing for the outdoors -- he doubted she'd gotten any more exercise in years than a daily waddle to the tobacco shop.

And yet he was ready to devour her.

He also knew there was no way to avoid what he was about to say; his need for money and his professional curiosity were too great.

"I'll take your offer," he said.

Her mood swing was awesome to see.

"Welcome aboard, darling," she gushed, running towards him all ajiggle, arms open for embrace, her aroma almost knocking him down.

"Wait, wait, wait," he said.

"My darling," Nilufer purred, wrapping herself around him. "What fun we're going to have. Oh, Burt, this is an adventure."

His mind knew he should pull away, but he let her engulf him for a dangerous interval. He could smell her, almost taste her, all that womanhood in his grasp ...

"I'm so glad you're with us," she said. "It will be a triumph. They laughed years ago when the first rumors of the missing chapter-folio came out. Imagine the astonishment if we prove the rumors true. If we succeed, and I think we will, you can tell Sotheby's where to go. They'll be coming to you on bended knee. By the way, my client wants you to have this."

She handed over an envelope. Horner found the promised 75,000 euro in cash.

"Your advance," she said. "You've got expenses, bills to pay."

He looked at her, then the money.

"Generous," he said. "Of course I'm nowhere near an answer as to where the chapter-folio might be. Any idea how much longer this translation of **The Secret of Suleiman** will take?"

"The going's getting tougher. The next set of verses, the imagery, is really slowing me down. Because I'm constantly watching for puns, word-puzzles that kind of thing, I take as long translating his description of a sunset as I do the kernel of fact we need. You know the Sufis and their word-play ..."

"When do you think you'll finish?"

"Next week, I hope. That isn't much help to you. You need to start."

"I have an appointment at Topkapi in an hour to examine the binding of the *Suleymanname*," he said. "I'll be able to tell if something was probably removed from the back ... even torn out."

"Wonderful," she said. ""Sounds like you're on your way."

"Let's hope so," he said.

"Burt," she said, coming towards him again. "You know you wanted to get on with the search from the beginning. Your eyes lit up like fireworks when I first proposed it the other night. Why maintain this facade of hostility?"

He couldn't answer her, but he knew he couldn't take another embrace.

"The work would go more smoothly if we could be friends," she said, in an uncharacteristic little girl voice, following him as he backed away. He almost laughed out loud.

"I'll be friendlier when I know who my client is," he said.

"All things in good time," she said. "Aren't you going to thank me for turning your life around?"

"Thanks," he said.

Someone once had told him if you stay in Istanbul longer than five years, you can't leave. Oh, you may think you're gone, but you carry the alleyways and the minarets and the memories within. The city's inside you, it reaches out into the world and finds you wherever you go.

But perhaps these events -- his poverty, the murder, this unsavory alliance -- were telling him his time here was up, that he'd best be thinking about a new life somewhere else. That's the lesson financial difficulty teaches, right? You've taken a wrong turn? What you're selling is not of value to anyone? A place no longer has need of you?

He knew he could never leave Turkey.

"It's getting late," he said. "I've got my meeting at Topkapi."

She turned and looked squarely at him for the first time today. The eyes were smaller than normal, the mind deep in calculation, even as her purple lips beckoned to him, tempted him to fall into disaster.

"There is one small thing," she said. "When you do talk to the police, I would appreciate your leaving my name out of this."

Most of the other tourists present had gone back inside, to hear a Turkish combo rehearsing for the dinner show to be staged in the tower's cupola.

"Is that a warning?"

"I think it's a ... gesture ... critical to our new project together," she said.

He said nothing.

"We'll talk in a day or so," she said.

He didn't respond, feeling her hair and flesh brush past him as she headed inside, reminding him that much as he truly disliked this woman, disliked the way she thought and played and presented herself to the world, he was also drawn to her like an addictive drug, as strongly as a decade ago ... when he'd been so blinded by the lust he hadn't paid much attention to her dark side. Her blue-jeaned thighs disappeared through the doorway, the labyrinthine maw of the city at his back, the declining afternoon and the burnished water reminding him of the first time he'd seen Istanbul 30 years ago. And now, standing here, it was possible to imagine the world had not changed in 30 years, the world was old and he was young, 1,000 forking paths of possibility stretched away from him, and all he had to do was decide which to take.

When had the choices begun to narrow? And why was it, once ignored, those possibilities were gone forever, life was like a machine set in motion, each movement of the mechanism fixing everything harder and faster, diminishing the range of choice?

By the time he came down the circular staircase, Nilufer was gone, most of the tourists had departed as a result of the religious heckling, and the street imam and his followers had taken a break, looking lost, unemployed, devalued. Despite Horner's earlier admonitions to Genghiz to drop him and then go look for paying fares, the driver was waiting on the street. Horner had the pleasure of telling him he could come back to work fulltime, because he was back in business now. And their next stop would be the manuscript collection at Topkapi Palace, to make a direct inspection of the *Suleymanname.*

Genghiz was pleased to accept the offer of re-employment.

*   *   *

Chapter 12

He had half the leaders of Islam on edge, and yet he was nobody.

He had been raised by a peasant family in Saudi Arabia, in the desert city of Ho'fuf, and so Arabia was in his blood.

But the street was in his blood too, the dirty street and the back alleys of poverty, the hopelessness of being an outsider, being marginalized. There was nothing in his birth or upbringing that made him anything more than the bottom of humanity.

But now he saw himself as a citizen of the world, and hundreds of millions of people listened to his every word and watched his every move.

He had been famous for only ten years. He had risen to fame as a folk poet and singer, all the time wearing his Bedouin scarf and headwrap. He had begun to recite his poems and sing his songs on market days in the many towns of the vast Arabian peninsula. He blended a mix of lost love and found love of God that passed the censors. His cassettes and DVDs were circulated hand to hand until they went on sale in stores.

It was then the government had adopted him as their unofficial ambassador to youth. They loved how he could sing as well about Allah as he could about his broken heart, about worshipping a girl from afar whom he could never expect to meet.

Suddenly his music and the videos became lavish and exciting, an odd mix of Hollywood and Bollywood and Islamic surrealism that began to reach outside the Kingdom, into Iran, Afghanistan, war-torn Iraq and even Central Asia. And even as this happened, and he even became a wealthy man for the first time in his life, he knew it was not the end. He knew it was just the beginning, and that he was intended for something much bigger, something so big that he could not even say it to anyone, lest they think him crazy or dangerous.

But he knew it to be true.

*　　*　　*

Chapter 13

"So you decide to work on Miss Nilufer's project?"
Genghiz asked as they maneuvered en route.

"Yes," Horner told him, still uneasy with regret. "She's
aroused my curiosity about her manuscript. Made this
appointment on Monday, before I went to Torkelson's. I used
my connection through Karaman, the former minister. My
visit will cause a flutter ..."

Topkapi: the old fortress of the sultans still stood in a
heavily forested urban park on a promontory overlooking the
Bosporus, while an exploding city lapped at its margins. The
poplars and birches, now nearly half-bare, would have
looked at home in Saxony or the Loire Valley. With gray and
dun stone and cement, the outer walls, gatehouse parapets
and slate roofs showed as much resemblance to the Balkans
as to the Islamic world or Asia.

Horner walked through the third and innermost gate,
the *Babussaade* -- Gate of Felicity -- leading into the once
forbidden sanctum. He turned into the Mosque of the Agas

which now housed much of the imperial manuscript collection. Only last week the Islamic Front had proposed in Parliament that its current use was blasphemous, and that it be reopened as a practicing mosque. The move had failed by only seven votes.

Ozbudun, the museum curator, and two of his assistants, Mr. Gunes and another whose name Horner didn't get, were already there to greet him. Ozbudun, scowling until he realized Horner was approaching, now plastered on a patently false grin of greeting.

Ozbudun was an effeminate man in his 40s, bald halfway onto his waxy scalp, with a severely edged Van Dyke beard lending a Mephistophelian quality to his features; he moved and spoke with hands clasped before him, and walked with an exaggerated girlish scurry.

"I must tell you this is quite irregular," he said. "Normally this sort of thing must go to the Minister for approval. In the current religious climate, we are even more cautious. But you have been so insistent, and ex-Minister Karaman said it was urgent, and I must take his word. I hope you appreciate the inconvenience this has caused."

"I certainly do."

"What sort of ... project ... are you undertaking?"

As they entered the manuscript room, Horner cleared his throat.

"A potential client is offering a manuscript reportedly bound by Suleiman's master binder --"

"You mean the great Mehmed b. Ahmed --"

"The very same. I wanted to examine the *Suleymanname*, and personally photograph the binding, particularly spine and folio joints, the foreleaf, that sort of thing. In order to make a comparison, and a verification."

They were now approaching the glass cabinet containing the *Suleymanname*. They stood there at the case for a minute, awkwardly.

"Might this material," said Ozbudun, "fall within repatriation laws?"

"I think not," lied Horner. "Its origin is Central Asian, not Turkish. If so, of course, I am honor bound to inform you."

Ozbudun nodded at him, looking through slits of eyes.

"I wasn't aware that the master binder had done any work in Central Asia," Ozbudun said.

"Nor I," said Horner, wondering if he would be caught in his own lies.

"May I examine?" Horner asked. Ozbudun duly snapped his finger, and Gunes produced a keychain which was sent to rattling as several locks were opened, and the case was opened. Horner pulled out his penlight and magnifying glass. Ironically, the manuscript was open to the chapter-folio depicting the formal presentation of the fabled solid ruby chalice of all the Persias, the *cam-i Jamshid*, to Suleiman the Magnificent.

Just three days ago Horner had read Nilufer's translation of the **Secret of Suleiman** recounting this same cup's involvement in a near-assassination of the sultan. But in this chapter-folio now spread before him, years before the alleged attempt, Suleiman sat serene upon a gold throne, surrounded by a swirl of Persian calligraphy, viziers and guards. All eyes were riveted by the treasure itself, by Suleiman holding the ruby cup in his hand, this moment perhaps more than any other capturing him at the zenith of his power, his domination of three continents.

A placard in the display case noted the ruby cup had later disappeared forever, one of the great mysteries of Topkapi.

Horner spent a good ten minutes in his examination. He quickly focused on the space between the spine of the book and where the chapter-folios were sewn together. As he slid his finger along the taenia inside the spine, covering the sewn joints, he could not help but sense a gap at the end of the volume.

Looking at the empty thread holes at the back of the volume, he sensed a widening of those holes alone, a stressing that could have come from violence to the volume -- indeed, from a final chapter being pulled or torn out.

Horner then made two requests: to see the files on the restorations done on the *Suleymanname*, which had been carried out every half-century or so; and, as a long shot, to personally remove the taenia covering the binding joints and examine it.

Ozbudun puffed and fluttered about the impossibility of either.

By the time Horner had come back out into the street, winter was indeed in the air. The sky was now the deepest aquamarine, pouring a blue light over the Aya Sofya Mosque just across the street. Old Hagia Sophia, the Great Church of Byzantium; the blue air hung over its primordial bulk, over the minarets added later by the Turks, over the dome drab and squat with the sediment of 1,400 years.

Religious picketers seemed to have driven November's few tourists away, making the place even more desolate. But the immensity and solitude helped Horner focus his thinking to more immediate things. And his central thought was this: that although he was ever more distrustful of Nilufer, her client and her motives -- he now thought her project might have merit after all.

* * *

Chapter 14

Maria was home when he reached there, but not for long, because she was working the night shift that night. She was covering the Turkish Parliament in extended session; the coalition government was struggling to fight down another no-confidence vote from the Islamic Front over its failure to win admission to the European Community. He hated these kind of nights. Life seemed turned upside down.

She hadn't yet noticed him come in, so he secretly observed her for a moment.

God, how he still loved her. Again he let himself fall into the possibility that she really didn't love him, that for whatever reason she was pulling away, that this would all end someday.

Then he took himself out of that place, getting back to the realization that gave him some sense of peace, at least for the moment.

So what if she didn't really love him anymore? He still loved her. And wasn't that enough for him? To have the experience of loving this person who was with him?

He watched how she moved as she prepared to leave for work. The job had changed her, especially when she was on duty; until she unwound, her movements were tighter, more martial, her voice informational and unmusical. Seeing her grow ever more engulfed in a career she professed to love, he had to conclude that in her deepest self she didn't love it, that she was aggrandizing it to avoid a deeper emptiness.

But now as he watched her, the light of sunset flooding the apartment briefly overcame her career facade, and he had glimpses of her as she really was. As she bent over to arrange clips and papers in briefcase, her walnut hair swung in a brightened veil. She was trim and glowing, still looking like the hiker she'd been when they first came together, even though now both of them were always too busy to get to the mountains. And he could see the artist, the potter she'd been in the spare time she now never seemed to have.

She was exceptionally beautiful, the result of her infectious laughter, her green eyes and her athletic build somewhere between dancer and gymnast. She also had a quality -- seen in expression of eyes, set of mouth -- he described as her aura of wisdom, a person who saw through surfaces to the essence. That was what had drawn him in, and

drawn them both to Sufism; and what had so frustrated him
when the door to her deepest feelings almost always was
closed.

As she sorted through the papers, she also broke out
of her officious role enough to wad up unwanted clippings
and fire them towards a trashcan. She was muttering about
them out loud as she tossed them, and it was engaging to him
to hear the remnants of her Chicago accent, but stretched out
or even softened by the many years of working in Farsi and
Turkish and Arabic. The accent was a source of
embarrassment, something she'd labored to erase; but it was
rooted so deeply that echoes of it would always be there, in
her English.

Then she looked up and saw him, and the spell was
broken.

"You scared the hell out of me," she said, flustered.
"The police were just here."

"What? They said five."

"I suppose they were early. They went for coffee.
What do you think they'll ask?

"I've no idea," he said. "Routine things, probably. How
long had you known Raine Torkelson? Who were his friends?
Etc, etc."

He hung up his jacket in the closet.

"Did they talk to you at all?" he asked.

"No. Why would they?"

"Oh, just that Raine Torkelson was urgently trying to get in touch with you when he was killed."

She didn't answer that immediately, continuing her bustling in preparation for departure.

"How would the police know that anyway?" she asked.

"Only if I told them," he said.

"And you haven't," she said.

"No, I haven't. But shouldn't I?"

She exhaled.

"No, I don't think you should."

"Why not?" he asked.

She appeared to be trying to contain herself.

"You know I can't do my work with police on my tail," she said. "This country is slowly sliding into extremism and I don't know who to trust in the government anymore. Not even the police."

"What's more important -- journalism or justice?"

She didn't answer.

"There <u>was</u> a murder, after all," he said.

"Justice is very relative in Istanbul these days," she said.

"Funny," he answered. "Nilufer had a similar comment."

"Then we agree on something," she said.

He almost told her that he'd agreed to work for Nilufer. But he envisioned the conversation, and it wouldn't be pleasant. To bring it up now would be disastrous.

"I won't mention your name to the police," he said.

"Thank you," she said. He wanted to keep her there a few minutes, but it was clear she wanted to leave.

"Have you thought any more about the story?" he thought to ask.

"Which story?"

"About the Iranian pillaging of the ruins at Ararat."

She looked at him an instant.

"I've thought a lot about it," she said.

"So what were the Iranians after? Why would they violate the border to ransack some ruins? Especially after the Israeli attack."

She only shook her head.

"Could it be disinformation?"

"Ask your friend Nilufer," Maria said.

"That was catty."

"Burt, Nilufer Oz, no matter how brilliant she is, is poison. She does the lowest kind of work now --

"Political advertising, p.r. --"

"Like Goebbels did. I did some asking around today. Turns out she was the Salvation Party's dirty trickster in the last campaign, fabricating all kinds of garbage. Luckily it didn't help, and they lost. Though this new government seems as bad."

"I'd never heard this about Nilufer before," he said. "Not that it surprises me."

She was still shaking her head.

"Burt, you don't mess around with police, especially when you're a foreigner. And you don't mess with the queen of Turkish disinformation herself. You're putting yourself at risk ..."

"I like risk," he said. "That's why I live here to begin with."

She was looking at him with amazement.

He concluded he had killed her cooperation by mentioning Nilufer's name.

"Oh. Before I forget," she said. "A Mr. Gunes called."

"Gunes, from Topkapi?"

This was unexpected.

"Yes. Wanted to talk about a manuscript."

But before he could collect his thoughts, the police were back.

*　*　*

Chapter 15

They were two; an Inspector Aziz, and a Sergeant Ekmekci, who served as the Inspector's aide.

The men were both short and slim, the Inspector showing some gray in his hair, the Sergeant at least 15 years younger, but otherwise not memorable in the slightest, both wrapped in shades of gray and brown wool and cheap polyester, like thousands of Turkish men who streamed around him on the streets and at the busstops and in open crowds.

They entered in deference, bowing and uncertain. They approached as would have tradesmen, tentative, uncomfortable to be in a foreigner's home, a home they would probably judge to be an abode of wealth.

Rich aureolin light suffused the apartment, carrying the room, with its tapestries and ceramics and Ottoman furniture 300 years into the past. The effect was magic, totally inappropriate to what was going on here. He wished he had a camera.

"Have a good night," he called to Maria. She waved goodbye, and was gone.

"Your wife?" Inspector Aziz asked. All of their conversation was in Turkish.

Aziz now became clearer to him, with an elfin quality, a face triangulating to the "v" of the chin and peaks at the top of his ears. Hair, feathery and close to the head, was combed down in front, adding to the boyish, clever air.

Ekmekci was round-faced behind tinted glasses, bushy black hair and full moustache hiding his features, a Turkish everyman found at soccer matches or downing raki in a corner bar.

"In a common law way," Horner replied.

"May we smoke?" Aziz asked.

Horner consented, knowing Maria would protest were she here. Both men instantly lighted up.

"How did you get my name?" Horner asked this as offhandedly as possible.

"That is police business," Aziz said. "Do you have identity papers for yourself and your woman?"

Chastened, Horner went and found his and Maria's U.S. passports.

"Could I have your full name?"

"Bertram Earle Horner."

Ekmekci was writing on a form, copying directly from

the passport -- but formalities seemed to require the questions be asked aloud anyway.

"Place of birth?"

"Dubois, Wyoming, United States. November 20, 1960."

"Length of residence in Turkey?"

"25 years."

And so it went for some minutes, as the minutiae of who he was and where he had been and what he had done was extracted, as he was categorized according to the parameters of the Turkish police investigation manual. There was a lulling, almost soothing effect to the Inspector's voice, as he alternated long stretches of routine information-gathering -- about Torkelson's work, friendships, sex life, personal habits, background -- with occasional pointed probes that cut to the heart of the murder.

The sensitive questions included: How had Horner heard about the murder? And with whom had he discussed it? And when had he last seen him alive? And what was the nature of the two men's relationship?

And Horner made the fateful decision to conceal that he had been in Torkelson's apartment before the police; to conceal that he had heard the murder taking place over the phone; to withhold that Torkelson had been urgently trying to reach Maria on the morning he died; or that Torkelson had spoken with Nilufer.

Nilufer had been right. Horner should have had a lawyer for this.

"And Monday at the AmCham luncheon was the last time you saw him?" Inspector Aziz asked, as they neared the end.

"Yes," said Horner.

"Were you aware of what Mr. Torkelson might have been working on, as a reporter?"

"He said he was working on a story about Ali Nuraddin."

"The Saudi rabble-rouser."

"Yes."

Inspector Aziz turned to the sergeant. Both he and the sergeant exchanged glances. Aziz himself made notes.

"What might the story have dealt with?"

"Some secret surrounding Nuraddin. Some secret that would destroy him."

Aziz went to his briefcase, and began shuffling the contents with vigor. His energy unsettled Horner once again.

"You mentioned a friend, a driver. Genghiz Akcael. This name sounds familiar."

"Oh?"

The Inspector was flipping through the sergeant's transcription. Horner wondered if his harmless reply would prove dangerous to him. Why was he focusing on Genghiz?

"But I know that name from elsewhere ---" said Aziz. He was looking to his aide again for assistance. "Wasn't this Akcael once a policeman?"

Horner paused a moment.

"I think he was, years ago."

"Of course," said the Inspector. "He's handicapped, correct? A war injury?"

"Missing fingers, from a terrorist bomb he was defusing," exhaled Horner.

Sergeant Ekmekci had started to write more energetically in his notebook. Was something being said of great significance that Horner had missed?

"Was Mr. Torkelson a drug user?" Aziz had then asked, abruptly.

"Not that I know. Why?"

"Some were found at his apartment."

"What kind?"

Aziz looked bemused at Horner's questions.

"*Haoma* liquor. Are you familiar with it?"

"The old Persian hallucinogen? I've heard of it, sure. But I didn't think it even existed anymore."

Horner now remembered the curious bitter smell on the killer's breath, the glasses on Torkelson's table.

The darkness outside was total now. Only the west

showed the faintest aurora of light to suggest a departed day. Traffic was swirling down the Cevre Yolu, towards the Bosporus Bridge, bound for Asia. The ships on the Bosporus were fully lit, new hotels above Dolmabahce Palace holding a promise of exotic diversion he found puzzling, for they were the same hotels found in capitals all over the globe, stale in their sameness. But this was the wonder of Istanbul: to infuse all, even the cliched, with the lure of mystery. Forgotten by the world in this century, Istanbul constituted a world of its own, and seemed self-sufficient, for an instant.

"Inspector," asked Horner, sensing the interview at an end. "Who do you think killed him?"

The Inspector looked at him a few seconds, so intently that Horner wondered if he had inadvertently revealed something about himself, his withholding of information and evidence.

"Who do you think killed him?" the Inspector responded.

"Journalists make enemies," Horner said, certain this was a straight answer and yet uncomfortable with the sudden scrutiny he'd brought on himself with his question.

"I shall keep that in mind," said the Inspector.

And so the two policemen took their leave, saying that it might be necessary to talk again, and asking if Mr. Bertram Horner could be so kind as to please advise them if he planned to travel, and suggesting that Mr. Horner might also want to advise his attorney of their conversation.

Horner could make no reply.

"Very well," the Inspector said, nodding in farewell. *"Iyi aksamlar."*

"Iyi aksamlar," breathed Horner. And they were gone.

*   *   *

He stood there at the closed door for a time, hearing them walk down the stairs rather than take the electric lift. In fact, he stood there for a good five minutes, a statue, eyes fixed on the door, the words of the last hour spinning through his memory. Was there someone other than the taxi driver who could place him at the crime scene before the police? Would he have to explain his presence there, his lie in concealing it?

He called Genghiz, relating to him the interrogation and his apologies for drawing him into it.

"No problem, boss. Tell me. Who question you?"

"An Inspector Aziz. Sergeant somebody."

"Ah," said Genghiz, making a tut-tutting sound. "This is very bad." And Genghiz proceeded to tell him Ferruh Aziz was probably the best detective in Turkey, having earned a law degree and been offered promotions to the prosecutor's office many times, promotions which he had declined because he liked detective work so much.

How comforting.

"This also says many things," continued Genghiz. "To put Ferruh bey on case means they think it of importance. That he came to see you means you now in his mind. He has photographic memory. He sees linkage, relationship everywhere. Deductive powers."

The conversation ended shortly thereafter. Horner had a beer and read the *Herald Tribune*. Then he dialed Atilha Atalay's home, interrupting the attorney's dinner. But Atilha couldn't talk. He had to leave in a minute to spend the evening at Istanbul Hospital with his brother, who was dying of a stroke.

"Meet me at my office at nine tomorrow," Atilha said.

Then Horner remembered the message Maria had given him from Mr. Gunes about the Topkapi manuscript. Gunes had helped Horner on a project a few years back, in the good old days of easy money -- he probably thought Sotheby's would be good for some extra income this time around, too. How wrong he was. But Horner didn't want to miss the opportunity.

Because Gunes might be able to get the *Suleymanname* restoration file for him, if he was hungry enough.

The calculation was correct. Gunes, a widower living in a rented room not far from the palace, was ready to strike a deal before Horner could even finish his proposal.

"I will call as soon as I have it," Gunes said.

And when he did, Gunes promised, they would arrange a time for Horner to inspect it at length.

*   *   *

Chapter 16

He knew he could not sing about love and God forever.

To be real, he had to step down into the real world, so that he was doing more than giving people a temporary escape from reality.

He had to help them change reality.

And so he began to speak and sing about things political, despite the advice of everyone around him. They warned he would lose his audience, put himself in danger, lose his wealth.

And while all those things were true, he had no choice. His heart told him to do more.

But just the opposite happened. His talks, which were really sermons, drew more listeners than the imams and the politicians.

His initial message was simple. He appealed for those who called themselves Muslims to come back to their Allah. But he avoided the superficial and puritanical judgements that had turned off so many Muslim youth. Instead he painted his vision of Islam the compassionate and merciful, declaiming that men were commanded by God to show love and compassion, and leave the judging of other men to Allah alone.

Miraculously, he did not lose his audience. He increased them. And so he took the radical step of saying that the true meaning of jihad had been lost, stolen by the terrorists. He said it was not an external battle but an internal struggle towards righteousness, to express love and compassion in all spheres of life, and to build a society on that basis.

He said the wealthy could redeem themselves by sharing their wealth with the poor.

And while his audiences now surged, across borders, drawing both Sunni and Shiite and even outside the faith of Islam, this final massage proved too much for his homeland. The Saudi government turned on him, saying he was now a heretic and expelling him from the country.

Though this saddened him, he remembered how the Prophet had fled from his own city of Mecca to avoid being killed, and taken refuge in Medina.

And he was further gratified to see how his audiences grew, how the money still poured in and the invitations to travel increased.

He was tempted to finally throw off his scarf and burnoose and show his face to all. But something kept him from doing that.

Because he realized that in his invisibility and disguise, he was becoming the projection of all his viewers wanted, no matter how contradictory. He realized that his mystery and hiddenness could deliver his mission sooner and more powerfully.

By being invisible, he was touching every heart with his own heart, and that was the most powerful tool of all.

*   *   *

Chapter 17

And so Burt Horner was now truly alone for the evening. He poured a large Scotch to clear his head. And his mood did lift a bit, helped upward by a sienna autumn moon rising above the waters and the city. Seafood cooking smells rolled over from the apartment next door, freshly-caught sea bass.

He read, he dozed, he made some notes about the *Suleymanname*.

And now it was midnight, sooner than seemed possible. How he wanted Maria to be with him. But he wouldn't see her until dawn.

Solitude drew him back to the subject he'd been avoiding.

He retrieved the DVD dropped in Torkelson's stairwell, a memento of a murder, a reminder of something that if he'd had any choice, he would never have known about.

Only two lights were lit in Horner's study just off the

living room, two small desk lamps with amber shades giving the room the look of a chamber with ceiling lost in darkness. More light was pouring in from the night cityscape than from inside.

He hoped against hope that this DVD was what Torkelson had wanted to get to Maria; but knew that it probably was not.

The soundtrack, which began before the video, affirmed that. A lone *ney*-flute in falling note summoned up out of the darkness another time, another awareness than the one conveyed by this eclectic apartment in this most cosmopolitan of cities. Far from being political or explanatory, the tape was of the last annual performance of the whirling dervish ceremony from the Mevlana Society in Konya, Turkey, a group dedicated to the perpetuation of dervish dancing.

As Horner's mind began to drift, the dancers moved deeper into their rite -- now become white hemispheres spinning in orbit, souls rising through the cosmic spheres, attaining ever-higher levels of spiritual enlightenment...

Now the *Sema* had ended and the life of the great Turkish mystic poet Rumi was being reenacted in documentary fashion by actors beneath domes and minarets, onion-arched porticos, wine-carpeted cells and prayer rooms. As Rumi, a tiny baby born in Afghanistan journeyed west to flee Genghiz Khan and the Mongol horde, all things began to drift together in Horner's head -- the Anatolian and Central Asian past ... the lure for him in mysticism ... the death of Raine Torkelson.

Where, where in all this was the meaning of the death of Raine Torkelson? Despite its ritual trappings, was Torkelson's death only about a political conspiracy of the present, a news story that would never be printed?

His last thought as he fell asleep, DVD still unwinding its particular vision of history and prophecy, was that nothing was random, that the task was to find the pattern binding one item to everything else, no matter how large the pattern, even if it be the design of the universe itself. Even if the pattern be expressed no more clearly than in a celestial explosion of blue and white tiles on a mosque ceiling, or luminous hemispheres spinning white through the black void, narrated by the filigree of an alphabet that was the expression of the sheer magical, poetry and geometry repeated a million times over ...

*   *   *

Chapter 18

Maria, rather than waking him when she returned at dawn, let him sleep another hour on the study sofa, so when he did finally awaken, the sun was burning through the gauzy layers of mist and cloud that the night had laid down.

Still half asleep, he thought he heard sounds he couldn't quite identify, sounds of distress. Was she crying? He got up and went into the bedroom. She had her back to him, and beside her was the opened album of her life in Iran, an album he hadn't seen in years.

"Bad night?" he asked.

She shook her head and blew her nose.

"Just feeling blue," she said. The album was open and showed a Sunday outing in the Alborz Mountains with her late husband's family. No one in chadors; black-haired mother in law with a silk scarf, father-in-law in elegant suit. Her husband Medhi had on a cardigan and was bent over, supporting their child as he took a few steps.

She saw Horner looking.

She closed the album, put it under the bed. He came over and held her for a minute.

"God," she was able to say, as she stood up. "Would you like breakfast?"

"What time is it?" he asked.

"Almost eight. What happened with the police?"

"I'm late to meet Atilha," he said.

"Bad enough to be seeing a lawyer?"

"I'll tell you tonight," he said.It was only when he went back into the study to get his wallet that he remembered to bring along the dervish dancing videotape, and the embroidered illustration of the old dervish being stabbed by men in caftans, which he'd found at Torkelson's.

"What are you taking?" said Maria.

"The prayer cloth and DVD from Torkelson's. I hoped it was what he was trying to get to you when he called. Now I don't know ..."

Horner had had the cloth expertly cleaned the day before. Now, more clearly, down went the old turbaned dervish, inevitably being driven to the floor by the hail of blades. Blood poured from exploding wounds in the neck, cheek and lip. And still the killers pushed the knives into his arms, hands, shoulders, while they seemed transported by the act.

But the cleaning had brought out more detail. For

while the caftaned murderers' lower faces were hidden, their eyes were exaggeratedly large and pink, even without pupils as far as he could tell.

"Is that Farsi?" he asked Maria of the embroidered text below.

"It's Dari, actually," said Maria. "or some dialect of classical Persian. A series of tributes. Titles."

"Can you understand it?"

"Something along the lines of: 'God the Abaser, God the Humiliator, God the Judge ....'"

Horner looked at the lead killer's face, and again large empty eyes transfixed him. Was this man blinded by cataract?

"A Dari snuff tapestry?" She still had her business suit on, and the question came with the authority she displayed with her news sources, the side of her that so distressed him to see at home.

"I think so."

"You kept it from the police?"

"My prints are all over it. I picked it up before I knew I was walking into a murder."

"Lord," she said, shaking her head and going into the bedroom.

He ejected the DVD and brought it into the bedroom while he showered and dressed. Maria wanted him to stay, and part of him wanted to as well, but he needed to see Atilha. He prepared to leave, carrying a pastry, but paused in the doorway.

"The biggest question in all this remains you," he said. "Why was Raine Torkelson wanting to see you before he died? What did he have that he wanted to give you so badly? Surely not this cloth and DVD?"

She looked out the kitchen window a moment, the exterior light heightening her features.

"Why you of all people?" he continued. "You, a competing journalist at a rival news organization?"

"God knows," she said finally.

She turned and looked at him, and there were so many things at work beneath the surface of her face he couldn't begin to interpret them. She simply shrugged.

"You're tired, aren't you?" he asked.

"Yes," she said. And although he knew there was more to it than that, he decided to drop if for now.

"We'll talk tonight," he said.

* * *

Chapter 19

To think that this boy who was scum of the Saudi earth, an urchin from a desert Bedouin backwater now had hundreds of millions listening to him, turning to him for guidance.

All was happening as had been foretold in his heart.

His first trip outside the Kingdom after his exile was to Sudan, that vast desert place clinging to the Nile for survival, the true birthplace of the pharaohs.

Sudanese organizers had thought they might have to bus in a crowd, so uncertain they were of an audience. But instead, they had to call out the Army to control fans and the curious who had begun to gather at the Khartoum parade grounds two days in advance. And who eventually numbered 200,000. While half the audience was under 30, for the first time the other half was older, meaning he was beginning to reach everyone.

As the Sudanese gathering swayed to his song-poems and cheered and wept at his chanted appeal for rebirth in the *political and spiritual worlds, his eyes and voice were broadcast on satellite, reaching millions of foreign viewers.*

And it was then that his supporters in Egypt, Algeria, Pakistan and even Palestine began clamoring for him to come to their own countries, even as some politicians in those countries began to wonder if the Peaceful One was a threat.

And he thought to himself in those days, yes I am a threat. If your world is the world of yesterday and today, then I am a threat to you. But if you are ready to open your hearts to the kingdom of God on earth and tomorrow, then I am no threat. I am your partner and your brother.

Come join with me.

*   *   *

Chapter 20

"Murder, murder!" someone was shouting in the distance, as Horner's driver, en route to Atilha's office, insisted on plowing through the congestion of Taksim Square rather than take a side route closer to the water. They must have spent a quarter hour getting through the square itself, for it also served as the central bus terminal where tens of thousands of commuters made their transfers.

Murder, Horner thought, suddenly transfixed. Torkelson's murder?

Taksim was also the gathering place for newshawkers and orators wanting to rant. Today the crowds were transfixed by breaking news, screeching out of radios and hot off the press tabloids. Horner couldn't help but have the car stopped so he could find out what was happening.

"Murder, murder!" a ragged hawker was shouting, and as Horner bought a tabloid and the driver switched his radio on to a news station, he saw the grim truth. Not Torkelson, but something just as ominous.

The Turkish Minister of Defense had been blown up in his motorcade today outside Ankara. Suspicions were pointing towards Iran or its allies inside Turkey, because the Minister was the most anti-Iran man in the Turkish military, or the government for that matter.

Though this news was from far away and about a man he did not know, Horner lost his breath for a moment, wondering if there was some linkage to the other murder much closer to home.

As they approached Atilha's office, Horner's mind kept wandering back to the embroidered dervish killing, and Nilufer's manuscript. And the blood, the knives, the killers' eyes. And to whatever predicament he was now falling into.

Atilha Atalay maintained a solitary practice, occupying a two-room office with his secretary. The walk-up office was spare, the waiting room stacked with files.

"My long-lost friend," said Atilha, rising from his desk. "When did last we meet?"

"Almost a year."

Over the office presided the customary portrait of Mustafa Kemal Ataturk, father of the modern state, eyes glaring. Another hero's photo also graced the wall: Albert Einstein, hair electrified, eyes softer here, smiling. The Einstein photo made a separate statement. Atilha had abandoned his foreign studies in advanced physics to save the dying family law practice, on which assorted relatives depended.

"I should say, what with going bankrupt, stumbling into murders, etc. How can I help you?"

Atilha was all forehead, graying hair curling over the collar, luminous eyes above his moustache.

Ataturk's eyes, Einstein's eyes, Atilha's ...

It was <u>eyes</u> he was remembering, but he wasn't quite sure where from. Was it the man with whom he'd collided outside Torkelson's flat that awful morning?

As best as he could recall, the eyes in the dark stairwell had been like a blind man's ... not alive. Iris and pupils smaller and lighter than normal, whites larger. And like the embroidered dervish killing, might they have even had that ruby cast?

Had the same cabal of ritual killers in Nilufer's 400-year-old manuscript gotten Torkelson? And so were Nilufer -- and Horner -- working for that same cabal ... or someone who wished to know about them ... or stop them?

Horner explained his insight, then the entire story of Torkelson's murder.

Atilha shook his head.

"You are already in jeopardy. Unexpected cards are already turning up. The police have visited just three days after the murder. Your fight with Torkelson will come to light, if it hasn't already. Worst of all, Ferruh Aziz is heading the investigation, and he's quite clever."

Atilha walked to the window for a minute, waved to an unseen child playing there in the courtyard, then turned to Horner, who saw him silhouetted from behind by the outside.

"Other factors are also wild cards. First, the poetic inscription on the DVD. Those are three of the 99 names of God from holy scripture, used by several Muslim orders in their mystic rites. Our criminal code allows extraordinary legal powers to protect the state from religious groups. Although the Islamic Front is fighting to have all that repealed ..."

He sat back down.

"Another red flag is Nilufer. She carries political baggage, through her ties to the former government. But you know this too..."

Horner sipped his coffee.

"Now to the missing chapter-folio from the *Suleymanname*. Is this search reputable?"

"The search itself seems to have merit," said Horner. **"The Secret of Suleiman** that Nilufer is translating apparently confirms the existence of the missing chapter, why it was removed. It's the client who is disreputable."

"Who?"

"Probably someone with Iranian ties."

"Iranians are all over the news today," said Atilha.

"Which news?" asked Horner.

"General Ishanoglu. You didn't hear?

"Yes, but just the headline."

"It's all over the television. The most anti-Iranian Turkish military leader was blown up in his car, just outside Ankara. He was the last one arguing against closer ties with Iran, and for a closer embrace of NATO and Europe. These are dangerous times. So you think your client has some tie to the bad side in Iran?"

The reminder about the general's killing sent another chill through Horner. If a five-star general wasn't safe in his own capital, how safe would Horner be?

Atilha's silent television screen showed the Ankara blast site cordoned off, a blackened hulk of a car that was once a Mercedes, dozens of onlookers.

"Our client," said Horner, "could be dissidents, terrorists, mullahs, I don't know. But it also tells me the great Iranian antiquities search of 35 years ago is underway again. I want to know what they're after. This is the big one, Atilha. I don't want it to get away again."

Horner brought out the embroidered *Qur'an* cloth with the dervish murder, while Atilha played the whirling dervish video on his office player. Horner examined the enlarged killers' eyes on the cloth, keeping his collision at

Torkelson's stairwell consciously in mind. Though the lighting and settings were different, Horner was increasingly certain that the man on the stairwell had the same enlarged eyes. More than anything his belief hinged on the rosy emptiness, a fixed luminous stare ...

"Shrunken pupils and pink eyeballs suggest <u>haoma</u> ecstasy," Atilha ventured. "The old drug of Persian revelation. Didn't the police say they found traces?"

Horner nodded. Together they examined the embroidered killers, victim, blood, wounds, and the Dari text below:

Ar-rahman
ar-rahim
al-malik.

"Three of the 99 names of God," Atilha said, beating him by a few seconds. "The 99 names of God, whose repetition could unlock the mystic world, a uniquely Islamic tradition based on Muslim holy scripture -- the *hadith*."

Atilha turned off the video.

"How bizarre," he said. "The cloth looks like a reenactment of the death of the mystic poet Rumi's mentor and muse, Sems of Tabriz. The DVD is a simple documentary of the annual whirling dervish dance in Konya. What tie it has to this murderous sect I don't yet see."

Horner's consideration of the parallels between Torkelson's own death, and the embroidered dervish murder scene he'd found there, and the murder tattoo and illustration in Nilufer's manuscript again washed over him like a cool tingling stream. And that realization, while it should have been like a warning bell driving him away, was instead making the whole project more tempting. For it held out the prospect of a truly major discovery, which some thought worth killing for, and a client was paying well for.

"Strange coincidence you should bring all this to me," Atilha said. "You remember my longstanding interest in the calligraphy around the base of the dome, at Sems' shrine in Konya. The Semseddin Tabrizi Mosque. I've always felt a secret Sufi message was encoded there, in the calligraphy of God's 99 names. I'm close to unraveling at least the first few characters, which I'll tell you about in a minute. But probably no coincidence the hidden message is at Sems' shrine ..."

"A message from beyond the grave?"

Atilha smiled. He had taken a pipe from his pipe-rack, and was tamping in the tobacco.

"Your joke may be close. And now your embroidery, which looks like new speculation on Sems' disappearance -- one of the great mysteries of Islam. Sems, a wandering holy man blown in from Central Asia, who confronts great poet-thinker Rumi in the street -- and so stuns Rumi with a tirade against traditional religion, this great leader undergoes a sea change and is impelled full speed into mysticism. Am I boring you?"

"Not at all. I've read a bit of Rumi."

"Rumi invited Sems into his home that night, and the dialogue went on for weeks, just the two of them locked in a room. Rumi didn't return to the religious school during that entire period, upsetting his followers. Imagine what would happen today."

"When the mystic dialogues had gone on for months and Rumi showed no sign of returning to work, a group of followers kidnapped Sems and drove him away. Rumi traced him to Damascus and brought him back, but the same secret talks resumed. At that point plotters again kidnapped Sems."

"We aren't certain what they did with Sems, but the story is he was stabbed and thrown down a well. It was always explained as an act of Rumi's most ardent followers. A simple question of jealousy, then. Other accounts accuse Sems of being a sorcerer. But that seems to be slander, for nothing in Sems' or Rumi's lives shows anything but lofty impulse. Unless the friendship was a case of homosexual obsession ..."

"Now," said Atilha. "Back to your embroidery of Sems' killing. The *haoma* the police mentioned to you points further east, and much further back in time. The Persian magi used it for religious vision ..."

Before Atilha could continue his thought, his assistant Huseyin burst in on them with a look of utter distress on his face. Atilha's brother had fallen into a coma, and the lawyer would have to leave immediately for the hospital. Horner fully understood, let him get ready to go.

They walked down to the street together. As Atilha climbed into the first cab to pull over, he paused a moment and looked at Horner.

"My longwinded story about Rumi and Sems kept me from telling you about my discovery in Konya," he said.

"You were going to tell me what you'd deciphered from the inscription at Sems' shrine."

The lawyer managed a slight smile, but more one of tragedy than humor.

"Would you believe a chemical formula?" the Atilha asked wistfully, as he prepared to close the door and leave them. "I detect the beginnings of a complex chemical formula, hidden in Arabic calligraphy of the 99 names of God."

*   *   *

Chapter 21

Horner might have spent the rest of the day researching the *Suleymanname,* plotting his next move, but there was a telephone message from Mr. Gunes at the Topkapi Museum asking him to come to the Oteli Divan bar at five. He had very urgent matters to discuss with Horner about the *Suleymanname* manuscript file.

It sounded like he had secret information about the missing folio, that it really existed.

Genghiz drove him to the Divan. When they got to the bar, Gunes wasn't in evidence. They called his office, then his apartment. It wasn't until 9 that night, when Horner was back home, that someone finally answered.

It wasn't Gunes but a woman, and she was nearly incoherent. Against the backdrop of weeping and wailing, she managed to tell Horner that Gunes was dead.

"Dead?" Horner asked, starting to say more, but arresting himself in mid-word.

The crescendo of Islamic keening in the background

was overwhelming.

"Someone kill him," she began to weep. "Who are you? Who are you?"

She was calling to a police officer Ekmeci in the background, to come to the phone.

Good God. The same Ekmcci who was on the Torkelson murder investigation, who had been in Horner's apartment the night before?

And with his breath being sucked out of him, his heart now pounding, Horner slammed down the phone, wondering if Gunes had caller ID on his phone? Would his sister say something incriminating about his call? Did she know his name? Would Inspector Aziz stumble upon the connection, intuit the relationship?

What in God's name had Horner inserted himself into?

Was it worth the price?

* * *

The idea that Gunes' caller ID would bring him into a second murder sent Horner into deep despair. Or just as bad, the possibility that Inspector Aziz had already put a tap on Horner's line, because of possible Iranian involvement in the killing. Horner knew nothing of Turkish wiretap laws, but surely the security forces could do whatever they wanted, if they suspected a threat.

And just as bad, now the authorities would wonder why murderers and plotters were connected to Topkapi, and even to the *Suleymanname.* Would this wreck Horner's quiet search for hidden treasure?

Horner really needed to talk to Atilha about all the legal ramifications, and he called him to set up a face to face meeting, because none of this could be discussed on the phone.

But he couldn't reach Atilha, whose mobile phone was turned off, and no one answered at his office.

Horner imagined the scene at Mr. Gunes' apartment. Wailing women and his body being prepared for burial. How had the murderers killed him? Another ritual killing, like Torkelson's? A gunshot or a stabbing, obvious to everyone as a murder? Or something more subtle? Being run over by a truck, or poisoned?

Would anyone have any idea why Mr. Gunes had been killed?

Within hours the police interviews at Gunes' office in Topkapi would show Horner's name in the appointment book of Mr. Ozbudun the curator, that he had made a special appointment to see a treasured imperial manuscript. Plus phone records would show several phone conversations with

Horner, including one making an appointment to meet just a few hours after Gunes was dead.

And now Gunes murdered, on top of Torkelson.

Two murders in less than a week tied to Burt Horner, American expatriate art appraiser, tied through murders to murky treasure hunts and Iran.

Should he be on a plane out of here, thankful to have 75,000 euro in his pocket and still be alive?

He picked up the phone to reserve a ticket to Rome. He knew the flight schedules, he could be on the plane by midnight, long before the police had made all the links and connections.

But once he'd made the reservation, he just couldn't go any further. He couldn't start packing.

He sat as though paralyzed in his chair. Despite the danger, he couldn't let go yet. The potential payoff was too big. Maybe he still had a few days. Maybe that was all he needed.

The only way he could dull the fear and paranoia was through drink. He had four scotches, in rapid succession. It took him into a gauzy haze.

He called Maria's office, but the bureau said she was out interviewing the leader of the Salvation Party and wasn't expected back before eight.

Murders aside, the hardest part of his work with

Nilufer would be avoiding damage to his relationship with Maria. They'd confided virtually everything in one another. Now a wall was being erected, by virtue of this new alliance.

He thought about these things as he waited on her to return home. Evening crept towards midnight. How he hoped Maria was working late, and her tardiness didn't imply something more serious. What a mess he was in. She was his closest confidante in the world, and yet she was barely part of his life of the last five days, less than a woman who he deeply distrusted and yet who was now his employer. But he sensed that his very mention of Nilufer would drive her farther away.

As he waited for Maria, he watched the television evening news for a moment's distraction. Enraged to have been finally excluded from the European Community because of its "non-Christian culture". Turkey was reported to be about to sign an Accord of Friendship with Iran, reported in a WPI wire service story that Maria had undoubtedly written.

But the murders of Raine Torkelson and Mr. Gunes were nowhere to be seen, and General Ihsanoglu's killing was now being blamed on Kurds, not Iranians. Had the censors squelched any coverage that touched on matters of national security ... or murderous religious sects?

*   *   *

Maria came in around eleven that night. She saw the bottle of Scotch, undoubtedly detected his rosy glow, and shook her head wordlessly.

"I had another visit from the police today," she said evenly, dropping her bundle of clippings by the front door. "How the hell did they know where to find me?" she said.

"They got your vitals last night."

She slammed her purse down on a table.

"You seem awfully flip about this," she said. "But I can't have cops messing in my work. Visiting my office, no less. I had some explaining to do with the bureau chief. Of course he would be the one to meet them at the door."

He ignored her, pretending to read, but the drink had blurred his vision and he couldn't make out what he was looking at.

"You should know there was another ritual killing today," she said quietly.

"Oh?"

"Some fellow at Topkapi. The censors are all over it."

"Who?"

"A fellow named Gunes. Don't you know him?"

Horner shook his head, unable to breathe. She was watching him closely.

"Is anyone reporting it?" he asked, having a hard time

speaking.

"Not if they want to stay in business."

"How did you hear?" he was able to ask.

"My grapevine."

He spent a good five minutes regaining his composure.

"I should tell you," he said after a minute. "I've decided to go ahead with Nilufer --"

Her face was stricken.

"I know you're not happy. I'm not either. But the search has merit. More evidence is turning up, that something was removed from the *Suleymanname*. I was over at Topkapi today --"

"Burt ... she's poison ..."

Her anger seemed to be fading into sheer bafflement at his behavior.

"You're right. But she pays very well --"

"Do you know where the money is coming from yet?" she asked.

This question gave her pause. He thought he could see her making the same linkages he'd already made ....
Nuraddin, Torkelson, Nilufer, the *Suleymanname* search, the pillaged ruins at Ararat. Despite her anger, her journalist's curiosity was being pulled in.

"Maria, I think this is my big one. My big Persian treasure hunt. They paid up front."

"How much?"

"75,000 euro. Cash."

Maria erupted with a gasp. She puttered around in the kitchen for a few minutes, then sat at the counter separating kitchen from living area, eating a sandwich.

"Iran is dangerous stuff," she said without looking at him. "They already have an undeclared war going with the U.S. And Iranian money was being funneled to the Salvation Party in the last election. That party has been playing footsie with Iran for years now. Although the Fatherland coalition is doing the same thing too now. They're both doing anything to placate the Muslims without holding new elections. After what the Israelis and Europeans did, the Muslims would win in a alandslide."

A period of silent eating followed.

"Any luck on your story?" he asked.

"The pillaged ruins? I'm going to Dogubeyazit tomorrow and sniff around."

"Alone?" he asked.

"I normally work alone."

"But this is the kind of stuff that got Torkelson killed. You're a foreigner, a single American woman."

"Torkelson was sloppy, he left his tracks all over everything. He was flying in and out of Tehran, asking touchy questions about Ali Nuraddin. I haven't been to Iran since

1981. They've forgotten who I am."

"They'll remember really fast if you start doing what he did," said Horner.

"My Iran coverage never carries my byline. Raine's always did. He'd still be alive if he hadn't slapped his name on everything."

"You can't go out there alone," he said. "Didn't you read about the attacks on the American tourists at Cappadoccia?"

"We're all ultimately alone," she said.

He didn't respond to that immediately.

"Why don't we work together for once in our lives?" he finally said. "You know as well as I that this whole thing probably comes together. The Iranians have got their big archaeological treasure hunt going again, after 35 years. You want to stop the Iranian mullahs, I want to know what they're looking for, why they're pillaging archaeological sites. I know more about ruins and pillaging than you do. Let's go out there together."

She didn't say anything. She reached into her briefcase to pull out a sheaf of clippings.

"I saw WPI's story about Turkey and Iran," he said. "Why would the Turks sign a deal with a theocracy?"

"Burt, that's the Europeans fault. What did they expect would happen, if they locked Turkey out? Turkey has been sucking up to them for 30 years, and now they get shafted by the EC. Oh, I understand the Europeans are afraid. But now they'll make their worst fears come true. Europe needs a healthy new economy to bring in. Turkey needs markets. If Europe won't open up, then the Turks look east and south."''

She went into the bedroom.

How much he wanted the evening to end on a softer note, the two of them moving closer together. Odd as it was at his age, he wanted them to be a family, he wanted the distance of two adult professionals going their own ways to be diminished, back to what it had once been.

But as if driven by malevolent destiny, the phone rang not a minute later, and it was Nilufer, saying she had translated the latest section of **The Secret of Suleiman**, and he simply had to come over to read it that night.

Despite his attempts to placate her, Maria didn't even say goodnight to him when Genghiz buzzed to say he was down below, ready to drive to Nilufer's.

* * *

Chapter 22

As he took his campaign to a fever pitch, many things in faraway places began to happen, in response to him or in spite of him.

In Yemen he read that the Turks were about to sign a pact of friendship with Iran.

This, in two countries that shared so much and yet which had been rivals and enemies for more than 500 years.

What to make of these things, in these waning days of the old world of yesterday and today?

He was not a politician, and yet he aimed to remake politics. He was not a conspirator, and yet he was daring to do what conspirators had tried and failed to do for many centuries.

He decided to do only what he could.

For now, the faraway plotters and schemers were beyond his reach.

But if all went according to plan, one day their cacophony would become a great harmony, a huge orchestra of many notes and voices joined into one greater symphony.

It was the symphony that God had written, and if he Ali Nuraddin were blessed, he might be the conductor, to bring it to the ears of all mankind.

*   *   *

Crack the heart of any atom: from its midst you will see a sun shining.

-- Sayed Ahmad Hatif

"But did Dashti get the secret from Sems of Tabriz?" I asked, my first words in nearly an hour. "And what was this secret? What was it Dashti sought with such fervor, that it could drive him to the murder of one who had never lifted a hand to anyone?"

"Dashti sought what we are told is the ultimate secret of illumination,"Bayram said. "He sought something called <u>the very-light of God</u>."

-- The Secret of Suleiman

Chapter 23

When Horner awakened the next morning, he could hear Maria in the living room, on the phone. Something was happening at the bureau. It was 6:49 am.

"There's been a Turkish Cabinet shake-up," she said, standing in the bedroom door. "Ministers of Defense and the Interior will be replaced by religious figures. The government is trying desperately to buy off the fundamentalists, without holding elections."

The night before still floated in his memory ... Nilufer's translation of **The Secret of Suleiman** still showing no discernible path to the missing folio of the **Suleymanname** ... yet directly linking Torkelson's murder and the dervish DVD to ritual killings by a heretic medieval Sufi group called the Dashtiya -- a kind of holy communion of death, in pursuit of the spirit.

He'd wanted to talk to Maria about it, but she'd been asleep when he got home from Nilufer's, so in the end he let her slumber.

"This is so big they want me to stay and cover it, but I've made my plans," she continued. "I'm going out east today no matter what. Did you have fun with Nilufer?"

"Cabinet shake-up?" he asked. "Are you leaving now?"

"I told them I'd come in the office this morning, but I'm out on the noon flight. I'll be back to finish packing."

"I'm coming with you," he said.

"Suit yourself," she said, without emotion. "Would you like to bring Nilufer along, too?"

He didn't say anything.

"You'd better call about a ticket," she continued. "By the way ... my Defense Ministry contacts came through with photos of the ruins at Ararat. They're in the bedroom. I hope my sources don't get shot by the new Minister."

She snapped her briefcase shut and left for the bureau.

The day was rainy, abysmal. The relationship being in danger brought up a flood of sentiment as he thought about Maria. He'd been so preoccupied the last few months he hadn't really allowed himself to feel it. Back in the bedroom, he looked at her clothes hanging in her closet ... her few accoutrements of beauty in the bath. He held her nightgown for a moment ... remembering their first night together, six years ago, in a tiny hotel on the beach at Kasos, in the Greek Islands. He hadn't wanted to go there to begin with, fearing the summer crowds of Germans in string bikinis and gold chains. But he'd had one of the best times of his life. They'd stood on a balcony overlooking the harbor, with her in this same nightgown, the steam of the summer Mediterranean coming up at him, and he'd felt so happy, so young, totally drunk with life

And now she was going to Ararat. Her suitcase stood in the corner of the bedroom, open, partly filled. She was booked on a noon flight to Ankara, with a change for Erzurum. She'd take a bus to Ararat from there. Folded garments were ready to be put in, and a bundle of work papers. Folders of clippings, dispatches, old newspapers, Ipod.

On top of the batch was a month-old *Newstime* story by Raine Torkelson about Ali Nuraddin, the Shiite Peaceful One, snapshots of a rally in the Iraqi desert outside Karbala. 350,000 people had come to hear him speak, rivaling the senior Iraqi Ayatollah's appeal, and surpassing any living Iraqi leader.

We are all orphans of God, Ali Nuraddin had told his followers, his lower face wrapped in black scarf, his eyes luminous and huge, *but together, no earthly king, no caliph, no dictator can withstand our power. The Kingdom of God knows no borders, and speaks all languages ...*

He found her Defense Ministry photos of the Ararat ruins. They included stark aerial shots, of stony mountainous terrain, the empty escarpments and abysses of eastern Turkey. He was astonished she had been able to score with her military contacts to get these photos. He could even make out the ruins themselves, which Raine Torkelson and Burt Horner and now she wished to know more about ... tumbled outer walls of a mountaintop fortress-settlement ... expanses of flat ground within the walls ... roofless fallen structures.

There were also photos of the evidence of hasty and recent excavation and pillaging: freshly turned earth, stones pulled from wall and frieze, signs of jackhammers and stone saws. He might have thought they were after the stones and friezes themselves, but no, they had been discarded, thrown aside, some broken and smashed. Nothing appeared to be missing, based on these photos; the looters seemed to have been looking for something contained within the walls or buried in the ground.

Were they looking for the lost chapter of the *Suleymanname*? Or the "greater treasures" to which it led? Had they been found?

Other shots of a topographical nature followed ... scarps, rifts, drainages winding down into the basin of the Murat, Lake Van. He fingered glossies of Dogubeyazit taken from above, of Erzurum, of the border area with Iran, all marked in felt-tip pen. Nothing as focused and as baffling as the pillaged site itself.

Nothing at all, except for the only close-up in the batch ... a shot of a piece of stonework. It was a frieze, the stone carvings above a doorway or gate. But when he saw it, and realized what it was, he very nearly lost his breath. For it was the last thing he would have expected to see here.

Central to the frieze, which had assorted designs that seemed to be of Seljuk origin, was the depiction of a turbaned man with a dagger through his heart, with his killers dancing around his corpse and the mystic number "99" calligraphed below.

*   *   *

Chapter 24

And yet, in his moments of doubt and melancholy, he feared that the forces of the past, the forces of fear and conspiracy, might prevent him from achieving his dream.

The great powers were planning their own interventions, not of the spirit and of the heart, but of force.

Every day, the stories of America sending its legions and mercenaries into the Kingdom and into Iran grew more frequent.

There was no guarantee that the side of right and good would be able to stand up to such forces, for in history, the record was mixed. Did good win out in the affairs of men, when men had free will?

Those who thought God would intervene to favor the righteous ones were naive. God did not send his hand into earthly affairs, except by sending certain messengers and prophets to talk about the world that could be. Otherwise, the choice was up to mankind.

The only way to prevail against armies and missiles was to make the case to everyone ... even to those who feared him, and thought they were his enemy.

His only chance was to appeal to the hearts of every man, and then see if the tides of history could shift.

* * *

Chapter 25

Rain was beating against the windows in a torrent. Horner packed, then called Nilufer, wanting to touch base and maintain the illusion of working with her, without revealing his plans.

"Making any progress, dearest?" she asked.

He explained the photo of the frieze with the murder of Sems of Tabriz and the number "99" that kept cropping up in **The Secret of Suleiman** that Nilufer was translating. But he didn't mention Maria was on the story, or where the ruins were located.

"How did you ever find that out? If those ruins were so hush-hush?"

"I'm good," he lied.

"I think it's a long shot," she said. "Could be a red herring."

"Maybe," he said. "But I still don't have any other leads."

"Whatever you say, darling," she said. "That's your

department. This political funny business makes me nervous. I hope we don't have a coup or something --"

The conversation ended just before Maria returned at 10:30.

He told Maria about what he had found in the photo from Ararat, and how it linked to Torkelson's murder, and the manuscript that Nilufer was translating.

"So it's all a package," she said. "The whole ball of wax. Like you said all along."

He basked in this accolade, the only one she was likely to give him now.

"The only questions left," she continued, "are what does this have to do with Ali Nuraddin? And what are the Iranians looking for?"

"Maybe we can help each other on that," he said, wishing she would overcome her jealously of Nilufer.

"Maybe."

Finally they departed. Genghiz picked them up on the curb. The rain was torrential. Dampened from their sprint to the car, they exuded humidity that covered the windows in fog. Blasts of driving rain and tire-spewed wastewater hit the windows.

Though they pulled up to the terminal an hour early, Horner groaned when he saw the glut of bodies at the ticket counter. Horner told Genghiz he'd see him in two or three days. They agreed Genghiz would wait for Horner's call at the Mihrimah taxi stand. Genghiz was to avoid either his or Horner's home.

Horner got the last seat on the flight, seats filled nine-abreast. Aside from the driving rain, the takeoff was delayed by the arrival of a half-dozen olive-green military jet transports, landing from the east. Horner wouldn't have paid much attention, but Maria commented, and other passengers were watching too.

The Turks weren't saying much, but he knew they were taking note. What could it mean? A coup? A military move?

Horner tried to scan the passengers for anyone who could be an undercover tail. He didn't recognize any, but then, he didn't have Genghiz' sixth sense.

His last thought before they lifted off was, Were he and Maria finally on the trail of Persian treasure he had sought in vain for 30 years? And at the same time, could they keep outrunning whatever had gotten Torkelson, the Defense Minister ... and Gunes?

*   *   *

Chapter 26

After they had touched down at the Ankara airport, surrounded by yellow grassy scarps devoid of a single tree, they sat for half an hour in a smoke-filled transit lounge in the tiny concrete airport, much smaller than Istanbul's huge terminal. A small crowd had gathered by the windows overlooking the airfield to observe uniformed troops being loaded onto transports, perhaps bound for Istanbul or other cities. Again, as on the flight out of Istanbul, many were watching and few were commenting. Turks weren't effusive in their public expression. But they knew something was up, and their silence made him uneasy.

The abrupt announcement of the departure of their connecting flight broke the interlude of waiting; all the passengers had to run out onto the tarmac to board. Then Horner and Maria were up and away again, on the second leg to Erzurum, where they would arrive in mid-afternoon to begin the final stretch, another good four hours on a bus to Dogubeyazit. Once airborne, he saw the remaining clouds dissipate rapidly, the rippling steppe and mountain valleys etched with the golden colors of late-autumn afternoon. The hour-long flight went quickly, Horner suddenly feeling as though a burden had been lifted from his shoulders. God, it was good to get out of Istanbul and civilization. He should have done it sooner. This was the lesson he always learned from travel, and then somehow forgot: liberation.

If only the exhilaration could be perpetuated, the ecstasy of the new, of change. But the lesson of his life had been that the feeling came only fleetingly, and must be savored when it did.

His mood was reinforced when they landed. For though Erzurum hadn't a tenth of the life of Istanbul or Ankara, what it did have was remoteness and difference, a settlement floating on the oceanic steppe, raw mountains on every horizon, a stronger taste of Asia. Altitude and cold arid wind combined to wake him from the familiarity and softness of the west. The severity of Central Asia seemed much closer here, the verdure of Europe and the Mediterranean far behind.

They caught a taxi to the bus terminal and walked down the arcade of assorted little bus company ticket offices, each hawking their destinations like rugs in the bazaar. They chose the first departure for Dogubeyazit, on something called Sultan Lines.

At the station they were further immersed in eastern Turkey: women in scarves, a few in *purdah*, men with the beards and skullcaps of the Hanafi or other sects. But there were Kurds and gypsies too, even refugees from the ethnic wars up north and the insurgency in Iraq. The crowd was at least half poor and rural, and the stares at the two of them as foreigners were direct.

And there were dozens of soldiers in transit, their leave cancelled or reserves called in, bound for the big bases at Malatya and Erzincan, Sivas and Diyarbakir, to remind Horner of the changes in the government back in Ankara. But the movements might be routine enough, too, for even though the country was officially at peace, there was plenty in the neighborhood to keep them busy, with squabbling ethnic enclaves in the fallen Soviet empire, Iraq in turmoil, and now Iran.

This is why I'm in Turkey, Horner thought, watching the flow of exotic humanity.

Once he was on board the bus they were underway, spinning first with the late afternoon traffic out of the old city, so he could see the local landmarks -- walls of the long-fallen Byzantine fortress, minarets of the Cift Minareli Medresse theological school -- and as a reminder that all this had once been overrun by the Mongol hordes, a Yakut theological seminary dating from 1310. The invasions and

occupations of Erzurum were almost too many to recount --
Arabs, Armenians, Byzantines, Mongols, Persians, Romans,
Russians and Turkish tribes.

To their south the sun-etched peaks of the Karasu-
Aras and the eastern Toros loomed, to the north the wall of
the Pontics beyond which lay the Black Sea. But the true lure
for him today was east, and east up ahead was yet an
undefined roll of golden light and abyssal valley, gilt
morning-land. At the center was the misty bulk of the highest
mountain of them all, the biblical Ararat, its vast cone glacier
swirled in the clouds of day's end, stark blue sky beyond.

He felt good again. He reached over to kiss Maria and
she responded, hesitantly in the beginning, then with more
fervor. The huge bus flowed over the landscape and the
smooth swells of Highway E-23 like a magic carpet, floating
down the great trans-Anatolia axis road, the main artery to
the Iranian border from Ankara, following in the footsteps of
the fabled Silk Road.

*   *   *

Chapter 27

The only real stopover came at Agri, by day a drab little settlement in the muddy steppe, but at sunset transformed into a stark plain of silhouettes, a center of half-light fading off into endless flatness, while all around circled the remote walls of mountain and peak. Out on the steppe, scatterings of nomad tents could be seen. Dogs barked and sheep and goats bleated as they were herded towards some sleeping-spot.

Both Americans got out, to stretch, to be stirred by the winds of evening. While the steppe was now falling into darkness, the roiling peak of Ararat 100 kilometers east -- their final destination for tonight -- still caught the full damask light of sunset on its summit.

"Quite a view," she said.

"Makes it all worthwhile."

"Americans like to think they're the only honest nomads left," she said. "Then you see Turkey, and you remember most of the human race began as wanderers, and a few still actually live it, the old way."

"You mean without RVs," he said.

Horner and Maria drank carbonated water, then climbed back on board for the final leg. Horner slipped in and out of sleep, then woke up when they began the final approach to Dogubeyazit. The other passengers seemed to come to life too, for Dogubeyazit was the end of the line, unless one was headed for Iran just a few miles beyond.

"I take it you're not going to cross the border," he said, half in jest.

"Not tonight," she said. And she squeezed his hand.

*   *   *

They climbed down off the bus into the little square of Dogubeyazit. It was about eight in the evening. A few businesses were still open -- primarily *kilim* carpet shoppes, keeping their doors open in hopes the evening bus would bring in tourists. And it had, from first appearances; themselves, and a Bohemian looking couple from northern Europe, en-route east.

Taxi drivers, a *kilim* vendor and shills for hotels swirled around Horner and Maria and the other couple.

Maria was waving them away like flies.

"We're going to the Tahran," she said.

The Hotel Tahran stood low, undistinguished from the rest of the block of stone and plaster save for a tiny sign. A *kilim*-shop was next door, and the owner, just closing his iron shutter for the night, rolled it back open when he saw them. He came at them, cringing and leering in anticipation.

"Here we go again," she said.

The teen-aged desk clerk insisted on claiming no off-street rooms were available, when it was clear from the reservation book the hotel was empty.

Maria won her point, when she said they'd go elsewhere. An off-street room became available.

"Charming fellow," Horner said, after the clerk left them in their room that looked out on a little courtyard.

They took a minute to inspect the concrete bathroom and shower, the slightly sagging bed, the double window with gauzy curtain. Maria turned on the radio, which only caught one channel, playing a mournful *ney*-tune, accompaniment to a dervish ceremony. She turned it back off.

"I always forget to bring music," she said.

Tour complete, Horner reached into his bag and brought out a bottle of brandy.

"Party time," he said.

"Why you foreign infidel," she said.

They had a drink before dinner, giving the stark surroundings a temporary rosy glow. And he was happy she was loosening up.

*   *   *

The hippies they'd seen upon arrival were just checking in as Horner and Maria came down to go in search of a dinner. He got a better look at them, in the light: late 20s, the man with an untrimmed rust-colored beard that puffed out from his face as though electrically charged, blonde hair cut in a bowl shape, like an Amazon Indian. The girl was also blonde, but curly, wide-eyed, with unsoled suede boots like an elf would wear.

He snuck a peek at the passports: Danish.

Maria decided they should head to the Hotel Isfahan, which had the best restaurant in town. The dinner could have been nice had there been anyone else there. But the two of them ate alone, and so the waiters hovering nearby made them self-conscious. They felt uncomfortable talking with an audience, and so didn't talk at all.

Walking back to the hotel, the night was cold and clear now, stars shimmering in the bowl of space. The moon was out, illuminating the ghostly summit of Ararat to their northeast. Horner swore he could smell the snow itself, blown down on the night winds from the glacier.

"I'm glad you came after all," she said, as they walked back to the hotel, hand-in-hand.

"What are you going to do tomorrow?" he asked her.

"I'm going to my military contacts at the garrison. See if I can find out why the Turks are covering up this pillaging ... and to confirm it was Iranians who did it."

"From your photos, looks like the looters were after something hidden in the walls or floor."

"Interesting," she said quietly. "But now your turn, Burt. How are you going to spend your free time in Dogubeyazit?"

He sensed she wanted to make sure he wouldn't be tagging along as she made her rounds.

"Oh, I'm going to look up an old friend. See if I can get out to the ruins themselves."

"But the word is out: Visitors aren't allowed. Is it worth a bullet to find out?"

"You saw this landscape," he said. "How could they close it? The murder of Sems on the frieze in your photo is the first parallel I've seen anywhere of the mention in Nilufer's translation. Who gave you that photo, anyway? The Army?"

"My lips are sealed," she said. "He'd be shot if word got out."

The desk was closed and dark when they got back to their hotel. With nothing else to do, they went up to the room, undressed and climbed into bed for a few moments of reading. He had a Lawrence Durrell novel, she was rustling her infernal clippings. Then they turned out the light, arms wrapped around each other, began to slip into sleep.

Somewhere in that interval between consciousness and sleep, the sounds of distress -- no, of lovemaking -- penetrated Horner's slumber.

A couple in the silent building was in full moan, bed squeaking, headboard thumping the wall. Involuntarily Horner wrapped himself more tightly around Maria, began ever so slightly kissing her from behind, though slowly, lightly, as if done in dream. He didn't want to move too fast, he wanted to give her time to catch up to him.

"You men," she whispered, breaking the silence. But she didn't resist, and he moved his hands to her breasts, her belly, feeling her undulate ever so slightly to his touch. Up and down he moved, teasing, then gripping, the breasts that were her special gift, the belly as enticing.

She jumped a little when he moved lower, the sounds from her throat thickened. He knew she was with him now, but he was in no hurry.

Now the definition of his hearing was washing out, less focused and distinct. He heard the sounds from down the hall, he heard the sounds from the woman next to him and from himself, but they were all part of the same thing, the same experience. The very tip of himself probed at her gate, teasing and rubbing, and she was telling him there was no need to wait, she wanted the plunge but he held back, wanting more than that. And when he thought she could wait no longer, he rose from the bed altogether, yet holding her hand, and pulled her to follow him away.

They walked across the room to the window, the gauzy curtains now luminous with moonlight from above, the world beyond wrapped in the oriental haze of curtain and moonlight. He seated her facing him on the cool radiator ledge, she gave him one leg for each hand and he held her there, braced her, at last giving her what they both wanted. He thought she gasped, but it might have been in his own mind, his own breast. Her head was back against the window, the window was slightly open, the cool air was washing across their hot skin and raising goose bumps, little trills of cool tremor on their legs, backs, even as the fire burned at their center. Now he was really in her, her eyes were moons without pupils, gone off somewhere, and he was driving it up into her, into the curtains and the courtyard below and the mud roofs washed with moonlight and the bath of stellar night washing over all. He was making love to it all, to Ararat and Turkey and the moon and the crazy earth he had come here so many years ago to find. She was moaning and he was moaning and somebody somewhere else joined their wail, the wail towards the earth and moon and God. He didn't remember breathing at all in the final passage, standing poised at the yawning abyss of his own death and of hers. All time was suspended, all life was in abeyance, as they reached out together for that thing, the one treasure left uncaptured, the wonder ever beyond their grasp.

Afterwards, embraced but half sleeping on the bed again, he wasn't sure if they had actually made any sound of their own, or had been utterly silent in the act.

*   *   *

Chapter 28

Horner and Maria were able to have breakfast together the next morning. Yet the closeness of the night before was already chilled by the intrusion of daylight ... and work.

But before they parted ways, they worked out a rough partnership, since they were both trying to find out more about the ruins. She would talk to the local police and military to confirm that Iranians had carried out this raid, and if so, which Iranians, what they had been after and why it was being covered up. Horner would approach his local archaeological contact, Sahin Taskiran, to see what he knew.

Horner hired a cab to take him to find Taskiran, at one time a good wholesaler of antiquities from the east, but now the curator of the enormous 17th century Isak Pasha palace ruins. Ararat towered clear and pristine in a blue morning sky when he walked out onto the street. The town displayed much more life than the night before. People were at the bazaar, buses and motorcycles were rounding the square, an early load of Iranian tourists had already come over the border and been disgorged, only to make their way to a kiosk selling Turkish girlie magazines. The women stood giggling in chadors in the gutter while the men pawed the magazine racks.

The drive to the palace reminded Horner where he was. From the artificial horizon imposed by the town's buildings, the taxi burst out onto the desolate valley floor, bordered by jagged peaks. Simultaneously all of humankind fell away into the enormity of the raw east, the expanses of the valley of the Murat River.

Ararat, the Karasu Aras and their sister mountain ranges ran north into the Caucasus and down into the massifs of Persia, sun, snow, serrated teeth of rock cutting the sky. The amphitheater of the mountains rolled off into the flatness of the far valleys, unveiling all the gray and pink and ochre bones of earth, memories of the planet's creation and unending transformation. The natural landscape, like the human, spoke violence, tumult, cataclysm.

As they approached, the ruined Isak Pasha palace floated like a sepulchral oasis on the valley floor, ravaged by time and a hundred pillagings, minarets and domes yet sending a message to God in the architectural language of Islam. And Horner remembered what it was, more than anything else, that constituted the beauty of this part of the world for him.

It was fear, he thought. *Man and history and geography were all more frightening here. And that is why I love the east,* he thought. *It frightens me ...*

The taxi dropped him off at the front gate of the fortress where Taskiran was the curator, the massive arched portal that led into the ruined compound; out across the valley, morning clouds were beginning to gather at the summit of Ararat.

"My very good friend Bertram bey!" erupted Sahin Taskiran, almost running out of his office to embrace his visitor. "I praise Allah, you have been brought here!"

"My good friend," said Horner, as they slapped backs. "So you've become a government employee?"

"Ah," said Taskiran ruefully. "We must accept what Allah brings us. And to me he brought the realization my sustenance would not come from what you Americans call the private sector. So he showed me the way to government, and a steady -- though modest -- paycheck."

"Business bad, eh?"

"Bad?" laughed Taskiran. "How can something that disappears be bad, or good? It does not exist! Please. Come. Sit here. We will have a coffee, and discuss old times."

A minion was dispatched to bring coffee and cakes. The coffee was classic Turkish, dark heavy syrup. Taskiran's hands were enormous and reddened, copper-gray moustache and a head of hair suggesting Georgian parentage.

So they could speak privately, Taskiran led them out through the gate, walking around the perimeter that seemed man's puny efforts to lock out the emptiness of the world beyond. The tumbled battlements confirmed that landscape had won, and this fortress was now as desolate as the territory outside.

And it was there that Horner told him that a client was very interested in a curious frieze, of the fallen Sems of Tabriz with a dagger in his heart, and calligraphy of three of the 99 mystical names of God. The depiction was known only in the frieze and in an Ottoman mystic poem.

Taskiran didn't recognize it.

"Where's this frieze?" he asked.

And Horner said the frieze was at a ruin site in the Tendurek range to the south, that the military was keeping secret.

Taskiran laughed, a tremendous guttural release. Everyone in Dogu knew these ruins, he said. But people had stayed away for centuries. It was considered a place of evil.

"Is this why the Army has closed the site off?"

Taskiran spat onto the dry soil.

"The story is the same as it always is, the bastard Army and the bastard secret police, may they rot in hell." And

Taskiran followed with a brief litany of his own battles with the security forces. He, being a man of the left, had been imprisoned, tortured, in the days of the anti-Communist military regimes.

"What's the big secret they're hiding?" Horner persisted. And Taskiran replied that while he did not know, it couldn't be good. It involved criminality, or scandal, or plotting, or some other intrigue. This was the only possible truth, he said. The wind was whistling through the fallen pillars of the pillaged palace.

"My client is paying a lot of money, to learn about those ruins. Can you take me there?"

The curator looked out on the vast panorama, the wind coming hollow and brutal out of the very teeth of the mountain range opposite him. They could have been the last two men alive, in the rubble of earth, so devoid was the scene of softness or humanity.

"If for no reason than to piss off the bastard Army of Turkey," he said, "I will take you there."

And for emphasis, he flung his unfinished coffee down to darken the stones.

*   *   *

Chapter 29

As they drove south of town towards the Tendurek range, Taskiran repeated that the site was not really newly discovered. Its existence and approximate location had been rumored for as long as anyone knew. But tradition and superstition had kept people away.

What was the superstition?

"That it was a place of evil," said Taskiran. "Ritual killings, human sacrifice, fire worship."

But an industrious and un-superstitious researcher from the Ministry of Culture had persisted only a few months ago in locating the ruins, without terrible difficulty, after a search of some days. But not long after, the ruins had been pillaged, and then the secret police had taken over the site and put a clamp on all information about it.

"The poor fellow got packed off to Istanbul," said Taskiran. "I think they beat the hell out of him, if they didn't kill him." The local police were given orders from the security forces to block all visitors, while the intelligence forces took over the site itself. The report went out that the ruins were closed.

"What do you think he found?"

Taskiran didn't know. It had become a government thing, an Army matter. The ruins were closed.

Had he heard that the raiders had come over from Iran?

No, he hadn't. But Iranian spies had been rumored and whispered about in Dogubeyazit for years now, so it was not impossible.

Using Rifat, a hunting guide from the adjacent village of Ortadirek, they would approach the ruins discreetly. Rather than hiking straight in from the main road that ran to the south and thousands of feet downhill of the site, they would come in from the north, literally from above, crossing the spine of the Tendurek range.

This approach was much shorter, and the only possible way to avoid the authorities on guard. But the journey crossed rugged terrain. At this time of year, with winter coming on, a storm could turn it impassable, even endanger their lives. But with good weather, the hike in and out could be done in a day.

The second concern was just as hard to read. In order to make the best time, they'd have to traverse briefly through Iran.

They drove south, on the highway that led ultimately
to the town of Van and the huge lake with the same name. At
Ortadirek, the range of Tendurek spread east-west before
them, the highest peaks to the right in Turkey, a lower left
flank rolling off, magenta and convoluted, into Iran. At
Ortadirek they picked up Rifat, a Kurd who while young, was
missing two front teeth and had a huge pale scar across his
cheek. He looked like he'd lived two lifetimes to Horner's one.
But he was in top physical condition, huge rib-cage from
years at high altitude.

Then they headed back down the highway. The road
began its climb into the range, and immediately went to dirt.
This slowed their climb, though Taskiran kept up his speed to
outrun the dust following them like a boat's wake. As they
went from the flat valley up into a canyon mouth, the road
began to escalate up the canyon-side, winding, the expanse of
the Murat valley rapidly disappearing behind them, the world
become a narrowing arena of rock and cliff.

Above them, at the canyon's head, towering walls of
cloud had built up heavily on the approaching range, adding
the illusion of enormous altitude; the clouds had so totally
engulfed the mountains above 7,000 feet that the upper
reaches of the range were lost to sight. This was typical,
Taskiran explained, especially with a strong wind, since
moisture from the Black Sea or Mediterranean condensed

here. And this explained why the ruins had been obscured for so long.

When they were about ten minutes above the valley floor -- the higher elevation giving rise to a scattering of pines and even spruce here and there -- the canyon and main road abruptly turned right and west, beginning the approach to a pass about ten miles further on, and then the descent to Van. But Taskiran turned the truck left off the road, to the east, and after a torturous five minutes inching up a dry wash, parked behind a pile of rubble.

"You can reach the ruins by the main road west," said Taskiran. "But the climb from that side is wretched. An overnight trip. This way we can complete by dark. Plus from the west we would pass the secret police camp, downhill of the ruins."

They were not yet under the shelf of cloud, so the sun shone bright and warm. The canyon walls had cut off the wind, turning the air spring-like. Landscape, sunlight, setting brought back memories of his own childhood, of hunting trips in Wyoming's Wind River Range, a state he had thought he'd forever left behind but that he carried in his memories, speech, being. His excursions into the alien, while he loved them for their raw edge, always brought an uncomfortable realization: even as an exile, he'd always be an American, searching out here for the exoticism his homeland had lost, reaching for the thrill of risk.

They started on a trail leading up a small rise and then angling slightly east. They crested the first flank, through a loamy meadow of tufted grass, gnarled shrubs. It gave them some perspective, allowing a panoramic view back north, of the valley, of a scattering of tents, the dusty track of lonely roads across the steppe, of Dogubeyazit in the foreground and beyond, Ararat, now also clouding up. Ahead, to the south, the vaulted meadows ran up into the lowest shelf of cloud. In the shadow of granulite boulders, patches of snow remained from an autumn storm.

"We'll be crossing into Iran for a stretch, once we crest that next ridge," said Taskiran. "Clouds should hide us."

Out here, Horner thought, borders were such an absurdity. They'd changed so much, the very states themselves had risen and languished and ceased to exist; why bother?

The hikers came into the clouds now, and Taskiran announced they were in Iran, or close to it. A border marker had been placed along here, but until he saw it, he wouldn't know for sure.

Rifat the guide found the marker a good distance off to their west. They were definitely inside Iran.

As they came up under the cloud, the whole nature of the place changed. The cloud began hitting them as a pearl mist, and the higher they went, the less defined the world grew, dropping from the sharp-edged clarity of desert mountain to a place of vision and dream, hints of Scotland and Scandinavia.

They continued on, finally cresting the ridge and turning back towards the west. The clouds were a dense fog here, and Horner wondered whether the guide would have trouble finding his way. For the landscape changed dramatically, and the treeless scarps of the other side now became small stands of conifers, balsam spruce sheltering patches of snow, with alpine meadow between.

"Welcome to Turkey again," Taskiran said. They stopped to have a quick lunch, of bread and cheese. In just the time they were seated there, the sky lightened and the sun began to break through. The world below remained lost in cloud.

"Allah is with us today," said Taskiran. "We'll be at the ruins in an hour."

And so it was, in the hour that followed. Bursts of radiant sunshine lit them from above, while the clouds below kept up a curtain for anyone who would have observed them from the valley. They came in and out of the spruce groves, spotting hawks and a pair of mountain rams. Then the forests and meadows ended in a sheer basaltic face. Rifat took time trying to find his trail at the edge of a zone of basalt and tumbled boulders, charcoal sand and rubble. Hardly a plant was growing there, while just behind them, a forest flourished.

"This area is bad for rockslides and avalanches in winter," said Taskiran. "Trail disappears every few days."

At last a way to pass was found, and Rifat the guide went up ahead of them, checking footholds in the striated rubble of the landslide. The clouds and fog returned, almost in the blinking of an eye, and the landscape again went bleak and unearthly.

As they walked on through the deepening fog, so profound now it seemed to herald nightfall although his watch showed only noon, Horner felt all color washing out of himself. The trail was taupe, the sand from the slide was gunmetal, the wind and bitumen scarp of rock all sprang from the same dismal paintbrush. For an instant his sense of up and down vanished, and he had no feeling of being on a radical slope, in fact a rock face. For in the final 15 minutes of the walk, they weren't walking at all, but literally inching sideways, faces towards the wall, backs out into the abyss, depending on their precious toeholds across this face, fog all around them, rock now dripping with condensed mist. Horner was shivering. The temperature must have dropped 20 degrees. His fingertips were even getting numb, as he gripped the rock at face level.

"Bertram bey ... keep moving."

Horner forced a step sideways, feeling the empty space beneath his heel, obscenities on the tip of his tongue. And he actually did curse with the relief of the passage, once he had rounded the bend. But his fear disappeared when he encountered Rifat, leaning against the buff stone beak of a primordial eagle's head weighing tons, sculpted from this very earth and mountain range.

The fog had begun to open again, enough to reveal the ruins spread before him across a small mountaintop plateau, stone heads gazing off to the south, heads that had laid here perhaps 2,000 years, heads with the echoing eternal loneliness he had seen other places ... at Nimrut Dagi and Persepolis, at Luxor and the Parthenon. These were the heads of warrior-gods, peaked helmets with earflaps, stylized formal curls of beard, pursed full lips and fierce brows and the beginnings of classical profiles that had come full bloom with the Greeks. But hints of it were here too, a quality of warmth, the sense these dead stone gods felt the tragedy of what they were and what they gazed out upon. Above all the tragedy came from the empty eyes, gazing off into the fog and the void of death and eternity. Still they warned the intruders from the south not to trespass, or they would be laid waste.

"Magnificent," Taskiran said, coming up behind him.

The word broke Horner's rapture, and he began to

think. How would something so ancient and forgotten have relevance to his search? What did the murder of Sems of Tabriz from a millennium later have to do with this?

*   *   *

Chapter 30

While Rifat stretched out for a nap at the base of the eagle, still in the shadow of the accursed cliff, Horner and Taskiran came down through the grove of fallen heads to a group of ruined structures. Horner was already searching for his frieze, the one from the photo, and he immediately found it, on an archway that seemed to serve as the gateway from the west. But he found it twice again, above doorways, one he would have guessed was a granary, the other a shrine.

The structures were in good condition, suffering hardly any of the ravages of time.

"Bizarre," Horner said. "Historical mish-mash."

"Of course. The statuary is ancient, 3rd century B.C. But these buildings are the strangest thing. The architecture is Seljuk Turk, from the 13th century."

Horner agreed. From the outside, the temple had the feel of a Seljuk mosque. The entrance, marked by an archway capped with the Dashtiya frieze -- apparently the one he'd seen in Maria's batch of photos -- was a portal into blackness.

Horner translated the Persian inscription surrounding the insignia:

God the Abaser,
God the Humiliator,
God the Judge ...

They now walked into the darkened shrine, complete with Seljuk arches. The exhilarating feel of the outer ruins gave way to something else here ... a mournful, almost squalid foreboding. The granitic altar -- really a broad platform in a recessed prayer-area -- had no correspondence to Islamic practice. A stone bowl was raised above the surrounding platform, interior blackened by soot.

Taskiran pointed out the configuration of the platform and surrounding stone floor, which had been torn open at intervals, presumably by the looters.

"A crematorium?" Horner asked, remembering the photos in Maria's suitcase. This was the same stone platform. It had to be.

Taskiran was nodding his head, though more in tune with his own thoughts than what Horner had said.

"The rumors must be true," Taskiran finally said. "Sacrifices once took place here. Fire worship."

"The bowl," Horner said, "looks like something I saw

in a Parsee -- Zoroastrian -- temple down in Mumbai. But I didn't know Zoroastrians were into fire sacrifice."

"More likely an Iranian magi heresy. The ancient Iranian priestly caste took over Zoroaster's movement after his death and turned it to their own secret ends -- with things like fire sacrifice. They were forever co-opting and subverting other cults. But to think they tried to incorporate Islamic elements, from hundreds of years later, into their horrors! We were always taught the Persian magi were swept away by Islam in the eight century. To find signs of them from hundreds of years later is revolutionary."

But Horner knew, based on Nilufer's translation, it did make some sense. For according to Nilufer's translation, the heretic Dashtiya had revived parts of the magian rite, with their own aberrant innovations. This might be the architectural proof.

While Taskiran remained at the altar, Horner moved around the room, searching for more in the Dashti shrine, the place they had continued their own search for, or shared their secret of the thing called in Nilufer's translation the "very light of God". He spent some time studying the friezes, trying to glean from the swirl of Islamic designs whether more hidden meaning dwelled there, an unseen connection to the fallen Sems of Tabriz and his dagger-wielding killers.

As he sat pondering one of the friezes of the stabbing

death of Sems, killers' daggers upraised, old dervish fallen to earth under the rain of blows, a play of light on one of the killer's stone faces brought more detail up, and he saw that the assassin wore a scarf across his lower face, while his huge eyes glared heavenward in the transport of this ecstatic ritual killing.

The true face of Ali Nuraddin was also half-hidden; did this mean the Islamic Peaceful One was really of the Dashtiya, a sinister and messianic sect?

Was this Ali Nuraddin's deepest, darkest secret, that Torkelson had been on the trail of?

Just as importantly, Horner thought as he stood looking at the violated walls and ripped stone and earth floors, why had the Turkish government covered up evidence of such a pillaging? To avoid offending Iran, if the Iranians had indeed done this? Was Turkey now so afraid of its neighbor that it would look the other way when its borders were crossed?

Horner was also trying to fathom what the raiders had been looking for. Since they'd left the friezes undamaged, those hadn't been the objects of the raid. He could only guess, by the fairly small cuts into stone walls, that the searchers had been looking for an object or objects, rather than a frieze. As he examined the fallen stones, he could find no evidence of inner spaces that might have contained anything so precious as to motivate this ransacking. The excavations in the ground were less informative. For all he knew, they had indeed found what they were looking for. But the fact that eight substantial holes had been dug could also indicate the raiders had been blindly searching and had been unsuccessful.

And the last, and perhaps most telling question, occurred to Horner when he had left the temple-mosque to look through binoculars down at the security police camp to the northwest, ostensibly set up to keep the curious away from the ruins. If the raiders had come from Iran to violate this site, why were the Turkish security forces now arrayed on the <u>Turkish</u> side of the ruins, instead of on the Iranian side?

Why would they be wanting to keep their own countrymen out? Why were they not watching the Iranian border?

*   *   *

Chapter 31

It was well past dark when he made it back to the hotel. The clerk told him Maria was up in the room waiting, and had been for some time. But Horner delayed his ascent of the stairs to place a mobile call to Nilufer in Istanbul.

"When are you going to level with me about our project?" he was asking, over the breaks and static and occasional bursts of verbiage from a crossed conversation, a Turkish mother and daughter wailing about a relative's heart attack. He told her the outline of his discovery.

"Where in God's name are you?" Nilufer asked, sounding breathless and euphoric, like she'd just run off a dance floor to take his call. "We can't do this on the phone. I've got the key to the missing folio, Burt -- and so much more. You need to be on the first plane tomorrow to Antalya. Meet me for dinner. The final key. It's here, in ***The Secret of Suleiman***. I know now why they're paying so much."

"You've said this before," he said. Although he was speaking English, he thought the desk clerk just a few yards away was taking an undue interest in the conversation.

"Darling, I can hardly hear you," she said. "Speak up, please. I'll be at the Marina Hotel -- dreadful advertising conference, I promised them months ago I'd speak. But I'm bringing the manuscript --"

"I don't want to fly to Antalya," he said.

"Have a drink on me, wherever you are," she said, ignoring him. "We're in the home stretch. Our retirement, darling. Monte Carlo, Barcelona, Gstaad. We can kiss this dreadful place goodbye, and leave it to the extremists."

"I hope we live that long --"

"Can't do this on the phone, darling," she said. "I can only hear every other word. Someone's at the door. I want you in Antalya tomorrow. To the victor go the spoils."

"Christ," he said. "You've been stringing me along on this goddamn thing for weeks now --"

He heard the dial tone, realized she had hung up on him, or been cut off.

He dialed Atilha's home, but just missed him. Atilha's wife didn't expect him back before 10 or 11 that night.

He climbed the stairs to the room, went in.

Maria was seated on the bed, notes and clippings spread out. She grunted in his direction.

"Have a good day?" he asked.

"Shorter than yours," she said. "Where've you been?"

"I went up to the ruins," he said. "Thought I might run into you up there."

She made a snorting sound.

"Did the military tell you anything?" he asked.

"You first," she said.

"Why play cagey?"

She took offense.

"You didn't waste any time calling your dear partner," she said. "I thought you might have popped in here first, since you're about four hours late."

"You could hear me on the phone?"

"I think everybody in the town heard you," she said. "Have fun with her in Antalya."

"To hell with Nilufer," he said. "We made it up to the ruins. I think the raiders were looking for the lost chapter of the *Suleymanname*, or the greater treasure that it points to. I can't tell if they found it. But the frieze of the Dashtiya is there, in at least three places. Looks like an ancient Dashtiya sect stronghold. And I saw the Turkish secret police camp below the ruins. But it's on the wrong side of the ruins, if they want to keep out Iranians. It's there to keep out Turks ..."

She was running her hands through her hair.

"And there's more," he said. "One of the dervish killers in the frieze wore a black scarf over his mouth, like Ali Nuraddin. Do you think he could be part of the Dashtiya sect my poem talks about? Could that be the dark secret Torkelson was onto?"

"Scarves are awfully common. Palestinians, Bedouins, Baluchis, Billy the Kid ... it would be tough to nail Ali Nuraddin on a scarf alone."

"But when you look at all the clues, the leads, there's too much of it," he said. "Everywhere I turn ... dervishes, mystic poems, altars, Torkelson killed by terrorists in scarves. I can't ignore it."

"Let's not talk about it here," she said. "I'm starved. So let's get out of here. Then maybe we can play show and tell."

*   *   *

Chapter 32

They ate dinner at the Hotel Isfahan, as the night before, and again were almost alone. The kitchen had very nearly shut down when they arrived at 8:30. The only other guest was a fiftyish Scandinavian-looking man with goatee and glasses who'd been reading the paper when they came in.

The man and Maria exchanged greetings. Maria introduced Major Engholm, from NATO. He invited them to be seated, but Maria answered for them, saying no, they'd respect his privacy.

After dinner, Horner and Maria went for a walk to the edge of town under the chill sky of a starry autumn night, moonlight rebounding off the glacier of Ararat. They shared his brandy to keep warm.

"I want to know what you found out," he finally said.

She was shaking her head.

"Nilufer's project is totally out of hand. You're mucking around in strange work. You'll get your head blown off."

He couldn't discount that.

"Maria, so are you. We're all onto the same thing..."

"But I'm not on her payroll, and you are. Burt, she's taking mullah money, exactly which group I haven't figured out yet. But she's not working for the good guys."

"I agree," he said. "But I'm smarter than she is."

"Don't be so sure."

"I have a plan," he said.

"God," she said.

She was looking at him as if he might have gone off the deep end.

That wasn't a good feeling.

"We had a deal this morning." he said. "Now your turn."

She took a swig of his brandy.

"I started with the police," she finally said. She'd asked some contacts why the ruins were off-limits. And she'd been referred to the Army. Then she narrated how after her fruitless approach to the Army -- they'd stonewalled everything, and even turned threatening -- she'd been at a loss. Sitting in the hotel lobby, she'd been forced to strike up a conversation with the Danish hippies. And it turned out they were there to visit the girl's father -- Major Engholm. He'd come to Turkey on a project related to the ruins. They'd even introduced Maria to him.

"Engholm was terribly uncomfortable when I first met him. You know Danes. But over lunch he warmed up, and let slip that the area had caught the attention of NATO by coincidence --"

"My friend told me a Culture Ministry guy discovered the ruins on vacation," Horner interrupted.

"That's true," she said. "But Torkelson wasn't onto antiquities, he was onto something bigger. Apparently his sources in the Defense Ministry told him about this border violation. NATO surveillance satellites had detected an Iranian incursion with three helicopters and maybe forty men, landing at the site, and they queried the Turks. The Army didn't know shit about it. NATO demanded they let a team come down and investigate."

"Engholm's well regarded by all the Allies," she added. "He's a satellite border surveillance expert. He did some very good work in Iraq documenting Saddam Hussein's moves against the Kurds, and the Kurdish refugee movements."

She stopped talking while a man smoking a cigarette passed them on the sidewalk.

"NATO was able to get their man down here, but he hasn't been able to investigate. It could have to do with the problems with the European Community, I don't know. They're in a standoff. As far as Engholm is concerned, Turkey is in breach of its treaty with NATO. He's going to present a report to that effect to the NATO Council in Brussels."

"That's serious stuff," he said.

She nodded.

"Did you show him your photos?" he asked.

"He'd seen them ... but only a day or two before me. But he's not a ruin specialist; he's a satellite border specialist. It doesn't look good, Burt. You and I might have to find a new country to live in."

And that's how the conversation ended. The idea of NATO and Turkey in an intelligence chain-of-command dispute was beyond his expertise. Leave it to Maria and others to figure that one out.

But cover-ups aside, he was most concerned about the site pillagers and what they had been after. Had they found the greater treasures that he too was searching for? Or had they failed ... and was that why murky Iranians had hired Nilufer to translate Yunus' poem and help the search?

And what did the evidence of ancient cremations -- or even human sacrifice by fire -- have to do with any of it?

Unless it had some tie to the very-light of God?

* * *

Finally my eyes moved to the light itself, atop an altar with carved chalcedony base ... and though it came clearer for me, its mystery was only heightened. This was nothing more, I thought, than a small star captured and brought here; a star captured out of the sky and set here to burn in this altar. It seemed to be enclosed in a clear glassine sphere, and either stood or floated just above the altar. The light streamed out of it in a uniform and awesome emanation, throwing white heat and light to all the room. The walls back where I stood were warm to the touch from it ... and I sensed if I drew much closer I would suffer the danger of being burned, or blinded.

-- The Secret of Suleiman

Chapter 33

At dawn the next morning Horner and Maria took the first bus out to Erzurum, to catch a mid-morning flight to Ankara. At the Erzurum ticket counter they encountered Major Engholm, who was waiting on the same Ankara flight.

"I've been ordered out of the country," he said to Maria, then laughed, his righteous Danish face shaken by tension, embarrassment, Horner couldn't be sure. He'd been out in the sun too much, and his bald pate was peeling in crimson patches.

"Good luck," she said.

Horner hadn't decided whether to meet Nilufer in Antalya on the Turkish coast yet. He could see it would do further damage to his relationship with Maria, since Antalya like Kasos was one of "their" places, another spot where their love had blossomed six years ago. For him to be flying off for a tete-a-tete with Nilufer in Antalya would serve as the crowning blow.

During their hour layover at Ankara -- made longer by

the loading and takeoff of yet more military transports, just as they'd seen on their trip out -- Maria was at one pay phone at the far end of the terminal, calling her bureau in Istanbul for the latest; he was doing his own calls, trying to reach Genghiz, but to no avail. Neither one of their mobile phones would work, not even in the Ankara airport.

At that moment, Horner recognized a man at a coffee shop who he was sure had been with them on the bus from Erzurum to Dogubeyazit two days ago. Were undercover people -- even Torkelson's killers -- on him?

He then decided he would have to go to Antalya after all, to meet with Nilufer and see what she had. There was no way to avoid it. He'd gone this far; he'd take one more look.

When Maria finally walked over towards him, he knew something was very wrong and he didn't compound it with the news of his decision. For her face was stricken.

"Burt," she said. "You have to break with Nilufer."

"What?" he managed to say, trying to hold her.

"I can't say much now. But she's in too deeply. Inspector Aziz was put on leave last night, and Torkelson's murder investigation has been quashed, for reasons of national security ..."

Inspector Aziz on leave? Did this mean Horner was off the hook ... or in even more danger? But he couldn't stop now; he was too close.

"Maria, I needed her money. Now I just need one more look. I've gone this far. I'm two steps ahead of her."

Maria was shaking her head, the crowds swirling about her. He could see tears.

"It's me or her, Burt. Make your choice."

"Maria, how can you say such a thing?" he blurted, embracing her. "I made my choice when I chose you to love." The two of them stood together, caught in an errant ray of morning sunshine coming down through an airport skylight, looking to all around them like a couple made for one another, the tall Wyoming exile turned art sleuth and the green- eyed Midwestern gamine glowing with life and extended youth. But while he thought he saw new moisture in her eyes, she didn't return the embrace.

"Maria," he whispered. "Trust me just as I trust you. I just need to finish what I started. I just need a few days to crack this thing; you've got to have faith ."

"This isn't the age of faith," she said.

"I'm clean," he said.

"I know you're clean, Burt. But Nilufer's working for the devil incarnate."

"Ali Nuraddin?" he was able to ask. "Is he trying to overthrow the Turkish Government?"

She flinched slightly as he said that. Did that mean he had hit the nail on the head?

"Turkey's only a part," she said. "I warned you about that woman. She wasn't to be trusted. And you let her suck you in deeper and deeper--"

"I know what she's about," he managed to say. "I went in with my eyes open."

"Burt, don't you realize what's happening? The only reason you aren't already dead is that the conspiracy is letting you finish your stupid quest, because they want what you want and they realize you might actually find it. Torkelson dead, Gunes dead, General Ihsanoglu, Aziz on leave and maybe dead soon. They could kill you right now, they could have killed you ten times in the last week. They are using you to lead them to whatever it is."

He realized in that moment she was absolutely right. What a fool he had been, to think he was outrunning the killers.

But still he couldn't let go. He was too close.

"I thought we were in this together," he said, embarrassed at how lame it sounded.

"I'm just a reporter, Burt. I can only do so much. You're in with saboteurs and murderers now."

"So come away with me," he said, meaning to sound romantic but sounding ludicrous to his own ear.

"What?"

"I'll get out, if you'll come with me."

She was so sad; she was watching him die.

"Let's be romantic," he said. "Somewhere appropriately exotic. The South Pacific. The Greek Islands. Start all over."

She was shaking her head, unconvinced. He thought for a second she laughed, but then he gleaned it was more a spasmodic thing, closer to a sob.

"Maria, if you give up the reporting, I'll give up my work for Nilufer. So we can have a life again. Like it was before ... like it could be again."

She looked down at the floor.

"I'm serious," he said. And for a second he thought he had her back ... had her with him on the way to new life, away from all this, fresh and in love.

"My plane's leaving," she said, looking towards the gate, leaving him feeling like he'd been hit with a brick. "Burt, I hope you'll change your mind. Don't let the treasure kill you."

She was backing away from him.

"Maria," he pleaded. "I need one more look at Nilufer's translation. I told you I had a plan. I know antiquities better than she does. This is something I've waited on for 30 years."

"And you really think you can outsmart these killers too?"

Yes, he still thought he could outsmart them. But he had a fleeting thought: was he delusional and obsessed with greed, and so doomed to die once he found what they all wanted?

She looked at him a moment longer. Then she was on the bus, out to the plane.

As his own layover lingered on another ten minutes, he wondered if he would be able to go through with any more of this. The idea of Nilufer was the last thing he wanted to deal with, the last person in the world he wanted to see. For hadn't she done this to him? Hadn't she wanted to break them up?

Maria was right about everything, he thought. He would take this one last chance to get to the missing folio, and then get out.

On his way to the departure lounge, he passed a small gaggle of people in the corridor. Shouted comments indicated someone was in distress.

Looking over the heads of the shorter crowd, Horner could see a European man being dragged away down a hallway by a trio of men in shirt-sleeves, perhaps security agents, perhaps paramilitary types. Whoever they were, their captive had such a look of incredulity on his face that it was almost comical -- as in, Imagine me, of all people, submitted to such injustice.

It was only as the man was pulled through a door which was immediately slammed shut, that Horner acknowledged in his own mind who the man was.

It was Major Engholm, and his NATO passport was apparently no protection against whatever violations -- or dangers -- his captors had in store.

*　*　*

Chapter 34

Oh, the conspirators would not rest, thinking that through their alliances of force and fear, higher good could be done.

While he had many things to contemplate and plan as the days now quickened towards their culmination, he saw that the Turks were contemplating leaving the Christian West and allying themselves with the Iranians.

What did such things mean for him, and the truth he was telling the world? Was this a new dawn for him, or a new danger to be confronted?

In the end, while he took note of all these developments, he decided they were only more symbols of the disorder preceding the great unification that would come. He had his own followers in both Turkey and Iran, and beyond. What did it matter what the small men lurking in the palaces and ministries did, in these times of turmoil?

And yet, he knew deep down, that any one of these

moves could be his downfall. The world was still driven by force and intrigue, and he would need to be wary.

* * *

Chapter 35

As the plane banked out over the golden Mediterranean for its final approach to Antalya, the afternoon sun washing from the snowy Toros peaks down to the beaches and bay, Horner was desperate, wanting to warn Maria that Engholm had been arrested, meaning that Turkey was turning against NATO and the West, and all that implied for both of them and their work, their very lives.

At the same time, he wanted to win her back.

But in his frenzy he acknowledged that Maria had been right: he'd made his choice, and he'd chosen Nilufer. And yet he couldn't let Maria go, not this way.

God, her life might be in danger now. For all he knew, she was the only outsider carrying Engholm's discoveries about the ruins and camp – that the Turkish military was covering up an Iranian incursion into the bizarre ruins at Tendurek.

At a loss, he poured down as many shots of Scotch during the flight -- three -- as the stewardess would allow.

That was about the only way he could deal with this mess now.

The plane was already taxiing to the terminal. The day was magnificent, summer still in full sway here, tarmac attendants wearing only shorts and t-shirts as they unloaded luggage in the afternoon sun. The date palms around the airfield moved slightly in the breeze.

Once through the terminal, he hired a cab and asked to go to the Marina Hotel where Nilufer was staying. In a few minutes they entered Antalya's old center of Kaleici, deep in afternoon shadow. Kaleici was truly a Greek town, minarets notwithstanding, from *bouzouki* music echoing from the tabak shops to the squid hung up to dry in the sun by sidewalk cafes ... reminiscent of points farther south, the old Levantine coasts of Syria, Lebanon and Israel before they'd become armed camps. November on the Mediterranean had a special character: summer had moved from its worst heat of August into a softer but more soothing warmth.

The light and color of the coast brightened his spirits momentarily. Then he thought of Maria, and how much he wanted her here with him. He dialed her mobile number, but only got her voicemail. She had to be back in Istanbul by now. But she might have seen his caller ID and let it roll over. God, what a mockery this was, to be drawn back to this place by a woman he now despised, even as Maria, the one he loved, the one whose love with him had flourished here six years ago, was leaving him.

The taxi dropped him at the Marina Hotel, an Ottoman mansion restored to full grandeur. The soft waters of the harbor lapped just beyond. Fishing boats were just coming in, and markets were drawing their end-of-day customers. At the ornate registration desk, he learned Ms. Oz was registered but away from her room. She had indeed told the hotel Mr. Horner would be arriving, and to have a key for her room made available to him.

"Ms. Oz indicated you would be staying with her."

"It was a misunderstanding. I'll take any single you have."

The clerk sniffed and began a search. There was a room available, but he couldn't recommend it as highly as Ms. Oz's suite.

Horner took it anyway, as well as the key to the suite. He tried again to use his mobile phone, but there was no dial tone, only a high whine, as had been the case all day. He gave the operator Maria's phone numbers and asked for the clerk to ring him when he reached Maria. But the landline circuits to Istanbul had also been out all day, he was told. So he had the hotel send Maria a telegram, the first time he'd sent one in decades, instructing her to call him immediately.

He stopped off first at his own room, then went up to

Nilufer's suite. He knocked, but getting no answer, he let himself inside.

The view from her balcony was breathtaking: the little harbor bathed in lutescent sunlight, air filled with the smell of ocean and orange trees on the corniche. The semicircle of the harbor enclosed yachts and fishing boats, an etched, swinging horizon of masts and rigging, the jingling of sail-pins and winches in the soft breeze, an almost glassy ocean showing only the slightest hint of swell. Oleander was blooming, sparrows and chickadees darted from his balcony railing off into the sky. He could hear girls laughing down below. Behind him, stone and plaster houses marched up the limestone cliffs between cascading shrubbery, olive trees, vines, to the plateau where the city stood ...

Horner decided to enjoy the declining afternoon from his adversary-partner's balcony after all, to collect his thoughts in advance of what would have to be a confrontation with Nilufer. He poured himself another Scotch, fixed a snack.

The pattern, though yet partly veiled, was coming clearer, and if given enough time he would unravel it, to see it blinding and stark in its symmetry.

From the immensity of that thought, the first step towards parting the veil came in a small way to him, a simple flash of light on a woman's jewelry, a tiny door opening in his mind, just as she was opening the door to the suite, shouting with glee to find him there, sweeping over to embrace him. It was not an idea he was yet ready to voice, but it grew and took shape within, like a pearl in the oyster, a gem created in the black fires of the earth. Even as she poured the champagne, gushing her victory sounds, he kept it single-minded within, polishing, refining, until the moment came when he could put it to use.

* * *

Chapter 36

"That's my old Burt," she said, pouring the umpteenth drink of the evening; the sunset had long gone away into the ocean, the bowl of stars now spread over them, yellow glows of the town's windows and lanterns playing out onto the black water and the rocky beach. Horner and Nilufer were looking at the remains of a gourmet seafood dinner they'd eaten there on the balcony.

"When I first walked in you were white as a sheet. What a dreadful time you've had. Bus rides, airports, fights with girlfriends ..."

He stifled the impulse to rebuke the vigor with which she described his troubles. And he was falling down into a restricted tube, the result of too many different kinds of alcohol imbibed. The food tasted like whisky, and he could hear a rushing in his ears that he'd thought for an hour was the sea but was really the noise in his own head.

"You've been under too much pressure, worrying about money and Raine Torkelson and clients and all sorts of things," she continued. "Remember how I told you to live like me ... enjoy the moment, take the good fortune that comes your way, and don't question destiny? Here precious, have another drink."

She seemed so confident, so supremely victorious.

"But as soon as you read this concluding section of the *masnavi*, all of your troubles will drop away," she said. "You'll be like the fool crying in his soup who then looks up and sees those stars out there, the enormity of the cosmos, the infinities of time and space rendering our little travails ludicrous--"

"That's a tall order," he said.

She had come up behind him and was massaging the back of his neck. She had doused herself with extra perfume if that was possible, she was like her own universe of perfume, moving in a cloud, tolerable only because they were on this balcony in the open air.

"I want to know who you're working for," he said.

She laughed drunkenly, spraying saliva onto his neck. But he could feel her warmth up against him, the tremors in her breasts as she shifted position. Her breath, a mixture of a dozen gobbled fruits and assorted liqueurs, grew hotter in his ear ...

"The same people you're working for."

"This thing has "plot" written all over it. People are

being killed. Over a fucking manuscript. That's a cover, isn't it? Is this some intelligence thing? Are you being paid by the mullahs or Ali Nuraddin? Because if so, I want out. I don't do spy work."

She laughed again.

"I was beginning to think like you," she said. "It is a lot of money, even for the *Suleymanname.* And if that's what got Torkelson killed ... I just couldn't believe it was worth murder at the time --"

She took a long swill of her drink, then fell against him, lost her balance, clutched him for assistance. He brought her up, their arms remaining entwined. He felt himself weakening ...

"Now I know why the money's so good," she whispered.

"Confess: the Iranian Revolutionary Guard is paying us," he rambled on, fighting to maintain his train of thought. "They backed your party, your ex-President, as I recall."

She gasped in mock outrage. She pushed him, laughing, then came to him to plant a drunken kiss. His tongue tasted her mouth, her lips, before he pulled back.

"It's time to cut the client out," she said, breathless.

"What?"

"The old double-cross," she said.

"Double-cross the Revolutionary Guard?"

"Burt, I know the real secret now. Our dear patron wants the manuscript because it shows the way to the greatest treasure of Asia, a treasure immeasurable in value, a treasure to which the missing folio is only a shabby guide, a treasure that will blind you with its beauty and mystic power."

"Who the hell are the Dashtiya?" he asked, half-ignoring what she was saying. "Come clean with me."

"Dashtiya," she hissed, swirling her hands around her in a dance of the seven veils, sans veils. Then she broke down in laughter for a moment. She arched her eyebrows, slid back into darkness of the suite, beckoning with her finger. "All secrets are now to be revealed."

She had the translated *masnavi* in her hand.

"I hold the key to the greatest treasure of Anatolia and Persia, the blood of the heart of Asia, a magical object lost to man for 450 years without which no one can rule this half of the earth."

He reached for the manuscript, but she put it behind her back; he was suddenly so dizzy he thought he would fall.

"Nothing comes for free," she said, batting her eyes.

"Give it to me," he said.

"Make love to me first," she said.

"I'm still in mourning," he said.

"Make love to me, and ye shall receive the greatest

treasure."

He wanted to pour out a thousand insults, but was silent because she had him now, he wanted to bury himself in her, be swallowed and wiped clean of all that had happened today, this week, this month ...

"What treasure?" he asked.

"It will make you a hero beyond your dreams," she said, "as rich as Croesus..."

"What," he asked. Her lips were puckered for a second kiss; a free hand had loosened her gown, and it was falling away. He lost his breath to see it all again after so long, the great red- nippled breasts swaying and the hips a god would have killed for; if anything, time had turned her more voluptuous.

"Horner, the things I do for you," she whispered.

He was vanquished ...

"Make love to me, and you shall have the ruby chalice ..."

"The ruby chalice," he heard himself say.

"The chalice of the Aryan light," she sang.

"Name its true name," he heard himself saying.

"The *cam-i Jamshid*, o unbeliever," she whispered, her drunkenness and delusion now unloosing all manner of portentous and faux-sacred blather. "The ruby chalice of all the Persias; the precious cup of the foundation of Iran, from which drank Cyrus, Darius, Xerxes, Alexander, and every conqueror who followed, up to Suleiman; the chalice of the continents intersected, of a race, a people, a dream, the light of Zarathustra, the drop of God's blood, the red sunset frozen in stone, the very nexus of earth's power..."

"Ahh..." he was able to say as she unbuttoned his shirt, brought his pants down to the floor; he kicked out of the shoes and socks ...

"Take me, and you receive it, and thus the key to the earth; the *cam-i Jamshid,* Horner, lost by Suleiman after he won it from the Persians in 1553 and they ceded it to him forever and named him *shahanshah*; mysterious goblet lost for all those years; the cup that Alexander wept to bring to his lips, because in its rosy light he could see all the way to the heart of India, and back to his father's chill fortress in Macedonia; he saw the beginning and the end of all mankind in its mystic lights."

Horner made some kind of sound, he didn't know what.

"Take me, find it..." she said.

"By god," he said. They tumbled together, falling back towards the bed, and his cries of hunger sank muffled into the mountains of her bosom, thighs; he spanked at her and tried to crush her when there was no way she could be crushed, she was all womanhood itself pulling him in only to conquer him. She engulfed his first thrust so wet and smooth it was like he was in air, he was in ocean, and they both made rough and bestial sounds that must have been audible down on the beach. As he slammed at her he could see her eyes afire, her mouth slack; she was way back deep somewhere, off in her obsession, this was what she had wanted for so long, she was crazy as a loon and so was he. How had he fallen so far?

Each thrust sent her bosoms rolling up headward, like a storm, a tide. On and on he and she rode, pouring out of that room and up into the sky. Clouds, moonlit fleece bounced around them. And though he wanted to say this lovemaking was an abomination, it was bedazzling in its evil; it dripped with titillation. And while she wrapped around him, while they streamed across the clouds and saw the armies tramping through the night, tramping east and west for 5,000 years, shields and banners blown to dust, lit by the icy moon of death, it was all spread out before them, from Scythia down through Bactria, Sogdiania and Chorasmia, all the ancient and mystic lands at their feet, theirs, theirs, wrapped in this treasured cup and this kiss...

And when they lay there after, moonlight dying, shadows falling darker so the night was like a prison from which no one would ever escape, as the magic spell sank into a foul cloud of evil, he remembered the tiny gem of knowledge he carried in himself.

Looking over at her, spent in her lust, falling into a snoring slumber like the sleep of Polyphemus, he thought this, as he had a few hours ago on the balcony.

He thought: Your partners had Torkelson killed; and our partners mean to use and betray and then destroy me, even as I complete your search for you. It is you who are the killer, the betrayer, the viper in the garden; and though I lay in your arms, I shall have to slay you.

He thought this at the first stroke past midnight. She fell into the deepest slumber like death, while he strode to read the secret poem leading to the fabled treasure of which she spoke.

*   *   *

If you escape the narrowness of dimensions, and see the "time of what is placeless," you will hear what has never been heard, and you will see what has never been seen.

-- Sayed Ahmad Hatif

And if you be accurate in your measure
Wrapped in truth you will find the treasure
The heart of the world, in my poetry hid;
The sultan's ruby chalice, the cam-i Jamshid.
Then gaze deep into the poetry of God's 99 names,
To find the secret of the very-light,
of the stars' endless flames.

-- The Secret of Suleiman

Chapter 37

By three, Horner had finished reading and was meditating upon the meaning of it all, in the light of a single lamp. The Mediterranean night was soft and springlike, stars up in the black cloudless sky. Only a few lights from the marina played out on the black surface of the Gulf of Antalya, quivering tails of comets, oscillating waves of light.

Past and present were now so entwined as to be a single tapestry. For Nilufer's translation of **The Secret of Suleiman** narrated a 1566 visit to the same ruins Horner himself had climbed to just yesterday -- and where Iran, Turkey and NATO were involved in a strange game of cat and mouse.

Though the individual elements continued to throw up a screen of confusion, a single beacon now outshone everything else, and might provide a touch of illumination, were its implications not so baffling. The *very-light of God*, repeatedly mentioned in **The Secret of Suleiman**, the holy grail of a heretical quest underway for 700 years ... what did it mean?

Add to that a lost ruby chalice coveted by both shah and sultan, treasured both by Turkey and Iran for millennia ...

He had done it, hadn't he? He had begun to open the veil obscuring a millennial quest, a quest that he had subconsciously known would someday reveal itself to him, if only he persevered. Or had he? The mind plays tricks at night, in the wee hours. The most outrageous scenarios can take shape, without the limits of daylight to bring them back to earth.

As if reading his thoughts, Nilufer awakened long enough to stagger to the bathroom. On her way back to bed she noticed him in the chair.

"Darling, you've finished it," she said, voice gravelly with much consumed liquor. She made her way to the decanter, poured another shot, downed it.

"And now the question is: Where? Where is our marvelous buried treasure?"

Horner looked out through the opened door onto the black water of night.

"It's in Istanbul, isn't it?" she asked. He didn't answer immediately, for he was almost certain that the translated final couplets, together with the missing chapter-folio from the *Suleymanname* and perhaps even the ruby chalice, weren't hidden in Istanbul -- or in the pillaged ruins at Ararat

-- but somewhere else.

"If the missing chapter exists at all," he said.

"You're being impossible," she said, taking another belt straight from the decanter.

"You've given a new meaning to the word nightcap," he said.

"I'm celebrating," she said. "First I want you to admit the treasures are hidden in Istanbul, probably Topkapi, then I want you to come back to bed." She was slurring her words again, but managed to flutter her eyelids.

"I guess so," he said, seeing she was fixed on Istanbul.

"You'd better know so. That's why you're here to begin with, darling. You know art, you know Sufism, you know the riddles. I want to hear more conviction..."

"My hesitation doesn't have to do with that," he lied. "I'm just in no position now to go prowling through Topkapi again. I used up my chits to get in there once before. For all I know I caused the murder of Gunes. My name is surely in his appointment book."

"Don't worry," she said. "I've plenty of connections. Topkapi is ours. Now come back to bed."

He grudgingly did so, yet unlike the first seduction, the edges of this encounter grated unsoftened by the haze of liquor. He did his mechanical best, and was mercifully reprieved when she fell back into her epiglottal snore. He let her sink deeper, then quietly extricated himself from bed.

He dressed, picked up her translation and left the room, went down and retrieved his luggage from the closet of the other room he hadn't seen since he checked in. As he passed the front desk, the night clerk was asleep.

The slightest hint of light was just coming up over the Toros Range when he stumbled out into the street. A trio of cats were quarreling over a fish-head in the gutter. A bird pecked at a banana peel. But he didn't see another human until he had made it up to Sarampol Caddesi, the main street running out of the old town center.

He woke up a sleeping cabbie in front of the Hotel Aphrodite and was driven to the open-air bus terminal in the new city. There, life stirred. A few kiosks were already open, and an overnight bus from Kayseri was just pulling in. Two others bound for points north and east were loading up.

Horner bought a pastry and some mineral water, grabbed a just-arrived issue of *Cumhurriyet*. While the Saudi ruling family was reported to be in Switzerland, more riots had broken out in Egypt, and a new military government was being formed. In Turkey, the Islamic Front claimed enough petition signatures to call new elections, which they would most likely win outright. And the Fatherland and Salvation parties were already mounting a legal challenge.

But most ominously, Ali Nuraddin the Peaceful One

was bound for the borderless expanse between Yemen and Saudi Arabia, in the valley of the Wadi al Jufrah close to the very source-land of Islam, where he had summoned an assemblage of his followers, amidst rumors he was finally going to unmask himself and make a "major announcement" to the faithful.

Horner placed a coin phone call to Atilha in Istanbul, who fortunately was at home. The call roused the lawyer from sleep.

They spoke for about five minutes, as Horner described his discoveries of the last three days. The Turkish lawyer went from curiosity ... to a decision to meet Horner that afternoon at a secret location.

He tried to call Maria again, as he had just after arriving in Antalya. But their apartment phone was dead or off the hook, the news bureau wasn't answering, and her mobile kept rolling into voicemail.

Then Horner boarded the first bus leaving.

As the eastern sky brightened in a radiant arch of incarnadine and gold, he was well on the way to his next destination, the city where he was reasonably certain the final verses of the translated poem and the missing chapter from the *Suleymanname* were hidden, with its own secrets and scandals ... and where, if the translation were truthful, the solid ruby chalice of all the Persias also waited.

The city where these things were hidden, and where he would meet Atilha, was the final resting place of the Mevlana Jelaleddin al-Rumi, the home of the dervishes Rumi had inspired. The city was called Konya.

*   *   *

Chapter 38

And now, as the final days rushed towards him, Ali

Nuraddin flew across the raw mountains and desert to where

the masses awaited his ultimate revelation. He remembered

how it had all begun only a few years before in the villages

surrounding Ho'fuf in Saudi Arabia. In those days he did not fly,

but traveled like the people, by bus or by foot, across land not

so unlike that now below him. He would travel to the nearest

market city, and he would find a place opposite the market. And

there he would connect microphone and amplifier, and begin to

recite his poems, or sing his songs and play his guitar. On that

first day, his audience had been a goatherd and three children,

and he thought, My road is so long and this beginning is so

small, will I ever reach my destination?

But he enchanted those four listeners, and more people -

- men missing teeth, or with scars across their gaunt faces, or

ravaged women who were as veiled in mystery as he with his

scarf and hood – paid attention. They said he had the voice and eyes of heaven, and the words of a prophet, and they became so affectionate to him that they did not want him to stop, and they wanted to accompany him when he traveled to his next market day.

The world, he would sing, is wrapped in fear and greed and selfishness; only through a revolution of love would it be restored to goodness, and the true believers allowed to join Allah in Paradise. They listened as the words flowed from his mouth, first as though they were his own words but then as though the words were coming out of the listeners themselves, or echoing thoughts that had long resided in their own breasts.

And when one of those early days was finished, a humble and poor imam who had listened from a tiny mosque doorway asked him to stay and shelter there, for he had the gift of the divine. And the young man did so, as new to this place as if he had dropped from heaven; yet this was now his home, the place from where he would begin his campaign.

His campaign was only to bring more love into the world, into a world and life that had given so little love to him, a lost orphan. To him the idea of Allah was nothing more than the purest love, love for even those who hate... and he thought if he could help bring that love into the world, then his own small life might be justified.

Chapter 39

Konya -- Horner hadn't been here in a decade at least. But it was fitting he conclude his search here.

The bus made its way through the jagged scarps of the coastal Toros -- pine-covered hills and cloud-tipped massifs, pallid marble and gray granite cliffs lit by a sun impossibly bright, even for December.

By early afternoon Horner and his fellow passengers -- all humble Turks -- were making their descent from the Kizilorem highlands towards the edge of the steppe, at the entry of which spread the city of Konya. What astonished him was the size of the city, for it appeared enormous -- vast suburbs of modernistic apartment blocks, broad avenues, streets jammed with pedestrians. But he knew it was deceptive, for Konya hadn't been of great importance in Turkish affairs since the fall of the Seljuks 600 years ago. Even now, the tiny city airfield had only one flight a week, to and from Istanbul. No, in the modern world, Konya had fallen to become just another regional distribution point. The swelling population was another reminder of the growth of Turkey itself -- now approaching 75 million people.

From the bus station he took a cab to the only hotel he had any experience with -- the Konya Oteli, just a block from the whirling dervish museum. The hotel was surrounded by *kilim* shops and private homes.

Horner's room was small and clean, though a precipitous come-down from the night before. The *kilim* on the linoleum floor looked unchanged from a decade ago. The walls were hung with cliched obligatory prints of the Mevlana Jelaleddin Rumi, head wrapped in high white turban, silver beard flowing down to a point below his chin, sparkling eyes gazing up at the heavens. Invariably the background was of the stars of space shimmering behind pointed minarets.

After a bite to eat, Horner went to the whirling dervish cloister founded in Rumi's name, now a state-run museum, and browsed about. The green dome of the tower above Rumi's tomb -- the green was truly closer to a turquoise -- glinted with mid-afternoon sun. Mercifully the sun was warm, because at this elevation -- about 4,000 feet -- the chill of winter in the shadows was like he'd felt at Dogubeyazit.

The low outer walls and their quaint chimneys stood as they had in *The Secret of Suleiman,* when Suleiman's spy Yunus had visited here 400 years ago. The turquoise tiles of

the green dome were as fresh and bright as the day they'd
been fired in the 13th century. The fountain in the courtyard
still bubbled, allowing the faithful to wash before they
approached the inner sanctum of Rumi's tomb. About a
dozen religious pilgrims were there this afternoon, peasant
women in shawls and their men in dark suits. At the entrance
to the actual tomb, some were shedding their shoes in
preparation for entry, while others washed at the outdoor
fountain.

At a nearby kiosk selling whirling dervish
memorabilia, Horner recognized stacks of duplicates of the
whirling dervish videotape he'd found at Torkelson's murder
scene. For a second he studied the sales clerk, as if some
secret were hidden there.

Then he looked back up at the green dome, the beacon
of this place, the defining architectural feature. He was
remembering the couplets of Nilufer's translation, the lines
he believed would lead him to the hidden treasure here ... if
not within these very walls, then somewhere in this city:

Ye fools seeking truth in sultan's lie
go to sultan's cloister, 'neath green sky

While Nilufer had been misled by the "sultan's
cloister" to think it was connected to Suleiman the

Magnificent, and Horner himself didn't quite know the meaning of the phrase either, he <u>was</u> certain the green sky was not the sky of Istanbul or the dome of any of the innumerable mosques there, but the green dome of this tomb.

Shoes off, he continued into the entryway leading towards the sacred sepulchre. Dashti the medieval heretic sorcerer, and even Yunus the Sultan Suleiman's spy, had both undoubtedly passed through this very chamber. Reading the next inscription, Horner wondered if in retrospect the whirling dervishes might have been too open, too trusting of those who visited here:

Come heathen, fire-worshipper, sinful of idolatry
come. Come even if you broke your penitence a hundred
times. Ours is not the portal of misery and despair ...

Now Horner moved deeper into the shrine, moving down a gallery of artifacts from the poet Rumi's life. But the dominant presence in these rooms was the tombs themselves, at the far end of the gallery -- in the Pivot of the Spheres beneath the green dome.

In the Pivot, today's pilgrims were being swept up in varying degrees of fervor, and the guards were trying to hold back two nearly hysterical peasant women bent on kissing the silver stairs leading up to Rumi's marble casket. One would feint while the other dodged, and while one was thwarted, the other finally succeeded in kissing the silver step. But blocking their approach to the casket was a restraining fence installed at the end of the 16th century.

Beneath the dome, a huge green turban on one casket indicated where Rumi's entombed head lay. Two of the peasant faithful gathered there were now eyeing Horner with a curiosity not at all benign -- perhaps his scrutiny of the place had betrayed his motives as being less than devout. Oh, they had no idea why he was there -- but they knew he wasn't one of them.

Had the guards been watching too? Horner couldn't say.

If the treasures were here, however, they didn't jump out and advertise themselves. In a moment of horror, Horner had a vision of them hidden in the caskets of Rumi's family and others associated with the founding of the whirling dervish order. How could he and Atilha ever open a casket, in a place of such reverent faith? For all he knew -- considering the chilly relations of the Mevlevis and the Turkish Republic -- these guards were intelligence officers themselves. What scheme could Atilha possibly have in mind, for gaining entry?

No hidden manuscripts or ruby chalices were in evidence.

And yet... couldn't they be hidden here nonetheless? All he was seeing was surfaces ... and yet the whole message of this room was what lay beyond the surface ... hidden cadavers, mystic ideas, magical powers. Why couldn't it all be right here, within ten feet of him?

He realized how much he would need Atilha's knowledge of Sufi code and imagery to help him answer that question.

He came out into the chill afternoon, to further explore town until his friend arrived. And as in the preceding days, he could see no evidence of anyone observing or following him.

*   *   *

Chapter 40

In the days that followed those early performances, Ali Nuraddin felt the circle of his power growing like the magic and music of his words; he saw the faces multiply, until almost everyone in the village and from the surrounding desert and even from the coastal villages now came to hear his songs and homilies. Some even brought their tape recorders, and the words that they believed to be straight from Paradise were recorded and taken home and played and replayed in the park and the alleyways and even in the distant fields.

And then his fame spread beyond the confines of the valley into the other parts of the province of Hasa, over the dry mountains and off into the deserts to the south and west. And hundreds now traveled to hear his message, not only the Shiites who were numerous in these parts, but also peasant Sunni Wahabis who were the dominant group in the country. And the rumors of miracles performed multiplied ... that he had spoken with the dead, or brought back messages from the hereafter, or even held a poisonous serpent without fear of his own death.

And some had begun to call him by the name, even though in the beginning they only whispered it, for to say it was to make it stone, bring it into daylight, invite some kind of retribution if it were not so. But still they whispered it among themselves, and he heard the whispering, and was puzzled by it. He heard it even as the simple songs of faith and love came out if his mouth and went into the ears and microphones they now arrayed in front of him, he heard the whispers even as he heard his own words echoing off through the hundred electronic chambers where his sound was now captured.

No, no, he would say, trying to dissuade them.

And only when he was alone, in the quarters the imam gave him, where he would receive his petitioners, did he allow himself to voice it, did he allow himself to shape the name in his own mouth. Each time he did it he was terrified, terrified that such expectations had been placed on him by humble and desperate people, people who had no hope left in life except that some divine rescuer would come to save them. How could he ever do that? He was only a singer and a poet and man of pure faith, yet still only a man; but these people needed him to be more.

What they needed him to do was fulfill the destiny of the name. And though he did not know whether they were fools to place so much faith in him, or whether they could see something in him that he did not yet see in himself, he could not destroy their hope. And so while he would not assume the name they were giving him, he could not stop them from saying it. He could not take away their hope.

The terrible new name they gave him was **mahdi,** the rightly guided one, and they said he had come to bring justice to the earth after a sleep of a thousand years. Was this what the god he loved so much, Allah the compassionate and merciful who was the inspiration of his poems and songs, who was the guiding force of his own small life, meant for him to do? He would do only what was in his own heart, and let any higher mission be revealed to him.

*   *   *

Chapter 41

"When you told me what you'd found," said Atilha later that evening, as they ate dinner in a kebab-grille, "particularly the closing couplets of Nilufer's translated poem, the account of the heretic Dashtiya holy place, the bizarre light ... I knew I had to join you. That you might also be on the trail of the ruby chalice of Jamshid was just icing on the cake."

An astonishing chill had fallen over the city at sundown. Even though Horner was wearing a sweater, it wasn't enough in the unheated restaurant and he pulled his overcoat over his shoulders. Atilha looked uncustomarily rumpled, the waxed moustaches a bit drooped, the usually ironed shirt creased with the wrinkles of a day's travel.

Before they got back to the subject of the search, Horner pressed his friend about the cryptic warnings about Nilufer Maria had voiced. What was the plot? Atilha could only speculate that perhaps the extremists were attempting to carry out a silent coup, and overthrow or subvert the government.

"I do know that the investigation of Torkelson's murder has been quashed, for national security reasons," Atilha added. "Inspector Aziz was given a leave of absence, he was so enraged. He's quite an honorable man. He fears someone is subverting the national police."

"Turning back to your search," continued Atilha. "Just as I was leaving Istanbul I was able to reach my friend Demircan at the Mevlana Society here. He's expecting us at the tomb at 8:00. He's promised a payoff to the security guards, which the Mevlevis do to gain private entry at night. Naturally he'll be held responsible if anything's missing tomorrow."

Horner was able to finish a beer before it was time to walk over to the museum gate. Atilha lit up his pipe as they stepped into the park, now empty of all but a pair of pedestrians.

"Unless Nilufer's translated manuscript is a fraud -- and that's quite possible -- I think we're onto a potentially cosmic discovery --"

"You mean the ruby chalice?"

"Yes, well, that too, from your point of view. But I'm speaking of the Dashtiya and their holy secret. Their motive for volunteering to murder Sems of Tabriz."

"The secret of the very-light ..."

"Exactly. Whatever it is, it squares with my own studies at the Semseddin Tabrizi mosque, just a few blocks from here. My fascination with the mosque -- which I started to tell you about the day the police interrupted us -- deals with a curious section of tiled calligraphy in the sarcophagus area, where Sems' body is interred. An otherwise typical section of sacred inscription -- the 99 names of God -- in Arabic script."

Atilha lit his pipe.

"From your reading of Nilufer's manuscript -- and the ghastly embroidered dervish scene found at Torkelson's," Atilha continued, "you've found that the 99 names of God are of some importance to the Dashtiya sect, for they appear to chant it during their hellish ritual murders. Why they've taken this most mystical and sacred of Islamic traditions into their heresy we don't yet know."

"But long before you stumbled into this, I'd sensed the script near Sems' sarcophagus had anomalies which were the key to a secret particular to Sems. Certain letters and numbers in the script, for no discernible reason, had been given a black highlighting, making them stand out slightly to the eye. For most people, if you can't read Arabic, all significance is lost. Originally I thought the letters were a code giving some clue as to who had murdered Sems in 1247. Yet try as I might, I could make no sense of the message there."

"Through sheer exhaustion I'd abandoned that line of reason not long before you called me regarding Torkelson's death. After wasting five years on the murder code theory, I cast all that aside in favor of something I should have recognized long ago."

The lights at the Mevlana Museum were still out. Atilha was awaiting a signal.

A single light now flashed at the entrance to the former monastery. Atilha took note, emptied his pipe against tree-trunk.

"I'm digressing," he said. "The point is, as I looked at the rather sophisticated and impenetrable code above Sems' tomb, suddenly the initial part of the code jumped out at me, like a blast of cold air. Seeing it, I thought: Atalay, you stupid fool. Any first year chemistry student would have seen it --"

The men were walking in step towards the Mevlevi Museum.

"You said the code was chemical," Horner said.

"I did," Atilha answered. "Why didn't I understand earlier the hidden secret dealt with alchemy? How could I have been so stupid, to forget that one of the greatest fascinations of early Muslim culture was in the realm of alchemy, the precursor of our own modern chemistry?"

"So far I've only been able to understand the tiniest

portion of the code," Atilha continued. "And what I've uncovered so far is this: Al2O3. Only the first five characters of a 99-character formula, the ultimate meaning of which I can only guess at ..."

"$Al_2 O_3$? What's that?"

"Aluminum oxide," said Atilha. "A mineral which, in the context of the discoveries of our search, has become quite important ... whose characteristic color derives from replacing a small number of aluminum atoms with chromium ... whose color is red ... I'm talking about transparent red corundum -- the gemstone ruby -- the point at which your own quest now intersects with mine, and perhaps with a thousand other truths. You seem to be on the verge of discovery of the long-lost *cam-i Jamshid*, the ruby chalice of all the Persias ... entwined with buried scandal surrounding Suleiman the Magnificent, and new scandal surrounding Ali Nuraddin, the Peaceful One. That in turn is linked to the Dashtiya secret of the very-light of God, perhaps given to Dashti himself by Sems as he was murdered. And I meanwhile have uncovered the first bits of a formula that seems at least to be advanced chemistry, if not verging on astrophysics, adorning the memorial mosque of the same Sems, who inspired one of the greatest outpourings of mystic insights in human history from the pen of his beloved admirer, Rumi. At the door of whose tomb we now stand."

Chapter 42

Demircan was a loyal keeper of the whirling dervish flame, a man who made his living as did half of Konya -- by selling *kilim* carpets from all over Central Asia. But his first love was the dervish order. And he respected Atilha as the rare outsider who could have been one of them -- as indeed he had been, during a period in his early twenties -- before he married and began his law practice in Istanbul.

Although time was of the essence, Demircan insisted on serving tea to his visitors. During these moments, Atilha fabricated the reason for the visit, not too far from the truth: Horner was an art collector, and wished to examine some of the relics first-hand.

The old Turkish man looked to be around 70. When he shuffled away for a moment to find some sugar for the tea, Horner leaned over to his friend.

"If we do find the missing folio or missing sections of **The Secret of Suleiman** here, how will we ever get them out?"

"We'll have to be inventive," whispered Atilha, studying the closing couplets of Nilufer's translation. Now Demircan had returned, and led them into the gloom of the shrine, lit only by two bulbs and Demircan's flashlight. The turbans on the sarcophagi threw looming reflections onto the ceiling above, and set up shadow-plays as they slowly walked down the arcade of calligraphy.

Even as Atilha carried on the drone of conversation with Demircan -- a guided tour by the grand master of the dervish order, accompanied by rant of saintly trivia -- he was simultaneously focussed on the lines of the translated poem; he revealed that in periodic asides in English.

"The key is the use of the word 'sultan' here," Atilha said, almost full voice in English. Horner flinched, for the old man was watching them. "Don't worry, he doesn't understand a word of English. No, the repetition of it is intriguing, and suspicious. I hope Nilufer translated this well. Not that I don't trust her knowledge of Chagatai. But now we're in the realm of puns and puzzles. The slightest misinterpretation and she loses the whole thing. That works against her finding the treasures, of course. But also against us. At least she has the original to go back to, if she's lost. We have nothing but her English."

"Not so," said Horner. "Last night I stole her working draft of the closing couplets. She knew the puns and clues were critical here. This was the most important part of the whole damned thing and she didn't want to screw it up. She was uncertain enough about her English equivalents to leave the Chagatai originals in parentheses. She said she spent as much time on that closing poem as on the preceding 30 pages. She tried to preserve as much of the word order, the alliteration, the original rhyme as possible."

Horner pulled out the unedited version from *The Secret of Suleiman* .

Ye fools seeking truth in <u>sultan</u>'s lie
Go to <u>sultan's</u> cloister, 'neath green sky;
If to the missing pages you wish a <u>guide</u>
(<u>delalet</u>)
Go to the coffin of the <u>sultan-child</u>
(<u>sultan-velet</u>)

"A curious and awkward construction in the original just to get a rhyme: *sultan-velet*," said Atilha, the closer they came to the Pivot of the Spheres, the holiest part of the shrine. The rich calligraphic panels were lost in shadow now, the stained glass windows black as obsidian. "This is key; *guide, delalet, sultan-velet*. The word *velet* is odd. Slang now; really means brat, or kid. An urchinish connotation."

"Nilufer thinks it means Suleiman's son Selim, his final

surviving heir and subsequent sultan. She thinks the pages might be in Selim's tomb in Istanbul."

"She'll be searching the rest of her life. I think you're right, the green sky is here. But why call this the <u>sultan</u>'s cloister?"

They stood in the medieval gloom, as though 700 years had never passed. The only reminders of the present were the lettered signs for tourists in English and Turkish, denominating who was interred where. Dozens of Rumi's heirs were preserved in the arcade leading back to the entrance. And here at the Pivot of the Spheres lay only Rumi himself ... and his loyal son ... who created the whirling dervish order to honor his father's ideas the only way he knew how: by ritualizing them. The devoted son who'd defended Sems against the gossips, who alone had mourned when Sems was murdered by those seeking his precious secret. The son who knew he couldn't give anything to the world other than worshipful service of his father, and so who lived as his extension and surrogate.

And who in return was buried here beside his father, beneath the green dome.

The son whose name was curious, sounding of royal blood -- Sultan Veled.

Horner didn't breathe for a number of seconds, as Mr. Demircan stood with them reverently before the two coffins, that of Rumi and his son Sultan Veled. And then he knew only one thing the urgency of which made him keep outward composure -- voice even, measured, nonchalant, even if the vocal chords and throat were constricting with excitement.

He had to get to the casket of Sultan Veled -- the *sultan-child, sultan-velet,* the pun on *velet* and Veled revealing all -- he had to get Demircan out of here for a few minutes.

Atilha was making polite conversation with the old man, but Horner could keep his secret no longer. He said quietly in English that what they had come for was somewhere in the catafalque of Sultan Veled. And while Atilha didn't break his conversation, his nod and glance to Horner indicated he was now finding some pretext to let Horner accomplish what he needed to do.

The sarcophagus was of white marble, but a green silk coverlet lay over it, topped by the giant green silk turban befitting Sultan Veled's importance to the whirling dervishes. If it was anything like the other funerary vaults Horner had studied, it would take five men to raise the lid. Moreover, desecrating the shrine would be suicide. While he was now convinced the missing folio of the *Suleymanname* was hidden here, Horner for a sinking moment entertained the idea he might never see it.

While Atilha and Demircan now talked heatedly about Rumi's poems -- a contrived debate about whether the *Divan-*

i- Kebir or the *Mecalis-i Sab'a* were written first, Atilha's strategy of distraction -- Horner quietly stepped over to the lesser vaults, those of the Rumi family and their bodyguards who'd come on the westward trek away from Genghis Khan. He was searching for signs the folio could be hidden somewhere outside the sarcophagus, perhaps under the coverlet.

His heart leapt again when he saw there were votive niches long since abandoned when the coverlets were put on -- niches where flowers, tributes, gifts could be left. Surely such niches had been included at the two greatest tombs, the focal point where thousands had come to worship and touch until a silver fence had been erected in 1597 -- 30 years after Yunus' time.

He needed to get inside the fence.

The contrived argument had achieved its objective; Demircan was going to take Atilha back to the museum library, to settle the argument once and for all. Horner would have no more than several minutes to do his work.

As they walked back towards the entrance, the old dervish had clearly forgotten Horner was even back there. No, the most immediate question was whether a special alarm system had been installed behind the restraining fence, a trip-wire or weight- sensitive system that would ring a bell somewhere. Horner could see nothing. Finally he gambled and stepped over the fence to begin his search.

If an alarm sounded, it was nowhere nearby.

Sultan Veled's tomb-cloth was immense, dusty and heavy. Clouds of dust swirled in the beam of the flashlight as Horner made his way around it. The end was devoid of votive niches, so he made his way down the sides, keeping his ear attuned to signs of Atilha's return. Here he could see at least two recessions. The first was full of dust and withered vegetation, perhaps floral offerings from the 15th century. And in the second, he found only more dust and a corroded tube, about 18 inches long, of what he would have guessed was copper or brass because of its green encrustation.

Using a pocket handkerchief, he tried to wipe it clean. A protrusion bulged at one end ... perhaps a corroded metal clasp or hinge. As he rubbed, this one was coming cleaner than the tube proper. Then the corrosion, which wasn't corrosion at all but desiccated, rotted leather, fell away.

While also corroded, but not nearly to the depth of the other materials, an exposed imperial seal showed itself distinctly through the layer of green. He could make out the magnificent "S" with its grandiose flourishes etched into metal, the "S" of an imperial *tugra* such as the world had never seen.

The imperial seal of Suleiman the Magnificent.

Working at the end of the tube, Horner realized he

would never be able to get it open here. While it was possible this was some other votive to Rumi's son from the long-dead sultan, Horner hoped not. The tube could easily hold missing pages, rolled up, from the *Suleymanname.*

He made a quick search for other treasures -- the pages of Yunus' poetry, or the ruby chalice itself. But short of being inside the casket, these things were nowhere in evidence. His only discovery was the cylinder, and the cylinder was sealed. Temporarily witless, he could think of nothing to do other than hide it in the outer courtyard. But once there, he thought that rash. In fact, he could see Atilha and Demircan just settling their argument in the lighted office.

The tube in his overcoat liner, Horner met them as they came out into the courtyard. Demircan hadn't even realized the American had stayed behind.

For courtesy's sake, Atilha allowed the private tour to go on for another half-hour. But finally the Mevlevi leader led them to the outer gate, wishing them well on their visit to Konya. Then the two visitors walked back outside the compound. If the missing folio of the *Suleymanname* were contained within the cylinder ... and Horner couldn't entertain now the possibility it wasn't ... the author of Nilufer's translated 16th century poem must have personally hidden them there.

Chapter 43

In the privacy of Horner's room, they worked with penknives for nearly an hour to loosen the tube's top.

At last Horner withdrew a rolled cylinder of parchment. Realizing the brittleness of the paper, he had already run the shower to steam up the bath and bedroom. While this humidity would do some damage to the pigments, it was the only fast way to soften the paper to allow it to be unfurled. With the clock approaching midnight, however, the two men began to slowly unroll and flatten the pages.

Inch by inch, gauging the brittleness of the paper as he went, Horner brought it flat, and weighed it down. Several times a portion began to crack, and so he bombarded it with steam from the shower. It wasn't until the task was complete that Horner could concentrate at all on the content.

Rather than the final pages of Nilufer's translation of **The Secret of Suleiman**, this was the missing chapter-folio of the *Suleymanname* ... and if not that, one of the greatest forgeries of all time. For both the panels depicted Suleiman in illustrations stylistically identical to the manuscript Horner had examined personally at Topkapi only a few days ago. One edge of each page showed the tears where they had apparently been ripped out of the binding of the imperial biography. No, Horner concluded; if this were forgery, then it had been an inside job, a palace production, done contemporaneous with the _Suleymanname_.

While Atilha focused on the text -- in Persian, with Arabic script -- Horner couldn't help but be mesmerized by the two illustrations. For while they depicted Suleiman, they showed other things as well.

In the first panel, the aged Suleiman and the young Persian Shah Tahmasp, together with an imam who might have been the heretic Dashti himself, were signing a pact. On the table where they signed stood the *cam-i Jamshid*, the ruby chalice Persia had forever renounced to the Ottomans in a treaty 12 years previous. According to the text, this ceremony had taken place in a secret location, a palace in eastern Turkey. The year was 1565. But what was most astonishing was that the two enemy rulers had ever physically met, and in such utter secrecy.

But if the implications of the first panel were unprecedented, the second panel gave him a sense of *deja-vu*. For in this panel, the same three men -- Suleiman, Tahmasp, and the imam - held the ruby chalice jointly, and above their heads, just as in the surreal narration in Nilufer's **Secret of Suleiman** which Horner had only read last night in Antalya. That in itself was hard to understand, the joint holding of a treasure Suleiman had taken as booty from defeated Persia a decade before -- but here apparently symbolizing the pact never published or rumored, a seeming union of the two empires that had known only war and stalemate for centuries, one the protector of Sunni orthodoxy, the other the redoubt of Shi'a Islam.

Politics and religion aside, what was more astonishing in the illustration was that a beam of light -- presumably the divine light described in **The Secret of Suleiman** about the heretic ruined temple at Tendurek -- was emerging from the *cam-i Jamshid* and streaming into the distance. But the drama did not stop there; for at the terminus of the beam of light, a ball of illumination and fire had arisen, indeed nothing so much as a small sun, a star fallen to earth.

Atilha translated:

And so, the treaty between them signed
Blessed by higher power, stars aligned
The two peoples jointly share the might
The destiny of the Turks, wed to the Aryan light.

So shall they subdue the whole world
As Allah decreed in holy word hurled
From heaven to earth, given to one
Shadow of God on earth, the great
Suleiman.

Mosque in Paris, muezzin in Rome
Chant Q'uranic suras at St. Peter's dome
Dervishes will return to homeland Spain
The earth shall unite, singing mahdi's
name.

Praise the sons of Safavi and Osman
Bring Asia's heart back into one
Now the secret of God's ruby light
Is the sultan-mahdi's sword,
His world-empire's might.

* * *

The total blackness of a moonless night had fallen upon Konya. It was two in the morning, and still the two men pored over poetry and manuscript, seeking the answer.

"What do you make of it?" Horner found himself asking. "The beam of light?"

Atilha smiled, rubbed his tired face.

"Ruby laser, particle beam, or medieval science fiction ... take your pick."

"Didn't," continued Horner, "you say the chemical formula calligraphed at the Semseddin Tabrizi mosque mentioned ruby?"

"I did."

"What's a ruby laser?" Horner asked.

"You pass light of a precise wavelength through a polished ruby rod, to excite the atoms within and then augment the light wave, thus generating a laser beam. Lasers come from Einstein's theoretical work on stimulated emission. Very esoteric."

The imponderability of that kept them silent for a few minutes. Atilha spoke first.

"Lasers are only part of it. The encoded formula I've been agonizing over all these years -- because I'm certain now that's what's on the dome of the Semseddin Tabrizi Mosque, a formula -- goes well beyond ruby and lasers. It's 99 characters long."

They paused for a time, the awareness of the hour suddenly making itself felt in their aching eyes, stretched faces...

"What do you make of the references to the *mahdi* in the missing chapter?" Horner asked. "It's come up several times now ... the Dashtiya plan to co-opt the *mahdi* when he arose, and then this scheme to seduce Suleiman the Magnificent into serving as *mahdi*."

"Disturbing. Shows definite Persian influence in the conspiracy. The *mahdi* is hotly debated, sacred to Shi'a legend, disputed by many Sunni. Back when the split in Islam was widening over the proper leadership succession in the 9th century, many Shi'a maintained allegiance to the vanished 12th imam --the *mahdi* -- saying he was merely in a state of occultation in his secret tomb and would arise to vanquish the infidels. An Islamic military messiah."

Atilha lit up another bowl of his pipe.

"But back to Nilufer's translation," he said. "We've made sense of the first four lines. They got us to the missing folio. But the folio doesn't mean that much without the treasure and the rest of Nilufer's. Let's take the final couplets:"

... Muse loses vision in cold tomb
Dead muse's secret becomes man's doom.
If Allah should ask to hear your wisdom
Say these words and save his kingdom:
Ardor and ecstasy lend pattern to the world;

Poetry without ardor and ecstasy
is merely a mourning song ...

And if you be accurate in your measure
wrapped in truth you will find the
treasure
The heart of the world, in my poetry hid;
the sultan's ruby chalice, the cam-i
Jamshid.
Then gaze deep into the poetry of God's 99
names,
To learn the secret of the very-light,
Of the stars' endless flames.

"I know it's dangerous to jump," said Horner. "But the last three lines about the 99 names seem to point to your Sems of Tabriz mosque, the calligraphy you've been studying."

"They do," Atilha said. "But I want to be sure of the preceding ones ... particularly the middle."

"Such as, 'Dead muse's secret become man's doom?'" said Horner. "One man's doom, or mankind's? A warning perhaps?"

"That points to Sems again," said Atilha. "Sems was Rumi's muse, his inspiration. He carried a secret that Dashti killed him for, the secret of the very-light. The secret which the translation said would bring earth's dark end."

"What does that mean?" Horner asked.

Atilha only puffed his pipe.

They paused for a minute. Atilha opened the window to let in some of the cold steppe air. Horner could see the stars in the black sky shimmering in the heat released from the room, rising up into the night air. A dog barked in a courtyard two or three houses over. Otherwise, Konya was utterly asleep.

"The poem's so literal in the last seven lines," said Atilha. "A specific road map. But he's playing games with those previous lines. Like 'Muse loses vision in cold tomb'. What the hell is that? Sems the muse isn't actually buried at his tomb; his body was never found."

"Muse loses vision in cold tomb," responded Horner. "Maybe the Sultan's poet hid his poem and the ruby chalice in Sems' tomb."

Atilha puffed on his pipe a minute.

"You've lost me," he said.

"Muse loses vision in cold tomb," continued Horner. "The muse/poet loses -- or rather hides -- his vision -- his poem -- in the cold tomb.'"

"Then everything does come together," said Atilha, "at the Semseddin Tabrizi Mosque. It's about five blocks from here. Beautiful little Seljuk mosque. If it weren't for that building across the street, we could see it from the window now."

"But where in the mosque are they hidden, the last part of the secret poem, and the ruby chalice? Not just sitting on the casket, like the missing folio was at Rumi's tomb?"

"As for that, something draws me to the Rumi lines quoted in the middle of these closing lines," said Atilha. "Nilufer told you in the original they were more boldly calligraphed than the rest of the text. 'Ardor and ecstasy lend pattern to the world/Poetry without ardor and ecstasy is merely a mourning song.' Even she underlined them in her draft. So they stand out to the eye, making it jump down there."

"A trick?"

"More like a gateway," said the Turk. "A password, to be delivered somewhere. When would Allah ask such a thing of us mortals here on earth, at the physical, earthly level? Help me, Burt. Come down from the stars."

They both stared at the lines of verse again for a quarter hour, but to no avail. Horner's eyes were swimming from two nights without sleep. Even the adrenalin couldn't keep him up.

"So I come back again to the last two lines," Horner finally said. "They seem to tie it all together."

"They do," Atilha finally said.

"They square with your own theory about a formula hidden in the calligraphy on the Semseddin mosque dome. The translated poem practically spells it out.

"Then gaze deep into the poetry of God's 99 names
To find the secret of the very-light,
Of the stars' endless flames."

Atilha was only puffing on his pipe.

"What's that, anyway?" Horner asked. "Fusion?"

"If you take it literally."

"How else could you take it?" Horner asked.

"I don't know," said Atilha. "We'll have to sleep on it, get to the mosque tomorrow and have a look ..."

Horner sensed the Turk certainly knew more than that; but he had his own reasons for silence. Atilha finished emptying his pipe out the window, then excused himself to his room, just next door. Horner lowered the lights, but kept the poem at his bedside, running his eyes over the poem in the glow of the bedside lamp. But it was useless. He'd been at this too long, the stream of association was broken.

Sleep came to him only after an interval of rolling in this thoughts of the day: his loss of Maria ... his adultery with and betrayal of Nilufer ... the long trip up from Antalya ... the discovery at Rumi's tomb. And all that was infused with the stream of words, of poems, of rhymes and visions, that somewhere, in their artifice, held the answer to what they sought.

*   *   *

Chapter 44

And now, ten years and so many villages and
performances later, Ali Nuraddin's time was at hand ... his time
of revelation, to unmask himself and reveal his full message.

The Bedouins and tribesmen and villagers of Yemeni and
Saudi border provinces had begun to pour towards the
gathering point for days, and his pilot flew over them so he
could see the multitude encamped on the deserts of Yemen on
his behalf. In their numbers they had created a new city, and
had lit cooking fires and hung laundry out to dry, becoming a
new army, a new horde, ready to follow his message.

And when he landed and rode out to their encampment,
he could hear the wail of their radios while the dust of their
buses still converging on that place darkened the air. A stage
had been set up on the back of a truck; and it was from this
place that he would reveal himself and his message.

He found himself in a strange state of transcendental
calm, trembling with the import of what had come to him as in

dream. For his words and actions today could forever change the world, the lives of everyone who heard him. The image of his face and the sound of his words would be relayed to a hundred million faithful, in their own tongues, and for the first time would they gaze upon him unveiled.

All was in readiness.

He let them wait for a little longer than usual, for this the performance of a lifetime; and as he waited behind the black curtains he could hear the rustles of anticipation that came from the horde.

As he kept them waiting, and in order to prepare himself, he sought to imagine waking from a cave tomb in a mountain not far from here, awakening from a sleep of a thousand years. For a minute, he took himself down into absolute darkness, as close to death as he could come, until sparks and memories danced before his closed eyes. More than anything else, he decided as he meditated, to be occulted was to be concentrated; these centuries of sleep had given time to focus his powers on the mission that awaited him.

At the deepest pit of blackness, he asked himself if he would have the strength to carry this forward?

But when he opened his eyes from his imaginary occultation, and when he came out of his tent into the solar blast of sun unimpeded by anything but the driest of north desert air and the bluest of God's sky, the natural amphitheatre of Dhofar filled with 300,000 to hear his unfiltered words and see his face revealed ... he felt the strength flow from them and from the world.

They were with him on this.

They were waiting for it, as they had waited for a thousand years.

*   *   *

Chapter 45

It couldn't have been two hours later when Horner was awakened by the first call to prayer, because the sky was still ebony. Even the stars seemed snuffed out by cold blackness, leaving only one or two of the strongest visible now. He heard the muezzin's call, amplified by cheap loudspeakers, the jump in the voice telling him it was badly recorded. But even with the touch of modernity, the call was as old and powerful as the first one uttered by the freed black slave Bilal on the Arabian plain 1350 years ago. Horner lay there for a time, his eyes closed again to soothe their intense burning, the mark of not nearly enough sleep in the last three weeks.

How he wished Maria were here with him. Sometime today he would call her, try and talk her out of her intransigence. To avoid the painful vision of their relationship at an end, of her withdrawing forever into whatever it was that had taken her away from him over the last year or more, he let himself construct the best outcome possible: All hidden treasures found, all secrets revealed. It would set him free at last, to overwhelm Maria with his good cheer, his victory rush. The discoveries would truly be liberating; at the very least, enough money to protect himself from the need to scrabble every day for cash. Maybe he would start over somewhere else. Morocco perhaps, or Spain? And if that weren't possible, India; maybe India had enough of Islam left in its stones to make him feel at home.

The blackness was brightening to gray when he finally got out of bed, stumbled into the shower. By the time he came downstairs for breakfast, Atilha was already in the dining room, cracking his boiled egg, reading a German travel magazine, for the newspapers hadn't come in yet.

"Any more ideas about the poem?"

"A hunch, yes," said Atilha. "I won't know until we get to the mosque."

Horner ordered a plate of toast and eggs, received it in less than two minutes.

Afterwards they nursed their coffee and tea for a time, watching the street grow lighter with the arrival of dawn. When they went outside, the first newspaper kiosks were open, already gathering small bunches of customers at this hour.

"What's happening?" Horner noted the unusual fervor of the news-buyers.

"Mecca finally fell last night," Atilha said, "Egypt had another military coup. I thought you knew."

"I heard some of that on the way up yesterday," he said. "Radio said the Saudi Army was running things in Mecca, after the royal family left."

"They were," said Atilha. "But they turned it over to the Wahabi imams yesterday. The imams get to deal with Ali Nuraddin's request to make a pilgrimage to Mecca. A turnover will probably happen soon in Egypt, too, the Muslim Brotherhood is poised to take over. Egyptian Army could try and hold on but most of the troops will go over to the Muslim side. The only question now is Turkey. A coup here seems inevitable."

Horner stood in line long enough to get a paper. But the object of the buyers' attention, which he gathered from their whispers and talk, wasn't events in the big countries but something further south.

While he read the first dispatches, he heard the radio the vendor had put on, in itself unusual at this early hour in this most staid of religious cities. But even Konya bowed to the 21st century ritual of broadcasting a major event in the making. For in a wind of sound the radio was carrying a breathless on-the-scene report from points south, the Voice of Yemen reporting from near the Saudi border. Horner knew the station, had heard it over the years on his travels. But this was something else entirely.

The overlay was the Turkish translation. But beneath that sound thundered a peroration, a rant of poetic lilt, delivered in a dialect of classical Arabic. At times it verged on a cry, the kind of passion one only hears in coverage of Third World soccer games and in the voices of desperate politicians in faraway places; at others, it fell to a soft whisper, hardly audible above the intonations of the commentator.

The import of the broadcast was just as surreal as the delivery itself. For the radio was reporting that the *true mahdi* -- the mythic savior of Islam, the harbinger of the arrival of the Islamic end-time -- had risen in Yemen, where he had been revealed to the faithful at dawn today.

The crowd at the kiosks -- young men with goatees, silver-haired older men in the Hanafi skullcaps -- had little to say, shaking their heads as the events of the night were recounted.

The *mahdi*, said the commentator, was an orphan folk singer from Ho'fuf in Saudi Arabia who had been infused with the occulted spirit of the 12th imam after a sleep of 1,100 years.

His name was Ali Nuraddin.

* * *

Chapter 46

In the name of Allah the Compassionate and

Merciful, Ali Nuraddin cried, his voice flying off into a plethora of

systems and speakers and echoing all the way to the mountains.

In the name of Allah, came the cry back to him.

It has come to me in a vision, he cried.

Tell us, o rightly guided one, they said.

We must upend the world with the love of Allah, he

sang.

Teach us, they cried.

We must be the sword of his love, he said, taking away

the black burnoose for the first time in five years and showing

his face to the world ...

And now the time of words was gone, for the moment

gave way to a vast roar, a sound undifferentiated into idea, this

a feeling continental. As on cue, he raised his hands up into the

wind of sound and a thrust of his admirers came up onto the

stage and covered his robe of white with a cloak of black, and they placed a black turban on his head; and then was given to him a flag-banner of black silk furling in the clear wind, an obsidian strip of silk that said more than any words could attempt.

Lead us, o mahdi, they shouted; bowing, he accepted the task. And now at his right and left hand appeared twelve children; all orphans from the scorched face of the earth; on their backs he would rebuild the faith of the Prophet.

Where will you lead us, o mahdi? they cried.

To Mecca, to Jerusalem, to the whole world, he cried, and in their answer they echoed him a quarter-million-fold.

As he stepped down into the company of his followers, those who had prayed and dreamed of him, their strength and their need poured in and he felt energized by them.

It was now as though a great river had lifted him up, and he was being borne along by the river's strength. Part of himself was laughing at the ease of it.

So easily, was he the mahdi, if that was what he was meant to be ...

*   *   *

Chapter 47

The report was so disturbing to Horner that it now colored the scene and morning with its own manic brush, even though the sun was coming up bright and clear through the last yellow fluttering leaves of the oaks and birches in the park at the Semseddin Tabrizi Mosque, amidst a sky deep blue, shining down on the earth tones of Konya and its streets utterly open and unthreatening in aspect. A half dozen men were scattered in the park even at this early hour. One had his ear to a radio. Vendors were opening night-grates from shop windows across from the park. Wares were being set out for display on the sidewalk. Horner had to will himself to concentrate on what Atilha was talking about.

" -- gotten entirely out of hand," Atilha was saying. "I hope this Saudi entertainer knows what he's playing with. God help us."

The mosque was compact and simple, befitting its individualist namesake, Sems of Tabriz, this the memorial to the sharp-tongued dervish who wandered the streets of Central Asia, searching in vain for an intellect exceeding his, until he met Rumi. Member of no school, movement, sect. Immune from any need for adulation. Atilha and Horner came into the foyer and removed their shoes. Beyond it, the open meeting room spread, lit by large windows. A dark-domed nave opposite held the empty casket, for his remains had never been recovered after his disappearance in 1247.

Looking up at the base of the dome, Horner could see the calligraphed 99 names of God -- and with some difficulty, the highlighting of certain letters that Atilha now believed composed the hidden formula. Who had placed it there, so ingeniously? Not the followers of Dashti; they'd killed Sems to gain the secret. It must have been the Whirling Dervish order ...

"*'If Allah should ask to hear your wisdom/Say these words and save his kingdom,'*" recited Atilha under his breath. "When would Allah ask to hear your wisdom here on this earth, but through an earthly teacher of his laws and ways, an Islamic catechist? An imam, of course. We picked the place last night ... this mosque. There's our man now; Allah's teacher. Imam Fahir, puttering about in the morning gloom. He's gotten to know me over the years ... Atilha bey the nutty lawyer from Istanbul, come to pore over the inscriptions on the dome."

The imam took no note of them until they were upon him. He was lighting a candle in the recess where Sems' coffin lay.

"My good friend," said Atilha, coming up behind the holy man.

"Atilha bey," said the small cleric, bowing. Atilha introduced him to Horner. The imam in turn invited them to come into his quarters for a cup of tea. They did so, squatting on kilim and pillows, a modest collection of sacred texts on a single bookshelf. Fahir's sleeping quarters were just off this room.

"You have come again, to study our calligraphy," said imam Fahir with the slightest pomposity, and Atilha smiled, without agreeing.

"Imam Fahir," he said. "I've been studying the artistry here for many years, and I have not yet understood the genius of those who created it."

The imam nodded, in this compliment to the architects and calligraphers of long ago.

"But I think I've gone about it the wrong way," said Atilha. "I've always asked questions of you, in the search for truth. Yet I've never given you an answer."

The imam's eyes had widened slightly, and his head was cocked, as though the relationship had just been changed. For he was, after all, a teacher. And these visitors couldn't help but be students.

"Imam, I wish to tell you something, in the hopes that

it be the answer. Listen to my words..."

"*Ardor and ecstasy lend pattern to the world,*" recited Atilha in classical Persian. "*Poetry without ardor and ecstasy is merely a mourning song.*"

The imam spent the longest time just looking at the two visitors, a face wrapped in incredulity almost verging on the hostile. For an interval, Horner thought they would be asked to leave. The only sound was the ticking of a huge grandfather clock, audible out in the meeting room.

"Do you know those words, imam?" Atilha asked. The imam said nothing, visibly shaken. He seemed not to know how to compose himself. If these were words of special significance to him, he clearly had never expected them to come from such men as these, secular men of the world, one of them even a foreigner. The whole nature of the equation was now changed.

The imam rose slowly and led them back out into the mosque, first to the front, where he locked the door against visitors, then over towards the tomb alcove. Once there, he paused before the marble wall.

"Those words were part of my rite of training, when I took this mosque," he managed to whisper. "I was told only that those words had been handed down from the time of Rumi and Sems themselves ... and that perhaps one day I was to reveal something to the one who spoke them to me, and if not, to the young imam who would succeed me. But I did not think this would come in my lifetime, for it had not come in 20 before me."

The imam paused, as if trying to remember more through the confusion of his discomfiture. Then he seemed to be counting wall stones, from the top and then the right side of one wall of the funeral nave. When he had made his choice, he gripped one of the marble panels and sought to pull it loose.

With some grinding of surfaces and a small cascade of falling dust, he slid the stone out, revealing a compartment within the wall, like a shelf. On the shelf was a wooden box with corroded brass seals, likewise marked with the seal of Suleiman.

The imam presented the sealed box to Atilha, bowed, replaced the stone in the wall.

"My task is done," he said, and seemed prepared to have them depart with no further comment. Anticlimactic, in a way, Horner thought; to think a chalice of solid ruby weighing hundreds of carats from which Cyrus, Alexander, Genghiz Khan and Timur had all sipped might be contained within, together with the conclusion of the secret mystic poem -- it all seemed rather matter-of-fact now.

"Might we leave this here with you, Fahir bey, while we find a way to properly accommodate it?"

But Fahir bey would hear none of that. The box was their property now, and he wished it gone. The most he could do was to provide a burlap bag that had once held potatoes. Which they took, stepping out into the sunlight of the park with their new burden.

A few more men now occupied the park benches than when they'd gone in, perhaps perplexed to find the mosque doors closed on this most unusual of days. More than one pair of eyes watched them exit. And though Horner tried to tell himself this was normal, he'd been stared at brazenly every day during his residence in this part of the world, still he felt as though the whole thing were too open, exposed, vulnerable.

Once back in the room, he and Atilha began the task of opening the box, more formidable than the brass tube of the night before. But it too yielded its secrets. First exposed was a lining of what had probably once been the finest of silks, now rotted into a tangle of threads and shriveled cotton padding. Within that was a circular sheaf of ancient manuscript, tied with a withered ribbon. And within that, like the pearl within the oyster, was a small cup -- in fact, a small concave drinking-dish -- of red translucent stone.

Though Horner had not seen the original of Nilufer's **The Secret of Suleiman**, he had seen Nilufer's xeroxed copy. And he had no reason to believe this manuscript was not an authentic portion of the other. But even though the secret *masnavi* held the answers to all he'd been searching for, still he found himself drawn to the ruby cup, as had so many before him. For there was something almost tragic in its simplicity and restraint, considering all the agony of its history. Not a vulgar shimmering goblet, nor even a chalice, reflecting any imperial artistry of the scale that had built Persepolis -- this was something much older and simpler, a small dish with an almost Neolithic quality that happened to be of solid ruby, the possession of a proud tribal king who was fortunate enough to have had it, but not much more.

The surface, if it had ever had a mirror polish, had long since gone dull. For the finish was like nothing so much as the buffed feel of a piece of glass washed on a beach for 20 years, transparency diminished, iridescence reduced to that of stone rather than gem. But the finely-scratched finish made it that much more precious, for in the scratches of the ruby surface Horner could feel the weight of 3,000 years, the grinding violence of the continent of which it was the heart, the reality of the rise and fall of each of the conquerors who had sought its mystic powers. He could imagine those rough and deranged men actually pressing their desperate lips to its own, in their search for its fabled spell.

"Mankind is so small," said Atilha, breaking the moment of reverence. And so for a time they left the ruby chalice of all the Persias, the heart of Asia, the *cam-i Jamshid*, to rest unadorned and unrecognized on a cheap manufactured bedspread, while they went about the task of separating the final pages of the secret poem. And this proved especially difficult. Passages were indeed lost to corrosion and rot, for the author had used paper and ink not nearly of the quality of the *Suleymanname*. In fact it was afternoon before they felt they had finished and began to look towards the next step.

"You're in the driver's seat now," said Atilha, noting the afternoon sky had suddenly gone as gloomy as the morning had been bright. "If you're indeed certain Nilufer is in league with conspirators and murderers, now you can extract all you want from her. For in the missing folio of the *Suleymanname* alone, you have a priceless piece of antiquity, and one which reveals political and religious scandal. In this simple cup, you have the most valuable archaeological find of this decade. In the secret poem's final couplets, yet untranslated, you have the key to the mystery of the cup's long disappearance. You can dictate your terms to her ... to the world."

"If the killers let us live that long," Horner replied. But he couldn't help but be moved. More than the completion of just another special assignment, this find had grown to be the vindication of a dim, slogging lifetime, a life of slights and petty humiliations, of defeats and inevitable disappointment. Here, here in his hotel room he grasped more of a victory than had ever seemed possible.

"As a Sotheby's man, can you put a value on the cup?"

"Off the scale," Horner said. "A national treasure for both Iran and Turkey, missing for 450 years. At auction we might put a floor of, say, $250 million. But it would never go to auction. The deal would be behind closed doors, with one of the governments. Lawsuits about ownership would go on for years."

They contemplated that for a moment, until the siren-sound of the afternoon call to prayer brought them back to earth.

They focused on the next move. Atilha voted for a trip to Ankara that night. The longer they stayed in one spot, the greater the likelihood Nilufer or her clients or the Iranian cabal would track them down. And so, copies of the manuscripts made and mailed to one of Horner old Sotheby's friends in the U.S. for safekeeping, they were on a bus to the capital by sunset, the cup for which thousands had died just to sip from its magic bowl now wrapped in protective toilet tissue in Horner's duffel bag and the manuscript pages protected in an artist's portfolio. Horner's only other significant move was to make a mobile call to Nilufer's apartment in Istanbul when they stopped for ten minutes at a nondescript Anatolian town called Kulu. Not certain whether she'd have come back home upon gradually deducing that Horner had taken the treasures for himself, at least he would leave a message.

She answered in person.

"You miserable cheating bastard," she shouted, beyond herself.

"Tell me about it, dear," he said. "This is your client's punishment for killing Raine Torkelson."

"You're unspeakably stupid," she spouted.

"I have it all," he said. "All we were searching for, and more. I want you to tell our client who they need to deal with now."

All she could emit was a congested eruption of noise, the vocal manifestation of rage beyond words.

"Tell the client I'm ready to deal. If I don't hear within 24 hours, I'm gone forever."

She was actually sobbing now. He saw his busdriver waving the end of the rest-stop.

"I've got to go now," he said.

"You American bastard," she managed to say. "You don't know what you've done."

"Tell me how I reach the client. Then we talk."

"God, you're killing us," she howled.

He hung up the phone, running through the dusk to

catch the bus bound for Ankara, capital of the endless steppe, as the first drops of a rainy night fell to chill earth. On the final leg to Ankara, the bus radio reported the latest news: the Islamic Front in the Turkish Parliament, denied new elections, had called on the armed forces to join with them in forming a new provisional government more representative of the Turkish people.

The military had not yet responded. But units of the Turkish military were being deployed in all major cities and towns, particularly those in the more secular western provinces near Istanbul.

*　*　*

Chapter 48

Even as Atilha raced through a translation of the final passage of **The Secret of Suleiman** in his adjoining hotel room, the final passage found in the Semseddin Tabrizi mosque in Konya, Horner made two late-night calls to Istanbul. Outside his Ankara hotel window, where he sat in the dark, the lights of the capital wound over hills and into canyons, the haze of winter dimming the farthest outreaches of the city. His first call was to Maria at home, but when he received no answer, he wondered if perhaps she hadn't already moved out, as she'd vowed. He called her office on the off-chance she'd be there, and he was right. Workaholic to the end, she was almost alone in the bureau.

Her voice now had a tone of distance, even of distraction. The implication was she would allow him to make his gesture, his overture; then he must go away.

"Where are you?" she asked.

"In our favorite chain hotel," he said, paranoid someone else were listening. "Maria, you're in danger.

Torkelson's killer will soon know you and I are threats. Engholm has been detained. Right after your flight left Ankara, paramilitary types were dragging him down a hallway at the airport."

She didn't comment.

"I've got it all here," he said, aware of the artificial pep he'd put in his voice, sounding phony and desperate even to himself. "Everything I set out to find, and more. Maria, this is unbelievable. The story of the decade."

She laughed, but her laughter went into a strange piped-sounding echo as his mobile line crossed with two Turkish men arguing about a shipment of detergent overdue from Mersin.

These lines are probably tapped, he thought.

He fingered the beer bottle from the mini-bar, sat in the dark room high up in the hotel in Ankara. The lights off in the distance looked like beads thrown to the ground, draped over hill and hummock.

"Are you there?" she asked after a minute.

"Yes," he said, but he couldn't think of anything else to say. Her wall of detachment was wearing him down.

"Burt," she said after another minute. "I'm very busy. In case you hadn't noticed, quite a bit going on besides your own personal quest."

"A new government in Turkey, Saudis and Egyptians

collapsing, a new *mahdi*," he said. "It's all one event now, isn't it?"

"I told you there was a plot, Burt. A very big one, bigger than either one of us understood two days ago. I told you to make a choice, and you did. You went with the plotters."

"I'm a free agent," he said.

"You're their employee, or rather tool," she said. "They want what you have and they'll absolutely get it. You are only the tiniest of annoyances to them. And there's nothing we can do to stop them. I'm going to have to leave Turkey tomorrow ..."

The crossed-line arguers' volume rose now, and he could hardly hear her. He told the men to get off the line but it was clear they couldn't hear him.

"Burt," he heard her say in a lull. "At least you had a choice. I have none. Time is very short now. I am being asked to destroy my own ... and I have no choice. It is a truly horrible assignment. Shall we say goodbye now?"

The line was wavering, and three more conversations now rolled into theirs and he thought he had lost her.

"What? Destroy what?"

He couldn't hear her.

"You are destroying both our lives," he almost shouted, hoping she was there. "We had something. You don't end it this way. This isn't like you."

"It's far bigger than us now," she said, returning but barely audible.

Now the four-line crossed babble was ridiculous, and the volume went so loud that he held the phone from his ear. The lines were clearly being played with.

"Maria," he called, but she was gone in the noise.

"Rest," he then heard her say, talking over him because it seemed she couldn't hear him. "Burt, you sound awful. Good night, love."

"Maria," he shouted, in spite of himself. "Meet me at our island ... meet me there in three days." While he couldn't name it on the phone, she would know he was speaking of Kasos, between Rhodes and Crete, where they had spent the most idyllic days earlier in their relationship, when he had money and she wasn't being consumed by her job.

"I doubt it, Burt," she said.

"Meet me there," he said. "I will wait for you."

"I do love you," she said, and then was gone.

The world was ending, and she'd said she loved him. Had he heard her right?

The world falling apart, and those words from her were enough to make him feel alive again.

Had he heard her right, or just dreamed it, in the desperation of no sleep, an obsessive quest, the threat of impending death. He reposed in the sweet thought this too might all turn out well tomorrow ... that she would understand him, and readmit him into her life. In fact he reveled in the feeling, the nicest he'd had in a long while, a mood like the world was smiling at him from all quarters. He wanted to stay here in his imagination of Maria and be done with the logistics of negotiation and dealing that would have to come after.

But what had she been talking about? *I'm being asked to destroy my own*, Maria had said. And when she left Turkey tomorrow, where would she go? What was she talking about?

Was he coming unhinged mentally? Had he really just spoken with her? He even checked his call log to confirm in his own mind that he had talked to her number.

A knock at the hotel door startled Horner. For a second he felt trapped, desperate, even searched for a way to escape. But it was Atilha, handing him what he said was the first ten pages of the final section of the secret *masnavi* they had found in the mosque in Konya, handwritten in English. He'd be bringing it in as he completed it. Horner read the first lines, prepared for a lawyer's prose, but he'd underestimated Atilha, for Nilufer had found her match. This man truly could have been anything he wanted to be, and he'd chosen to be a Sufi intellectual dilettante, who paid his bills by lawyering.

Alone again, Horner paused for a moment, watching

on the silent screen of the television the latest from CNN. He'd left the picture on for most of the night, soundless, the same sequence of news stories repeated again and again. Only now did he again let his eyes focus on what he was seeing.

He'd seen it repeated in every headline wrap-up, the same footage from Al Jazeera TV, as this network often did in its hungry search to fill up a nonstop newscast. But the repetition meant the pictures were working themselves in deep, making themselves felt behind the eyes when eyes and mind did not even pay them note anymore.

The footage purported to show the black-robed *mahdi* Ali Nuraddin and his huge entourage moving north from the Yemeni desert towards Saudi Arabia late that afternoon. The invasion force was bizarre enough, an advancing sunset-illumined wave of flatbed trucks and old school buses, open pick-ups and vans bearing a multitude dressed in black, followed by thousands more on foot, horseback, even some rifles thrust into the air and criss-crossed bands of ammunition. The *mahdi* himself rode in the heart of the mass in a black Chevrolet Impala convertible, and he was waving as he pressed westward with his black banner, hood and trunk bedecked with garlands of flowers flung by the receiving masses.

And then the final shot, before the headline wrap

moved on to the new governments in Saudi Arabia and Egypt ... the forward-striding bodies of 12 child imams who were accompanying the *mahdi,* 12 little orphans from Central Asia and the Middle East superimposed by Al Jazeera TV on a panoramic shot of the advancing human wave, so they seemed to float above their continental flock, as levitated angels. The whole thing had become a choreographed ballet, brilliantly done.

This little show has been finely calibrated to appeal to some deep coding of the archetypes, he thought.

This was the last thought he had before he realized new footage had now been inserted, close-ups of the unmasked *mahdi* himself. Although this was he first time Horner and the world had been able to look at this man's face, there was something oddly familiar about it, as if he had known this youth somewhere else.

I'm being asked to destroy my own, Maria had said. And as the memory of those odd words combined with Horner's sense of knowing this Saudi messiah at another time, revelation poured like a tumbling avalanche of ice crystals into every cell in his body, as he gazed for an instant upon the face of the square-jawed young *mahdi* himself, arms stretched up to heaven in a summons to his people to rise up. For Horner looked upon the face of the 30 year-old *mahdi* Ali Nuraddin and saw in the play of multicolored pixels the same face in a halo of photos around a bedroom mirror, the face of the boy constructed out of semiannual letters and Polaroid photos: Horner looked at the face of the *mahdi* Ali Nuraddin and knew it was Ardeshir, long-lost son of his own lost love Maria, and it was clear the boy's great mission was now being played out. For Maria was the mother of the newly-risen *mahdi*, and she had been somehow called to destroy him, and all Horner could think to do was to dial her up and marvel in awe at the news.

Her line interminably busy or blocked, his impulse thwarted, he retired to bed as he read the secret poem's final words, the answer to all he sought.

*   *   *

It came to me in dream
my vision of the end,
the death of all creation
in God-light's awful spin;

For as the imam chanted
the 99 names of God,
the whole world fell in worship
of mahdi's flaming rod.
I saw the beam of white
cast on enemy camp,

I saw the sword of fire
thrown from ruby lamp.
Light poured out to westward
and struck the enemy's tents.

It blinded them in fury,
and swallowed them in wind.

The cry of a thousand was wretched,
the cry of ten thousand worse,
the field of earth's rich bounty

became mankind's black hearse.

For the fire did not stop there
but opened a hole in air,
It drew all things inside,
within its writhing lair.

Victor was merged with vanquished
and yesterday with tomorrow;
the only sound I heard at last
an empty wail of sorrow ...

Chapter 49

Now it was time, and he leapt to fulfill what he heard in his heart.

With his voice trembling, he called on his camp of 300,000 followers to march with him to Mecca the holy city, to begin a massive global campaign of civil disobedience to overthrow the existing order of fear and force with the pure love of Allah.

To all my brothers and sisters he cried, I ask you to peacefully conquer the world of fear, of greed, of terror and of hatred. Gently overthrow those who are not with us, and show them the righteous way. Do not attack them. Use force only in self defense.

But his words were drowned out, drowned out by the fact that many of the followers wished to crown him the mahdi, the reawakened twelfth imam.

And as was to be expected, his call threw the world into chaos. The religious authorities in his Saudi homeland said he was doing the work of Satan. And he triggered vast and disordered uprisings in many cities where the skyline was marked by minarets and the call to prayer.

Now he had showed his hand and his face. The world was trembling. Would the outcome be the vision he had seen in his heart for all these years ... or something else, the dark inverse?

*   *   *

Chapter 50

For most of that night Horner rolled below dreams in the depths that lie beneath for all of us ... the ether of unconsciousness, closer to death than life.

But somewhere towards dawn he rose into a lustrous vision of a beach framed by blinding white pillars of chalk and limestone, beyond them an aquamarine bowl of water that faded off quickly into the indigo depths of the Mediterranean. He could hear a fisherman singing in Greek, the old language of Odysseus that was almost a vacation for him from the complexities of Turkish and Arabic. He dreamt that Maria was at the water's edge, looking off to the horizon where the Toros Mountains of inland Turkey cut the lower edge of the sky with their serrate tops. How much he loved her; how much he wanted her, even while her own heart was torn.

For she loved another, she had just told him; she loved another across the water.

Then she came walking to him, bending over him where he lay on the sand, shutting out the blaze of the sun with her corona of hair blown in the wind. He tasted salt water drip from her hair onto his lips, felt it on his cheeks. Or was it her tears he tasted? Or were the tears his, as in this dream he realized what he had lost, what he had never had?

As he rolled in the sorrow of that, she was caressing him awake, even as he lay in his Ankara Huxley bed. And then in a rush he realized it was Maria in the flesh, here with him in the daylight world.

"I caught the first flight out of Istanbul," she whispered into his ear. "The desk clerk was very friendly ... gave me an extra key. He called me Mrs. Burt Horney."

He couldn't say anything, couldn't get his breath, only holding her to him, separated from her by the sheets of the hotel bed. He could smell the remnant cigarette smoke of the aircraft cabin, the slightly sour smell of a journalist who'd been up working all night and just escaped on the edge of the world's latest revolution.

"I was afraid if I didn't get to you now," she said, "I'd never see you again."

"Is it that bad?" he asked.

"Burt, the world's ending. It's beyond me, you, anyone. It's like an act of God."

"Maybe it is an act of God," he said. He paused before asking her about last night, if she'd seen Ali Nuraddin revealed, the scar across the cheek and lip, the scar and the face that for Horner revealed him to be Maria's long-lost son. He wanted to ask, but it seemed almost obscene now, so soon after their reunion.

"Thank God you came to me," he said. "I was going to leave this morning for Kasos, any way I could get there ... fishing boat from Antalya if nothing better. And pray you made it."

"And what if I hadn't made it here?"

"Sooner or later I'd have gone to Europe. Praying you were alright."

He was counting on customs and border surveillance to be less rigorous by that route, enabling them to transport his find and to flee the rising whirlwind of Ali Nuraddin. He had the original manuscript pages stored in a small artist's portfolio, and the ruby cup was compact enough that he could hide it in his small duffel bag.

"Did you see Nuraddin revealed?" he asked softly.

She nodded, biting her lips to contain the emotion that lay within.

"And you know?" he said.

"I think I've known for two years," she said, the tears now flowing more freely, although she did not sob. "I knew and didn't want to know. Can you believe I almost prayed that he'd died in that orphanage ... that he was gone forever, yet in that way preserved in my memory, my little boy, the angel I created and loved?"

He held her.

"Does anyone else know?" he finally asked.

"I have to hope not," she said. "Or he'd not have gotten this far. Although everyone's heard rumors of a secret."

"It would be the end of his Revolution," Horner said.

"It would be the end of him," she said. "Imagine the holy inquisition over that revelation. Not only is the *mahdi* the son of an American, he is the son of an American reporter, whore of the Great Satan and the CIA."

"They would execute him in a minute," she added.

"Do you think Torkelson knew?" he asked. "Was that why he wanted you so urgently that morning?"

"If Torkelson didn't know, perhaps he was close to knowing," she said. "The heirs to the ancient Dashtiya Brotherhood, who now call themselves the Elect, killed him because he was so inquisitive. Digging in Tehran and everywhere else. He was onto Nilufer, the pillaging of the ruins. They knew he was the enemy."

"And why haven't they gotten you?" he asked, horrified at his line of thinking. "You're hardly a friend of the mullahs either."

"The Elect aren't mullahs or fundamentalists," Maria said. "They aren't even Muslims. They are an ancient Persian cabal trying to use Islamic religious fervor for their own ends.

They still dream that Persia could rule the world, and with them in charge."

"Don't the ayatollahs know this?" he asked.

"They have no idea. They are being used."

Atilha's knock on the door jarred them into the present.

* * *

Chapter 51

Atilha too was overjoyed to see Maria had come to be with them, and he hugged her with as much affection as he would have a daughter. For she too had been in the Sufi study group that had brought Atilha and Horner ... and Nilufer ... together for the first time years ago.

The lawyer waited until the Americans had bathed and packed. Then they went down to the Ankara Huxley's sumptuous buffet breakfast. If there were any authentic Turks present, they were few, for the only people who could afford the Huxley's prices for rooms and meals were foreigners on expense accounts.

"You heard the coup rumors from the hotel staff?" Atilha asked.

"Not rumors anymore," Maria said. "If the new military-Islamic coalition hasn't been announced already, it will be soon. A suspension of the Fatherland government, for national security reasons."

"God help us," breathed Atilha. "Last night, watching

Nuraddin on television, I had the most terrible vision. That here was my new leader, in his turban and scarf. That I a Turkish lawyer would be ruled by a Saudi mystic poet. Something out of the Middle Ages."

Horner almost spoke, but Maria's stricken look kept him silent about her son's identity. Instead, he repeated Maria's comments about an enormous plot to overthrow governments and make Ali Nuraddin the *mahdi* of all Islam, and the fact the Nilufer was involved, almost certainly working for the Iranian mullahs. He assumed the search for the folio of the Suleymanname was part of the plot, for it led to the secrets about the Dashtiya temptation of Suleiman to serve as *mahdi*, and the ancient pact between Turkey and Persia, and ultimately to the *cam-i Jamshid*, without which they believed no conqueror could hold the heart of Asia.

Even as they engaged in the outwardly placid ritual of breakfast, Horner wondered if their lives were in danger even now. He scanned the room, almost sorry he'd picked such a conspicuous place in the nation's capital at such a momentous time.

Speaking of Maria," said Atilha. "*Herald Tribune* carried one of your stories today." He handed it over. Horner read, "Turkish military now allied with region's Islamic sweep?" The story was centered around reports that the Turkish military had held discussions with Iran about a new military alliance to replace NATO.

"Jesus," he said. "You can't keep writing articles like that. They'll have you in jail for sedition."

"That was my last," she said. "I should have caught the midnight to Frankfurt last night. But I came to be with you."

"Are we ready," asked Atilha, "to say the rise of the *mahdi* and the fall of Egypt, Saudi Arabia -- and Turkey -- are the work of the reborn Dashtiya, or someone following in their footsteps?"

"We call them the Elect now," said Maria. "They've managed to channel public discontent and religious fervor to their own ends."

The conversation was interrupted by a trio of Army trucks, canvas-shrouded beds loaded with troops in combat gear, rumbling down the street towards downtown.

"Coup preparations?" Horner asked.

"It's looking like that," said Atilha. "While travel may be difficult today, you really should be out of the country. And Maria for sure. They'll not let her file reports like that any longer --"

"I think Kasos is the safest, via Antalya," said Horner. "They won't have the smaller towns under such close surveillance yet."

"Better to leave now than later," said Atilha. "There's always lots of confusion here in the initial days of a coup.

Your Kasos plan might work, if you do it today."

Atilha changed the subject back to the 99-character encoded formula on the dome of the Semseddin Tabrizi Mosque in Konya. Based on what he'd read of the translated manuscript the night before, the ruby laser was not the end of it, not the very-light of God in itself. The laser was only an element, a tool. Though the poet was only equipped to describe a ball of fire where the ruby light struck, Atilha wondered if the Sufis hadn't gone into advanced particle physics. As he talked about things like plasmas and carbon fusion, Horner tried to jot notes on a napkin, because the esoteric formula was beyond him.

"I'm especially worried about the opening verses of the final section," Atilha said. "The 'writhing hole in air', 'yesterday merged with tomorrow.' It's more than imagery. As soon as you leave, I'm going to the Hayrettepe University library ... they have a decent physics collection."

"But Atilha," said Horner. "Do you believe two Sufi dervishes 800 years ago could have divined the secrets of astrophysics and fusion and lasers? Be honest with me."

The 21st century Turkish Sufi sat and thought for a moment.

"Burt, there were always stories that the most developed Sufis had achieved out of body, time travel, major chemical reactions and so on. At the least, ancient Arab and

Persian scientists were playing around with ideas of relativity, cloning, the theory of evolution."

"But you aren't answering me," said Horner. "Do you believe scientists or mystics could do any of that 800 years ago? And if so, how?"

Atilha smiled again.

"The true Sufis believed that in the highest stage of spiritual enlightenment, time, space and the physical universe could be manipulated, through meditation and thought. They believed the highest souls had achieved oneness with God, and could be instruments of his power, which was absolute."

"Do you believe that?" Horner pressed.

"It doesn't matter what I believe," Atilha said.

As they finished breakfast, Horner voiced his uncertainty about traveling with priceless antiquities like the manuscripts, and particularly the Cam-i Jamshid. He wondered if Turkish customs in Antalya would give him a hard time.

"I'm not worried about the Greek side at all. It's Turkey."

Atilha agreed.

"And should you be ... detained," Atilha added "... you're in a much better bargaining position if you have the cup in a safe place."

By now they were out in the lobby, the bustle of morning check-out giving everything a driven, harried air. Maria and Atilha went back up to the rooms, to get the remaining luggage.

Horner noticed a Worldwide Courier kiosk over by the concierge. Two Turkish women uniformed like flight attendants stood, awaiting business.

"Do you deliver to the Greek Islands?" Horner asked one.

"We deliver Worldwide," she said robotically.

"Kasos?"

"Worldwide," she said.

"How long?"

"Second business day," she said.

"What about customs?" he asked.

"Turkish customs you clear here. Greek is different. You have to pick up at the terminal there."

"You mean you can clear something here?"

"At this desk," she said. "We are both customs agents."

Horner fumbled in his carry bag, brought out the ruby chalice of all the Persias.

"Can you box?" he asked.

She pointed to an array of boxes she could offer.

"Would you like to fill out a declaration?" she asked.

Horner began writing. He identified the cup as

provincial glassware, valued at $50. He insured it for that amount.

"Can I see the glass?" she asked. Hesitating a few seconds, he unwrapped it for her.

She held it up to the light.

"Where you bought this?" she asked.

"... Konya," he said.

"You have receipt?" she asked.

"Uh... uh... perhaps in my room, or bag."

"And you paid $50 for this?" she said with rising tones, her partner now looking at the ruby cup. Now the two of them were talking in Turkish dialect. There were exclamations.

"Is there a problem?" he asked.

"We can't believe you pay $50 for this," she said.

He felt himself melting, wondering now what to do ... whether to grab the cup from them and bolt from the lobby. Did they have authority to seize antiquities?

"I ... just can't locate the receipt," he said. "Perhaps I shouldn't ship it."

"I'm from Konya," she said. "Where you bought this?"

"Konya Oteli," he said. "The shop there."

"Owner is a criminal," she said. "He should be in jail."

"I'm so sorry," he said. "Thanks for your help."

She wouldn't let go of the cup.

"He is a criminal for charging so much to tourists," she continued. "Old Konya glass like this you can buy for $5. My uncle sells it."

Horner only breathed.

"The export duty is 10% for $50 export of glassware," she said.

He paid her $5.

He watched as the ruby chalice of all the Persias was thereby shipped to Burt Horner, c/o the Hotel Poseidon, Kasos, Greece.

He watched the box be labeled, stamped, sealed, and thrown into a small bin that would be taken to the Ankara airport that afternoon and shipped to the Worldwide Mediterranean hub in Rome, then on to Athens and Kasos the next day.

Now Horner madly dialed Genghiz, but the circuits to Istanbul were blocked and the operator said it might be two hours before they opened. That was too long. Horner wanted them to catch the first flight to Antalya, and they had little more than an hour to make it ...

Atilha and Maria came down with the remaining luggage, borne by a bellboy. After checking out, Horner let the bellboy call them a cab from the taxi-stand, while they both embraced the Turk and wished each other well. But time was of the essence now, and their leave-taking lasted only a minute, before they went their separate ways, Atilha to a local university library, Horner and Maria to the airport.

"Bon voyage," said Atilha to both, knowing it might be many days, or longer, before they met again.

*   *   *

Chapter 52

Horner's taxi driver shot into the morning traffic, claiming he knew a shortcut through the city that would save fifteen minutes from the hour-long trip to the airport, and a bit in fare too. And so off they sped, descending with the gathering flood of rush-hour traffic into the winding canyons of Ankara, airport-bound.

The driver had told the truth, for the main route visible off to the left and downhill seemed obstructed by military movements. Horner was ahead of schedule when they emerged from the other side of the city and raced down the airport highway, between huge dry hills, yellow grassy buttes. While there was heavy military traffic, it was all coming towards him, Ankara-bound. Troops brought in for riot control?

"Part of me feels strange, going with you to Antalya," Maria said, watching the yellow arid grasses of Anatolia shoot by the window. Horner felt his heart stopping again, for the second time today.

"Where else would you go?"

"Mecca," she said. "The press pool was organizing a flight last night. I almost went."

"Do you want to get shot?"

She didn't attempt an answer.

"Maria, you yourself said the world was ending. You'd have no journalistic immunity or protection in Nuraddin's new world. I'm sure they've got you on their list already. It would be insane."

Her jaw was set, and he could see his words were not penetrating.

The trip to the Ankara terminal was always agonizing, especially if one was late for a flight; the 30-mile trek seemed like 300. That was why Horner felt himself rise with irritation when the driver slowed down no more than halfway there, and despite Horner's questions, turned off to the right onto a dirt road.

"What the hell?" he asked in Turkish. "We need to go to the airport."

The driver nodded apologetically, yet kept up his detour until they were out of sight of the highway and behind the ridge of hills that defined the north of this valley. Horner assumed the man was stopping by to visit a friend, or pick up a package to mail at the airport. Horner knew the routine and it pissed him off. But rather than a nameless little village or a farmhouse, they pulled up to a desolate spot where two other cars and a half-dozen men waited, smoking cigarettes.

Three of them wore black scarves over the lower halves of their faces, revealing only their eyes. The other three wore no disguises.

Looking at the scarved ones, Horner could only think of Ali Nuraddin.

"Good God," said Maria.

But of the other three Horner's first thought was police, for they had the look of government about them -- tough and mustachioed to a man, with short haircuts, cheap suits like Inspector Aziz. Yet honest police wouldn't have done this off the road. Their capture would have been forthright, in his hotel room or at breakfast.

Then he thought of the fall of the government, murky dealings, and that made more sense. As soon as the car stopped, the three men in black pulled Horner and Maria outside, frisked them, took their passports and identity papers. As the search went on, a curious bitter smell like fermented wheat or bread drifted up to Horner's nose, a smell that triggered memory, a scent of deja vu ... but only when he connected it with the black scarves. In a rush he recalled the morning he'd found Torkelson dead, the collision with one of the killers in the stairway, his breath heavy with the Persian hallucinogen *haoma*.

The man who had dropped the prayer cloth with the embroidery of Sems of Tabriz being stabbed to death ...

One in particular was glaring at Horner, and when their eyes locked for a second, Horner knew it <u>was</u> him, the one he'd knocked unconscious on the stairs when they collided. But did this man remember him? Was this meeting coincidence ... or had he been on Horner's trail ever since, and only now had made his move?

The same man -- perhaps Torkelson's killer -- opened Horner's and Maria's bags and cursorily searched them; the leaves of the *Suleymanname* were unwrapped, briefly examined and put back in the bag. One of the other men kept the bag with the treasures.

The lead captor held Maria and Burt at gunpoint while a portlier young man without scarf was nervously talking into a cellular phone in Farsi.

The man on the phone was gesticulating towards them.

"He's arguing about treasure," she said under her breath. "Apparently they were expecting more, with the manuscripts."

This inane discussion went on for nearly two minutes while they stood there in the Anatolian sun. If they knew he had found the chalice and yet he didn't have it, they could torture the truth out of them in the most gruesome way. God, they could threaten Maria to pressure him. He was sick he'd pulled this greedy stunt, sick he had put them in even more danger. Sick he had been so stupid to think he could get away with all this.

"Apparently a flight is leaving for Iran," Maria said quietly. "They have a schedule to keep. Their superiors will be angry at a delay, and angrier over the loss of the chalice."

The portly young man, now sweating rather profusely, came towards them, forcing a smile.

"You have treasure?" he asked in broken English.

"Treasure?" Horner heard himself feigning.

"A treasure cup," the man expanded.

Horner shrugged.

"What cup?" he said. "All I have are manuscripts."

The false smile was flickering; now discussions about the advancing hour resumed, in Farsi, between the chubby man and Torkelson's killer.

The scarved man cursed, opened the back door of a vehicle, and motioned with his pistol for Horner and Maria to get in.

"Could I see a badge?" Horner asked.

His answer was to be handcuffed, then literally kicked into the middle of the back seat by Torkelson's assassin, surrounded on either sides by captors. Driving back down to the highway, they turned towards the original destination, the airport.

*   *   *

Chapter 53

Horner's back throbbed with being kicked, because the man had caught Horner with the narrow heel of his boot just to the right of his spine, in the kidney. He hadn't taken a deliberate blow like that since adolescence, and he was in shock at this physical affront. To take his mind off the pain, he studied his surroundings, the details. The cars were new. He hadn't noticed government plates. When they finally reached the airport, they drove past the passenger entrance and headed instead towards the air cargo terminal.

"You're shipping us somewhere?"

Horner's humor was ignored or not understood. They drove to the security checkpoint, slowing down but not stopping at the guard post. The military guard nodded and admitted them on facial recognition, disappointing Horner because he'd hoped to see an ID flashed or some such that might tell him who was in charge here.

Horner and Maria were both strangely calm, serene, through all of this.

They were driven around a vast hangar used for

Turkish Airlines air cargo, and then taken straight out onto the tarmac.

Over by the passenger terminal, he saw a Turkish Airline plane parked, the one they were to have flown to Antalya. But their captors took them in the opposite direction.

It was a magnificent craft, Horner had to admit to himself, a snow-white 747 with the most tasteful of royal blue markings on its nose and tail. "City of Isfahan," identified in both English and Persian script just below the cockpit, had its huge rear cargo bay door just being raised, and a single mobile stairway led up into the fuselage.

The Iran Air freighter was surrounded by at least ten plainclothes guards, automatic rifles drawn. The time was early morning at the beginning of winter, the sun bouncing off the white fuselage and the silver wings still wet from the rains of the night before. The huge turbines were just beginning to turn, a sound that had always given Horner just the slightest bit of thrill, the anticipation of departure.

It had the same effect this morning.

Their captors took them over to the mobile stairway, their hearing overwhelmed by the whine of the engines as they started their turn. He'd never been this close to one when starting, probably because there was danger the big fans would suck a passenger in the front or incinerate them with the backwash, so commercial airlines didn't submit their paying patrons to such risks.

But what amazed him most of all, as he climbed that stairway into the huge Persian jet, the whiteness of it like Moby Dick, the magical Farsi inscriptions and the airline logo of the mythic Persian bird that had adorned Sufi robes and *kilims* since time immemorial, what amazed him more than the danger of the engines turning so close to him and the guns pointed vaguely in his direction and the fact he was being kidnapped, was the woman at the top of the stairs waiting to welcome them on board.

She should have been no surprise, for he had suspected her all along. No, the surprise was because she was apparently as much a captive as he and Maria, and more so because she had obviously been submitted to significant torture and abuse. For her once-luxuriant hair had either been mostly burned or cut off, her face with the pouting lips he had found so odd and yet alluring was darkened with a bruise across one cheek, her luminous left eye appeared swollen shut, and in overall aspect she looked utterly broken and forlorn.

As he looked at the captive Nilufer, it began to dawn on him that he was responsible for her punishment -- his double-cross and disappearance having left her vulnerable to the same forces that had captured them and were now leading them onto the Iranian jet freighter. And seeing her in that state, the stakes of what he had done suddenly became even more extreme. He saw now that he would undoubtedly have to surrender all he had gained, just to survive and to protect the others close to him; even survival was not guaranteed. And not only had he put Nilufer and himself in jeopardy, he had drawn Maria into the net.

Nilufer was also handcuffed, and another member of the Elect held her upper arm as she was displayed there in the aircraft doorway for the two of them to see and contemplate as they climbed the stairs. Completing the symbolism of Nilufer's downfall was the fact she'd been forced to wear a traditional Shi'a black chador, and the surprise was as much the severity of the garment, as seeing Nilufer forced into the political conformity and submission this cloth implied. It also gave her the aspect of a martyr, a Hester Prynne scorned for her sin, a Joan of Arc bound for fire and the stake.

Whatever her other qualities, never had Horner thought of Nilufer as ascetic ... but today, she looked it.

"I warned you," Nilufer said softly, as they were escorted up the stairs and past her.

He attempted to reach out and touch her arm, but they were both handcuffed, so all they could do was look into one another's faces for a few seconds.

And then the leader of the assassins rammed Horner through the door with a full body blow, knocking him to the floor of the aircraft hold. Horner lay there a minute, stunned, gasping for his breath until one of his other captors expressed a limited kind of mercy and helped him up. Maria too was brought aboard and they were all made to strap in, for their captor and nemesis -- his name was Hamza -- told them they would be flying to Iran, and the air was rather choppy that day.

*   *   *

Chapter 54

He made the following speech, which was broadcast to the world.

To my brothers and sisters of the faith:

The heart of the world has been broken. Yet just as we can heal our own hearts with the truth of Allah's love, so can we heal the heart of the world, by bringing the truth of Allah's love into our everyday lives.

Brother and sister Muslims, I say to you, open up your minds. For there is no greater tool of Allah's love than the minds he gave us. He gave us brains that we might think, invent, create. And he gave us freedom of choice so that we might be more than slaves to him. Brother and sister Muslims, set yourselves free for the glory of God.

To the leaders of Islam he said:

If you have been doing Allah's will by showing mercy and compassion and love above all, then peace be upon you. But if

all you have done is judge others and inspire fear and
narrowness of thought and increase divisions among men, then
you will face the wrath of the supreme judge.

To the rulers of the Arab world he said:
I hrow off your greed and your lust for power. If you
have been blessed with power, use it for the good of the people.
If you have been blessed with riches, then it is upon you to share
half your wealth with those who do not have it ... to build a
better world, with schools, hospitals and nurseries.

To the rulers of Iran he said:
Shame upon you, who had the opportunity to do God's
work but instead gave in to greed and fear and lust for power.
Throw off your false faces and your lies. Cease your preparations
for war. To those who work on nuclear bombs, thrown down
your tools and come out into the shining light of the love of
God.

To the Jews of Israel and the world he said:
I tell you that I am one of you, so do not fear me. I am
Jew and a Muslim at the same time, for in Allah's eyes there is
no such division. Come pray with me side by side and come do
good with me and make peace with me. Soldiers of Israel, lay

down your arms and come into the arms of me and your Muslim brothers and sisters.

To the Palestinians he said:

My dispossessed brothers ... If you wish to return to your beloved homeland and call it your own, then leave behind your weapons and your anger. Walk with me in peace towards your Israeli neighbors. Let us all sit together under the olive tree and drink the tea of God's love.

To the Christians of the world he said:

I tell you that I am one of you, even if you do not know or believe me. For I revere Jesus as much as you do. Join with me to hasten the days of Revelations. The love of Allah is the love of Jesus. Come pray with me side by side, and do good works, and make peace with me.

To the rulers of America and the West he said:

Believe me that I want peace and freedom among men more than I want my own life. Know that I will fly to the sun and the moon to bring peace and freedom to this world. I call upon you to give up your fear and your greed and your arrogance, to lay down your arms that injure so much of the world, and to open up your treasures to help the poor. Come join with me to build the shining city upon the hill, so that all the world may share in its freedom and riches.

And then he said to everyone:

All of you, put away your fear and divisions and come with me to Mecca, where we begin our Revolution.

Come with me.

* * *

Chapter 55

It was a beautiful early winter morning, the kind of sunrise you can find only on the Asian steppe in December, a combination of elevation and aridity and the convoluted folds of earth all merging to give everything a clarity and definition not found anywhere else in the world. The skies and air were particularly clear from an overnight rain.

After Horner and Maria were brought on board the 747 at Ankara's airbase to join Nilufer as prisoners of the Elect, they were flown east at low altitude in silence, into the morning sun rising into the sky. The heart of Turkey spread out before them now, this land that had been their second home in exile from America. They were flying so low they doubted they were higher than the Pontics to the north, while below, they could see the yellow tumbling canyons of Anatolia, and off to the south, the beginnings of the labyrinths of Cappadoccia.

"Sit," ordered Hamza their captor, who Burt whispered was probably Torkelson's murderer, as he ordered them into crude sling seats that hung from the walls of the gutted aircraft. He bustled throughout the cabin, revealing with his entrances and exits major activity underway through a door to the rear, which led into the cargo bay. As the door swung open, the captives could see a group of the Elect in camouflage, some unmasked, in quiet conversation over maps and charts, or in uneasy silence.

"The Elect have been very good at infiltrating everybody on all sides," Maria observed.

"But you get your wish," Burt said.

"Which one?" Maria asked.

"A free trip to Persia," he said.

"Shut," snapped the gunman in Farsi, and he kicked Burt so hard in the shin that Horner briefly thought about rising from his seat and attempting an attack, even if doomed.

But he didn't, for such an expression of anger would almost certainly result in more pain and death, and so he simply lowered his eyes and studied the floor of the hold with an opaque stare.

Then Hamza the assassin sat on a battened shipping container, pawing through the Americans' bags and effects. For the longest time he sat with the captured treasures, first studying the centuries-missing chapter-folio of the **Suleymanname**, depicting Suleiman in his long-hidden pact with Iran and the high priest Dashti to dominate the world for Islam. He commanded Nilufer to translate aloud the final couplets:

And so, the treaty between them signed
Blessed by higher power, stars aligned
The two peoples jointly share the might
The destiny of Turks, wed to the Aryan light.

So shall they subdue the whole world
As Allah decreed in holy word hurled
From heaven to earth, given to one
Shadow of God on earth, the great Suleiman.

"Praise Allah," Hamza said to no one in particular.

But then he drew near to Horner.

"Where it is, you fuck?" he whispered.

"Where is what?"

"The treasure cup," he said.

"I couldn't find it," Burt said, while Maria wondered if by miracle the agents who must have been on them at the Huxley hadn't seen him ship the cup to Kasos?

Hamza tried to slap him, but Burt pulled back, so only his chin was caught by one of Hamza's overgrown fingernails, so that it cut Burt and left a line of blood, which slowly began to drip down his face.

"Without cup," Hamza said, "you and your friends die."

Burt sat, blood dripping from his chin.

Now the man who had held them for the last hour, the man who had probably killed Raine Torkelson, who had dropped the prayer cloth revealing the bloody cult of the dervish killers, who had been waiting for this moment, rose from his sling, eyes glistening, and put his pistol to Burt's head.

"Where?" Hamza asked.

"You can't fire away in an airborne 747," Burt said.

The man duly put the gun barrel in Burt's ear and pulled the trigger, which only clicked in an empty chamber, or misfired.

Maria screamed involuntarily, the noise and pitch of it startling her captors much more than the misfired pistol. Hamza glared at her, and she thought he was going to begin torturing her. But then he turned back to Burt. And as Horner tried to regain his composure, the killer and his two colleagues burst out in an adolescent gale of cackling laughter.

"Hamza isn't concerned with the niceties of jet aircraft technology," Nilufer said in a hoarse voice.

Hamza cocked his pistol again.

And it was now, desperate to give them at least a

fighting chance, and to end this abuse of Burt and Nilufer, that Maria spoke.

"Get my old leather purse," she told Hamza and his attendants in Farsi, which after some discussion was duly produced.

"Separate the lining," she said, "and reach inside." She knew that there he would find a crude and scuffed ruby-colored dish about the same size as the sacred antiquity Horner and Maria had shipped out only that morning.

Warily, Hamza probed into the lining, felt the inner firmness revealing a small circular object that the original search must have taken for a woman's compact ... as she intended.

He pulled the chalice replica out, and held it up to the light.

Horner almost said something, for a few seconds stunned and confused to think that Maria had somehow kept the real ruby chalice ... but in confusion, he held his tongue.

"Let him have the cursed thing," Maria said. "It isn't worth dying for."

As soon as Hamza fully comprehended what the object was supposed to be, he laughed idiotically, clutched it to his breast, again held it to the light, and then poured some seltzer water into the cup and drank it down.

"You are smart American whore," he said to Maria,

and winked.

Now he dropped back into his seat, where he began to play with a ghastly pink-stained stiletto dagger, perhaps the very one that had killed Torkelson.

With great flair, he removed his shoes and socks and began to clean his toenails with the blade.

As they continued their flight east, the 747 climbed well into the sky. Eventually the passengers recognized Erzurum, and could pick out on this arid day the same route Horner and Maria had taken by bus to Dogubeyazit three days ago. The four-hour bus ride went by in minutes now, until on their left side the snowy massif of Ararat appeared, seen now from above, not below. And to the south, the range of Tendurek, where the Dashtiya temple and mysterious encampment lay hidden in eternal cloud.

"Where are you taking us?" Horner finally had the courage, or foolishness, to ask.

Hamza glowered at him for a second, then went back to his toenail trimming without answering.

"We are honored guests of an Iranian ... faction," Nilufer said in her diminished voice, which still managed to capture a hint of her innate irony. "I overheard we are to stop somewhere and pick up a delegation of Revolutionary Guard. Then we and the ruby chalice will all be taken to Ali Nuraddin. We are the Elect's gifts to the new mahdi."

Then Hamza stood up, and while standing, did an asinine little pirouette. He gave his prisoners a look of false pity, before he took the manuscripts and the other treasure, gently repacked them in their protective portfolios, and carried them into the rear of the freighter. As he left, two more of the Elect passed through the cabin on the way to the cockpit.

Thereupon ended the first interval of the captives' conversation with Hamza. The likelihood that they would again see freedom, or even survive, looked quite doubtful. The likelihood that this ruse of the false chalice would succeed -- which Atilha had forced on Maria even as Horner was shipping the real thing to Kasos -- was so slim Maria hadn't wanted to think about it. And when it was found out, she feared, they would be in even greater danger.

She only hoped that there were no professional jewelers amongst the mullahs and terrorists who now had them. The false chalice was a garnet replica, itself at least a hundred years old, that Atilha had managed to find during that single afternoon in Ankara for just this kind of emergency. Maria was later to learn that for several centuries there had been a cottage industry in making copies of the ruby chalice, in the hopes that one would be so skillfully made it would be declared the real thing, bringing riches to its fabricator.

And while Horner was apoplectic to know when and how and why his friends had done such a thing, he could do little more than stare at Maria in mystification ... and perhaps a little admiration.

Then Maria took a few moments to pray.

*   *   *

Chapter 56

When they were well inside Iranian airspace and Hamza had left them alone for some time, Nilufer felt confident enough to start talking. And she said that the ruby chalice was a bonafide treasure, and the Elect were superstitious enough about its powers that they believed the Peaceful One needed to have it in hand for the plan of revolution to succeed.

"How long have you been working for these people?" Horner asked.

"I was never sure," she said, "until I was ... detained ... last night. I'd hoped it was the CIA that was paying us. I was wrong."

"So the Elect are the Revolutionary Guard?" he asked.

"My God, Horner," Nilufer sniffed, "is that the best you can do? No, nothing so mundane. The Elect are a tiny secret society, all that's left of the Zoroastrian high priesthood, the old fire worshippers, magi now masquerading as a sect of Shiites. They still think Persia should be the center of the world. But their old Zoroastrian worship of fire and light seems to have morphed into an obsession with lasers and fusion. Most of the ayatollahs don't even know about this, much less the government or the people. The Elect are deeply infiltrated into the Iranian nuclear program, and always have been. Just like they tried to seduce Suleiman 500 years ago, they tried to seduce the Shah 30 years ago when he decided to go nuclear, and he almost fell for it. When he wised up, the Elect joined the Islamists and helped overthrow him. That's why he had SAVAK pillaging the tombs, looking to understand their plot."

"And now?" asked Horner, trying to absorb all this.

"They've managed to seduce the ayatollahs into their quest for ruby enrichment, fusion, particle beams. Again they've played on Iranian memories of grandeur lost, Shiite ambition, belief in the mahdi. Quite a mix, to say the least."

"How did they find us?"

"Their plants in Turkish intelligence must have had taps and tails on my place and yours, your driver Genghiz, and certainly Maria. I gather your call to her bureau last night did it, of course. You might as well have put your whereabouts on a billboard."

Horner ignored the barb.

"Why did they want the manuscripts?" he asked.

"For obvious reasons," she said. "They are incriminating historical evidence of the first secret Turkish-

Persian alliance. The Elect don't want their second alliance to fail."

"The Shah's SAVAK had been on the same trail 30 years before," she continued, "when his agents had been gathering intelligence on the Elect and its ancient cabal. But the Shah was overthrown before he could find it."

The new Elect, she added, also wanted the manuscripts to help find and decipher the formula associated with the 99 names of God. Apparently they had not yet gleaned it was hidden in the calligraphy at the Semseddin Tabrizi mosque in Konya.

"The Elect," she said, "believe the formula was theorized -- or intuited -- by the Sufi alchemists 700 years ago, and holds the key to the process of stellar fusion ... the very-light of God. It was the same secret Sems of Tabriz shared with Rumi, the secret for which the Dashtiya murdered Sems in Konya."

"At the least," she concluded, "they believe the formula and perhaps the precise curvature of the ruby chalice may hasten Iran's ability to enrich vast quantities of uranium for their arsenal using ruby lasers, a theoretically possible and much faster method than anything the Americans or Russians have ever perfected. They sincerely believe the Sufis intuited shortcuts to major discoveries, which they can recreate through modern methods and reverse engineering."

" At best," she whispered, " it could lead to things like particle beams as described in the missing folio of the Suleymanname. With that kind of power, the Elect and their unwitting Iranian dupes could upend the world order."

"So Ali Nuraddin is their man after all," said Horner, looking quickly at Maria as though he had offended her.

Nilufer looked woefully out of the window.

"Only he has the answer to that one," she said to no one in particular.

*   *   *

Chapter 57

It was now coming to its end ... or its beginning.

He was encamped with 300,000 followers near the Saudi border in Western Yemen, preparing a triumphal midnight flight to Mecca.

As his followers encircled Mecca, he was working on the sermon he would deliver tomorrow, the dawn of the new order.

He would call for a peaceful overthrow of corrupt governments across the Muslim world.

A massive telecast was being readied to carry this message around the globe.

He read that the Americans were claiming that his intent was to create a multinational Islamic caliphate, and they said that as something to be feared.

The time was winding down to the final moments. His vision was still not yet born, for many forces were gathering to oppose it.

Yet it was his moment of truth. His entire existence, and that of all those who followed him and feared him, was now *focused down to this single point of light.*

It was now.

Even as he readied himself, all the old things, the things of the world of yesterday and today, were in chaos. Stock markets were falling, the price of oil was soaring, armies were being gathered.

A man of peace, now it was his time to go into battle.

Would Allah be with him? Or was he the newest martyr, another story to be added to the long chronicle of tragedy and defeat in this world?

Chapter 58

"Sounds like the Apocalypse," said Horner.

"The Elect intend to present the *mahdi* with the ruby chalice before he speaks at the Kaaba tomorrow," Nilufer whispered. "At some point in the near future, once he has established himself as the true *mahdi,* they will blackmail him with their proof that he is half-American and heretical and a fraud; if he agrees to obey them, he will be allowed his life and leadership of his movement as a figurehead. If he does not, he and his American mother will be killed. He will be declared a martyr and replaced with a puppet of their own liking. "

"If he cooperates, no government will be able to deny them," she intoned, now far back in her dark hooded chador so that only her single huge unbattered eye shone out from within. "And if the Elect martyr and glorify him, they may well be able to accomplish more than he ever could."

And sometime after she finished talking, the plane began to descend over the Iranian desert, landing at midday on an airfield unmarked by anything other than a pair of prefabricated barracks. It was 20 miles from the nearest city, Shiraz to the southwest, which Horner recalled he had visited occasionally during his youthful trips to these parts.

But the seemingly anonymous spot took on a spectacular irony when Horner was able to look off to the north, out the windows on the other side of the aircraft. He interpreted for his friends a dun-colored set of ruins barely distinguished from the landscape around them. In a recognition that made him laugh in irony, he looked out upon Persepolis, the once-grandiose and now forgotten symbol of Iranian myth and imperialism, the old capital of Cyrus and Darius. The fallen Shah had staged the exorbitant 2,000th anniversary celebration of his rule here only three and a half decades ago; his Islamic successors had consigned Persepolis to the closet of embarrassments, an unwanted reminder that Iran had been here long before Islam.

"Why Persepolis?" Horner asked Nilufer.

"Because it has a huge runway far from any towns or cities, the same runway the Shah built for his stupid anniversary. And it was special to the Zoroastrians, too."

And that was the last time Maria and Horner ever saw her, for she was taken off the plane immediately thereafter and driven off into the desert in a Jeep.

About half an hour later, they heard a single gunshot,

small arms, undoubtedly a pistol, echo through the air. Although they could not be sure, they assumed Nilufer had been shot.

For the longest time the two were held on the aircraft at gunpoint -- and periodic knifepoint -- by their black-scarved guards long after everyone else had departed; they breathed the now-stale air, and suffered as the temperature inside soared, from the arid sunlight pouring in through the windows.

Maria had much time to contemplate the execution of Nilufer, her long-time rival for Horner's love, though he would have denied that. And though she had been Maria's enemy since they'd all three met in the Sufi group ten years ago, her death produced such a sorrow in Maria that she could not understand. Indirectly, she thought, her son had caused Nilufer's death. And so, though Nilufer had always flirted with the forces of political darkness, Maria felt oddly that she too had killed her somehow. She hadn't wanted the woman dead, or abused. She had only wanted her out of their lives.

She had gotten her wish, in the most ghastly way.

Towards the end of their captivity on the plane, Hamza returned, perhaps from the execution of Nilufer. For about half an hour, he amused himself by commencing knife-throws in Horner's direction ... only to hold the handle and not release.

Each vicious little taunt produced further moronic laughter from Hamza and his assistants, as Horner would inevitably flinch or blink.

At the end of this sequence of abuse, Hamza spat a gob of saliva onto Horner's face.

"That for Abu Ghraib and Guantanamo," he said.

Mercifully, towards sunset the captives were ordered off, loaded onto a bus, and driven to a barracks that would be their brig. The black-scarved gunmen of the Elect escorted Horner and Maria inside. Though it did have bars on the windows, it also had a severely battered but still operative old Grundig television console that would broadcast the Nuraddin worldcast on MTV Mideast, his old fans from folk-singing days.

"Sit," Torkelson's killer commanded them, pointing to the spot on the cement floor with his pistol. When Horner hesitated, Hamza hit him hard in the back with the pistol butt. Horner gasped and fell against the wall, but recovered himself.

"Are you okay?" Maria whispered.

He managed to nod. They both sat down.

The sun was going down now. Their guards stood, the ringleader with pistol cocked and pointed, the others smoking Indian cigarettes. A cinnabar desert glow washed over the 747 now dark and silent, over the cluster of buildings. Horner said the declining light poured through the window and illuminated Maria as he had never seen her. Never, he said, had he thought she looked angelic, but she did now.

"You do not look like someone of this planet," he said.

"Shut your fuck mouth," said Hamza, and he hit Horner in the neck so hard that Horner coughed and choked for about ten minutes. Then the Iranian and his aides drifted outside.

*   *   *

Chapter 59

The blasted shards of Persepolis had slipped into the languor of the millennia. The three guards had remained outside for more than an hour now, and so Maria felt free to stand at the barred window, through which she could see the few standing columns of Persepolis that loomed against the desert and mountains of north Fars. Horner remained seated on his haunches against the wall, occasionally dozing, occasionally watching the television.

"The Peaceful One is resting," the television intoned. "His day was arduous."

And so they waited for their execution. The only signs of life surrounded the airstrip. The Elect had erected an outdoor television screen to monitor the Nuraddin telecast, which was being run live on MTV Middle East, the same music channel that for the last five years had helped make him a celebrity far beyond his Saudi base, and its false colors played against the sere backdrop of the desert. The captives saw replayed footage of the night before, mahdi advancing, child imams flanking, while split-screen inserts showed crowds gathering at assorted places: Almaty, Tashkent, Cairo,

Algiers.

The names of the cities shifted constantly -- Bishkek, Amman, Dushanbe, Khartoum -- and the faces in the crowds changed too, the fezzes and purdah of a dozen cultures spinning out their possibilities, sunlight altering in the different time zones as earth spun into night.

As night fell, the pace of human movement in their field of vision quickened. A smaller jet landed, and was being refueled and serviced.

Who was it?

And the enormous screen too was now a panel of light and energy against the deepening purple of the desert night, its luminous rectangle become a window into mass dream. The crowds to witness the mahdi's coming had grown, and a buzz of global conversation washed across the oceans of heads, children still gesturing at the cameras, faithful gathered in clutches.

Even as Maria pondered, now the screens showed her son arising from his siesta. She saw the shadows of the Bedouin bodyguards as they held parade position near the huge black tent that was his quarters.

"Nuraddin had a hard day," intoned the MTV anchorman, a Dubai-based DJ in tank-top and jeans.

And a moment later her son the mahdi emerged, now in his black robe and hood, but face forever unmasked. At that distance he resembled his dead father more than she realized, the man to whom she had been wed almost three decades ago. Not only was it like she was seeing her grown son for the first time; she was seeing the ghost of her dead husband, a man dead so long the vividness and clarity of his image stirred up memories she didn't know she still carried.

Nuraddin shook hands with the Bedouins, then the throngs of admirers pressing at the line.

She commented on how she felt as emotional as she had in memory. Horner agreed and said years had come off her face, and her veneer of the career journalist had been swept away.

And now, as they waited there watching dusk fill up the Persian desert air, the scarved gunmen of the Elect served them the most bizarre of meals, consisting of half-heated Iran Air dinners, the mashed potatoes still frozen in the center.

While Maria watched him, Horner chewed and swallowed, still watching the panorama.

For lack of anything else to do after eating, he too prayed.

*   *   *

Now they looked out on the expanse of the camp, towards the broken remnants of the shrine of the Persian conquerors, ruined for millennia. The edge of the mountains shifted against the turning bowl of space. A vast winter moon emerged from the eastern reaches of Fars, and rose into the sky.

"In Zoroaster's time," Horner whispered, "the Persian magi would have been drinking the sacred <u>haoma</u> at about this time of day, to break down the barrier between the mundane and cosmic."

And indeed, their three guards could be seen drinking from a common bottle, whether beer or their own mystic brew, and they were whirling in a crude dervish dance. Was it in anticipation of the Americans' execution? From time to time, as if to warm up, they would take shots at the wild cats wandering the scrub surrounding the ruins of Persepolis, and an occasional tortured shriek told them one had been hit.

Sang a muezzin on the huge MTV screen:

Mosque in Paris, muezzin in Rome
Chant Q'uranic <u>suras</u> at St. Peter's dome
Dervishes will return to homeland Spain
The earth shall unite, singing <u>mahdi's</u>
name ...

All this they saw, saw, and tried to understand, before

Hamza their ultimate tormenter, his scarf finally removed and the whites of his eyes wide and pink from his ceremonial drug, emerged out of the darkness like a visage from magian nightmare and spat at them through the bars.

"The empire of the Elect is born tonight," he jittered to them in Farsi, winking, waving his knife with dried blood on the blade.

Ar-rahman
As-rahim
Al-malik
Al-quddus
As salaam ...

Now the controllers of the big screen switched to a different broadcast, on Al-Arabiya satellite. It had a totally different tone than MTV ...

"The senior clergy of both Shi'a and Sunni Islam," said the broadcast anchor, "are in consternation as to what to do with the earthquake that Ali Nuraddin has unleashed. They are about to read an unprecedented joint statement."

Then the Nuraddin screen went blank for a few seconds, followed by a scroll of Farsi, Arabic, Dari, Urdu and English texts rolling across a green background.

"A special message to the faithful, from concerned religious leaders," said the text. It froze on the screen, and was being seen everywhere from Mauritania to Indonesia.

At this point appeared the Hojayatollah Varhesti, the highest religious authority in Iran these days. Varhesti was a looming and corpulent man, evident even beneath the black drapery of his robes, and he wore a white turban for this special evening. He had a full gray beard streaked with black, and his eyes twinkled this evening, so that by a stretch of the imagination, he seemed almost benevolent, a Shia St. Nicholas.

He put on a thick pair of reading glasses, and then looked into the camera before turning down to his text.

"My greetings to the faithful of the world," he said in Farsi, inclining his head slightly as though to convey sincerity, while simultaneous interpreters translated into a half-dozen languages. "I come to you this evening, full of concern, urging calm and quiet deliberation about the unprecedented events of the last several weeks. ..."

And so he began to recount the short life and rapid rise of Maria's son Ali Nuraddin, the proclaimed mahdi. As he spoke, Maria was remembering a home movie she'd brought out of Iran with her when she was exiled, and which she now had in her purse, if for some reason she should need it. It depicted her 26 years ago bouncing her child on her knee at a Baha'i gathering, the same child who now led a religious movement. Also in her purse she carried her baby Ardeshir's child passport from the United States, which she had kept all these years in the hopes that it would somehow bring him back to her.

*   *   *

Chapter 60

As he was *putting* the finishing touches on his sermon, he saw what his so-called Saudi brothers had to say in response.

The religious leaders of the Kingdom, joined with their everlasting opponents the Iranian Shiites to do a joint broadcast.

The grand ayatollah of Iran said

"I declare tonight that the man called Ali Nuraddin has no right to speak for Shi'a Islam. So all who hear him must cover their ears and stand back and resist."

The great Sunni imam of Mecca said, "Do not be seduced by sweet words, for beneath the flower of poetry waits the serpent."

So that was what he faced. He would be like the Prophet, chased from his beloved Mecca by those who would kill him. Or Jesus, who was turned on by his own sworn *disciples.*

So be it, he said to himself. So be it.

*   *   *

Chapter 61

As the television was switched back to MTV Mideast, Horner and Maria looked at her son, now shown cross-legged on a prayer rug watching the televised sermons in his own tent. Instead of the anticipatory glow of hours ago, in the monitor they could see how tired he looked now, more tense and depleted, the crush of what he was taking on visible to them even now as it came to an end. Was he doubting himself, in the final hour? And, more importantly, was his doubt a lack of sincerity? Although Maria did not agree with what her son was doing, although she could not stand with him in his crusade, at least she could stand aside if this were his sincere belief. But if this earthshaking revolution of souls was spawned in his mind by base ambition or dark design and not by his divine call, then she hoped God would have mercy on his soul ... for she would not.

And as she watched this she was desperately running through in her mind if she had made the right decision, to remain silent ... if her boy could be turned to good, if he should be allowed to achieve what destiny now brought him.

She thought fleetingly what the mothers of other demagogues had thought of their sons. Had the mothers of Napoleon and Tamerlane been horrified enough at what they stood for to oppose them, or had blood ties and ignorance made them defenders of their offspring?

But such considerations were not to be. For now a small squadron of about twenty men who she recognized to be Iranian Revolutionary Guards, passengers on the smaller jet that had come in earlier, approached them. They were carrying rifles and they commenced to speak outside earshot with the hallucinating captors even as the prisoners could hear the whine of the smaller jet's engines, an unmarked DC-9 parked near the 747, being started.

"I think this is it," Maria said to Burt.

An argument now developed between the two groups.

They were able to hear the word "trial" repeated, but nothing else.

Suddenly the Revolutionary Guards drew their weapons on Hamza and his colleague. An interval of shouting followed, but the outnumbered Elect, drunk on haoma, stood down.

Now two of the Guards came over to Horner and Maria. One of them wore an unctuous, bizarre grin, as in supplication.

"Lady," he began in halting English, speaking to them

through the barred window.

She nodded to them.

"The Islamic Republic wish to apology to you."

"Excuse me," Maria said in Farsi.

As she translated for Horner, the Guard said that there had been a mistake. They would now be taken to Yemen.

"Yemen?" Horner protested.

The Guard ignored him, speaking instead to Maria as their detention room was unlocked. Horner's nemesis Hamza now staggered over to give him a final taunt with the knife again for a few seconds, until the lead Guard slammed him in the gut with his rifle butt, then put handcuffs on him. Hamza fell to the ground, drooling. Then the Americans were taken, still handcuffed, to the DC-9, while the Revolutionary Guard took possession of the 747.

Horner and Maria were ordered into seats opposite one another. Several of the Elect were allowed to join them. A Revolutionary Guard crew was piloting the plane, and several others stood guard at the cockpit. Maria was given a black scarf to cover her head.

"What the hell is going on?" Horner whispered.

Miraculously, Hamza and most of the scarved murderers of the Elect were ordered to remain on the ground, and as Horner and Maria looked out their windows while the plane began to taxi, their worst tormenters receded into the darkness. But Horner still could not take his eyes off the man who'd killed Torkelson, and perhaps Nilufer, and had tortured him all day.

"I gather the Revolutionary Guard just got new orders from Tehran," Maria said. "Most of the ruling ayatollahs are now backing away from Ali Nuraddin, and they said we are his problem to resolve. They said they had new orders to take us to Nuraddin. Hamza wanted to execute us on the spot."

"I'd like to execute that bastard on the spot," he said of Hamza, as they flew up over the ruins of Persepolis, into the fathomless black of the Iranian desert.

*　*　*

Chapter 62

For some time they flew southwest into the chill night, the stars above their heads, and spreading below them the glow of what cities, what towns, what countries?

Then for more time than seemed possible they flew over absolute blackness, while only stars shone above. It was as though they had left the planet and gone out into space.

"Can you tell where we are?" Maria asked Horner.

"Either over the darkest desert ... or water ... or both."

Their answer came as they banked over what must have been the Al Mahrah Range in Yemen, and then began their approach into the valley below.

In a late-risen December moonlight they realized they were looking down on nothing so much as a tent metropolis, the white canvas reflecting the moonlight and interspersed with the yellow and orange glows of bonfires and campfires and cooking fires, the portable city of more than 300,000 people that was now a fixture in the movements of Ali Nuraddin. This seemed a scene not out of their time, but rather a manifestation of an earlier day, an epoch of conquerors and hordes and vast Asiatic armies churning across the steppe, for goals that to a westerner might now seem unfathomable. Oceans of humanity, shorn of their ties to the land other than to blow like a vast dust storm across it, moving like the wind across the scorching dusty plains and summits that made up this part of the world.

"That is Ali Nuraddin's camp," Maria said to Horner, and he nodded. Then their mullah-captors and the pilot began to take them down, down in a heart-stopping descent to another nameless airfield, in the wastes of Yemen or Arabia, who could know in this emptiness?

Soon they and their Revolutionary Guard escorts and several of the Elect were riding in a van on a winding road that led to this vision of the past, this memory of a thousand years ago, at the edge of the Empty Quarter.

"Do they mean to judge us in the camp?" Maria asked, and Horner shrugged. When she asked the Elect, she got no answer, simply an impassive forward stare, forward to Ali Nuraddin, forward to the camp of the *mahdi.*

As they came nearer, they could first smell the smoke and the odors, of the cooking fires, of the meals that had been prepared in the desert, of boiled rice and potatoes and if the followers were fortunate, some bit of goat or bird to add richness to the broth. Add to that the baser smells of humanity, the smells of the body and of refuse, giving the scene an even more primal cast. And finally in the lights of their vehicle they could see these adorers now materializing on the side of the highway, still coming, mostly on foot, to wish the *mahdi* well on the eve of his departure for Mecca. And as the Americans rode closer into the mass they could hear the radios and the DVD players and Ipods ringing with the songs and poems and orations of the *mahdi,* these utterances that defined everything for his people, the utterances that were for them godly insight, rules for living, maps into the future.

And then they could see, as they passed through the outer rim of this vast encampment, the bearded men and the women in purdah, heads wrapped in black and blue and sombre silks, a tribal encampment, a coming together. Perhaps this was not too different from how Ali Nuraddin's adorers normally lived, in their wattle huts out on the desiccated land or chiseled from rock on the sides of gorges and abysses. No, the ease with which the pots had been hung above the fires and the tents pitched and huts assembled made clear this was only a change in location, not in lifestyle, for many.

In the poorer parts of the Middle East or Central Asia, these are the unnamed millions who trudge by the roadside, who await the arrival of a bus, toting a wrapped bundle, a straw sack of something like nuts or grain or another staple, the inescapable and profound weariness of the bearers and yet their acceptance of the burden meaning it is worth it, it is worth the effort to lug this sack so far ... for otherwise, one's family might starve.

And as they were in one of the few vehicles allowed in by the checkpoints that had been set up, those faces in the night peered back at the visitors, assuming they were of some importance to the migration, perhaps the Peaceful One himself. Horner by now had also wrapped his head in a cover, so that their foreignness was not so obvious, and they would hear the voices coming to them out of the darkness, blessing them in the name of Allah, for they assumed the visitors too had some role in this continental outpouring of faith.

And they came deeper into the camp, deeper into the heart of it, and the robed and turbaned figures would salute and bow and wave them onward, onwards towards the center marked by a raw uplift of land like a mesa. The tents of the followers ended at the foot of this mesa. There too, in a small enclosure of vans and RVs and floodlights and mini satellite dishes, stood the encampment of the few international journalists who'd been allowed into the *mahdi's* camp. If Maria had pursued this story to its end, she might have been one of them tonight. She could see familiar faces, who in turn looked back in curiosity at her vehicle, at the two passengers, wondering who they were. A few even rushed towards them, calling out questions in three languages, held back by Bedouins. The pursuers were the low end of the journalistic food chain, the stringers and German and British radio stations, while the television luminaries stayed behind under a tarp.

Among them Maria saw her friend Christiane of CNN International, herself half-Iranian, whom she'd known for many years as she passed in and out of Istanbul. She was obviously rehearsing her next satellite feed to Atlanta. Maria had to forcibly restrain herself from calling out to her ... about the letter.

Then, when they had come through a final phalanx of hooded guards armed with automatic rifles and bayonets, their van labored up the dusty road only 100 feet or so in elevation to its summit, a broad rock tableland where stood the huge black tent that they recognized from the earlier television broadcast, the tent of the *mahdi* himself.

"They are taking us to see him," Maria said to Horner, almost unable to form the words in her mouth.

At the top they saw no further evidence of security or force, save at the entrance to the tent, two huge Yemenis in turbans and holding scimitars. And though part of her rejected the theatricalism of this scene, a deeper part accepted it as honest and real, as real as anything else in their world. This one simply sprang from a different mind.

The camp guards motioned the visitors to follow them to the outer checkpoint, and after a brief discussion those guards parted and they were allowed inside. The Yemenis now led them into an outer room, filled with more men in turbans and skullcaps, these the assorted imams of village and town, men as poor and humble as the crowds gathered outside. The visitors could not say those eyes watched them with acceptance or love; no, a silence fell as the Americans were taken deeper into the tent, a silence produced they supposed by the fact they were strangers, they were apparently foreigners, and most disturbingly, one was a woman.

The tent was filled with the aromas of burning spices, a smell of cardamom mixed with incense, coming from the brass censers that burned in corners of each room. Now the visitors were told to remove their shoes, and they walked barefoot across a floor of carpets spread on the desert ground. Finally they came to stand in what they judged to be a waiting room, for there were petitioners ... all men, save one crippled woman who had been brought there ... seated on mats around the wall.

The Americans sat there for a time in silence, while the Elect were taken in first, presumably to present the ruby chalice to the new *mahdi,* and convey whatever message it was they wanted to give him at this time of triumph.

His meeting with the Elect lasted less than five minutes. The Americans tried to extract some meaning from that. Then the Elect came back out and were escorted outside and never seen again.

Now, while Horner was told to wait in a corner, Maria was taken inside. And now she knew her heart was full of thousand things, of fear and wonder and horror at this thing she had spawned. She was told to enter alone and then the mullahs fell away and she found myself walking down a narrow little canvas passageway that opened into a small chamber that must have been dead center of the tent structure that was the dwelling of the *mahdi*.

Her son Ali Nuraddin was alone, sitting lotus-style on the floor but with his face and hands touching the carpet in prayer. She did not know what to do, so she simply stood.

The room held a small folding military field bed, a portable washbasin, and a writing table with an opened laptop. Part of the ceiling of the tent had been pulled back, so that she could see the moon up through the canvas.

To his left was an enormous red leather-bound volume, which she assumed to be the *Qur'an*.

Now he rose from his prostrate position, stood, and opened his eyes towards her.

*   *   *

Her son was about six feet tall, bare-headed with short black hair and unlike so many of his supporters, clean-shaven. He was wearing a simple black caftan. He was an equal mix of her and her late husband Mehdi, she supposed, although he was taller than her, owing perhaps to some tall male genes on Mehdi's side of the family. As for nationality, his mixed American-Iranian parentage made him look like something else entirely, more Mediterranean, perhaps a Spaniard, perhaps a young Israeli playboy. She could see herself in his square jaw, the furrowing of his brow, although there was a curious imbalance in his face, of one brow more deeply furrowed, and one side of his mouth slightly lower than the other, because of the childhood scar.

He looked smaller and more vulnerable than he had seemed in the television broadcast. Like many rock and film stars, his power came from nothing so much as the size and definition of his head and face, which were perhaps larger than average, more distinct. And while he was tall, he was slight in frame and body, narrow in shoulders and if possible even narrower in hips, lithe like his father had been, almost bodyless beneath his robes. Again Maria remembered her dead husband, of whom she'd hardly thought since she'd left Iran, focusing her loss and misery on this boy, now 30 years old. It was like she had searched so long for her boy, and now found her dead husband instead.

His eyes were still heavy, with exhaustion, prayer, or sleep. And the effect of all this, in the darkness lit only by candlelight, was to give his face a peculiarly apocalyptic aspect, unusual for one so young and inexperienced. She saw it in particular in the eyes, the creased cheeks, seeming not a face of youth but rather someone who had seen and felt too much, too soon.

"By miracle after all these years," he said in halting English, "I received your letter from the CNN woman. And now you have finally come."

So Christiane _had_ delivered her sealed letter two days ago when she'd interviewed him. And he had read it -- and believed.

"You know who I am?" Maria asked.

He nodded, and she thought she saw the slightest hint of a smile on his face.

"How long have you known who _I_ am?" he replied.

"I think I've known for several years," Maria said.

He appeared amazed at that.

"You've risked much to bring me here," she said.

"And you have risked much to come. Will you have tea?"

She accepted, and went to sit next to him on the old

carpet that must have long rested on dirt like this, rather than in a formal home.

"Do you really remember me?" she finally found the courage to ask him, as she sipped the mint tea he'd poured from a pot.

He paused a moment before he spoke.

"What memories I have would come to me as dreams," he said. "I once called them my Dreams of Paradise. For in these dreams I was a small child and all was goodness and light. I do not remember your face, so much as your sound and your smell. The same for my father. Of you I remember your English tongue. I dreamed in English for the longest time, for that must have been the language you used with me?"

"It was," she said, feeling the most wrenching ties of memories come up in her, so that she didn't know if she could keep her composure.

"As you wrote in your letter, I remember you singing the song called "Love Potion #9". This song came to me in dream for many years. And then I finally heard it on the radio, and I had the most magnificent, terrible feeling ... that my mother would at last reveal herself to me."

Maria had trouble breathing, for she had indeed sung this to him.

"And I remember the English story book called

Scuppers The Sea Dog, he continued. "I dreamed this book, its illustrations, its story, for years. And then I saw it in a bazaar, a torn and beaten British version, and I clutched it to my breast like the *Qur'an*."

He laughed, and she tried to as well, but the reaction was something else, like a torn internal sob.

"And do you remember?" she asked when she was able to compose myself better, "when we were separated ... when you were taken away from me?"

This brought a long silence on his part, for she had no assurance that he knew the facts of their separation ... that she had been forcibly deported while he had been left behind.

"All I remember," he said, "is a time of great sadness. I was five then, correct? A time of injury. A radical change. Something vast and important taken from me ... a sense of wellbeing that came to an end. An end of .... comfort."

Maria now cried soundlessly for a time, her face in her hands, the loss and agony of all those years coming out now, the feelings of guilt over what she could not control, the deeply buried shame of what her deepest self still considered her abandonment of him.

He came over and put his arm on her shoulder.

"It is lost," he said very quietly. "But this was the will of Allah. In losing my parents, I found God. So we must be thankful."

She remained doubled over for a time, the tears slowing, the horrible burning pain fading gradually now into a resemblance of the ache she had carried for half her life ... the loss of her heart, her home, her only child.

He then asked her to come outside with him, for a time.

*   *   *

Chapter 63

He took her through a small passageway that led out into the night. A lone guard bowed to them, and they walked through the darkness over to the edge of the elevation where his tent stood.

At their feet were spread the encampments of his followers ... the sounds and smell rolling up to them, even here, now. Many were preparing for bed, for the midnight departure would come early, and if children were to witness it they would have to get some sleep.

But others were up, dancing and celebrating, prepared to stay up until the event.

"Are you not afraid of me?" she asked him in a whisper.

"Are you not afraid of me?" he replied.

She couldn't answer.

"All children fear their mothers," he said. "Even later in life. For you more than anyone else can destroy your child."

"Does anyone else here know about me?" she asked.

"For those so inclined, they sense something ... a buried secret. Surely you have heard these rumors? They have run in the press."

"If you knew," she said, "Why have you .... let me live? How can you risk all this?"

He shook his head slowly, then looked out over his followers.

"If you had listened to my words all these years, you would know violence is not my way. And you would know that my words and ideas are more dangerous to me than any secret about my parentage. I was not sure until your letter came where my mother was. To find out she was a reporter of some importance in the West was another shock. But to kill my own mother? I would rather kill myself."

She measured her words carefully, before she spoke.

"You know there are those," Maria said, "who call you the *mahdi*. But who want to use you for their own ends. There is even a group called the Elect who will blackmail you so that you will do their bidding. If you refuse, they will kill you and make you a martyr, and put their own puppet in control."

He was very quiet, and looked down at the earth. She feared that she had damaged whatever bond was forming between them by this statement. She wondered now if she could repair the damage ...

"I know of them," he said. "The misguided have always killed in the name of Jesus, and Mohammad, and Moses."

"This Elect," she felt emboldened to add, "conspires to bring you the world, but through treachery and force. They have been plotting to bring about your conquest since the time of Suleiman the Magnificent."

His rubbed his face with his hands, and coughed in the night.

"Plots, conquest, power," he finally said. "This fearful mentality is my greatest obstacle. It saddens me. These people you speak of have already come to me tonight, pretending to be my allies. They even sought to bribe me, by giving me this ancient treasure ..."

At this point he pulled out the garnet ruby chalice, the replica Maria had given to Hamza on the plane.

"It's false," she said. "Have it checked by an expert to make sure. I know where the real one is. It is worth hundreds of millions of dollars ..."

Should she have said that? Could she trust him this way?

He looked at the replica, then laughed.

"It doesn't matter," he shrugged. "I was going to use it to fund our welfare programs for the poor. But we will find another way. Already huge donations have been pouring in. The unfortunate will be taken care of."

"But this cabal of the Elect will not be easily stopped," she insisted. "They have been plotting this for 800 years. They are murderers, ritual killers. They are pagans, sorcerers. They worship lasers, solar fusion, not Allah. You are only their tool."

He thought about this for a moment, looking down at his feet.

"I believe you," he said. "Those who came in before you, I could sense their evil. So be it. But do you see those people out there? They speak and act through me. If I abandon their cause because vermin have come into the struggle, I abandon tens of millions. I must trust that God will show me the evildoers, and when it is time I will turn them away. But the time to march forward is now. I cannot hesitate, just because some of humanity in their imperfection wants to wallow in intrigue. The love of Allah must be spread, for the fear and hatred and anger in our world are so great that they threaten all of us."

She pondered this for the longest time, before she spoke her next thought, for she knew that in voicing it she would most likely set up the highest barrier between them. But she could not remain silent.

"My son," she said. "Your words are soft and sweet, but there are those who say it is all a pose, that you are not sincere. Many before you have called for love and peace and social justice and brought just the opposite. Many of those people out there would follow you if you commanded them to loot and kill in the name of Allah. How do you win over those who distrust you, or who hate you?"

He thought a moment.

"What you say is true and real. The loving world that I describe in my songs is still a dream, a vision. Most of us thought it possible when we were children, and I think many of us hope that it exists in the afterlife. But what of this world, this life? Is it always to be a fraud, a charade, a prison camp only ended by death? But it does not have to be that way. I swear to you I do not want money or power. I want only to appeal to the goodness that is in most men, in their hearts, the goodness that is the highest reflection of God. I want to bring more of that into the world. In this way I am an American, because was that not the purpose of the founding of your country? To bring the goodness of heaven into this world? If you should see me abandon that way, then come forward with the truth. Bring me down. I will deserve it."

Now he stood stark still, and turned and looked at her, his eyes unblinking, his face uncovered and scarred chin exposed as it had been at his unveiling only last night.

"Trust me, my mother. Watch me like a hawk. If I become pompous and intoxicated by ego, tell the world, strip me naked. But tonight I promise will not fail the world, as the world failed you and me. I will try to bring God's love back into this world, as long as I have life."

A wind rose up and blew the now-icy air across the rock summit where they stood, furling the sides of the tent, furling the tents of his followers down below and sending billows of sparks and dust up into the night. In spite of herself, she felt strangely elated.

"My son," she said, without premeditation, following only a sudden impulse, a flash of realization. "When I read and hear your words, sometimes you sound like a Sufi. Do you know of the Sufis? Are you one of them?"

And at this he began to laugh, the first time she had seen real mirth in his face.

"That is the most dangerous thing you have said all night," he said. "To have that known would do me more damage than to have an American mother."

"So you are one?" she persisted.

"Just as I am a Christian and a Jew and a Hindu and a Buddhist. I love the Sufis and their love for man and God. I have read the poems of Rumi. In fact, his own path inspired me to find my own path. Though I think he would disapprove of my immersion in the world. Good as the Sufis were and are, they always chose to keep too much of their wonderful love behind closed doors, in secret."

"But our world has fallen too far," he continued.

"People of love and vision cannot withdraw into secret societies, for the outer world is threatened as never before. Anger, hate, fear and selfishness are at their height."

"I am honored, to have you think I am a Sufi," he added.

Then her son Ali Nuraddin walked closer to her, and held her arm.

"I am only the skipper," he said more softly, "and those spread below us are the ocean of God's power and beauty. I may sail atop their storm, and carry their banner. But even if I am taken away and sink beneath the waves, this ocean at our feet will rise up anyway, for good or for destruction. Should we not help steer it to the good?"

As he expressed it, the logic came clear.

He paused a moment, and smiled.

"I consider you my mother, and my door is always open to you. I invite you to come with me, if you will. Maybe after all these years, we could recapture a bit of what was lost."

She tried to say something to that, but again broke into that hoarse wracking sob, the sob for lives lost, for love never given nor received. She didn't think she could live another minute.

He held her.

When she had calmed, he took her and walked her

back into the tent.

"I am so glad we have had these few minutes together," he said, his dark eyes shining like they had as her little boy. "I am so blessed to have met the woman who brought me my dreams of Paradise."

"I am so glad," he added, "to have met the woman who sang Love Potion # 9 to me, and read to me about Scuppers the Sea Dog."

"I thank you for all this, my mother," he said, and he embraced her, and bowed to her, and then he was gone, and she stood in the canvas passageway that led from his inner sanctum to the outer room where the other petitioners waited.

*   *   *

Chapter 64

As Maria came out of her interview she walked in a daze somewhere between dream and hallucination, and looked at the suspicious faces of the imams and others waiting there, and felt both a terrible sadness at the irreversibility of life and destiny, and at the same time a joyousness that her son did seem to be as noble as his words, even if he would bring the world into upheaval. Horner was there waiting and he came to her, and then the Yemeni mullahs escorted them back out into the night, to a waiting Jeep.

"You are now free to go," the elder Yemeni said, and bowed.

"Can you assist us in getting back to Turkey?" Horner had the courage to ask, and it was a valid question, for they had been spirited here in the midst of a revolution, and it would be difficult if not life-threatening to make their way back through Saudi Arabia to Turkey, and then Greece.

The guards conferred, and then held a radio conversation about the visitors' plight. As they spoke, a huge bonfire had been lit in the camp below, and hundreds of people now chanted before it, calling out to their mahdi rhythmically, to come out and speak before he departed for Mecca at the stroke of midnight.

And now Maria's eyes traveled to the press caravan, solemnly recording the celebration of the mahdi's army of faith. It was now or never for her. Although she now trusted her son and his motives and goals, in fact was moved and inspired by them, the chance of him being able to control the thing that he had unleashed seemed almost impossible, unless they all had somehow entered the days of Revelations. She looked at the people around her son ... people who days or months or years ago had been entranced by Osama bin Laden or Khomeini or the harsh elders of Wahabism. Did they really understand, much less subscribe to, her son's vision? Or were they just entranced with his charisma, with the possibility he was the mythical mahdi?

If she was to stop her son's Revolution of Allah, what better time than now, on the eve of its birth? All she had to do was step through the line of guards and into the gathering of reporters, her long-time tribe. All she had to do was go to Christiane, for she already knew of the child left behind, the lost days in Iran, Maria's blood tie to that land. All Maria had to do was tell her the awesome full truth, of parentage and conspiracy and murder, which would be the story of the century. All Maria had to do was to show Christiane the passport and the home video of her long-lost son in her purse; the whole spectacular report could be assembled between here and CNN headquarters in a few minutes.

Maria could stop this thing now that she had given birth to, more easily than tomorrow. She could do it now or never, if she had the courage.

As their guards continued consulting about transporting the visitors out of this place, Maria willed herself to walk forward, through the line, into the false light of the cameras. She willed herself to move, to save the world she knew. She willed myself ...

"This man will give you a ride to Sana'a," one of the Yemenis now said. And before them stood a friendly Bedouin with a truck, the passenger door thrown open in welcome.

Christiane meanwhile had come out of her broadcast van, and she was looking around for someone, perhaps a sound technician, perhaps a colleague from another organization. But then her gaze came over in Maria's direction, and Maria saw the correspondent look at her in curiosity.

Now, or never, Maria thought. Her heart pounded, as she felt a burden of years, of continents, crashing down on her.

Now, her head screamed.

Now.

And then, when Christiane might have been beginning to get the first inklings of recognition, when it would have been most appropriate for Maria to make her move, Maria pulled her scarf tighter around her face and moved into shadow, into the shadow of the truck's cab.

"Now," she said to Horner. "Let's leave now."

As they careened away from the reporters and the mob out onto the Sana'a Highway headed south and away from the melee, this young man, this Bedouin whose cousins were probably followers of the fallen Osama bin Laden and al-Qaeda drove them towards San'a, the Yemeni capital about four hours to the south, where he said they might catch a flight out of Yemen.

Maria's heart, her head, were collapsing with the choice she had made. Her tears were streaming again for the third time in a few minutes, her head was pounding, her heart felt as though it had been shot through with adrenalin and was now exhausted.

In that moment of curious desert peace when all truths were told, the very last thing they saw was the tail of a meteor flaming across the sky towards the northeast, a piece of fallen Aldebaran or another of the stars found and worshipped so long ago by the first magi ... celestial gems in the throne of Ahur-Mazd, jewels in the diadems of Jahweh and Allah. The meteor plummeted through the heavens far to the northeast, across Iran and Turkmenistan and Kazakhstan, across Kyrgyzstan and Uzbekistan, across all the broken pieces of the empire of the steppe where dervishes had once ruled -- before it was lost in the blackness of this night where all men found themselves, awaiting judgment by their Creator.

The things that followed in the next hours only shallowly registered in the Americans' consciousness.

*   *   *

Chapter 65

As they drove west towards San'a, Maria rolled in and out of consciousness, sheltered up against Horner. Numb from it all, Horner remembered his own duffel bag resting in his lap as they jostled in the Jeep. She felt him as he fingered the empty tissues and portfolios that had earlier held the missing folio of the *Suleymanname* and Nilufer's translated secret *masnavi*, and the ruby chalice of all the Persias, now perhaps on its way to Greece, or fallen into the hands of thieves. He reflected a moment, although he didn't say what he was thinking. Then he wrapped a blanket around her, and she tried to sleep again, dulled into numbness by his brandy.

Their Bedouin driver and savior shared the brandy.

Afterwards Horner would tell her that despite the fact that he had found -- and then lost -- treasures greater than most men dream of, he had been thinking of the woman he had almost lost, perhaps had already lost forever. He hoped the meeting with her son would have a completion about it, a closure to make it real and final for her. And he told her that what made him especially sorrowful was that he could see that despite the constrained circumstances and bittersweet conclusion, she might now be utterly free in her own strange way, free from the doubt and fear that had shaped her life in Istanbul. He was afraid that she might be pulled into fatal depression by the farewell of her son, by the awful suction that occurs when a loved one is gone forever. At the least, Horner was afraid that when she awoke in the morning she might be a different person. She might look at him strangely. She might leave him again.

Just before dawn, as they were nearing San'a, the radio reported that the mahdi's jet, the same one that had brought the two of them down from Iran, had risen up on the stroke of midnight from the black mountains and deserts of Yemen and flown due north, where it soared out over the flecked black surface of the western range along the Red Sea, and then out across the plains where the Prophet had received his divine visions. Sometime during their own hejira it had passed some thirty miles to the north and about 15,000 feet above the truck they were now riding in.

Even as they approached San'a, as the truck wound through dizzying gorges and abysses of the flanks of Jabal an Nabi Shu'ayb, Maria imagined her son Ali Nuraddin flying on his final mission, along the peaks of the Asir and the Hejaz, to his east the Arabian rifts and plains unfurling in the moonlight, and then the moony crags of the Harrat Rahal beckoning him onward. North, north he flew, and she fantasized his attendants had felt their destination before they saw it, for many on the plane had probably begun to ululate again, and then the lights of the unsleeping City of the Prophet had rolled out before them in a carpet of glory, not so far inland from the Red Sea. She imagined they would have been met at the airfield by a convoy of limousines, and then taken to a place for the highest pilgrims, a place once reserved for kings and sultans, and now for the party of the newly arisen *mahdi*.

When the Bedouin dropped Burt and Maria at the only decent hotel in San'a just as the eastern sky brightened -- the manager was the soldier's wife's cousin, and it was near the docks where in the disorder of tomorrow they expected to catch a flight to Dubai, and from there anywhere they could go -- they were given a vast but vulgar suite, a room of Oriental taste, silkish clashing patterns of gold rug and sofa. The only other thing memorable about it was that the air conditioning was stuck on "high," blowing air so cold and dry she feared it would suck the life out of them. She knew Horner wanted to talk it out, to try and put some shape on it all before they slept. But she could not. And so he lay her on the bed and put a blanket over her.

As the first light of dawn began to silhouette the distant Hadhramout horizon peaks with bronze and umber,

Horner fell onto the single bed still wearing his overcoat, coughed for a minute, and then sank into the most impenetrable slumber imaginable. Though exhausted, Maria drifted some time before she was free of consciousness -- rerunning scenes of her son walking with her ... looking into her eyes ... clutching her hand to say farewell as their two worlds hurtled in opposite directions.

*   *   *

Chapter 66

Beyond sleeping, she fell into a different sort of place. And though she dreamed, her dreams were so vivid that in looking back later, she wondered if instead she had been visited by a series of visions.

In the one she remembered to this day, she dreamed she brought her son the mahdi over to meet Burt Horner, only the boy was not grown, he had just entered puberty ... the exact age when his last letter had come to her. In another life, this boy might have become Horner's stepson. The boy was uncertain and deferent, a shadow peachfuzz moustache darkening his upper lip. His breath smelled of grape bubblegum, his hands were soft and slightly sticky.

Now he would be mahdi of all the world.

It was at this time that she began to speak to Horner.

And she said to him, "The future I give you is something no man has ever lived ... the chance to see what has never been seen, to preside over the coming of the millennium. For if you embrace us, you embrace the world ... and for that, you shall sit at the right hand of the throne of Ahur-Mazd."

The world was spinning now, like the orbs of space. She could see stars above, and she could feel the vastness of God's might ...

The throne, Horner answered, the throne of the world ...

"Join me," she said, "and sit at my right hand as my consort, my love. For I shall be the Valide Caliph of all the world, and my son shall be the Foundation of the Heavens. Join me, as my man, and we shall live deeper and more fully in one minute together than you have lived in all the years up until now ..."

And then Ali Nuraddin was lifting away from them and rising up into the sky, soaring like a comet, his face expanding to become a new constellation in the stars. She saw her son reaching out to her across space. And though he tried to say something, he could not, could not. So for the longest time she just reached up to him, thinking goodbye.

*   *   *

Chapter 67

It was not until sometime late in the following morning that Maria and Horner both awoke, still pondering what had really happened.

She was up first, and had on the single channel of Yemeni state television, monitoring broadcasts from Mecca. Horner came and sat next to her as the screen showed a white sea of the faithful whirling around the pivot of the Kaaba, the rotating masses of the world awaiting the master's oration; the commentator intoned that even as several other governments -- Turkmenistan, Algeria and at long last Syria -- had fallen overnight into righteous hands, the task now was to defend the Revolution from the infidels who would subvert it, and to fortify righteous governments that would follow the teachings of the Prophet, blessed be his name.

Another voice in the background was chanting the 99 names of God ...

al-gafur
as-sakur

al-'ali
al-kabir
al-hafiz ...

And as they watched the televised panorama of the searing streets of the holy city of Mecca, the camera followed a lone black Mercedes formerly of the Saudi royal family as it came down the avenue bound for the Kaaba, bearing the *mahdi* to his day of destiny.

"He has won it," Maria said, "My son is the *mahdi* of the world."

And Horner took that and thought, and found no reason to question it.

"This is a fact, Burt," she said, and he wrapped his arm around her tightly. "Should I have gone with him, to hear the multitude praise him? Did I abandon him even in this way?"

He couldn't say anything.

But whether it was right or not, she had not gone with her son, she had remained with Horner. And now, the morning after, she thought of manuscripts and treasures and lives half started and children lost, she looked into the wailing television and into the streets emptied by faith and into the land burned clean by the sun, she thought of what reality is, and of her own small destiny.

As the cry, "Allah akbar al mahdi!" could be heard in

the hot air out over the manic streets of a thousand desert towns, she watched as the screen depicted her triumphant son being swept through the wailing avenues of Mecca, the chant of the 99 names coming through on the television. Arriving at the outer fringe of the sea of white robes at the Kaaba, his car was absorbed, then conveyed deeper and deeper into the event by almost peristaltic motions, tens of thousands of faces pressing at the glass, scorched by the sun, eyes reflecting an absolute faith and frenzy that she had never had, never understood.

Then they had him out of the car and they were bearing him on their shoulders, his body being jostled by those who wanted to touch him, tear him apart in their ecstasy, and despite this melee the camera was able to zoom in on his face and she saw his eyes wide with their mission and his lips open and the black turban they put on his head, they had made a saint of him and they were reaching out to touch him, to capture a bit of his magic that they had given him.

at-tawwab
al-muntaqim
al-'afuww
ar-ra'uf
malik al-mulk ...

For an interval, the cascade of names they chanted was comforting, lulling, achieving even in the unenlightened the intended effect of lifting the listener to a different state of being. Forces were being marshaled, doors opened, mysteries revealed. Burt and Maria couldn't help but mouth the names as they heard them chanted, the names they had learned in their meditation group so very long ago. And yet even as they were ascending to a higher plane with the permutation of word and sound, something else was tugging at their awareness, some realization was screaming to break through with urgency ...

As the black-robed ruler came finally to the pivot of the Kaaba, the white-robed multitudes had ceased circling the curtained Black Stone fallen from the sky, and they stood mesmerized before the stage, also draped in black. The crowd and the muezzin were together chanting the last stanza of the 99 names of God, for now no one was missing save one, the only one, the last to come, the Rightly-Guided-One, and he remained just behind the curtain, the black curtain, but his voice suddenly ringing out over the oceanic chants of the masses.

"I thank you!" he cried out, his amplified voice thundering out over the chanting crowd. "In a few moments, we go forth to a jihad of spirit, a jihad of love and peace ..."

"In a few moments, we open our arms to the world."

The crowd was chanting the last of the 99 names of God, and the television viewers found themselves chanting too, as the electricity of the masses worked through them and made them all one, if only for those minutes.

Each name a number, each an element in a formula taking everyone closer to the 100th name, the name not uttered, for it was understood, the completion, and in completion the instant of separation of spirit from flesh, of the living from the dead, light from darkness -- to utter the 100th name, which was "God" itself -- was to leap off the precipice into His arms.

With the cry of the 100th name of God on his lips, her son Ali Nuraddin stepped out onto the awful sombreness of the stage draped in black, but holding a single sparkling red cup above his head in triumph, its glassy facets catching the sun and glinting in a roseate pinpoint, a tiny point of fire, a dwarf star brought to earth, to become the focus of all that swirled around it.

"But beware!" he shouted. "Because even at this beautiful hour, there are those who wish to corrupt you and me, drag us into plots and conflict. They wish to bribe us, and deceive us. When they come to you with their earthly treasures and their dark magic, listen only to your heart, which is the mirror of God's love. Do not be seduced!"

The crowd shrieked, more in excitement than in

understanding. But he did not stop there.

"This is our answer to the plotters. Retreat into your holes like the serpents you are! Do not stain this wonderful Revolution with your schemes and nightmares!"

And in a magnificent and unexpected gesture, he threw the garnet copy of the ruby cup out into the crowd's midst, where it went down in writhing froth of humanity, shattered, vanished forever into the sparkling light that washed over the children of God.

It was the same inescapable light that poured over Burt and Maria as they took the flight east from Sana'a to Cairo over the heaving cobalt waters of the Red Sea, as they made their curious slow-motion retreat, motoring inexorably away, away. The outlines of the world they had both loved now shrank and faded as they were pulled away from it forever, disappearing into the light and the blue, into the ocean of Sinbad and the ocean of the Bible, into the ocean of ardor and ecstasy.

*   *   *

Chapter 68

The ocean was without swells, flat and still as far as the eye could see, though the surface moved with rival etchings left by conflicting light breezes. From where they sat, the marine colors fell away in gradations of aquamarine, from the pale greens of shore water underlain by the same lime and chalk cliffs that lofted above water into the promontories of the island, to the strips of turquoise and then cerulean that reached out into the horizon. In the far distances, lakes of sunlight brought everything into gold and flame.

Save the geologic profiles of the nearest other islands, some so small they were known only to fishermen and navigators, the horizon line was also disturbed by the occasional bulked outlines of enormous ships in passage.

In a normal season, one would have expected them to be the cruise ships, the ocean liners that appeared on the horizon at dawn, by midmorning disgorged their pastel-garbed passengers for an orgy of shopping and lunch, then by mid-afternoon began to load up for embarkation again. But this was not a normal season; in fact, the cruise ships had stopped coming this far south and east.

Instead, these were ships of war ... titanic aircraft carriers, destroyers and cruisers and all the attendant vessels of support and supply, in their enormity and uniform gray colors suggesting a world gone less festive, more inclined to force. At night they seemed as motionless and grand as cities on a black plain, and only the most studied observer could detect their movements relative to one another, or the islands. Periodically volleys of aircraft would take off and patrol and then return to the carriers, on certain days splitting the air with unneeded maneuvers and stunts, but then gone before one's anger could work its way in very deeply.

"They look especially busy today," Maria said, lifting her eyes from the days-old *International Herald Tribune* that had made its way by mail plane from Athens that morning. The contents of the paper were uniformly ominous ... the disruptions of markets by the wave of unrest in the Middle East, European leaders at a loss for direction, a slow but inexorable drift into a war or wars that no one wanted or understood, much less knew what they would bring.

"It's still just show," Horner said, watching through his binoculars; he thought in the marine haze he could just make out the line of the Turkish coast in the east, but then maybe it was illusion, for they were many miles west. "I think NATO's trying to scare the Turks into second thoughts about allying with Iran ... or at least neutrality. And they want to keep Ali Nuraddin at bay."

It seemed not to matter, though. The advantage of the disappearance of the cruise ships was that the two of them had one of the most beautiful parts of the world nearly to themselves now.

Every morning they watched the fishing boats go out, and in afternoon they saw them come back, pouring their nets of iridescent catch onto decks and beaches ... the fishmongers making their day's purchases, the dogs snapping at the flipping minnows and the gulls who swept in to devour them. And at night Burt and Maria would feast on calamari and snapper and an unusually rich run of shrimp, which for some reason had come back in the eastern Mediterranean very strongly this year. Oh, there were a few other foreigners in the restaurants and little alleyway cafes, a few outsiders nodding to the bouzouki music or sipping the retsina and Greek wines that had been discounted because there were hardly any buyers this year ... but they tended to be the hard core, the ones who came every year, the German ceramicist and the British writer and the mature couples of mixed nationality who had hardly any conversation at all, they'd been together for so long.

Burt and Maria would start each day with a dawn walk down to the tiny cliff-topped beach at the Hotel Poseidon, a swim as the sun burned up from the eastern ocean depths, then a shower and breakfast of eggs and Greek pastries. Mornings were given to hikes up the cliffs into the gnarled pine groves that led into cathedral canyons of lime and chalk, to wild goats and periodic hawk's cries and in the farther reaches, a shepherd boy driving his sheep up an impossible incline of rubble and sage grass. Lunch was either a picnic up there, or back at the hotel, then reading or a siesta in the room with louvered bone-white doors that opened onto the balcony overlooking the dining terrace and the beach below. By later afternoon they walked along the cliff-trails to the town harbor, first to watch the fishermen come in, then to have a retsina and watch the sun fall into the molten western seas, then dinner at one of the dozen places in the harbor town.

Today, though, they had come back to the Poseidon after their hike, to have a cocktail on their own private balcony before going down to the town for dinner. For it was a special day ... the seventh anniversary of the first time they had come to Kasos together, and here decided to cement their romance into a permanent thing, a civil marriage.

Horner found a bottle of ouzo into the room and he

poured it into a single scuffed red vessel, a small and crude drinking cup that to the initiated would appear to be an object of great antiquity ... a product of a tribal vision at the beginning of the world, and therefore more precious than the gilded and filigreed creations of later, more worldly artisans.

As he brought the cup and the bottle out into the declining flamed bath of late afternoon sun, she looked at him and smiled, then looked out to sea as she spoke.

"It's not often," she said, "one can look out on war fleets and think, I could have stopped this."

He considered before he responded. And in the silence, she answered herself.

"But I look at what he has said ... a revolution of love and freedom and justice, creating the world that was intended for them in the Prophet's revelations long ago, but lost and distorted. While I wouldn't want to run to the *Qur'an* every day for guidance, I can't dispute what he is saying."

"But Maria," he felt compelled to say. "No one in human history has ever been able to create a regime of pure love and freedom and justice. Do you really believe he can do that?"

"No," she said. "But does that mean he should be stopped, undermined before he can try? Should he not be allowed to try?"

"And what he believes about the West?" Horner finally

asked.

"He doesn't hate the West. He just doesn't want us to tell them what to do, how to live."

"Then why are we preparing for war with him?" he asked.

"Because we can't tolerate someone outside our control. It's our greed and arrogance and lust for power, just as he says. Because we don't want to let go of what really belongs to them. Our companies, our client states, our mountain of treasure depends on them in part. We feel entitled."

He thought a long time before he said, what he said next.

"And the murdering?" he said.

"He had no part of that," she said, off into the air out over the patio and the beach and the ocean. "You heard how he challenged the Elect at the Kaaba. He put himself on their death list."

The sun, and the six months away from the horrible trial of her life as a journalist had done her good. The sun had brought color back into her cheeks, and her hair had picked up blonde streaks from the salt water and constant light he'd never seen before. She looked healthier. She smiled almost constantly, as she had in the early years.

She was much the more the woman he'd brought to

Kasos seven years ago.

"The way I see it is this, finally," she said. "Their world was reaching for the pinnacle a thousand years ago, and then it went wrong. It began to die. And it has been dying for a thousand years. And they have had to live in this structure of failure and resentment, generation after generation. They have seen the West take their knowledge and use it to dominate the world, when they could have been the leaders, the model. Whether this new religious rebirth is real, or the last gasp before they assimilate into modernism, I don't know. But they need to find their own way. If not my son leading them, somebody else will."

An old Swedish couple, retired architects from Stockholm, had come out onto the patio below and were standing against the sun, arms around each other. On the beach below them, a little Greek boy was shouting up to them that he had ancient Minoan pottery for sale.

"Then we drink to a world gained, and a son lost," Horner said. He held the true ruby chalice of all the Persias, the cam-i Jamshid, up into the sunset, the falling sunlight shooting amber through the ouzo lens contained there.

"The myth says you will control the world, if you drink," she said, and they both drank and embraced. And then he brought the cup down and there it stood on the table, now acting as a prism of amber and ruby, the fan-shaped corona of its magic light spread out the white marble table where it stood. And in looking at it, he sensed she <u>had</u> sacrificed a world, in order to save her son. And he had sacrificed a world, to have <u>her</u>. That was all; the curve of destiny and the curve of earth, in that ruby glass.

He left it there, radiant in the dying sun, as he took her hand and led her down towards the stairway that would lead them to the rocky cliff path, and then the town, and then their dinner, only now being poured still alive from the nets of the Kasos fishermen into the hands and buckets of the cawing island fishmongers.

*   *   *

Book 2

THE SECRET OF SULEIMAN

A mystic poem

By Yunus, private interpreter to Suleiman the Magnificent, Shadow-of-God-on-Earth

Translated from Chagatai by Nilufer Oz

*In the name of Allah,
the Compassionate, the Merciful.*

Folio One

*A caliph's crime
rests in episode lost,
in story repressed,
in memory quashed.
To find what was hidden,
by imperial shame,
read these verses about God's 99 names ...*

I who have now fallen to dust and fed the worms was once called Yunus, my Turkish clan name I need not give. To paper I took this quill most often in the employ of the Sultan Suleiman, the shadow-of-God-on-earth, for I the Turk-of-many-tongues was his second tongue, his extra pair of ears. If that baffle you, call me the translator, the interpreter. See me as a man of the shadows, close at hand, behind the curtain to be summoned when needed. Know me as a man who had no life, except at the sufferance of a greater life. Know that I was a man to be used.

But on this parchment I write not at the request of the

sultan, but at the impulse of my own heart. Indeed, there was a time when my master might have killed me for this very poem ... and another, when he might have begged me to write it down.

Where do I begin, then, with this sometime treacherous tale? If I am to tell you the whole story, I must begin before the beginning. Do I puzzle you again? I mean to say, the events that would lead to those in my story began before I knew to notice. For in the autumn of 1565, there was such an atmosphere of foreboding that while there was no concrete evidence, it engendered fear in the people, a mood that rolled across the city as sure as the tremors of the earth.

Some in the palace had even begun to talk of this foreboding on the night the story truly began. It was on own mind even as I sat on my balcony. And it was then I heard the first shouts below, heard the guard's whistle, saw torches flash in courtyard gloom.

"Murder! murder!" a voice wailed over and over, as if in a chant.

"Seal the gates!" cried another, thinking the assassin might still be within.

Then I ran down into the inner chamber, to be confronted with such as scene as I will never forget. For the shadow-of-God-on-earth was yet in his bath, but the bathwater was rosy with blood, and more blood was spattered upon the marble floor. And the sultan was still locked in the iron cage that surrounds his tub, constructed to protect him from just such an attack. The sultan was alive, but drenched in his own blood, and stood dazed in the coralline bathwater like a lost orphan. Refik the chief of the guards was fumbling with the sultan's own key to open the cage even as at his feet the murderous reptile, the failed assassin, lay in final spasm. For Hasan the sultan's bodyguard had already chopped off the attacker's head and it was a full ten feet from the rest of him. But the body was still convulsing, eyes open and staring, mouth twisted in grimace of death.

Shouted the court physician Adaoglu:

"Bring in ice and bandages!"

Whispered the grand vizier, the great Mehmet Sokollu Pasha:

"The beast managed to thrust a swords-point in. Our lord was at his mercy for nearly a minute."

But the sultan was alive and conscious. In fact, the wounds proved superficial, save one just below the heart that, had the sword's tip not been blunted by a rib, would have been death's entryway.

Yet even as the sultan's rescue was being carried out, the glint of a solid object in the tumbling cascade of blood drew our attention from our master's injuries to the sea of red at our feet. Had the killer's very heart fallen out, we wondered for a minute? For on the floor we saw the most ghastly and yet wondrous thing ... an object as red as the blood surrounding it, drenched with a man's emptied life and yet apart from it ... a small and scintillant treasure that stood solid and fixed, as though blood had been fused by the pressures of earth and time ... into mineral.

Rather than a heart, we beheld a cup of solid ruby that had been the possession of a most exclusive fraternity -- the handful of men who not only had aspired to the conquest of the world, but who had very nearly achieved it ... a vessel which had touched the lips of Cyrus and Darius, Alexander and Julius Caesar, not to mention the shahs of Persia reaching back to the very foundation of that ancient land in the dim mists of history.

This was the fabled cam-i Jamshid, the ruby chalice of all the Persias bearing the name of the primordial founder of the Aryan realm. And this magical cup had been in the possession of our lord and master Suleiman since his defeat of the shah Tahmasp in battle some twelve years before, in 1553.

"Assassin meant to steal the cam-i Jamshid," pronounced the grand vizier, and indeed, his insight appeared beyond question.

"Wait, my faithful Hasan," the sultan was able to say,

before Hasan went any further with the corpse in whose clothes this cup had been hidden. The sultan beckoned to his grand vizier, who brought him the treasure.

"Examine the body," he commanded to Mehmet Sokollu Pasha and to the physician. "Find out who this man is."

And so the bodyguard lowered the cadaver, and a group of minions and advisers oversaw its removal to the cellar medical chambers where it would be examined. The court physician's assistant was delegated to examine the corpse in all its aspects, a scribe was assigned to record the proceedings.

"And you, Yunus," the sultan whispered to me before withdrawing. "Stay with them. Learn about my enemy."

How much I wanted to stay with that magical chalice, instead of making a descent into death. For though I had laid eyes on it at its formal presentation in this very palace twelve years before, I do not think I had seen it since. Because the chalice was not meant for common eyes, but only for the eyes of the masters of the world. Its curved symmetry was nothing so much as a piece of a sphere, and the sphere it implied was the sphere of the earth. To call it a chalice was a misnomer, for it was truly a small drinking bowl. Yet so far as I know no commoner had drunk from it. I did not aspire to such heresy; but no, I simply wanted to savor it with my eyes, this curved red lens that refracted a red universe in its curve, this thing that had motivated the lords of the earth in an epochal quest for its powers. Indeed, we did not even know what those powers were, except that no man could dream of holding the earth without holding this bowl.

And that it was drenched in blood was only an aphrodisiac to me, for that was as it should be. Domination of the earth implied a cosmic level of violence ... and yet here it was so muted and abstract as to make conquest a mystic and almost reverent act.

Why, why did I want to gaze on it so? Why, why was my focus drawn back to it, instead of to the duties my lord had given me? Did I sense then what history would later bear out ... that this fabled artifact was not long meant for any eyes, but that its utter disappearance from the treasury would soon follow? Or in my attitude of humility and servitude did I harbor some overweening dream hidden in this object, some unhealthy fascination with the domination of the world?

The luxury of such speculation was not to be mine. Instead, my odd rapture at the powers of ruby became a night in the cellars of hell, where I spent many dark hours with the physician and others, examining the clothing, the shoes, the severed head and even the stained teeth of this mysterious visitor who had very nearly changed the course of history. At first the smell of his dried blood was overwhelming, the stench of his opened bowels horrendous. But as I grew accustomed to the horror of death, facts began to emerge about our guest.

"Not a Turk," muttered the physician Adaoglu, holding the head up to the lantern-light. "No elongated head, no high cheekbones."

"A Greek?" ventured his assistant.

"No," interrupted the grand vizier, lighting up a pipe. "Traitorous Persian, I would say. Maybe mixed blood from Yemen, Arabian coast."

The scribe noted all this.

"Or Armenian," I ventured.

"Perhaps," the vizier said. "I've had enough stink for one night. You faithful servants finish up."

We watched the glow of his pipe go off down the cellar hallway, partly envious that grand viziers can afford to do such things. But he was premature in leaving, for he missed the only clue that might have a chance of better identifying this man. Because after further washing of dried blood, we found on the cadaver's chest a tattoo.

Tattoos in themselves were not terribly unique, except by content; and this one, rather than carrying the usual range of Islamic designs or representations or words from the Qur'an, was something else entirely; a small illustration of a fallen man, apparently a Sufi dervish by the shape of his turban, with a dagger driven into his heart. And the number "99" was calligraphed below the body. The tattoo was not orthodox to my knowledge, it certainly was not sexual nor comic nor meaningful in any way except in its mystery, which was undoubtedly its intent. This, I immediately suspected, was the mark of a secret society, or sect, or code. To further complicate our work, the scars of an x-mark cut through this tattoo, as though the wearer or someone else had tried to expunge it with a knife-tip.

While it seemed to be the most promising discovery, do not think I was filled with elation. Because I knew that in my city, and in my empire, and in the world we inhabited, the sects and societies were nearly as numerous as stars in the sky. And though I would leave it to the physicians and guardmaster to prepare their final report to the sultan, in my own heart I knew that if anything, it was this fallen dervish tattoo that would take us in the direction of the truth.

*   *   *

The next time I saw the sultan was three days later, when I was summoned to the Hall of Whispers, together with Mehmet Sokollu Pasha, his vizier in the last years of his reign;

and Abu Su'ud, his counselor for the law. We were to tell the sultan of our preliminary investigation.

"Tell me, faithful. What of foreign intrigue?"

"My lord," said the grand vizier. "We suspect the hand of Persia in this. For none would so like to see you dead, and return the ruby chalice to Persian hands ..."

"If we take the surface of things as the truth," said the sultan.

Behind him, the waters of a fountain rushed.

"What, o master, would you have us do?" Abu Su'ud asked.

"You shall do nothing," said the sultan. "And no one shall speak further of this event of three days ago."

"As you wish, my lord," said Mehmet on our behalf. We all rose to leave.

"You, Yunus, stay behind," the sultan said. The others looked at me for a second, the grand vizier above all both envious and hostile. I felt conspicuous to be singled out this way. I do not consciously seek favors or dominance, for at heart I am a translator and scribe, not a politician.

Only when the others were gone and the door was closed did he speak to me.

"I read your report," he said, lost in thought. "While Persia is automatically suspect, this tattoo is also curious."

"Yes, my lord."

"Yunus the interpreter," he said, almost to himself. "You are the most important to me now."

"Pardon, my lord?"

But my question was only polite, for I knew what he meant. It was what lay behind the glance of envy and hate that Mehmet had thrown me, it was the reason I was standing here now. In the many years in which I had served as imperial interpreter and translator ... in the wars in Hungary, Serbia, Armenia and Libya... a special trust had built up between us, until I was more than an extension of his mouth and ears. Bit by bit, as the trust and relationship grew, as our minds functioned as closely to one mind as two can do, I had been given other assignments -- to find out this bit of sensitive information, or to carry that discreet message -- until one morning I had awakened to find my role had changed, and I had been drawn well into the realm of manipulation and subterfuge.

"As I said to the others," the sultan continued, "we shall do nothing, publicly. But you shall not rest until you find out who has sought to kill me, and why."

"Yes, my lord."

"You shall begin immediately," he said. "Loyal Refik will be your companion and bodyguard. While he is conspicuous here, outside these walls no one knows him. And he is as loyal as you, and stronger, if not as smart. If you need travel, and I think you will, go where you must. Refik will accompany you. For provisions and stipends, report to the imperial bursar in our garrison cities and present my <u>tugra</u>. You need answer no questions, my seal speaks for itself."

"Yes, my lord."

"If the Persians have mounted a plot, I want to be certain of their guilt. If true, it means war."

*　*　*

My first stop as I tried to follow the trail of murder was the royal archive in the Has Oda, a place I had spent many days in earlier times. These documentary treasures were only part of that which had flowed to the Osmanli sultans in their role as spiritual guardians of the faith.

In my visit, I even detoured by the treasure room, and was there granted a glimpse of the fabled ruby cup of all the Persias, restored to its place of honor ...

If only the eventual truth had been something buried in the archives and imperial artifacts; if only my search for the truth about the tattoo of a dervish with a knife in his heart had been a matter of poring over these sacred manuscripts of a dozen civilizations.

But it was not to be so.

"Master Yunus," my newly-named assistant, Refik, whispered over my shoulder, interrupting my reading. "We have found this among the assassin's belongings."

And what he handed me sent a cold chill through my body. While it was only a small gold seal, this was a seal of a particularly rare type, and though much as I wanted to discover that my own eyes had tricked me, or that I was mistaken, I could not escape what I myself saw and felt.

I was looking at the engraved seal of the imam muderri Ferruhzade, a Mevlevi Sufi master and professor of theology attached to the seyhulislam, highest religious body in the court. What was even more painful was the fact he was also a personal friend of many years. But what most disturbed me was this fact: Ferruhzade was and had been for some time personal Sufi tutor and counselor to my lord and master, Suleiman.

How and why would the priceless, sacred seal of the sultan's most intimate religious advisor be in the possession of the assassin who had tried to kill the same sultan?

I looked squarely at Refik, and sought some sort of explanation from this man I hardly knew, yet who was now my aide. He stood half a head taller than me, dressed in his uniform of balloon salvar trousers and scroll-toed slippers, a multihued vest without sleeves revealing part of the chest and all of the arms, not so much impressive in their size as in their hardness and contours, muscular cords, veins and cleavage. His nose was as prominent at brow as at tip, dropping straight down towards the mouth in the classic Hittite way. In fact, I had seen this nose in the ruins in Anatolia, the tumbled profiles of the ancient Hittite gods.

"Have you spoken to the imam?" I asked.

Refik rolled his eyes upward and clucked his tongue angrily, in the Turkish gesture meaning that of course he had not, and how could I have imagined he would do such an impertinent thing? And he was right. I was the one who would have to carry out such onerous duty ... to go to a holy man, with evidence that linked him, no matter how tenuously, to a murder and a failed assassination.

The question was how best to do it. The dilemma stayed with me for the remainder of the afternoon and evening in that summertime of two years ago, as I sat on my terrace pondering my next move, trying to find some way to avoid that which was inevitable. But fate would rescue me from confrontation, for it was there that the news was brought up to me that the imam muderri Ferruhzade, lifelong loyal servant of the prophet and spiritual advisor to our suzerain Suleiman, had just been found dead in his chambers, apparently poisoned by his own hand. And at his side lay a fragment of a poem in the mystic tradition which I took as no more than a simple and reverent farewell message, so thoroughly wrapped I was in shock and disbelief that to me in that moment, the unbelievable events were now unfolding like a dream.

> *On to two cloisters,*
> *First in city of thieves,*
> *Then vale of ecstasies,*
> *Thou pulled me east and up*
> *How I wanted to know thy name*
> *Calling out for an answer,*
> *and instead given only the pull*
> *Until I was afraid I might find*
> *What shouldn't be found*
> *Perhaps thy name e'er unutterable*
> *Wrapped in blinding bright...*
> *Come thou for me now,*
> *Mine father of light!*

* * *

As I pondered where to turn next, I made my way to the now-lifeless chambers once inhabited by the imam Ferruhzade. Especially lifeless for me, in that I remembered our good times together -- his arrival in the entourage of the fleeing Persian usurper Elkas Mirza, brother to Shah Tahmasp; my initial wariness of him giving way to friendship, when he and I had discussed politics and foreign intrigue there in his library or out on his quiet terrace ... all recollection now tarnished by his suicide.

As I puttered through the belongings he had treasured these many years, my hands traveled across the cool surface of his cedar writing desk, still littered with papers marked by his flowery hand in the script we Turks and Persians had adopted from the Arabs. I thought long on the meaning of life and death ... how abrupt his departure had been, everything ceasing in that moment ... slippers still in position by the small bed, ready for his feet to fill them ... a silver and ivory comb on the edge of his wash-basin ... the smell of his tobacco smoke, and an underlying hint of incense permeating the bedcovers, carpets, drapery. I held his Qur'an marked with the same seal as had been found on the dead palace guard, the special seal which was the signature of the imam. But nothing captured Ferruhzade the man so much as his books.

I pondered for a moment my own ignorance about Sufism, based on my childhood glimpses of the more flamboyant carriers of the label ... street-dervishes handling poisonous serpents or swallowing swords. But as I read, I realized there was much more to it.

For Sufism was based on an ancient Central Asian doctrine of shamanistic enlightenment not unlike Buddhism, although the Sufis would have said their way long predated Buddhism.

What a rich tradition these Sufis drew from, and what

a rich tapestry of thought had shaped the mind of the late imam. As I read the verse of these men, I too felt the pull of the mystic way, sensing a glimmer of what they must have felt, as they soared out of their bodies into the next world, as they sought to strip away the ceremony and ritual and rule-making of the conventional world. And though I was not a strongly religious man I felt my affinity with these Sufis growing, and my understanding of their separation from the restricted majority, of which I myself had been a member, also increasing.

And that is why I was so devastated, at the moment of my transport, at the instant of my first understanding, at the very point when I felt as though the <u>imam</u> and all his forebears were there with me, to see fluttering from out of this volume of poetry a piece of paper tucked somewhere in its leaves. That is why I was so stunned to see it fall to the floor with first a sense of revelation and then with a chill, for my own feeling of ascent had been so rich and fulfilling that I did not want to see what I now saw. I did not want to make out the inked sketch almost identical to the tableaux I had seen only once before, in a tattoo on the breast of the man who had tried to kill my sultan. But it was there, yes o my lord, I gazed for the second time in a fortnight on the sketch of a turbaned dervish slain by a dagger through his heart, while a circle of killers rejoiced at having done the deed, their grinning faces and arms reaching towards heaven, while below was calligraphed the mystic number "99", and three of the 99 names of God -- "God the Abaser, God the Humiliator, God the Judge."

*   *   *

And so now the djinn of murder would lure me into the realm of faith. What was I to do? I, a fishmonger's son risen to become imperial interpreter, was no one to be interpreting mystic poetry and threading through the permutations of Islam!

A direct approach to the Mevlevis was out of the question. I needed to know more before I could even ask an intelligent question. I required a guide in these matters.

And the only name that kept coming to mind was a man who was not even a Muslim, much less a Sufi, and yet who had been of assistance to my lord in negotiations with the Jews of Cairo and Baghdad in past years. His name was Rabbi Moises 'benShalouf, a Sephardic Jew whose ancestors had been driven out of Spain and been given safe haven in my city seven decades ago, during the Christian Inquisition. Rabbi Moises was the uncrowned king of Istanbul's Jews, and it was to him I would now turn.

We met in a tiny courtyard off the rabbinical school

which he administered, deep in the oldest part of Karakoy, the ancient Jewish quarter.

He wished me <u>shalom</u>, and I responded.

"Rabbi Moises, you are a learned man. You know much of the world of faith, including those not your own."

"You honor me, man of many tongues."

"I have come to ask you about one of my own," I said, and it was here his joking tone grew wary, and the twinkle of the eye was replaced by a guarded reserve. "I wish to ask you about the Sufis."

"Why, Yunus bey, do you come to me? How would I know much about the holy men of your own faith, and why would you trust me rather than one of your own?"

"Rabbi," I said. "I have learned there are times when we must stand outside ourselves to understand what we are. Strangers can sometimes see our ways in the cold light of reason."

"The Sufis are enemy to reason," said rabbi Moises. "For reason is an impediment to experiencing the ecstasy of God."

"Rabbi, would the Mevlevis want to bring down our sultan?"

The rabbi shook his head for a long time, rubbing his face, half-starting several times and then stopping himself.

"This is most unlikely," he said. "For the Mevlevi

whirling dervishes do not meddle in politics. They seek a mystical enlightenment that baser involvement in the world would only degrade."

I nodded, for it seemed true to what I knew of that gentle sect.

"And if it is not the Mevlevis who practice treason," I asked, "who might want to make it appear as though they were?"

Again he shook his head. And it was at this time I brought out the inked sketch from the imam's library, of the dervish slain by a dagger, and the number "99". I gave it to him, and asked what it meant.

"You bring me one of the great mysteries of Islam," he said. "The artist depicts the murder of Sems of Tabriz in Konya in 1247. Sems was the beloved companion of the great Rumi, saint of the whirling dervishes. These figures who cheer Sems' death had envied his friendship with the great one, that the two of them remained locked away in private dialogues for months at a time. For this, they killed him."

I took this and digested it, angry at my own ignorance.

"As for the number 99," he continued, "it must allude to the 99 names of God from Islamic scripture. Several mystic orders believe the recitation of the names can lift one into a higher state of being. But surely you know this?"

I had heard of such, but knew little.

"Is there a conspiracy against Suleiman?" he asked.

"Perhaps," I replied.

"Perhaps your questions are better answered in Konya," he said. "Rumi is the saint of the Mevlevis in Konya, the murdered Sems was his great love in that town. If you wish to uncover a plot by or against the dead Sufis, you might start there."

This was true. While a holy city, and the old Seljuk capital, Konya had also been home to intrigue. It was also where the late imam Ferruhzade had studied.

"Then I shall go to Konya."

"Great Yunus," the rabbi said. "Listen closely. Your sultan has been a friend of my people. Friends are few in this world, and when we find one, we are true to the death. If you should decide to journey to Konya, or on to Baghdad or any other place in pursuit of the answers you seek, I offer the aid of my brothers. We are scattered far and wide, and though small in numbers, I don't think there is a city in the world that doesn't number a few of us. But wherever you go, you shall travel as my friend, if you ask."

"My thanks, rabbi Moises. I will advise you."

He bowed in the Turkish form of leave-taking, and I responded. While what he said was true, I was hesitant to be any more deeply dependent on strangers in our midst. For though I thought the rabbi an honorable man, in the end I could not mistake our bond as anything more than a strategic one, and I feared that if I succumbed to his friendship, which was offered with the justifiable end of protecting his people, I might find that I had compromised my own interests, which in the final analysis were different.

*   *   *

FOLIO TWO

Clues led to God's city,
where Seljuks once ruled,
Now-ruined Konya,
where imams are schooled ...

When Refik and I first descended the piney hills of
Beysehir into the wide, shimmering plain of Konya -- on our
mission known only to the Sultan Suleiman himself, to find
out who had attempted to assassinate him -- it was then I felt
I was leaving the Mediterranean forever behind, and
venturing into Asia, into the land of steppe, caravan, cry of
man on desert. Indeed, though we were yet at some distance
I could already hear the call of the muezzins to midday
prayer, the voice of the fabled city, the summons of the
citadel of God.

Konya spread out before me as it had for 5,000 years,
yet showing only its most recent face -- the face of mosque
and cloister and Sufi holy place, of ochre walls falling into

dust, of dust blown across the flatness. Yet it also yearned to pull itself heavenward, because its width was lifted by the spires of Sultan Alaettin's crumbling mosque, and the Karatay Madrasa, and the Mosque-of-the-Slender-Minaret, and above all the turquoise dome of the spire at the Mevlana Monastery, its cobalt form sheltering the very tomb of the Mevlana Jelaleddin Rumi himself, he who was the invisible soul of this place more than any man had been. Konya had once been the center of his world, and of the Seljuk domain. But then with the arrival of the Mongols and after them the horde of Tamerlane, the Seljuk order had fallen, replaced in time by my masters the mighty Osmanlis who would rule all the earth -- yet who resigned magic Konya to the role of a backwater.

It was in this mood -- of reverence and a sense of impending discovery -- Refik and I made our descent on donkeyback into the city that would be our stopping place for some months, as we sought the secrets that reposed here about those who would kill our sultan.

*　*　*

My masquerade to gain entry into the Mevlevi Monastery founded by Rumi was this: I posed as a long-lost Mevlevi dervish from the outlands of the Azeris, and Refik as my bodyguard. I was the dervish Dogan, descended from a line of dervishes distantly related to Rumi himself, but so distant my deception would go undetected ... or so I was prepared to claim. I would say I needed to ensure my rites and practices were in conformity with those laid down by the master, Rumi.

The Mevlevi cloister is a magic place, both for eyes that have never known it and those who glimpse it every day. The walls and spires stand imbued with a gentleness and warmth assuaging all who fear fanaticism or intolerance. When one first approaches the cloister, as I did on that bright autumn day, the low stone outer walls do not present the impression of a fortress, though they are thick; because they are so low, they can easily be climbed and so do not intimidate. They are further softened by a series of domes on that low outer wall, and beyond them, small chimneys modeled as minarets, some emitting merry plumes of smoke into the sky from the living quarters of the dervishes who reside there. From outside, another row of larger domes can be seen behind that, and beyond, the dome and minaret of a mosque and the hall where the whirling dervish dance is performed.

But most memorable is the green dome itself, the turquoise-topped roof looming above the city beneath which shelter the remains of the great Rumi, and the order's other founders and leaders.

The master of the Mevlevi order in that time -- and thus the leader of the Mevlevis the world over, if he had wished to assert himself -- was Husrev Celebi, a direct descendant of Rumi. It was to him I would have to make my petition.

I left Refik at a lodging-house not long after my arrival, and made my fateful approach to the Monastery alone. How can I convey to you the surprise I felt when, upon knocking at the door, I presented my request to speak with the master Husrev ... and was instantly walked into the quarters of the master himself. This, before I'd had time to rehearse my fabricated identity.

The master, a stout bearded man in tall conical fez, rose from his reading of Rumi's Masnavi and opened his arms to embrace me.

"Welcome, o brother, from the long lost Caucasus," he said.

"I am honored, o brother of the faith and descendant of Rumi, for though my valley be far distant and lost in the mists of ignorance, the fame of your wisdom and stewardship has echoed even there."

Perhaps I had overplayed the role. For though the whirling dervishes were ceremonious, they were not pompous; indeed, as I had to remind myself, they were sworn to simplicity and honesty.

"And why, wandering brother, have you come to us?"

And it was then I expounded my tale. While I had feared an interrogation by a phalanx of imams rather than this one informal interview, it was a stroke of good fortune I did not have to face such an inquisition, for I would never had withstood their scrutiny. But Husrev was an open and unprepossessing man.

"The way of entry into the order is not easy," he proceeded to tell me. "Since I do not know of your master, or of his line, and so cannot be confident of the practices they imparted to you, could you tell me which rite of initiation you underwent in the Caucasus?"

I took a deep breath, and prayed.

"The first stage, o master, which I and all my brethren underwent at age 18, was that of the <u>muhib</u>, or affiliate. After an extensive interview and an investigation, the master determined I had the ability to be considered for affiliation. That was followed by a castigatory retreat of 1001 days, followed by 1001 days of penitential service to the kitchen staff, followed by the oath of allegiance and my investment as a dervish. The process in my case took six years, and in many cases, can take much longer."

"Have you planned on spending so much time with us?" the master asked.

I was truly discomfited by this question, and sought some way to answer it honestly -- no, I had not -- without jeopardizing my own chances of admittance.

"I doubt that you had," he answered for me. "For you, like me, are in the winter of your years and you might well pass into the arms of the Beloved while still on the path. So I must defer to your word, that you have done these things and are as you say you are."

He looked directly into my eyes as he said this.

"I speak the truth, o master."

"Very well, brother Dogan. You shall remain with us as long as you wish, to learn our ways and take them back to the brothers in your homeland. I shall have the dervish Bayram install you here in the cloister."

"My thanks is without limit."

My head swimming with the ease of it, I was escorted first to the dervish Bayram, a man a few years younger than I but exuding, as had his master, a sense of wisdom and above all tranquility that seemed to seep even into me, and calm my agitated heart.

Why was I agitated?

First because it had happened so fast, too fast in fact.

Additionally because of my sense Husrev had known from the very beginning I was lying to him; and yet he had nonetheless admitted me into this special place. And this speculation, which I had gleaned from his face and eyes as he searched my own, was spawning a thousand new questions. Such as, why had he let me in? Was he seeking to draw me out in some way, by letting me have my wish? Would I be under surveillance? Was I in danger?

As I was taken to my quarters, however, I knew no danger to me resided here. If anything, I was the danger, I was the introduction of contamination, I was the vermin of an entirely different awareness than the one the great Rumi and his successors had tried to foster.

*   *   *

For the cloister was utterly different from the communities I had known. Here no glittering potentates swept by, no windy ceremonies took place to blaring trumpets, no scurrying minions ran from place to place, no scimitar-bearing eunuchs or strutting janissaries sent messages of physical intimidation and force. No, all here had gathered for the express purpose of seeking the mystic knowledge of God, and were at the same time sworn to do good works in the society of men. Worldly power was not part of the formula.

I do not want to give you the impression these

dervishes and their novices floated around like angels with harps. No, that morning assorted sounds washed over me: clatter from the kitchen, where meals were prepared to feed the dozens of people who made this their home; laughter from the dervishes and the apprentices at a comic allegory I couldn't hear from my room; music, from rehearsal and practice of the whirling dervish dance in the great hall; the voices of debate and discussion, as assorted moral issues were bandied about.

"How long have you been here?" I asked the dervish Bayram as he took me to the single room at the corner of the courtyard that would be my home in the coming days.

"Nineteen years," he replied. And in our subsequent conversations I learned it was his choice to remain here, fearing the outer world would distract him from the quest.

"I'm told you are a linguist," I said.

"This is how I serve," he said.

"What tongues are yours?"

"Persian and Arabic," he said.

"And also mine," I answered. "This has also been my calling; to spread the word of God, and of Rumi, into the thousand tongues of ignorance."

I secretly cringed at my own pomposity.

"What good fortune," he said. "We would welcome your assistance in our translation circle."

He left me in my cell, where I placed my bundle of belongings. The tiny chamber, even at that time of springlike warmth, was still chill with the cold common to the high plateau of Karaman by night, and which never fully leaves the stones of that windswept place by day. Tea-pot sat on brazier, and fireplace stood ready to give warmth. Two high windows let in a bit of light from the outside world; and a blanket-covered pallet would be my bed.

For the remainder of the morning, I simply absorbed my surroundings. I smelled the cooking smoke, lamb turning on spits, dust heated by sun, pungent odor of hides and carpets in my room, camels and donkeys tethered outside the walls. Through my open doorway I watched the men of the cloister in burgundy caftans and fezzes. Birds spiraled though the leaves of the garden, and sunlight broke on the fountain.

Whereas my plan had been to lose not one minute in my quest here for the truth about the sultan's assassin, in fact I wondered whether I would be able to accomplish anything at all. For no sense of conspiracy floated in the air. Added to that, the master already knew I was not who I said I was; how could I accomplish anything on those terms?

And there was a third realization lurking, which I did not yet consciously recognize, but which would gradually take shape in the coming days, like the reflection on the surface of a pond settling from disturbance to mirror glassiness -- a realization which was a lesson, the lesson taught by a forgotten wise man: that we each change and are changed by our surroundings.

* * *

I was soon made a prized member of the translation group, where my aptitude with foreign tongues gradually made its way out and I became the uncrowned master of the translators. The others were astonished I might be the agent by which the teachings of Rumi could spread beyond Ottoman Anatolia, a dream which had not yet been obtained, in these 300 years the order had existed.

And Bayram and I became good friends, though I must tell you it was not a friendship of expediency, ingratiation or exploitation on my part to pick his brain for the secrets I sought; but out of my genuine admiration for his honor and decency, and his frank reverence for my linguistic ability, which he said was one of the manifestations of Allah.

The man was simply beyond corruption. If he made you a promise, he kept it. If he said something, it was the truth. He never spoke negatively about anyone, even those who merited denunciation; he did not give himself a boost up by pointing out the imperfections or failings of others.

I do remember an angry response from him once; to one of his young novitiates, who had sought to paper over his own self-hatred by religious attacks on his comrades, which Bayram confronted him about and called "wind of the fanatic." This boy was irredeemable, at least as a Mevlevi, and soon thereafter awoke one predawn to find his shoes turned outwards at his cell door, indicating he had until first light to leave the cloister forever and abandon his quest.

But most importantly for me, by my being with Bayram I came to privately question everything I was; me the clever mouthpiece, the minion of greater powers, one who had no opinions or center of his own but who had grown only by attachment to those more powerful. And worse, I had thrived in a world so twisted and duplicitous I could not help but carry its contagion. Do not think I expressed these thoughts to anyone in the cloister. Instead it was a solitary process, a dissatisfaction with myself that grew with the days, until it was a voice in my brain I heard more and more often, a background chorus as I went about my routine.

The power of this realization, and the wondrous new way of being that was revealing itself to me here, was such that I actually contemplated leaving my calling, and making my home here with the whirling dervishes if I could perpetuate the masquerade.

*   *   *

But the outside world, the world of schemes and plots and power and grandeur, would not let go of me. Refik and I had agreed to meet once a week in the whispering gardens of Meram, on the outskirts of the city, to keep each other apprised of our parallel investigations. And no sooner than our first meeting was it clear this man, this servant, was the agent the "real" world would use to pull me back. Not that he had discovered anything. But it was simply his awareness, his utter immersion in the everyday, that entangled me in what I wished to leave behind.

It was on our fourth meeting, as the leaves tumbled finally from the poplars and birches, as the spruce boughs quivered with anticipation of the frost that would descend from the mountains in the coming months, that things began to come clear.

We were strolling in the gardens where Rumi himself had once strolled, walking by the very waterwheel that had been the inspiration of many of his most beautiful verses. It was afternoon in late October, and because of the elevation, winter with its snows would soon be on us. We were mostly alone, as always on these walks, and would have taken no note of the man in the hooded caftan who stood on a bridge, seeming to gaze into a fishpond, but for the gust of wind which pulled the hood back to reveal his face.

"Look," said Refik, and I did. And I knew I had seen the face, yet I couldn't place it for a moment ...

"It's Alaeddin, from the ship," Refik whispered, and he was right, it was the sinister crewman who had darkened our ocean voyage ... by constantly sneaking glances at us, and loitering about our cabin door when he thought we were up on deck. And in the instant we recognized him, Alaeddin knew he was found out, and disappeared into the trees, Refik in fast pursuit, me following as best I could.

Within minutes we were in country as rough as that the first Hittites might have seen thousands of years before, craggy desert and buff-colored cliffs studded with windswept pines. Mercifully Refik captured Alaeddin after a quick struggle, and now the sultan's chief bodyguard held his dagger against the throat of this man, with his twisted off-center mouth and dark eyes like swirling pools of treachery.

"Shall we punish you the Arab way, and cut off your treacherous hands?" Refik asked, when I finally caught up with them. But the sailor's only reply was to spit in the dirt, in my direction.

"Who has sent you here?" I was able to ask, my breath so far behind I assumed it would never return.

While the first response was more spittle, Refik let the blade bite in, until blood ran down the crewman's throat.

"I work for the grand vizier," Alaeddin choked.

No more unexpected answer could have come. For while I had associated Alaeddin with wrongdoing and evil from the first time I'd seen him, I knew Mehmet Sokollu Pasha was the least likely to be plotting against the sultan. And so for a moment I felt relief. Mehmet Sokollu was a good man, he was no danger, thus his agent was no danger.

I contemplated setting this man free, with a warning to be gone.

But then he said something I could not ignore.

"I know you, Turk-of-many-tongues. Do the Mevlevi dervishes know you come from the court of Suleiman?"

This, of course, changed the situation. Alaeddin knew who I was, and could easily report that back to Mehmet Sokollu or even expose me to the dervishes. It was at this point I remembered my sultan's commands: I was to reveal nothing of what I'd done to anyone, save the sultan himself.

"And you shall be the Turk-of-no-tongue," I found myself saying, from clenched jaw. Refik knew what I meant, for in an instant he had taken the dagger into the mouth and scooped out the tongue from this wailing wretch of a man, and now he held it before me like a prize escargot, cut out at the root, blood pouring from victim's awful mouth.

If you believe removal of a man's tongue will silence him, then think again. For there arose from Alaeddin's throat the most horrible gargling mixed with the gagging and choking of one drowning in his own blood, a cry of misery such as you and I will probably never experience, a cry of shock and outrage.

We stood there for a minute or two as the import of what had been done sank in on us all; on me the initiator, on Refik the executor, on Alaeddin the victim. The ground was wet with spittle and blood. Refik was the first to speak.

"He can still write his report," Refik said, and I eventually nodded my agreement. With a swoosh of his scimitar, Refik removed the man's hands at the wrist, two swift clean separations, and as I watched my slave carry out the punishment I realized he was more alive than at any time on this trip; this was what he had been trained for, and there was no question, his eyes were alight with the horror of his task.

"I once heard tell of a man in Istanbul who learned to write with his feet," Refik said quietly, and though the result of this inescapable logic would only be more carnage, I assented, it was true, a man could learn to write with his feet. And so in swift chops, the feet came off as well, leaving Alaeddin flat on his back in the bloody soil, howling his awful wail of unspeakable agony, four stumps waving helpless at the sky.

"Such a miserable creature should suffer no longer

than necessary," Refik said, and this time around he didn't wait for my assent, for I could give none. I felt the blade as it broke through the flesh and bones of Alaeddin's throat, until the head rolled a foot away from the body, facing off to the east, eyes half open, the spot where it had once stood atop the shoulders oozing the most awful flow of blood and other humors from within the torso.

Even Refik seemed to come to his senses, for now he stood panting, shaking over the man he had just dismembered. Then, while he muttered something to himself which I gauged to be a burial verse from the <u>Qur'an</u>, he dug into the soft sand of the gully-bottom where all this had happened, using his bare hands and sticks to gouge out a depression wherein to place the remains of Alaeddin.

I meanwhile sat and watched all this from a perch on a nearby boulder, wondering if I would be able to go from this scene of carnage back into the Monastery that was my home of four weeks. Knowing the Sufis as I had come to appreciate them since my arrival, I feared the more advanced among them would instantly smell the stench of evil upon me; from my trembling hand and unsteady glance they would glean my corruption and secret.

*   *   *

FOLIO THREE

If there were any who had such perceptions, they did not evidence them upon my return; for my part I tried to stay as separate as I could during that time, choosing to remain in my room for seven straight days, in meditation and prayer. I well knew that Rumi, with his reverence for the teachings of both Jesus and the Prophet, could never have contemplated, much less condoned, murder. As it was with the order founded in his name, darkened only once by such a crime -- the murder of Sems of Tabriz 300 years before.

So I took my meals in my room, I pursued what translation of the <u>Divan-i Kebir</u> into Georgian I was able to undertake in my anguished state of mind. And the <u>Divan</u>, a mystical ode of more than 44,000 couplets, was an appropriate work for me to contemplate at this time, for it was the enormous composition Rumi had begun after the death of Sems. In fact, he had even used Sems' name as his pseudonym, and the work was a record of such torrential emotion that at times in my room, already remorseful over the murder I had ordered, I was overcome by it and burst into tears.

My friend Bayram came upon me at one such moment, and was given pause at the doorway.

"The passion of Rumi has overtaken you?" he asked.

I nodded, letting him ennoble my dark feelings. In fact, though I had long inhabited a violent world, this was the first time I had directly ordered the death of another. This strange experience awakened in me questions that must have slumbered in my heart for a lifetime, but never before finding expression. Suddenly I looked at the great men I had served -- the brave and wily admiral Khair-ed Din, assorted generals, pashas, and even my beloved sultan -- in a new light. The power of life and death was a terrible one; I thought about the leaders I had known and served who had sent thousands to their graves, all in a day's work.

It was at this time I made a signal decision: If I was to carry out the orders of my sultan, I would have to resume and even accelerate my search for the truth about the sultan's attacker or the imam Ferruzade's suicide, lest here in the bosom of righteousness I would abandon the quest forever.

*   *   *

Fate gave me my opening in our evening translation circle, in a discussion of one of Rumi's commentaries on a Q'uranic verse on the nature of light. It was then that I uncustomarily barged into the fray, with a recitation of the Persian poem I'd found in the dead imam Ferruhzade's chambers back at Topkapi:

On to two cloisters, first in city of thieves,
Then vale of ecstasies,
Thou pulled me east and up
How I wanted to know thy name
Calling out for an answer
and instead given only the pull
Until I was afraid I might find
What shouldn't be found
Perhaps thy name e'er unutterable
Wrapped in blinding bright...

Come for me now,
Mine father of light!

I knew I'd hit upon something with my recitation, for a buzz of whispers ran through the room.

"These words have a ring of familiarity," Bayram said, and another agreed with him. "You've forgotten the author?"

"If I ever knew it," I lied. "I don't know how it came

into the possession of the monastery library back in the Caucasus; perhaps one of the many gifts left by travelers. But I was taken with its beauty."

"This writer has been to Konya," said Bayram. "The city of thieves is Baghdad. But then he mentions the vale of ecstasies, which is of course Konya. And the cloister might have been ours. But the style is quite antique, the images not current. I would better expect it in the Sufi poems of 500 years ago; then the Prophet was often described as light from light, and from his light all prophets derive. I might think this poet was influenced by as-Suhrawardi...the Illuminative School."

I nodded, but wanted to know more, and took the plunge.

"Perhaps my esteemed brothers would help me better understand if I told them a curious design was also found with the poem."

"A design?" Bayram asked.

"Yes, brother. This one I had never seen in all my days. It was on a leaf of the volume, and it showed a turbaned dervish with a dagger through his heart, perhaps Sems of Tabriz, with the mystic number 99 calligraphed below --"

The gasp I engendered with that remark was followed by a collective rustling of papers...

"Never speak of that again," said brother Bayram.

"My brethren, what have I said?"

"Be silent on that," said Bayram; the questions had so discomfited the others that they were gathering up their papers as if to leave. Once again, I insisted.

"Brother Bayram, tell me, what have I found? Is this a thing of evil? Please, do not leave me in ignorance."

But their only answer was silence.

I came outside into the courtyard, watching the last shadows of my brothers disappear into darkness as they made their way to the lantern-lit rooms that were their homes; though I could not see it, I could feel the first snow of winter falling out of the sky onto my cheeks from the black void of night.

Allah, what had I said?

From the great hall I could hear the sounds of the sacred dance, and not yet ready for sleep I stood there in the shadows of a doorway watching the mystic dance, the whirling men in white making their climb to God, arms outstretched, heads inclined, eyes blank, feet turning as pivots; this the culmination, the highest point of the preparations that took a lifetime. In the kitchen the novices were cooking hundreds of bread cakes to be distributed among Konya's poor, a practice of charity this old cloister thought as important as the mystic rituals it taught inside, for while these men looked towards God, they knew they could not make the climb if they had not cared for their fellow men.

Then I returned to my room, where I made my toilet as always, leaving my shoes outside the door as always, hoping by the repetition of routine to ameliorate the frustration and insult I'd just suffered.

The fitful sleep I had was ripped by dreams that took me deep down into a churning place of anguish and uncertainty -- Alaeddin dying in the sand, the sultan's imam Ferruhzade dead by his own hand, the sultan bleeding in his bathwater. I was awakened long before dawn by a sound outside my door, and when I arose, knowing sleep would not return, it was then I learned that while the snow had fallen heavily overnight, my shoes had been turned outwards by the unseen visitor who'd awakened me, the whirling dervishes' irrevocable statement I had been expelled from the Madrasa, that I had only until first light to be out of this place forever.

*   *   *

FOLIO FOUR

Though I'd only been a "dervish" for two months, I suffered the same depression upon expulsion that the most devout brothers would have felt ... of this I was sure. And all the more painful to have winter fall just as my expulsion occurred. Though of course I was able to shelter in the lodging house where Refik had languished all this time, nonetheless I took to walking the frosted ground just outside the gate to the Mevlevi cloister, like Adam exiled from Eden, remembering with ever greater pain the higher way of being I'd glimpsed ... but only glimpsed ... as an unenlightened sinner and fool. The spruces and cedars were dusted with snow, the chimneys gave up their merry smoke into the wintry skies, the roofs of the mosque and the green dome of Rumi's tomb itself were white with snow. And I was locked out in the cold. Five times I sent messages in to Bayram, to please explain to me what I had done, but no response came. On the sixth visit, the gatekeeper did not even look up for my entreaty, but signaled with his stony stare at the ground I was to go away.

And so I went; but I also knew at least I was nearing the answer to my quest; for my mere mention of the depiction of the murdered Sems, coupled with Ferruhzade's poem, had engendered this reaction. If only I could catch a former colleague on the outside, then the veil of mystery might finally be drawn away from this affair.

It was in the third week of winter that Bayram came to me voluntarily, wrapped in the hides of winter.

"My brother," I said, ecstatic at the sight of him. "I'm honored you would leave the monastery just to answer my lowly request."

He nodded, and I could see, he wished to tell me something. But to speak with confidence, he made me leave Refik behind, and we walked the frozen distance to Meram ourselves, even as night was falling, and the ice-rutted roads danced with the light of a frigid moon in a sky so black and cold it was as though Allah had opened our earth up to his final judgement.

"I long sensed," said Bayram, as we entered the frozen gardens, now home only to a few lonely sparrows scrabbling for a last bit of sustenance in the snow before utter darkness fell, "in your silences and certain comments and behavior an ignorance of our ways that I ascribed to the naivete of the provincial. Now I am not so certain that was correct."

I said nothing in reply.

"When you quoted the poem I sensed your curiosity would lead you in a certain direction. And when you mentioned this insignia, I knew for sure. Although the agreement of the cloister and the order is to shun any who seek to introduce it into our practice, I knew from your surprise that the depiction of the slain Sems was truly unknown to you, and you were being condemned for a crime you had not consciously committed. I also feared you were not one of us."

I was silent.

"As a Mevlevi," he resumed, "I believe in freedom of choice; and so, while I do not know who you really are, I must trust my sense that you aren't evil; and so I have chosen to come to answer your question as best I can, in the hope you will be warned about this mark, and will, as we have, dedicate your efforts to seeing it does not thrive."

*   *   *

"The dervish who shelters in the arms of Satan," said brother Bayram, "becomes a third arm of the Deceiver himself; for just as he is versed in both the ways and style of God, so can he better hide the trickery and plan of the Betrayer".

"It is so now," said Bayram, "and so it was in the time of Mevlana Rumi himself."

"For it came to pass," he said, "that in the adult years of Rumi, both before his period of mystic awakening -- before Sems of Tabriz came into his life, and pointed him towards the mystic way -- and then after -- he was a lodestone for men in pursuit of the truth, a flame for the moths who wandered in the dark night of untruth and confusion. In the early years they wandered to him lured by the scent of his reason and scholarship, by the silver tongue that caused birds to pause at the windows of the Monastery to better hear his divine song. Then, later, they were drawn when the entry of God into his pen-hand unleashed the torrent of his sacred poems Fihi Ma-Fih and the Masnavi and the Divan-i Kebir and the other golden masterworks of his soul and tongue."

"Now," continued Bayram, "his reputation of freethinking, and his transcendence of dogma, caused a certain kind of person to come to him, among many. Best to call them discontented personalities, with the discontent having many sources. Often it was genuine, sincere and pure, the simple yet constantly thwarted human impulse to realize the innate yearning for truth we all have. But there were others who from Rumi's thunderous harmony picked out only certain notes that resonated in their own wounded breasts; and others so totally tone-deaf that they thought they heard in his symphony the lonely and broken rhythms that really arose from their private disease."

"The unhealthy seekers," he said, "might have sought power on this earth; they might have been driven ultimately by lust and greed, by the need for pretension, or for status, or for a guru who would think for them -- again, these you can name all day."

"Some years before the arrival of Sems, in about the year 1240, a young seeker had come unto Mevlana Rumi, and he resided in the Monastery. He was not yet a dervish, for the order as it is now did not exist. The young man was Ali as-Dasht, known as Dashti, and he was a Persian from the east of that land, from a village called Dasht in far Khorasan."

"Dashti announced upon his arrival that he had been schooled in the ways of the Ishraqiya, the Illuminative School. Influenced both by Aristotle and Zoroaster, the Ishraqiya taught that existence is a single continuum culminating in the pure light of the Divine."

"In Konya," Bayram confided, "Dashti was a promising student. Tall and handsome, brilliant and with a tongue already able to captivate, some saw a great future in him, as a teacher. Rumi himself was taken with him, and welcomed him on occasion into a group of older scholars and holy men who would be taken to Rumi's house for deeper discussion."

"In fact, it was Dashti's premature inclusion in such saintly intercourse that later caused him to take a different path."

"Dashti's profile grew. But those with Dashti noticed his interest had become increasingly drawn to that aspect of Sufism which has most caused us to be maligned and in some cases feared. For while Rumi was turning ever more strongly towards truth and an approach to God, Dashti could not help but be drawn to the magical manifestations of enlightenment, when applied to the physical world."

"While some so-called Sufis have made magic the center of their quest," said the dervish, "for Rumi and later for the Mevlevis it was only a facet, a manifestation ... in fact, a distraction from the real objective, which was Allah. It could not be an end in itself. Magic was appropriate only in the context of the highest stages of f'ana ... when the self had passed away, so that magic could not be employed for selfish ends. Dashti's interest in these matters, while noted, was hoped by Rumi and others to be a passing phase, something he would grow out of. For he was nowhere near the level of f'ana to be practicing magic arts."

"The arrival of Sems, meanwhile, generated a stir among everyone. The primary public reaction was anger, for Rumi took Sems home with him and just the two of them remained ensconced there for weeks, deep in secret discussion. And the motive of this anger was jealousy ... for Rumi's students wanted him for themselves, in the cloister."

"But," said Bayram, "a different kind of interest arose in Dashti, and those of like mind. Dashti and his incipient cabal believed Sems had stumbled upon a <u>secret of hermetic knowledge</u> that he was in the process of passing on to Rumi."

"Sems' detractors had long said he was a devotee of sorcery and had dark designs upon Rumi. But it is unlikely these intense conversations dealt only with the transmission of hermetic knowledge. Yet Dashti, in his ever more misguided way, fixed upon this as a treasure he wished to possess. More likely, the secret, if there was any, was only one detail in an entire body of knowledge and experience Sems was sharing. Dashti, however -- whether by eavesdropping or via some spy in the house of Rumi -- had fixed on this one item."

"And when the popular anger against Sems and his monopolization of Rumi again arose, a plot was hatched. Some of Rumi's own family even knew and approved of it. Sems was to be murdered."

"Now Dashti," said Bayram, "driven mad by his overwhelming need to know the secret of their conversations, volunteered to be allowed to carry out the death sentence on Sems. And so Dashti and his devotees kidnapped Sems. But they would extort from Sems the secret they believed he carried, the secret so important to Dashti that he would commit murder to obtain it, would murder the very man who had awakened the titanic flame of mystic love in Mevlana Rumi and inspired an outpouring of genius and love that nearly rivals the Holy Qur'an itself."

"And this is what Dashti did, on the last night of Sems' life; he sought to extract the precious secret from the old Iranian dervish' lips. Once done, Sems was killed and thrown into a long-lost well."

*　*　*

"But did Dashti get the secret?" I asked, my first words in nearly an hour.

"This we don't know," said Bayram.

"And what was this secret?" I was driven to ask. "What was it Dashti sought with such fervor, that it could drive him to the murder of one who had never lifted a hand to anyone?"

Bayram stood there in the hardening winter evening, while a slight breeze came at us with teeth of ice, and all nature seemed to draw down inside herself in preparation for a night that would be the coldest yet of the season, that would test man and animal alike and make us wonder as at like times whether we had all been forsaken by our father in heaven, if he would finally leave us to face the brutal extinction by no-light, no-heat, the utter absence of his life-giving warmth.

"Dashti sought what we are told is the ultimate secret of illumination," Bayram said. "He sought something called the very-light of God."

*   *   *

With that our conversation was at an end, because Bayram could not tell me the meaning of those curious words, only to say that the secret was of magical value, not spiritual. What he could tell me was that Dashti and his sympathizers had then been expelled from the followers of Rumi, and had traveled from Konya to the east, towards Persia from whence he had come, and had created a stronghold near Mount Ararat.

"From time to time," said Bayram, "reports came back that Dashti had founded his own anti-Sufi school, which he called the Dashtiya; borrowing from the 'school of illumination,' the Dashtiya were dedicated to the pursuit of this secret of the 'very-light'".

"The Dashtiya even allegedly said that darkness was merely the other face of light, that evil was merely a reflection of good, that Satan and Allah were both the true faces of the one God. They were even rumored in their secret rites to have blasphemed the name of Allah by the resurrection of the old gods of fire-worship, Ahura-Mazd of light and Ahriman of darkness, and to have conjured up the dark spirits of magian prehistory, the beast-headed daevas."

"And they sought the most ghastly way to enshrine their beliefs in ritual," said Bayram. For they made the original stabbing murder of Sems a holy act, capturing it in the very tableaux I had seen in a murderer's tattoo and a suicide's library. They had commemorated it in a hellish communion, staged during ritual reenactment of this killing. In fact, they were reported to stage human sacrifice as had the ancient magi in the days of Zoroaster, accompanied by the drinking of <u>haoma</u> and chanting the 99 names of God. For they believed that it was in the precise instant when flesh and spirit separate -- the very instant of death -- that God himself, the pure spirit, the embodiment of light, is most immediate and can be seen and touched by those still imprisoned in flesh.

But that was not the end of it.

"While their rite and theology was wicked enough," said Bayram, "the Dashtiya were particularly disturbing in their pursuit of worldly power; knowing their own interpretations held little appeal to the broad mass of people, they decided to thrive instead through the infiltration of all the Sufi and other Islamic sects, so as to someday orchestrate them according to the hidden plan of the Dashtiya."

"And what was the plan?" I asked

"<u>The Dashtiya</u>", Bayram said, "<u>would seek to ensure that when the true mahdi -- the rightly-guided caliph of the world -- arose to cleanse the earth, he would be in their thrall</u>."

With that told, my heart was as chilled as my body. The stories of infiltration, human sacrifice and pursuit of worldly power, told me the Dashtiya, for whatever reason, had been the perpetrators of the attempt on the sultan's life. The remaining question, however, was why; for a group so intense and clever would not have sought to slay Suleiman the Magnificent except as part of some broader plan. The why, however, was yet veiled in mystery. When Bayram said it was time for us to part, we both knew it would be forever, for there was no longer any role I could occupy here, and no further information for me to glean in Konya beyond the bizarre tale I had just been told.

Bayram never did ask for any explanation of who I really was or why I had come, but he must surely have known by then, as had the sheyh at my time of arrival, that I was not a simple lost Mevlevi dervish from the Caucasus. Perhaps, I like to tell myself now, Bayram saw the spark of goodness in me and trusted I would make some good use of the information he had reported. But whatever was going through this gentle man's mind, the handshake in the frozen waste of Meram that winter's night was our last; and it was the symbolic resumption of my journey ever farther from the world I had known, towards an end I dared not even imagine. I knew only that, much as my soul was now as lifeless and dark as this wicked night falling upon us, I would take Refik and we would close out our affairs here and head for the caravanserai at Sultanhani, to begin our journey east towards Ararat, and the home of the Dashtiya lo these many years after their murder of Rumi's beloved dervish-muse, Sems of Tabriz.

*   *   *

FOLIO FIVE

Are God's two faces,
one light refracted fine,
through man's flawed prism
into both horrible and divine?

At the caravanserai at Sultanhani, beyond the city of Konya, Refik and I joined a caravan headed east in December, the darkest month of the year. And my own mood as we set out east in search of the plotters against Suleiman was as dark as it had ever been in my life. Which is not to say God's creation did not do its best to lift me from my gloom. For even nature at her darkest can still bedazzle; and in those days as we moved into the rising sun, no ploy was spared by her to make me lift my eyes up and see the beauty of the world around me.

The steppe was frosted with snow and ice; but only slightly so, for in these dry reaches away from the mountains the snow fell only lightly, and not often; there was not nearly enough to impede the hooves of the camels as they trod surely east, their winter coats shaggy as bears from the high mountains. No, the dusting of frost was just enough to catch the rosy glow of dawn and the fiery descent of sunset and multiply their effects, transforming this cold dry plain to a world afire, magic times when, though the air was cold and we wrapped our stoles and burnooses tight around us, the crystals of ice caught the sunlight and shot it back like diamond arrows from a genie's bow. The mountains at the edge of the steppe were likewise burnished with the soft amber light of heaven.

I was continuing in my disguise as dervish, more by happenstance than by design. On the day we journeyed out to the caravanserai, I still wore my dervish's robes because they were the warmest I could find. I had grown quite accustomed to them during my time in Konya. But as I considered assuming a new identity, I concluded that to travel as a holy man would serve as well as any other calling, and might serve me better.

It was at the end of a lonely stretch beyond the caravanserai at Karatay Han that we met another caravan coming west, this one having begun its journey five months before at Tashkent. We made camp together for one night, while they brought us news of the road ahead, most significant a warning the snows had already been heavy when they crossed the eastern passes of Persia a month before, and were surely closed now. Among their wares were carpets from Uighur Turkestan, spices from the valleys of the Hindu Kush -- cardamom, cubeb, hyssop and assorted mints.

But most importantly, to my ears: they bore casks of Caspian wine!

As a result, the meeting of our two caravans became the occasion for celebration, and the sounds of diversion began to ring through my tent walls not long after sundown. As was the custom on a normal night -- since in the frigid blasts, there was little to do but huddle for the evening meal, then sink into a shivering slumber until the wake-up horn sounded before dawn -- I remained in my tent for a time, in the sullen company of Refik. He was sharpening his scimitar, and as the minutes passed and the scrape of whetstone on blade continued unabated, accompanied by the muffled shouts from outside, I thought I would go insane if I did not participate in the festivities.

Yet I was a holy man, a dervish; how could I possibly break my character, by imbibing of the wine my cold lips how thirsted for?

Refik's endless sharpening drove me out, my saintly role notwithstanding, and I moved through the shadows, watching as my cold lonely fellow-travelers stumbled and frolicked, the wine warming them for this one night of pleasure and indulgence.

In a foul and melancholy mood I found my feet carrying me to the outer fringe of the camp, to a fire that burned the brightest; to the fire of the gypsies who brought up the tail of our caravan, allowed to travel with us to provide extra manpower against robbers.

I noticed a pair of black eyes on me, and though I averted my glance with that recognition, I returned the gaze after a moment, for the eyes were still on me ... brazenly so.

The face was oval, soft and dusky. But the singular feature was her grin, one of invitation, so open and shameless I immediately assumed she was either crazy or a prostitute. In Anatolia, such a public glance from a woman could mean only that.

I turned to leave them, imagining the lamb on the spit must be about done now, back at the main camp. Even I, with my pompous flights of fancy, had to feed my hungry gullet or I would fall dead in the dirt. I made my way along the icy trail.

As I walked a form drew up beside me, and in the moonlight I could see the dusky face, the embarrassing grin I'd seen in the firelight.

"Won't you stay and dance with us, papa?" she asked. Her use of the word papa I found curious. Did she mean it in a religious way, or as recognition of my senior years?

"My feet couldn't keep up with your rhythms," I said.

"I think your feet could do quite well," she said, reaching over to stroke my beard and then give it a little tug.

And then the strangest thing happened, after this silly exchange. As we walked along, somewhat awkwardly, me knowing I could say no more without compromising myself, certainly not without damaging my pose as a dervish by consorting with a gypsy whore -- nonetheless something stirred in me I had thought long dead, forgotten. Indeed, the most powerful lust came up in me, and I, a gray-haired translator in the service of the sultan, felt like a panther licking his chops at the prospect of the morsel beside me. Lifted from the depths of tragic contemplation of only a few minutes before, I was like a beast in the night. My stride changed, my breathing quickened; even my nostrils flared.

We were coming into the light of the cooking fire. Others had taken some note of us. And though I burned with a consuming hunger, the eyes of opprobrium fell on my back. I stammered in confusion. The oval face with the berry lips of youth looked up at me; in the firelight I could see the smudges of dust on her cheeks and forehead all the better, I could smell her perfumed stink, but the thickness in my throat turned me mute.

"I must go now," I was able to say.

She looked at me expectantly.

"Later," I mouthed, lips flecked with foam.

"The fire," she said, and I agreed. We would meet by a fire, her fire I supposed. I wondered if I could wait until that moment.

*   *   *

FOLIO SIX

"Where will we go?" I croaked when later we met as planned.

She pulled me toward her tent, past an adjacent one where a group was playing cards by lantern-light. Because her tent was large, it surely sheltered more than her; I didn't want to know if the cohabitants were family, even spouse. It seemed not to matter, for they were all asleep. Lit by lantern-light, ceiling hung with herbs and garlics, the interior was filled with a smoky funk that was hard to avoid in this hard life on the trail. The middle of her tent was divided by a hanging cloth, and the left section further subdivided. She led me to a corner hidden from the rest with its own curtain.

Now I could see her better, in the firelight that came over the partition, through the divider. As I reached toward her to touch her, she took my hand and introduced my forefinger into her mouth and proceeded to suckle it a way such that I couldn't contain myself. I engulfed her in embrace, and my only incentive in breaking it off was to shed the clothes keeping us apart.

I smelled the reek of her and the gypsy tent, of unwashed hair and horsehide, of woolen carpets long unwashed, of perfume and body odor. It amazed me such a young woman if unbathed could approximate the smell of a grown man in the same condition. But none of those things were impediments to what I sought. Finally we tore away the garments and gazed upon each other.

I couldn't believe the serpent between my legs was mine. It hadn't glowed with such power in many a year. And she took note too, and circled her icy fingertips around it, sending a thrill of delight up through my legs and midsection, taking my breath away. And I looked at her, the black puff of hair between her olive thighs, womanly red nipples occupying the larger part of the rather tiny breasts she had ... at her small rounded belly ... at her cherry lips now wet with wine, glistening in the candlelight ... at her mouth slightly open, face flushed. Part of my frenzy came in holding myself back, for I knew with this particular woman if I let myself go I would nearly crush her in my desire, so tantalizing she was.

But we couldn't hold back forever, and, kneeling face to face on the chill pile of blankets and rags, we came together, shaft pressed up against belly. We attempted to kiss, our mouths crashing together, but we never quite achieved it, for our hunger and breathlessness were too great, we had gone long beyond the stage of kisses before we even touched hands. Instead our teeth and tongues tangled and bounced off one another and we released, frustrated, wanting much more. She brought my cobra's head down to her dark place, and let it feel the wetness that flowed there like a hidden spring, ready for my pleasure. But I pulled back, wanting to postpone a minute. Taking her ankles in my trembling hands I lay her back down on the bed and spread her soft legs, exposing her in the most vulnerable pose a woman can achieve.

From the chill air, my burning self touched another place just as hot, though hers flowed soft and wet, a mineral bath, a bubbling mud spring. I was as hard as stone with flesh wrapped around it, red and distended in sweet pain, but the warm drenching of her love took me in, bit by bit, our breaths taken away, my impulse now unstoppable, until with each stroke I had brought our bellies closer, me that much further inside.

Once in, I began the torturous friction we sought, together and apart, slowly at first, me still holding back because the impulse raged to impale her, ram her out through the tent wall and across the snowy ground, all thought lost to us, all memory obscured. She had turned me into a marauder from the steppe-horde, I had found her sheltering in a yurt as my ancestors must have done, I had burst in dressed in wolfskins, my breath hot with mare's blood and I would take what was mine.

And just when the pressure was too great, when the ending teased us to go further, further each time when we knew a blackness sheltered beyond, still we went and I could not ignore the thought that sprang from my flesh rather than my mind: Was I not approaching God from this alternate means? Was I not coming close to the celestial throne which the austere mystics found through whirling in the dervish dance, or the Dashtiya professed to find in the universe of the senses? Was not the full power of the physical world an equal path to knowledge of the divine, was it no coincidence the vocabulary of the mystics was of the hunger for the beloved, the love-drunk wastrel in the tavern of ruin? Were they not in the end the same, bringing the heavenly journeyers to the same point, if only briefly?

The explosion of our culmination was so intense that only after a time did I regain my senses, to feel the chill air on the perspiration that had broken out on both of us, to watch the flickering candle flames throwing shadow and ripple on the ceiling of the tent, to hear the mutterings of the card game that continued just a few steps away. Then I remembered my name and why I was there, noting my dervish's robes spread on the carpet; and with my recollection of that I began to wonder who it was that had drawn me into such a spell of passion and lust?

"Well," I was able to whisper, bringing the slightest smile to her lips.

"I have never made love to a <u>dervish</u> before," she said; and with that, both of us commenced an idiotic period of giggles that swelled into paroxysms of stifled laughter, she because she thought she had broken some terrible rule, though it obviously did not inspire any great fear in her (I imagine like all of her race she followed the gypsy rite, whatever that was, and not the Islamic); I was one more rare species to be added to her list of conquests. As for myself, the amusement sprang from a different source, my amusement at the irony of her statement, for she in fact still had not made love to a dervish, since I was an impostor. But more than that, the night's episode seem to burst my pompous bubble of mystic awareness, until I thought to myself: Yunus, son of a fishmonger, you shall never be anything more than a scamp and a trickster. Don't waste your time climbing the stairway of heaven; content yourself with the chambermaids, for that is where you belong.

That thought produced another outpouring of gasping laughter on my part, and she joined it, though we were stifling it so as not to arouse the sleepers and cardplayers any more than we already had. She had the clearest, most musical laugh I had ever heard on anyone, and it was absolutely infectious. She managed to milk the joke for another five or ten minutes, through occasional repetitions of the word dervish, which she found incredibly funny; and the way she was saying it, with a funny guttural gravity coming up out of her luscious throat, caused me to laugh like an idiot as well.

"You haven't told me your name," I said, pausing at the tent partition when I had risen to go. And she smiled coyly, sitting cross-legged on the pallet that had been the site of our fornication.

"Alev," she said, and I repeated it.

"Alev."

*   *   *

My secret still seemed buried when, the next dawn, we broke camp in a fog of hangovers coupled with aching chill. No one smirked or winked or sought to bring charges of scandal against me. Life moved along as normal.

Ah, but it was not normal; it was ecstasy. Seated on the camel, each rhythmic shift of the great animal's body reminded me of the night before. From time to time I would look back at the caravan-rear, hoping to see her there. But if she was, she kept herself well hidden.

After the day's journey, the caravan bedded down that

night a bit earlier than usual, to make up for the debauchery of the night before ... but I lay sleepless when Refik and everyone else snored, and soon I was stealing into the darkness to find Alev. We met in the steppe like two demons in search of blood to drink, making for a place to do what we had to do. We couldn't go to her tent that night because suspicions had been aroused and as for my tent, I did not wish to have Refik as a spectator for my fornication. So, in a frenzy, we found a boulder and, striking a compromise between lust and survival, we remained almost fully clothed yet unsheathed those parts that most urgently needed to meet, those primitive tools of flesh.

On those occasions when I wanted her but could not join her, I wandered the night wilderness in a primitive yearning, ready to take anything that presented itself ... a thawed melon, a sheep, a camel in heat. By God, what had become of me? I was like some lewd joke of Rumi's from the Divan-i-Kebir, the victim of a blissful and yet ridiculous curse that might drive me to stick my member into a beehive for the ultimate thrill. It is a miracle we did not die of pneumonia, yet the power of the lust was such it seemed to immunize us against other ailments -- all save one, an infestation of the tiny larvae that seem to dwell in the areas where sin is born, and punish its indiscriminate expression, little mites chewing and biting the hairy areas. Such a thing had not befallen me since my sailor days; I could not believe at my age, I was regressing down the scale of evolution, back to the goatlike behavior of the young male. At the same time, I did not regret this regression, compared to the alternative: slipping away into the black ether of senility.

*　*　*

As the earth fell into deep winter darkness, a new energy coursed within me. My immersion in this other person was proving not to be only a communication of the flesh, for I learned that Alev was quite quick mentally, with a gift for mimicry like mine that had served her in learning other languages. She too spoke a good Persian, as well Chagatai Turkish. She could follow Arabic.

She confessed that her tribe was moving to Khorasan, for they had heard great wealth could be made there. She had been born somewhere between Armenia and Georgia, and had been wandering ever since. No other family members were with her on this journey.

Each day we saw the great mountains of the east loom just a bit larger; and then other days, the mountains were lost in cloud, which told us snow was falling heavily. Soon our journey came to a temporary halt, when it was agreed we would make our winter camp at Kars. But it was on the first night, when I prepared to go out and do what I must, that Refik finally spoke from his apparent slumber.

"That whore will suck out your mind," he said to me, unbidden.

"I beg your pardon?"

"You've pumped so much juice into her you've lost your balance," he said, from his blankets, facing the wall.

"So you know?"

"Allah knows, the little children know, everyone in Anatolia knows," he said. "Your gruntings have become like the voices of the night, as regular as a clock from Helvetia."

I was dumbfounded. To think I had thought we were keeping a secret.

"Why has your soul taken up residence between your legs?" he persisted. And with that my embarrassment transmuted into a kind of anger. I exploded.

"I have endured your spoutings and prudery for months," I said. "What is your calling, o great saint Refik? Is the scimitar your only love? I have never seen such ... a young man, in the prime of life, shunning women as you have. What demon possesses you?"

He could make no answer.

I brought up this subject with Alev, and she at first ventured the opinion the mighty Refik was a sodomite. I couldn't believe so. But my curiosity planted the seeds of an idea which, had I seen the inevitable outcome, I would never have believed, until I saw it proven true some weeks later.

With the sun beginning to slowly struggle back towards the center of heaven from the frozen perimeter, still the snowy winds blew, still the glaciers of Ararat and the ranges of Georgia, Armenia and Persia stood like a white wall to the east and south. But a pair of hearts seemed to have been loosened in that winter -- warmed by the fire of love.

Love? you may ask. But that is what it was. For when the time came for all of us to part ... for Refik and I to travel south, to the area where we had heard the Dashtiya had taken refuge ... and the rest of the caravan to continue east, into the lands of Asia ... I realized I had fallen in love with Alev. Our violent union of the flesh had changed us both, and reached into my soul. The first night apart I sat in my lonely tent looking at the sultan's seal, the tugra which I'd used to seek replenishment of funds along the way. And I knew that in fulfilling my final commitment to Suleiman, the way ahead darker than ever ... I had let a priceless treasure -- love -- slip forever from my hands.

*   *   *

The arrival of spring can often be no more than a ragged end of winter. As we moved south from Kars, a period of mild weather brought rain to the valleys instead of snow, and high up on the mountains rain also fell, eating away at the snow that had blocked the passes east and south. But to call mud an improvement over snow is an exaggeration; for as we began our journey to the stinking village of Dogubeyazit, beyond which I assumed I would at last confront the Dashtiya, mud ruled the world, and it was then I vowed I would rather freeze to death in a snowdrift than flounder for a lifetime in mud. The earth had turned to slop, oceans of it. We lodged in a dreadful caravanserai, so dismal and filthy I thought we might fare better and in better health if we slept in tent again. But the rain and mud precluded that. So while Refik went out seeking the whereabouts of the Dashtiya, I remained in the low wattle compound, keeping an eye on our belongings, which I feared would be gone the moment we closed our eyes.

Finally Refik returned, and said he had not only found out where the Dashtiya were, he had found a tribesman who would lead us to the fortress of the Dashtiya, high up in the mountains to the south. We would begin the journey tomorrow, which lifted my heart, to think we would be out of this dunghill.

After a wretched dinner of gruel -- which took revenge

within an hour with sharp pains and the rushing of the bowels that made travel that much more miserable -- we fell onto our foul pallets, Refik with his dagger under his cheek to fend off anyone who would waylay us in the night. But sleep was not to grace us, for the stink of the other travelers and our periodic need to run to the latrine added the finishing touches to one of the most miserable nights I had ever lived.

Had the dysentery continued, I would have begun to fear for my life, for such can desiccate a man in a day or two. For me, at least, it subsided and then stopped; yet for Refik while it lessened it did not end, and had even begun to mix with blood. But he was a much younger and stronger man than I, and when he said he would rather ride a horse sick than shelter here another night, I took him at his word.

We were just saddling up the next morning when a delegation of turbaned men, including a fellow imam, came up around us. I could see from the aspect of the imam he had not come for theological discussion.

"God is great," I said. Their reply was to pin my arms behind my back and jerk me rudely towards an alleyway. Refik immediately moved to draw his scimitar, but his weakness and surprise at the attack caught him off guard, and they had him too. Our stupid guide was unmolested, although as I was dragged away I heard his shouts of protest, to the effect that we were paying customers and we hadn't paid him yet, leading me to think he was a bystander rather than conspirator.

We were taken to a mud cell at the edge of the village, robbed and beaten and then locked there, without water or food. The beating left Refik so weak he could not even get up to go to the slophole to relieve himself. And so he sank to the lowest level any of us will know, when we cannot even extricate ourselves from the effluent of our own bodies but must lay there stewing in it like a wretch. My first thought was that we had unwittingly reached the Dashtiya after all. But whatever the explanation for our predicament, Refik's fate was in more precarious balance. For the beating and weather had worsened his condition, and as I listened to him wracked by the ailment that first night, I wondered if he would survive long enough to face whatever our captors had in store for us.

*   *   *

Refik did survive the night, but just barely; yet he seemed moved that I, the master, would stoop to nurse him, the servant. All this, even as my entreaties to our captors -- a band of Shi'a rebels who seeing the sultan's seal thought we would serve as hostages to extract a bit of autonomy from our employer, Suleiman -- were ignored.

As the second night descended, Refik went into fever, and from then into hallucination; and so I had to listen to him as his mind came unhinged, as all manner of dark things welled up. He was swept with fever and chill, boiling with sweat one minute and then chattering teeth the next. And then the illness took him so low that it stripped away his final shred of dignity, and at the same time revealed to me the secret of his celibacy, the renunciation of the company of women that I had never understood. It came when he had staggered to the slophole that served as our latrine, but did not return. Fearing he had collapsed there, I went to retrieve him.

And so it was, as he lay sprawled in the dirt, garments open, I saw what he had so long concealed: he the fearless janissary and head of the imperial guards was in fact a eunuch, his bag having been cut off long ago and the remnant of his penis withered like the finger of a small boy, pink and tiny.

What a terrible secret for him to have to shelter, I thought. How had he survived the carousing and rape parties of the janissaries in his younger days? How had he begged off? For a eunuch had only certain roles in the palace, and they were all attached to the harem, not to protecting the most powerful man on earth. How had Refik ever accomplished this masquerade?

He finally began to stir, and it took him a full painful minute to comprehend he had last been found out. In a normal state, with his full physical powers, I think he would have drawn himself up and chopped off my head with his scimitar. But he could do nothing now; and so he let me try and wipe him off with a rag, and take him back to the straw pallet.

"One other knows the truth about me," he said, and I asked who that might be.

"The one who has meant life and death for me," he said, "the one who overlooked my deformity and made me the chief of the guards. To him I owe all my life..."

He meant Suleiman, our sultan, and while at one time those words would have echoed with resonance in my own breast -- for I was of like indebtedness to this ruler for whom I would give my life -- tonight they echoed as a kind of mockery, a reminder of the awful nature of such indebtedness, of the unnatural power of one man over another.

His fever peaked in that low period beyond midnight, when the night is at its deepest ebb; he seemed to regain his senses for a time. He even sat up in his bed, and spoke in a clear but strange voice. He was belittling himself for not having fulfilled his orders from the sultan, but then he answered himself, saying he had been given orders that should not be fulfilled.

"What do you mean?" I asked, thinking the nonsense of the last few hours was again overtaking him. "You were commanded to protect and obey me, as we carried out his mission. And you have done that well. If you're berating yourself for the capture, you weren't well at the time, it was my fault for not letting you rest in Dogubeyazit."

"Ah, master," he said. "There was more I disobeyed."

"And what was that, Refik? " I asked.

"My lord and master commanded me to kill you," he said, his face red with fire, his eyes alight with the sickness.

"Did he?" I asked, dismissing it; he was going back into his hallucination.

"He did, master. Before I left Topkapi my lord Suleiman commanded me to kill you, once your mission was completed. Once you had learned the secret of the assassin, and had prepared your written report to him, I was to have killed you, and brought him the report. But this is something I cannot do."

Can you imagine the feeling that swept over me, as I began to appreciate he was telling the truth? That a man I had trusted above all else, the sun in my universe, had commanded my own execution, to dispose of me once I was used up?

"Why could you not kill me?" I managed to ask.

"Because you have traveled with me as a fellow man, not as master and slave. And you have cared about my wellbeing. Lord Suleiman, great as he is, never did either."

I could say nothing, for there was nothing to say. In a way, this man who had been commanded to kill me had in fact saved my life, even as my quest had been the ruin of his. Everything he had believed in had been destroyed by me; now, even his reverence for the mighty Suleiman.

That told, Refik slipped back into sleep, the first real slumber he'd had in three nights. I hoped that accounted for the deepness of it, the curious sound of his snore. I tried to stay awake at his side; but I too inevitably slipped into sleep, since I'd had only barely more than he. I fell into a dark pit of unconsciousness where even dreams did not penetrate, a low rolling place of subterranean blackness. I was at the bottom of a well, and when I did come up, it was not because I was rested but in response to shouts and commotion in the far distance.

When I finally did emerge, I thought it was into dream, not wakefulness, for my love Alev had come back to me, to rescue me from the Shi'a.

I reached out toward her, expecting her to float diaphanous and disembodied outside my grasp, a spectre of memory and imagination. But then I touched her flesh, felt her lips as she came close.

I knew she was real.

"You are free, o dervish," she said, winking to me. And I was totally perplexed; I realized the commotion had been the conflict outside our cell door between our Shi'a captors and Alev's band of gypsies.

"What in the name of the Prophet ..."

She laughed, and said she had two things to tell me that would surprise me greatly, and give me great joy.

The first, she said, was that she was not really a gypsy but a Jew sent to safeguard me by Rabbi Moises in Istanbul, the Sephardi I had approached when I'd first begun my quest.

"Because of the nature of your journey, he was concerned foul play would befall you, and we were sent to assist you as we could," she said.

The second secret she was about to reveal, when one of her bogus gypsies motioned to us to come to Refik's side. For he had died in his sleep, perhaps hours ago, and was cold and stiff with death.

I was so overwhelmed by this news that Alev's second secret did not make its way into my awareness for a good long time thereafter; not until after Refik was buried, and we had left the pesthouse of Dogubeyazit and were underway to the Dashtiya fortress at Tendurek.

Alev told me she was with child, the child was mine,

and if nature took her proper course the baby would be born in eight months time.

* * *

FOLIO SEVEN

My story up until now has been a straightforward one; the account of a journey which I do not pretend was any more significant than thousands made by greater men and women than myself, for more noble cause. I say that, because what follows seems so difficult even for me, who lived these events, to believe, that I have read and revised this part of my <u>masnavi</u> to remove anything other than narration of what I observed with my own senses and intellect.

That done, you will find the tale fantastic nonetheless. For you, the reader, the choices are two: to believe what I say, or to think my senses distorted, for you must be assured there has been no effort at fabrication on my part. As for the latter possibility, I can only tell you in my humble way what eyes saw and ears heard, and tell you I believe I was in possession of all my faculties at the time and afterward.

As soon as we made our ways into the southern mountains of the Tendurek, I knew we had departed the realm of the known, and were entering a zone where other forces ruled. Though my gypsy-cum-Jew protectors continued with the frivolity that had made our caravan so lighthearted before, it was of little consequence as we climbed into the dismal passes and abysses that led to the place where Dashti and his followers had eventually retreated after the murder of Sems of Tabriz more than 300 years ago. The range of mountains constituted their own world apart from where we had been ... a place not entirely of this earth. So much so I ceased thinking of this mountain as a mountain, but more as an extension of the fortress we did not yet see; as though the range had been thrown up not by the hand of God but by the supernatural allies of Dashti, whomever they might be.

A perpetual darkness hung over the sky, and the endless clouds and mist prevented us from seeing more than a few paces up or down the trail. While rain had replaced snow, great melting glaciers still clung to the deep ravines and crevasses, and their dying faces generated further fog and mist to cloud our way.

Never have I seen the earth convey such an emotion of sepulchrous gloom and dread; never have stone and earth and sky been able to charge me with such foreboding and anguish. For two solid days and nights we climbed, enough verticality to obliterate memory of the world-down-below. This was a place of wall and abyss, of updraft and shadow, avalanche and slide; the few plants that survived here were twisted bits of life, lone tufts of shrub distorted by the awful climate into aberrations, shapes out of a nightmare. If there was any more significant life, we rarely saw it, only heard it -- the howl of a wolf from a distant ridge, the shriek of a bird in the grip of something larger, other cries and moans that we attributed to wind and rain, when in fact we did not know what they were.

Even our dreams on those nights on the mountain seemed wracked with darkness. Strange forms persecuted us in the prison of slumber -- men dancing to wild firelight, daggers dripping with blood ... or a dozen children dressed in white as if in the realm of the dead ... or men and women writhing in orgiastic display, that which was meant to be shared between man and woman become diversion for the slavering mob. What made it more chilling was that a number of us had these same dreams at the same time. Were they instead the memories of things long past to our race, or vision of future yet to come, wrapped now in the veil of dream? None of these questions could be answered, for the answer lay at the top, in the redoubt of the Dashtiya.

We came upon it late one afternoon, when our legs were stinging with the exertion of the climb, our faces with the assault of dank air. The statues of great beasts loomed out of the dusk at us, not so different from what we'd dreamed; their sighting even triggered a shout of recognition. The bodies of great stone men with the heads of eagles, wolves, bears; their stone eyes gazed out upon us in welcome. Beyond, more statuary loomed, this reflecting the memory of Greece and Alexander ... sensitive lips and eyes softening the countenance of warriors, perhaps the stone sentinels of Seleucus Nicator forgotten up here by the centuries.

But what drew us most was a glow of light that had illuminated our way from above for nearly an hour, a light that at first told us we were approaching a place of habitation, but the nearer we drew to it, the more we realized this was not the soft light of hearth, the light of man gathered around the cooking fire, not the light of lantern or torch. No, it came from within a building that, had I been elsewhere, I would have thought a Seljuk mosque; a mosque that could have come from Konya, its arched entryway surrounded by a frieze that at a distance could have told of the wisdom of the Prophet.

But this was no mosque, for such a thing as we saw could never have been a mosque as we knew it. It was not until I drew up close to the arch of the entryway that I saw the thing that told me I was so very near now -- for there on the frieze, in eternal stone, stood the etching of the murder of Sems of Tabriz, his dancing murderers and the mystic number "99", the same insignia from the tattoo of my lord's assassin and the mark falling out of the eerie poetry of the dead imam Ferruhzade in Topkapi, the very insignia that had brought on my expulsion from the Mevlevi cloister. Here it was, not hidden between pages nor veiled inside a man's clothing, but displayed openly, for all to see. And with it, these lines inscribed in Persian:

God the Abaser, God the Humiliator, God the Judge ...

Even Alev and her band had succumbed to the unearthliness of the place, and were stuck speechless, although the emanation of light from the temple-mosque was such as they had never seen in their lives. Its blue-whiteness fell on the swirling fog and the looming statues and seemed to give them a life of sorts, a spectral realm of unearthly beings that could have no benign intent. My protectors were afraid to go any further, though as far as we could all see, we were utterly alone; the only movement was the fog drifting in the wind, the beams of luminous white emerging from the archway and windows of the temple-mosque and rendered into columns of swirling misted brightness. No sounds came but that of the wind rushing up the stones from Persia and Iraq, from the burial grounds of Nineveh and Babylon, from Harran and Elam and Ur of the Chaldees, the wind off of faraway oceans and the dripping of melting snow. As the leader of the expedition, I felt no option but to step forward, through the threshold and into the realm of light which had drawn us to this spot.

As my eyes, accustomed to the dark weather and gloomy stone of the last three days, adjusted as I once came inside, I could identify the light only as coming from a source at the front of the temple. While I stood there, shielding my eyes and face from the glare, I felt in my flesh the sheer power of it, radiating heat from some distance. The room, laid out in the customary floor plan of a mosque or Christian church, was empty of furniture or adornment, save supporting columns for a dome roof and adjoining empty wings; the columns and roof carried friezes in cold stone, with none of the color or artistry of those places of worship in the world below. And the imagery depicted was such I could not identify it from the Qur'anic tales as we knew them, although I recognized two things from Islam ... a depiction of the fallen angel Iblis when he refused to bow down and worship Adam, as Allah commanded ... and a calligraphed panel with the 99 names of God inscribed.

Finally my eyes moved to the light itself, atop an altar with carved chalcedony base ... and though it came clearer for me, its mystery was only heightened. This was nothing more, I thought, than a small star captured and brought here; a star captured out of the sky and set here to burn in this altar. It seemed to be enclosed in a clear glassine sphere, and either stood or floated just above the altar. The light streamed out of it in a uniform and awesome emanation, throwing white heat and light to all the room. The walls back where I stood were warm to the touch from it ... and I sensed if I drew much closer I would suffer the danger of being burned, or blinded.

The tiny star had a hypnotic effect, too; none who came near it could help but be drawn into its spell and power, in wonderment at how such a thing could be; a star come to earth, a star for men to worship. I was drawn into a kind of manic rapture at its intangible symmetry, its eternity, its source which I did not understand. Having no other point of reference than my own life, I could see how someone could be drawn to worship this thing, whatever it might be, for it seemed not bound by the limits of the physical world I inhabited. And it was then, when I was in the steadiest part of the rapture, when I was beginning to forget why I had come and in search of what, that a voice came up to me from the side of my vision.

"Greetings, great Yunus," spoke a mighty voice in classical Persian; and when I turned to see who was addressing me by my given name, I wondered if I had indeed lost my mind.

An ancient man approached me, dressed in black robes; on his white head was a conical fez, but unlike those my fellow Mevlevi dervishes had worn. This one rose to a greater point, and was made of black silk so that it shone with the light of the captive star; upon its crown were embroidered symbols of the stars set in black space. As for the man and his face, had I been a peasant from the hills I might have thought I had seen Allah himself or one of his angels, so powerful was his countenance, with weathered cheeks, tangled white hair, and above all numinous eyes that, as he raised his head to face me more directly, seemed proof of the supernatural. His nose was prominent and hooked, and confirmed in my mind that this was indeed an Iranian, in aspect one of the original Aryans who had swept down out of the Hindu Kush to populate this piece of the continent, though he be dressed in the garb of someone else.

He was certainly no one I had ever seen before, but the effect when first seeing him was for me to think he was someone more important than any I had ever met before; more so than shah and vizier, than bey or king of Europe -- more so than Suleiman himself, who though he was the Shadow-of-God-on-Earth was a mortal man, while about this one you could not be so certain. Though aged, he appeared healthy. He wore only sandals on his bare feet, and so was open to the terrible chill and dampness of this place, yet seemed to be none the worse for it.

"You mustn't gaze too long upon the light, or it will blind you," he said; and as he came towards me, I realized perhaps some of his unearthliness of countenance and form derived from the fact he appeared blind himself. Yes, the special quality of the pallid rubiate eyes derived from the emptiness of someone who had lost all vision, the iris and cornea bleached or seared into rose cataract or perhaps merely reflecting the white light before me. Yet he knew my name, he knew where I stood, the loss of his vision seemed to be no impediment whatsoever to his perceptions and activities.

"Who are you?" I asked, and he paused a second in his approach.

"You know me, although you don't yet know," he said; and this set me to wracking my brain for some indication of what this riddle could mean.

"Are you of the Dashtiya?" I asked, and to this he only laughed, it seemed the greatest joke to him. As we were speaking, Alev and her warriors had come across the threshold, some with hands raised to shield them from the light, others with weapons drawn, wondering if this old man posed a threat.

"Are you of the Dashtiya?" I repeated; but he did not answer me, beckoning to us all that we should come with him and rest.

We walked out of the temple back up to the fortification, and into a windy room with coarse wood tables and benches, and it was there he said we would be fed.

The tables, as I have described them, were rough and dusty. They showed no signs of having been used in years. No kitchen stood adjacent -- only empty windows opening out onto the swirling night. The floor was nothing more than dank mud, the walls unadorned stone. He motioned for us to seat ourselves at the bench, prompting a few of our party to guffaw at the invitation, because of the improbability of its fulfillment. No one wanted to sit at a dusty table in a room unused for years, seeming more fit for livestock than men. Yet all I know is that one second we were looking at this desolation and emptiness, and the next instant a table held lamb, bread, wine and cheese; it was borne out by no one, it did not spring up out of the tables or appear in the blinking of an eye. It was simply there, as though it had always been.

There was a delay of some seconds as this was filtered by our minds; but then a collective gasp rose up, and two men even screamed and backed towards the door; others drew daggers for protection. They looked to me for guidance.

"You are a magus," I said, and again I received his empty laughter.

"Please, sit," he said to the men. Several men, tempted by the food, yet frightened by the magic, drew close, then held back.

Finally Alev sat down, the others eventually joined

her. As I moved to sit with them, the old man asked that I join him outside. My guardians seemed uncomfortable, and three sprang up to join me, but the man, saying no danger faced me while in his care, simply wished to speak with me alone.

While the old host and I stood out in the wet darkness, the men ate in virtual silence, for though food had been provided, none of the accoutrements of a civilized place were there. Indeed, no one was at ease, and the more nervous among them were continually swinging their eyes around, to see if anything was at their backs, or what trickery the magus would employ. A second thought ran through my mind; was the food from this source trustworthy? Might he not poison us all, and be done with the intruders?

"I do not poison my guests," he said, as if a participant in my thoughts.

"What is that light in the temple?" I asked.

"The very-light of God," the old man said.

"Tell me who you are," I repeated for the third time.

"Have you not guessed?" he asked, and though the idea forming inside me was so preposterous, I had to admit to myself, yes, I had surmised as he said, although I would never admit it. Though I still believed he could not see, his empty gaze was fixed steadily upon me. Out before us, the clouds and mist of this meeting place of Persia and Mesopotamia and Anatolia swirled with unholy vigor. Night was dark.

"Say it," he said to me, and I resisted the absurdity of it.

"Say my name," he commanded to me, and I could hardly resist him.

"You are Dashti," I said, "who was a follower of the Mevlana Rumi, and then driven away."

He nodded.

"You are 300 years old," I said.

"Older," he replied.

"There is no way on earth I can believe," I said.

"I have shed the ways of earth," he said.

That exchange was followed by more silence from us, as those guarding me drifted away to their own entertainments. As for myself, I was running through in my head what was the best approach to this man who claimed to be the apostate of Sufism driven from Konya in 1247, now resident on a mountaintop in 1566.

"Why did the imam Ferruhzade kill himself?" I asked.

"A hand other than his own took his life; the murderer feared what secrets he knew."

"Why did you try to kill my lord Suleiman?" I asked.

"I did not," he said.

"Why did you dispatch a man to kill the sultan who rules half the world?" I persisted.

"I did not send him," replied the man who said he was Dashti. "The assassin was a traitor to me. I would never take the life of such a great one."

"Your trickery is equally great," I said. "What is there to make me believe?"

"Because I would not kill one of my own," he said.

"You liar," I whispered, turning to face him. "How dare you slander the caliph of Islam this way -- the guardian of the shrines of Mecca and Medina?"

The old man calling himself Dashti laughed to himself a moment, and then stood to answer my attack. But rather than saying anything, he reached into the pocket of his robe, and pulled something out that he let swing for a moment in the light of the torches drifting out from the eating room, in the reflected starlight from the interior of the temple-mosque, in the empty light of his own ruined eyes that could not see yet could see far beyond anything I ever could; he let it swing there at the end of its pendant for me to see, his defense against the charge of untruth and murder, the proof of what he said.

My first reaction was to feel my own pockets, to make sure that what I carried had not been stolen from me; but it was there, safe, as it had been since given to me in Topkapi.

As we stood there atop that unearthly mountain at the center of the world, as the terrible light from beyond poured over us and this man beyond death grinned at me, I looked down at the item he held as proof, the proof he was no enemy of Suleiman but if anything an ally, the proof my quest had brought me in a circle, to the point of all beginning...

I looked at it, touched it, examined it in every detail.

Unless it was trickery I looked at the very seal of Suleiman, the <u>tugra</u> identical to the one I and only the grand vizier possessed, the one object as powerful to the bearer as the presence of the sultan himself. Now a third was in the hands of this Persian sorcerer, the man who claimed to be Dashti and who was more than 300 years old.

Only the sultan himself had the power to bestow his seal on another man. Never had one gone out of his possession, except when he gave it away, as a sign of alliance and blood friendship.

I wanted it to be trickery, I wanted it to be false, but the warm gold in my hand said only truth, truth, there was no other explanation but the truth.

*　*　*

Now time and space flee their bonds. What was solid, becomes only a bubble in the air, a fleeting glance in a mirror, once glimpsed but forever lost. Memory is dream is reality;

what happened I remember as I clutch a dream, as though time stood still, as though we were out of time.

We walked upon the mountain, Dashti and I, the mountain called Tendurek but it could have been Demavend or Ararat or Sinai, for he took me from the mountaintop high up into the air, and showed me many things.

We walked into the full force of the storm blown up at us from the nexus of the earth. We walked for a time there, above the ground, our feet brushing across the racing clouds, below them the black face of the land touched only by lightning and brief bursts of moonlight.

He showed me the whole world, though the world was small in its finitude, become a map by Piri Reis and not the spinning globe in space; for below me I saw Anatolia and Persia and Mesopotamia and Arabia, I saw India and Transoxiana and Khorasan and Mongolia; these the centerpieces of the world-island, and all the rest swirling about them. This was the heart of the world, the heart-womb of the Turks and Parthians and all our brother races, and to us it was our destiny to bring these shattered parts together, and thus subdue the rimlands round about.

Then I could see Cyrus and Darius and Xerxes and Alexander, I could see Seleucus and Antiochos and Mithradates and Julius Caesar, I could see Constantine and Justinian and Sal ah-din and Alaettin Keykubad, I could see

Genghis Khan and Timurlane and Mehmet the Conqueror; they all floated like spectres in the air, moving like us across the sky and across the earth, leading the ghost-legions. But as we watched, they faded away into shadows, into the wasteland of memory.

But see, he said to me, see the one who now has it in his grasp, and spread before me in the black air of space suddenly the palace of the Topkapi appeared, suddenly I could see Suleiman in a tower of the Babussaade, gazing at his globe that stood by his great window; he stood with his hand on the globe, looking out to sea; and this was Suleiman as I liked to remember him, a younger man, when the personal losses of wife and sons had not dragged him down so into the pit of melancholy and despair.

Still he has it in his grasp, said Dashti; the one man today who could rule the world; and yet he does not, because he is blocked by his refusal to see-what-could-be.

The next thing I saw in the screen of the air was the Safavid shah in Tehran, young Tahmasp; there he sat, alone on his jeweled throne, with nothing to do but commit treachery and mischief.

If only Suleiman were to see Tahmasp as his ally, said Dashti; why then, they could rule the world. For the Turks and the Persians were once united, in the Seljukid sultanate that was the marriage of two peoples; why not again, but in a

498

partnership 100 times greater, under the benevolence and fatherhood of Suleiman? Why do they not join, to rule all?

Then I saw Suleiman and Tahmasp in joint audience, Suleiman holding the mystic cam-i Jamshid, the ruby chalice of all the Asias in his hand and drinking from it, Tahmasp kissing the hand of Suleiman, and kneeling at his feet and calling him the Rightly-Guided-One, the mahdi.

Then the two, the sultan and the shah, held the cam-i Jamshid together, and as they gazed upon its ruby sides, a great light rolled over the earth, bathing the world in its glory; and the light brought the power over earth unto these two, and in turn the entire world kneeled unto them. Europe, Asia, Africa fell into the hands of the shadow-of-God-on-earth, the mahdi Suleiman, and his viceroy, the shahanshah, while 12 child-angels sang the victory of Allah.

And you, Yunus, said Dashti; you have yet to achieve your greatest destiny. For you shall rule as grand vizier of the whole world, and sit at the right hand of Suleiman and Tahmasp. Yunus Pasha, grand vizier of all the Asias, and the rimlands beyond; it is for you to take, if only you will.

And I looked and saw myself in the robe and turban of the grand vizier, and thousands were bowing down to me, the colors of their skins like the iridescence of a peacock, the babble of their many tongues like the 99 names of God spoken at once; over this multitude I ruled, and it was if I ruled as a sultan myself.

This cannot be I said, I am Yunus the lowly interpreter, the son of a fishmonger; how can I pretend to be a grand vizier?

And Dashti reminded me that Suleiman's once-favorite childhood friend and vizier, Ibrahim Pasha, had been a slave, the other viziers from more humble beginnings than me.

This is your destiny, he said, I have seen it; you shall be the mahdi's grand vizier, the right hand of Suleiman.

And he shewed it to me, in full: all the earth bowing down to Suleiman, and to me; Persia and Khorasan and Transoxiana were ours once again; Europe prayed to the call of the prophet, and the muezzins sang in Vienna, Paris, Madrid and Muscovy; all this was to be, if only the brotherhood of Tahmasp and Suleiman were affirmed. For a shattered heart, he said, cannot rule the body; the heart must be one, and then all will flow to it. The heart of the world is the cam-i Jamshid, the ruby chalice of earth herself, no conqueror can rule without it, yet it is inexplicably bound up with Persia, and to hold it, likewise to hold the world without holding Persia cannot be.

Then came only fire and smoke, the swirling winds of storm, and a world flying apart; a sound beyond our lives, the shriek of all mankind. Whether these had been my thoughts, or hallucinations, or his insanity in my thought, I do not know, for there was no speech, there was only the silent communion of minds; I was at his mercy, I was the tool of sorcerers and magi, of djinn and demons of the sky.

And so, my readers, I must leave you for a time; for these pages now carry secrets only few should see; as precaution against those who would use the power of God for evil ends, my final verses are hid in a separate place. When I came down from the mountain I knew what I was never meant to know; the secret of a sultan's rule, the secret of the earth's dark end ...

Ye fools seeking truth in sultan's lie
Go to sultan's cloister, 'neath green sky
If to missing pages you need a guide
Go to the coffin of the sultan-child.
Now dead poet's secret becomes mankind's doom;
Muse loses vision in cold tomb.
If Allah should ask to hear your wisdom
Say these words and save his Kingdom:
Ardor and ecstasy lend pattern to the world;
Poetry without ardor and ecstasy
is merely a mourning song.
And if you be accurate in your measure
Wrapped in truth you will find the treasure
The heart of the world, in my poetry hid;
The sultan's ruby chalice, the cam-i Jamshid.
Then gaze deep into the poetry of God's 99

names,
  To find the secret of the very-light,
  of the stars' endless flames.

*   *   *

FOLIO EIGHT

It came to me in dream
my vision of the end,
the death of all creation
in God-light's awful spin;
For as the imam chanted
the 99 names of God,
the whole world fell in worship
of mahdi's flaming rod.
I saw the beam of white
cast on enemy camp,
I saw the sword of fire
thrown from ruby lamp.
Light poured out to westward
and struck the enemy's tents.
It blinded them in fury,
and swallowed them in wind.
The cry of a thousand was wretched,
the cry of ten thousand worse,
the field of earth's rich bounty
became mankind's black hearse.
For the fire did not stop there
but opened a hole in air,
It drew all things inside,
within its writhing lair.
Victor was merged with vanquished

and yesterday with tomorrow;
the only sound I heard at last
an empty wail of sorrow ...

And even when I awakened from this nightmare, still I journeyed through a landscape of cinders and ash. O my lord, my master, my Suleiman; why had you forsaken us so? I repeated that name again and again, for it was that name that sent me to the ends of the earth, and in doing so, prompted me to see the earth's end.

Ever westward I journeyed, all secrets revealed. Retracing my steps, from the revelations of the mountaintop, I journeyed back down the steppe-valley wrapped in the summer of fire. Acrid heat, blazing out of the sky, seared the dead mountains, the baked plateau. All did roast in a haze of insanity. The few clouds loomed as djinns in the sky, their shadows on the parched earth like the shadow of death angel Azrael coming down to take us away forever.

And when the sun did not shine, yet the heat continued. It blew off the southern deserts night and day, fouling the air with dust and nettles. Sleep at best was only one or two hours a night ... and then we would resume our journey west as sleepwalkers, to the capital, where I knew I must return. This dark mood and climate hung on me even though I traveled in the company of my woman, even though our embraces filled the night. But the embrace of just two humans on the black face of the earth was not enough to lift the darkness of the world.

The days became weeks, the steps became journeys of a thousand miles. Time lost its meaning. We must have taken two months to return home, traveling with a west-bound caravan, bound for the capital Istanbul. And yet it was all in the blinking of an eye, for as we came unto the gates of Istanbul, it was as though I had just descended from the mystic mountain that morning, the words and revelations fresh in my ears. And though we were exhausted from the trip and I should have taken some days to put my own affairs in order, all I could think to do was to report to my master, and confront him with what I had found. Even though I now had a new wife, to add to my harem of one, this something that would require diplomacy and sensitivity, for my old wife Burju would be sent into shock when she were told ... even though I was a year older, and much had happened in my absence. But no, no, I stumbled through the desert of my life, my eyes fixed on one thing above all others; and that thing was the sultan, Suleiman.

And so it was I learned the sultan was not there ... while we wandered in the east, our lord had led our armies into new war in Europe, and that he was now camped there, again, arrayed against the armies of the Hapsburgs and their allies... And so I knew my own journey was not yet complete.

So north, north I traveled, a gaunt spectre of a man. Once burned by sun and heaven's fire, now I was condemned to continue my <u>hegira</u>, into the weeping valleys and damp bracken of the Balkan lands ... the place of cruel fairy tales, the dwelling place of evil spirits and wampyrs, curses and werewolves. Into this cursed place of a thousand nameless valleys I passed, this gloomy land that had darkened our own Turkish countenance to rule. Were I sultan I would be done with it, done with these scheming little tribes and their backward ways. I would leave them to their Jesus who was only a talisman for them, for so little did the teachings of Jesus manifest itself in the way they lived. Little bits of peoples, miserable little kingdoms and satrapies, fighting out their mountain feuds; in this morass we had spent our blood and treasure to rule?

Dreary little places with haunted steeples and evil cellars ... Panagyuristhe and Sofia, Krusevac and Belgrade ... through these places I journeyed for the final time, servant of the shadow of God on earth. And these subjects looked at me with their sullen stares of subjugation and festering resentment. To hell with all of you, I thought. The black rain fell out of the coal-colored clouds like the apocalypse, it rained and rained and the mud and the earth and the cloaking blanket of green were like to suffocate me ... the end of us, I swore, the end of the Turks, here in Europe.

And at my journey's end, I came upon Szigetvary and surveyed it from the plateau. A moon had at last come out, and the moonlight was arrayed upon the majesty and power of the sultanic forces deployed upon the valley floor. Moonlight shone down upon banners and tents, upon smoke rising from fires, upon the bending Drava River and the puddles in the roads that had brought this titanic force here, in the final campaign of Suleiman's life. A chill wind had come up, and it truly felt like the end of summer, autumn would soon be here. Frost had begun to burn the mountaintops of Musala and Midzhur, Bolotoy Kuk and Peleaga.

I descended from the high plateau into the valley, as the Turks were bedding down for the night. Hardly anyone save a few sentries took note of me, and when I showed them the sultan's tugra, I was allowed to pass, with a bow and flourish from them. Smoke from the cooking fires lay low here, forming a ceiling over the camp, and the firelight reflected off its underside, giving the scene the aspect of another world. But while the sights and sounds of this strange encampment beckoned to me right and left, I knew the place I must go, before another moment of my life could be led.

I came unto the sultan's pavilion, and it was there the janissaries allowed me to pass further. After that, through the gate of the white eunuchs, some of them now remembering my face and curious to know where I had been for so long ... finally into the anteroom of the sultan's great tent, where aides to the grand vizier and the <u>ulema</u> were gathered in a tight knot of whispered conversation.

At first they did not recognize me, so changed was I by the sunburn of my desert travels, and perhaps by the loss of weight occasioned by the fire that burned without and within. But when they did know me, they fell speechless, as though I were the messenger of dread news. Before I entered my lord's presence, I learned the truth: that the Sultan Suleiman was on his deathbed, and his grand vizier Mehmet Sokollu and others were there at his bedside, attending him to the end.

While they passed this news with the false gravity of courtiers -- who know that the death of a ruler can occasion changes in all fortunes, most especially theirs -- the news found me in another mood. The news of his grave condition did not strike me with any sadness, but rather with a confirmation of inevitability. For I had known, somehow, that I would find him this way, the master of the world -- weak and feeble in his final hours.

At last I entered his bed-chamber, the tent there hung with layer upon layer of damask and velvet, of kilim and canvas and silk to soften the damp night air of Central Europe, to keep any breeze or draft off him. I came across the carpets, past the glowing coals inside the brass lanterns, the smell of camphors and unguents, of potions and liniments rubbed on this body that was the body of the empire, to alleviate the inevitability of old age and death; even here the patter of whispers continued.

When Mehmet Sokollu saw me, he sought to motion me away and back to the door, as though my intrusion was not what was needed now. But Suleiman, despite his fever and pallor, saw me also, and beckoned to me with a shaking hand to come closer, which I did. And there, in the glow of the candles and lanterns arranged around him our commander, I saw him in his death mask, the certainty of his departure as fixed as the rising of the sun tomorrow. Death was heavily upon him, claws dug deep into the man's heart and lungs, and he was only being allowed to gaze out at us for a few more hours, like a small bird in the talons of a hawk, heart pierced, yet the last drops of life coursing through, enough to give a final impulse to the struggle to live.

"My servant," he whispered, and though I would like to say what I saw in his eyes was thankfulness and appreciation that I had returned to him, that I had performed my mission, I honestly believe what I saw there was surprise, astonishment in those dying eyes that I had survived to come and confront him with what I had found, surprise I had somehow evaded the death sentence Refik was to have carried out once my quest was completed and report written. My lord was looking at me with surprise and fear, as though I might in fact be among the dead, and sent to welcome him over to the other side.

"My lord," said Mehmet Sokollu, seeking to preserve the last ounce of strength in this the imperial body, "the physicians say you must rest now, for tomorrow the battle resumes, and your well-being is integral to the success of the army." But our lord was not listening, he knew the armies would follow their own destiny now, his had separated from theirs long ago.

"Leave us," the sultan hissed, and Mehmet was in turn stung to be talked to this way. Mehmet's response was to look at me with the hate and surprise he'd directed at me since that meeting in the Hall of Whispers, when my mission had first been declared nearly a year before. How dare you? his eyes were saying, how dare you be of such import that you remain alone with the sultan in his death-throes while I the grand vizier am ordered out like a scullery maid? But the sultan's continued hissing at him to be gone left him little time to sulk, and so bowing he withdrew into the outer room, most likely to try and eavesdrop and hear what would transpire between us.

"A man came to me in a dream" the sultan said, "only I could not see his face. And now I do."

"And why did the man come to you?" I asked him.

"He came to kill me," said the sultan. "This I have dreamed ten times, as befits the numerology of my birth; and now, dreamt the tenth time, it will come true. For, my servant, you have come to kill me, have you not?"

And it was then that I felt compelled to answer him honestly, for there was little motive in not telling the truth now. I looked him directly in the eye, and said,

"Yes, my lord, it is so," even as I clutched the dagger I had been bequeathed by Refik, and which I carried for the purpose Suleiman had already divined.

The sultan nodded there in his pillows, a sad smile upon his withered lips. His eyes were sunken black in bluish pits, and beads of perspiration dotted his brow and cheeks.

"I have saved you the trouble," said the sultan. "For I have also come here to die, and to atone for what I have done."

It was then I told him what I had learned on my journeys to the east, taking a full year of my life to complete: that the assassin of the warm autumn night a year before had been sent by the enemies of Dashti, the killer having once been of the apostate's flock and won back over to the teachings of Allah after spending some years in the grips of the Persian deceiver ... that the killer had sought to kill Suleiman because he had fallen under the spell of Dashti and the Dashtiya, their teachings brought to the sultan by the late imam muderri Ferruhzade ... and that the Dashtiya, while pretending to be loyal to the One True Faith and the Prophet, were in fact devotees of sorcery and evildoing, and served the ends of those who would harm the Osmanlis and mankind in general. Into their rite, I said, had crept corruptions of the flesh, orgiastics, ways that belonged to fire worship and to the bestial rites of prehistory the Prophet had tried to strike out 700 years before. And that, I concluded, was why I had come with dagger in hand, to complete what had not been completed by the assassin ... to restore justice and righteousness to the House of Osman, and end an imprisonment of the sultan's soul by the handmaidens of Iblis the deceiver.

That said, the sultan looked at me the longest time, before he in turn began to speak. But when he did, he told me the tale I now set out for you, a tale that atop what I had heard before, nonetheless struck me silent ... so that for the longest time, as the candles of the sultan's chamber burned lower and lower, as the wind and rain thrashed outside in anticipation of tomorrow's battle, as his life-force ebbed away, the whisper of my lord continued like a confession without end, a hissing of nature and of the wind, the wind in the leaves and the wet grass, the confession of a man who is about to die with a heart stained by wrongdoing.

FOLIO NINE

Some years ago, confessed the sultan, he had wandered the corridors of his palace, a lonely and melancholy man. As he gazed out upon his world from the latticed window that overlooked the sea, he knew he possessed as much of this physical world as any man can, for he had armies, fleets, servants, and treasure without rival; indeed, half the globe answered to his command. And yet he knew the limits of those things, for those most precious had slipped away from him, beyond the veil of life into the realm that lies beyond ... the viziers he had loved as brothers, only to have them betray him ... the sons he had loved best and yet been forced to execute when they did not obey him and the rules of succession ... the others who died of plague or of a broken heart, to see their siblings slain ... but most importantly his beloved wife Hurrem, who had been dead now a good seven years. Many a time he was forced to ask himself: Why have I been left behind, in the world of the living, when those most precious have gone onto the next world? Why has Allah given to me these years of loneliness?

But the answer was not apparent, in those early years. The answer could not be discerned from the cold winds that blew off the water, from the dead leaves that scuttled across the marble balconies and pathways of the Babussaade. The only response from the world was cold gray mist, the message being that nothing here held meaning for him anymore.

And it was in this time he turned to the imam Ferruhzade for counsel, for the imam seemed especially attuned to the emptiness afflicting the sultan, and seemed to hold the key, the answer to the void. It was the imam, speaking his native Persian, who reawakened in the sultan the awareness of the mystic quest, so that the world not be so hollow and desolate as the sultan's stricken heart made it seem. He reminded the sultan that God was as much here as in the next world, if only the eye were open to the glory of Him ... and that Suleiman must realize he had been left behind when all those he had loved had gone over to the other side, for a reason ... and the reason was God's plan for him.

He had survived because the sultan was destined for greater things yet, based on the numerology of his birth. As the personification of the 10, he was that rare individual to whom the exception would be given, so that which was unattainable for most men could be his, if only he sought it. All these things were told by the imam to the sultan in the dialogues that took place in the privacy of the gardens or the balcony or in the tower that overlooked Topkapi and all of Istanbul, to which the sultan would retire when he was feeling most forsaken. And these dialogues and his tutelage in the ways of the holy imam Ferruhzade, came to be the centerpiece of his life, eclipsing the countless physical pleasures at hand -- those of the hunt, or of the harem, or of food and drink, all his to have, if he wished them.

The sultan decided that above all he wished to make the mystic climb the imam offered, secretly hoping that in coming closer to God he might come closer to those who had left him behind.

And so began the initiation of the Sultan Suleiman into the mystic ways.

The imam Ferruhzade professed to be of a secret brotherhood of the Mevlevi, and so Suleiman began his instruction in the mystic climb to f'ana, utter extinction of self, through dance, and meditation and the recitation of poetry that through the sheer power of words broke down the dry surface of life and provided glimpses into the magical beyond. And many a night these rites took place high up in the tower, where no other man could witness, and only Allah and passing spirits might see the great sultan, bent by his years, whirling in the mystic sema, or swaying in the beauty of poetry or lost in meditation to bring him to a higher plane.

And this mightiest of sultans, the man who had subjugated half the world, fell into his newest quest with all the eagerness he had once shown for battle. This was his newest purpose in living, and so consumed him like fire.

He took everything on faith, and believed the imam's motives pure. What reason was there to think otherwise? And so the months passed and became a year; and Suleiman came to the point where he at least glimpsed the beyond, even if he did not grasp or understand it. Using the mystic liquor <u>haoma</u>, the imam was able to take the two of them out of their bodies, and to actually fly above the earth, above the clouds ... or to descend invisible into the darkest warrens of the city, into such places Suleiman had never dreamed existed. In the blinking of an eye, the imam could take him into the court of the French king, or the cabin of one of his own admirals at sea, or into the chamber of a Russian whore if he so wanted ... the imam could take him under the sea, to watch the great creatures there swim as if in a nightmare. Or he could bring the Beyond to them, and show these things reflected in a sphere of crystal, as well as things that had never existed, but might yet. He could summon up the dead, he could picture the unborn ... all these things were in the power of the imam.

And it was then the imam introduced the sultan to the concept of <u>gnosis</u> -- the highest awareness of God which was wrapped in secrecy, meant to be glimpsed by only a few able to bear its awful knowledge -- because the laws and restrictions binding the peasants and working men of the everyday were not suited to those whose minds and souls were greater. Coming into the possession of gnosis, the imam showed Suleiman the true world of God was not one of laws or restrictions, but nothing more than the beating heart of the cosmos itself, the swirling, ever-changing demiurge of creation and destruction, the endless alternation between night and day, between darkness and light, between flesh and the soul ... that the entire structure of the universe was the mind and body of God, moving in its evolution towards the highest perfection. In this cosmic world of spirit and the very-light of God, concepts of sin and restriction had no part. What had been known as sin was not sin, for acts of the flesh had no consequence; the struggle of man was either to immerse himself fully in the world of flesh in order to leave it, or to leave it through the ascent into light. Either way was valid, for darkness and light were the two manifestations of the one God. The worst tragedy was merely to remain mired in the constraints and regulations of the everyday, where most men remained, having no resources to do more. But for those great souls, like Suleiman's, the task was to climb totally out this world's limits, into that-which-was-not-yet-become.

Even as these things transpired, the sultan was perplexed. For the higher and farther the imam took him, the less talk there was of the Qur'an and Allah and the Prophet. In fact, the imam told him the Prophet and Jesus and Moses were of no importance, when one went to the higher plane. These statements did not cease to disturb the sultan in light of day, when he would awaken after a night soaring in the clouds, his head now throbbing as though too much wine had been drunk, his body weak and trembling for having been pushed to the limit.

And so the sultan finally felt the need to put his questions to the imam, and to learn what all this meant, if it no longer had to do with the Qur'an or with the Prophet, blessed be his name. What was God's purpose in leaving him here, in the physical, when the others had all been sent beyond? And what was the meaning of the rites into which the imam Ferruhzade had inducted him, for they went beyond anything he had ever heard of or dreamt?

And the imam, smiling, said the moment of final revelation had come. The evening was warm, as summers in Istanbul can be ... the city below was slipping into sleep just as the imam again took Suleiman out of his body and led him up into the moonlit sky. The waters of the Bogazi and the Kara Denizi caught the moonlight and sent it bouncing back to their invisible eyes. And it was then the imam Ferruhzade said that he Suleiman was now an initiate in a brotherhood to which few were called, for its demands were so awesome: the brotherhood of the Dashtiya. Destiny had declared that Suleiman and the Dashtiya would become one, in the completion of God's destiny.

And what is this destiny, the sultan asked? What is God's purpose in leaving me here when all have gone into the land of shadows; why do I remain, when I have done all there is to do, so there is nothing for me to do but to wait for death?

And the imam now laughed again, for he said Suleiman could not leave because he was not finished with his purpose on earth. Again he pointed to the numerology of Suleiman's birth ... that he had been born to rule, but to rule more than any had believed possible. For Suleiman had been left on this earth in order to bring the earth into one, under one ruler. He was to be the Rightly-Guided-One, the mahdi to cleanse the earth; this was God's plan for him. And if he departed this earth without achieving his destiny, then his soul would echo in the halls of heaven like a marble thrown into a tin pan. He would not be fulfilled, the plan of God would not be fulfilled, the universe would not move towards its necessary fruition.

But I have conquered half the world in the name of Allah, and now I am a sick and melancholy old man, said the sultan. How can He expect any more great things of me? And the imam laughed, and said, The tools have been given you, right under your nose; you could rule the whole world, if only you so wished.

And when the sultan asked what those things might be, he was told he possessed the ruby chalice of all the Persias, the cam-i Jamshid ... that this had been prized by conquerors since time immemorial not because of its precious stone, but because it held mystic powers as well ... yet only those who fully understood the source of its power could harness it, and thus conquer Asia, and thence the world around its rim. The secret of its power had long been lost. But now the secret was in the possession of the Dashtiya, and the Dashtiya would share that secret with Suleiman, so that he would at last use the beating ruby heart of Asia, the frozen drop of God's blood, for what it was destined.

What is that secret? the sultan asked. And how shall it give unto me that which no man has ever attained, and for which many have died by the sword? What is this thing that will so stand reality and history on its head, for my benefit?

It was then the imam summoned up a vision of the two enemies that, though weaker than Suleiman, had thwarted him for a lifetime, on east and west. To the east, the Shi'a Safavids, young Shah Tahmasp now sitting on the throne of Persia ... and to the west, the bickering kings of Europe, who had used little more than their wretched climate and landscape to deny him the conquest of their realms. But the Shah Tahmasp should be your ally, said Ferruhzade, for the Turks and Persians were once brothers together, speaking the same tongue as do you and I here ... and thus through Persia the power of the Seljuk Turks then extended into the mists of Asia. It is an error for the sons of Asia to see each other as enemies, for that way they split the heart. This has been the weakness that has denied you Europe, for Europe is your true enemy.

Then the imam summoned up another vision, and he showed the armies of the mahdi Suleiman marching against the fortresses of Europe. But the sultan did not march alone, for Tahmasp was at his side, as his emir, and together they held in their hands the cam-i Jamshid, together with a third man in a black robe and a high conical fez with the stars of space embroidered thereon. As the three joined hands on the cam-i Jamshid, a light spread out from the cup and onto the land, and where it touched, at the fortress of the Europeans, a horrendous fire arose, beyond flame, a ball of burning light like that of the sun in the sky. In this way was the fortress of the Europeans laid waste, and the armies of the Turks set free to overrun the northland.

What is this fire, this light? the sultan asked, and the imam replied, O my sultan, this is the very-light of God; and with it as your sword, so shall you achieve the destiny He wrote for you at the beginning of time. It is the gift offered to you now, for you have the mystic ruby chalice itself, and now you have the key to the secret knowledge to unlock its hidden power.

What must I do to gain the secret? the sultan asked, and the imam said this: You must join us forever, O my sultan, and declare the Dashtiya to be your brotherhood. You must protect us against those who would do us harm, who would call us heretics and apostates. You must take us above all others into your counsel, even as our sacred rite remains secret.

The sultan did not reply for the longest time, for no such request had ever been put to him, and with such force. But then no man had shown him such knowledge as this one had, nor harnessed such powers as this imam from Persia. And so the sultan, a tired old man confused by the sorcery of his imam, agreed. He would take the Dashtiya into his counsel, and in secret partnership with Persia, turn his furies on the Europeans who stood in his way. As the mahdi-incarnate, he would wield the very-light of God as his sword; and rain heavenly fire upon the Christian infidels.

*　*　*

FOLIO THE TENTH AND FINAL

The candles had now burned lower in their stands, and the winds and rain of the Hungarian night now raged unchallenged outside the sultan's tent. And though I wanted to say many things, the only thing that emerged from my lips was,

"My lord, why did you forsake us so? Why did you deliver your allegiance into the power of a cabal that has departed from the way of the Prophet?"

And as he looked upon me with sadness, I did repeat for him what I had learned on my long journey east, and what he now knew in his heart: the heresy of the Persian cabal, the sorcery, the secret rites where they had even sought to restore the old deities of the Iranian magi, Ahur-Mazd and Ahriman and the daevas with the heads of beasts. And I told him of their ultimate ceremony, the frenzy of human sacrifice by stabbing and fire, when flesh and spirit separated and the Brotherhood believed God was most immediate.

I also said that I had seen with my own eyes the sorcery of their very-light, the power of which I did not dispute. But I said to him with all my heart that this power was, while proceeding from God's majesty, taken from Him by murder and trickery, not by virtue and enlightenment ... that I had seen an unnatural man claiming to be 300 years old, perhaps their prophet Dashti himself, who if he be the same man had resorted to the murder of Semseddin Tabrizi in 1247 to gain the secret of the very-light, which Semseddin had come to share in mystic dialogue with the Mevlana Jelaleddin Rumi -- not as a tool for the domination of mankind, but as only one part of a body of mystic knowledge, the knowledge of the forces and mechanisms of the universe, God's universe, built on the principle of love and righteousness, not hatred and trickery, on the purity of principle and not the raw strength of evil.

Then I told him the story of my dream after coming down from the mountain, of the world destroyed by man's use of the very-light of God for unclean ends. I told him my dream made clear to me that part of the mystic secret Semseddin had given to Mevlana Rumi was the fact the very-light could only be harnessed by those of the highest perfection and enlightenment, and if that were violated the very fabric of the universe would be torn, and light would fall into darkness, and yesterday and tomorrow would be merged as one.

"I do not doubt the power of this light or their magic," I said. "But what they have done, as with everything, is to steal the fruits of the godly labors of the noble Sufis, to steal from them parts of the secret knowledge of the reality of God, and to employ them for base and selfish ends. And so, my lord, I cannot let you rain fire upon the Christians in this way, in alliance with the Persians and sorcery. In this way would you bring us down, into a fall I see nothing so much as a delivery of us straight to Iblis the betrayer. I cannot let you employ tools drenched in the blood of the Mevlana's muse, Semseddin Tabrizi; and that is why I have come to kill you."

The mighty sultan of half the world, the caliph of Islam and the shadow of God on earth, had covered his face with his hands. It was as though he were overwhelmed by the rightness of my words. Though he had no breath left in him, still he sobbed a dry rasp, in his way seeking forgiveness from the Allah to which he had been introduced at circumcision, the way of goodness and light. He realized how weak he had been, to allow such deceivers to gain power over him.

"Come to me," the sultan whispered, and he took my hand in his. "Loyal Yunus, you must do certain tasks for me now, for only you and I and the Dashtiya know of these things, and time is short. Only you know that they have come into battle with me here, and are awaiting my permission to establish themselves throughout the empire. First, you must take the sacred <u>cam-i Jamshid</u>, which I have brought here, and take it to a place where no one will find it for a thousand years. You must see these heretics are driven out of our lands, to never return. And you must tear out the final pages of my precious <u>Suleymanname</u>, for they are evidence of my wrongdoing and apostasy, and for those deeds shown therein to be known by my flock would only sow doubt and confusion among them about the true way. Tear them out now, while I watch, so that I will know it has been done .. and then keep those pages also in a place where none shall know of them, until men look at them across the gulf of history, as we do now upon the misdeeds of the Byzantines."

As he watched, I did the two things; I took the precious <u>cam-i Jamshid</u> and put in my cloak, wrapped in a scarf; and I tore the final folios of the <u>Suleymanname</u> from the binding, and also hid them on my person, to be disposed of as he decreed.

To see these things done seemed to have been his release, for he settled for a time into a semiconsciousness that began to deepen until I feared that he would die right then and there. But just as I sought to revive him, he opened his eyes one last time.

"Loyal Yunus," he said; "for this you shall serve as my grand vizier, for only you carry the knowledge of the danger of evil." And though I protested, he insisted I bring him paper and pen, and with his last bit of strength he wrote in his own scrawl such a decree, and had his <u>tugra</u> fixed to the bottom of it.

And even as he fell back onto his pillows with the final exhaustion, even as the death rattle sounded louder in his throat and I knew the moment had come, still I smiled at the irony that I the son of a fishmonger had become grand vizier after all, as Dashti had prophesied. I who had dwelt forever in the shadows was now the most powerful man in the world, if only for these few fading minutes. But he was dying, dying, there was no doubt about it. His breathing was ever more spasmodic, the opening and closing of the lips to take in air an ever more grotesque parody of life, sunken skeletal jaw trying to maintain what had long since been dead in spirit if not in flesh. Even after he had stopped breathing, the jaw still rose and fell for a moment more, in fulfillment of the Magnificent One's last command. And then, when I was sure he had in fact died, I walked out to the curtains, where I found Mehmet Sokollu and the others waiting: and I said to them he had died, to go into him to prepare his burial.

And while they did these things I listened to the whispers grow to a sound as strong as the wind and rains outside. The sultan was dead, the affairs of state must go on. I made no mention of his deathbed appointment, for in no way did I wish that job now held by Mehmet Sokollu. I only remained unobserved in one corner of the imperial bedchamber while the bustle that men carry out when one has just died, the bustle meant to cover up the finality and terror of death for those of us who remain behind, went forward. They fluffed the pillows and sat the sultan up as if ready to take tea. Cosmetologists were brought in to rouge his cheeks and comb his hair. The charade of continuity began at that point, and the next morning they went so far as to secure a Bosnian by the name of Hasan Aga, who was made to impersonate the dead sultan for a full month, until the heir Selim could come to Belgrade and meet the army of his dead father. Another minion, Cafer Aga, expert at forgery, signed the sultan's name so that the flow of decrees, orders and commissions never ceased even when the signer was dead. The embalming was carried out in utter secrecy, the entrails buried near the imperial tent.

Then, when the grand vizier was certain the heir Selim had indeed arrived at Belgrade, he ordered the impostor Hasan Aga to ride curtained in a carriage, pretending to be the ailing sultan, traveling south to welcome his son. It was not until they were four days from Belgrade that Mehmet Sokollu announced to the armies of Suleiman that the sultan had indeed died, provoking them to riot and weep for one entire night. Finally order was restored at dawn and they went on to the city of Belgrade. And for the entire month of November, the funeral cortege made its way back down through the Balkans, until my lord and master was laid to rest on November 28 1566, in the mosque that bore his name, at the side of his beloved wife Hurrem, who had crossed over into the next world so many years before him, and taken with him his reason to live.

* * *

REVELATION

This story has been too much one of death and treachery. It did so darken my life in that year that at many times did I wonder whether I would be able to remain on this earth, so woefully did I see it through the prism of that experience. But as I sit here at the distance of some time, I can see that this black period did have a beginning and an end; the beginning for me was the realization the sultan had fallen into the clutches of wrongdoing prompted by his own melancholy, the end of the spell his deathbed realization of what he had done.

And then he was dead, and gone forever. And it was as if a cloud had lifted off my own life, too, for I was free of my secret mission in the service of the man I had given my life to. I was free of the experience that had drawn me into its twisted dark ways, just as I was realizing I was not meant to finish my days on this earth as the ever-loyal servant. That I was a man of worth, with a mind and a soul as valuable as any. That though the laws and ways of men set some up above others, in my heart I knew that none was above any other ... and that if anything the pursuit of the trappings of power and majesty were the sure way to lower oneself on the scale of spiritual evolution. Not that I could trumpet this from the minarets, for I could not. Even though our Prophet had long ago taught that all men were equal before God, even though the central lesson of my hajj to Mekka the year after the sultan's death saw me stand in simple white robe on the mountain of 'Arafat, in worship and supplication, surrounded by emirs and merchants and stevedores and cutpurses, the lordly swept up in the sea of the lowest of the lowborn. We were all one, none having any more worth than the other, even though he or she be of grander presence or possessed of the idea they are of greater soul. We were all part of the one soul, and only through love of one another could anything good come for us.

This lesson even proved true for me, for I took the Jew Alev in marriage soon after my return to Istanbul, and thus created a harem of two. And though my old and loyal wife Burju did accept it in principle, it only gave her more reason to continue her pull away from me and into the affairs of our grown children. But with Alev, the cycle of life was begun again, and she brought me not one but two daughters, to me the white-haired interpreter who should have been bouncing only grandchildren on his knee. At last I entered life with the smile I had given up in my own childhood, when I sought to reinvent myself and rise from the life of the fishmonger's son.

For I finally realized that in all my years, in the service of the navy and then the admiral and then the mighty sultan himself, I had lost my smile. In fact I had lost myself. And this was the greatest loss of all, as I looked at the teachings of the Mevlana Rumi and the great Sufis, to whom I would have been forever a stranger had not this strange investigation taken me into their midst. For the most important lesson they gave to me, was one I learned very late in life: In order to know God, you must know yourself. Only then can the self pass away, and you rejoin the oneness of God.

I think upon this often, as I lay with my beautiful wife in the early morning hours, and hear the sound of her breath that comes from the soul of one who is fully at peace with herself, and possessed only of the desire to bring fun and laughter into the world. I think of this when I see my little babies at sleep, their faces possessed of the innocence of not knowing sin or selfishness, the innocence that streams directly from Allah onto their tiny faces. And I think this when I look out onto the panoply of my world, in these my final years. I see it in the tower of minaret, in the dome of mosque, in the glitter of sun on sea and the beating of gulls' wings in God's blue sky. I do thank Him that I was given the grace and good fortune to learn, and to possess, if only for a few precious years at the end of my life, what the mightiest man on earth never had occasion to enjoy, even though he held half the world in thrall.

*   *   *

Made in the USA
Las Vegas, NV
01 July 2025

24354056R00295